CW01219083

> Dear Tracy,
> thank you for all the times you have saved my life. Who knew the power of paracetamol?!
>
> With love
> Sadie Mx

SILENCING ANNA

Sadie Mitchell

Text Copyright © Sadie Mitchell 2018

Sadie Mitchell has asserted her right in accordance with the Copyright Designs and Patents Act 1988 to be identified as the author of this work.
All rights reserved
No part of this publication may be lent, resold, hired out or reproduced in any form or by any means without prior written permission from the author and publisher. All rights reserved.
Copyright © 3P Publishing

First published in 2018 in the UK
3P Publishing
C E C, London Road
NN17 5EU

A catalogue number for this book is available from the British Library

ISBN 978-1-911559-50-4

Cover design: Jamie Rae
Cover model: Kimi Armstrong

For my family and friends for helping to pick up the pieces, for my colleagues for their support and good humour and everyone who has given me words of encouragement along the way.
Also, thank you to Pat Craven for making me see clearly and allowing us to reproduce her work.

Contents:

An Introspective Retrospect	1
DylanWatts1982	18
Who is James Green?	34
That Love Affair	49
Death By Radio	71
Growing Up	78
Facing Forwards	90
The Bubble	104
Waking Up	121
Phone Call	128
Afterwards	137
A Wolf	146
Sinking Mud	162
Hannah	171
The Strings Tighten	184
Near Miss	194
The Warning	200
The Poison Spreads	217
From Bad To Worse	228
Best Behaviour	242
Looking Within	255
The Dominator	269
James Really Changes ….	283
The Admission	298
Time Out	317
Pretzels	336
The Escape	365

Elbow	388
The Fall	409
Frosty	419
Silver Lining	428
Love Never Dies	438
Further reading	
About the author	450

AN INTROSPECTIVE RETROSPECT

It's important to take stock of your life. How often do any of us actually stop, look around and really appreciate that which surrounds us? Not often enough. Imagine that all you know, your life, your experiences and your independence were about to be taken from you. Imagine that tomorrow your world will be gone. It's difficult to do, but please try. It's important to realise what it is that we have because life is so fragile and we never know what is just around the corner.

My name is Anna Bright, and I am telling you this story from my prison cell. It's not the normal kind of prison cell, and I have committed no crime. There are no walls in my prison, and there is no secured door, for I am locked away inside my own body. My thoughts, feelings and senses, they are all as they were, and the connection from outside to inside is working as well as it ever did, but the connection from inside to outside is broken. I can't move, smile or talk; my face remains inert and expressionless, unable to convey my emotions. A machine is keeping me alive by breathing for me; the tube into my windpipe feels uncomfortable and intrusive. I want to take a deep breath and sigh or yawn; I want to shout and tell others I can hear them, but no matter how hard I try, no matter what effort I make, nothing changes and no one notices.

Allow me to tell you how I ended up here. Quite simply, I slipped. I stepped on a wet floor in the bathroom of a hotel room, and I slipped and banged my head on the bidet. A bidet of all things! I suppose it is marginally better than a toilet, or maybe it isn't? I don't know if people even use them. I knocked myself out on a superfluous piece of bathroom furniture. Isn't that the most unexciting way to destroy the intricacies of my brain? I think so, but it is okay because the world outside my prison has been making up a far more exciting story to replace the wet floor/superfluous bathroom furniture one. The world outside my prison believes that I am the victim of a murder attempt, and according to the world, the would-be murderer is my boyfriend of eighteen months, James Green. I can't tell them this is not so, and it was simply an accident because I am locked in my prison, so I have to listen while the world makes up events that didn't actually happen. Oh, and James is probably going to prison and for a long time too.

People think I am asleep. I am not asleep; I am trapped. It's incredibly frustrating! Sometimes when I get really mad and want to shout 'I can hear you,' my heart rate monitor beeps faster. The only part of my body that still responds to how I feel and what I think is my heart. There is something quite poetic about that. It is so boring here, trapped, with the beeping and the rhythmic breathing of the ventilator, and all the alarms going off. I've been trying to work out how long I have been here, but I have no real reference. I think there is a shift change every twelve hours. I will try and remember how many handovers I have listened to about myself and divide it by two. Why not? I've nothing else to do.

The nurse who is looking after me today hasn't told me her name, but I think it is Viv. Some of the nurses introduce themselves which is nice, and when they open my eyes and shine a light on them, I try hard to catch a glimpse of their faces. I think Viv has blonde hair. The light shining thing shocked me at first. It's quite regular. Some nurses warn me; others just swoop in eyelid opened, light waved in front of my eye, other eyelid opened, repeat light waving. It's horrible, but a chance to try and see something. Apparently, it's something to with my GCS score. I don't know what a GCS is. Give me a GCSE any day, that's my speciality. The General Certificate of Secondary Education, because back before I became imprisoned in my own body by my altercation with a bidet, I was an English teacher at a very large secondary school. Was? I am an English teacher. I have no intention of staying here. As soon as I can work out how to get my body to respond to my mind, I am out of here and back to my life which I love very much. Thinking about my life makes me cry. I feel the sensation of crying, the welling up in the chest, the lump in the throat, but nothing happens. I want to feel tears streaming down my face. I want snot. I want a wobbly chin and a high-pitched voice.

It's visiting time. I hear my mum's brisk clip-clopping. I know which boots she is wearing, and that feels nice, that I can see in my mind's eye what she has on her feet.

"Hello darling," she says, "mum here." She sounds like she does when she leaves an answer phone message. I giggle inwardly, the only outward sign is a slight quickening of the beeps; I know how much she hates leaving a voicemail. She takes my hand in hers and continues chatting in her self-conscious answer phone voice.

"Darling, I... I want you to know that James still denies what he has done to you," her voice is cracking now, sobs are forming in her throat. "We aren't going to let that evil pig get away with this. Look at you; look at you, my beautiful girl." Wracking sobs now and her head is on my arm, I can feel her tears wetting the sheet. My poor mama, I want to comfort her. She sounds so desperate.

"How could anyone hurt you? How? You have been through so much; I should have protected you." If only I could tell her that it was an accident, I think she would find some peace.

It was an accident, but in a way, James caused it. Our relationship had gone from something that seemed too good to be true, to something dark and toxic and the consequence of that is this. Me being trapped in my body, James being accused of something he did not do and me being the only person who could help him. Some would say it's poetic justice.

****

I met James in September 2009. My best friend Chloe had persuaded me to go to her brother Tom's thirtieth birthday party; it was a fancy-dress party which made me even more reluctant to go. Chloe managed to get me to agree eventually by making me an outfit, which took her ages, and guilt tripping me about all the effort she had made. I was a cowgirl, and Chloe was my horse. She made it so that we were part of a pair and she promised to look after me. I hadn't been out with friends for over a year, and Chloe was doing her best to help me to move on and get back out into the world after the worst eighteen months of my life.

After a few glasses of wine, we took a taxi to Tom's house, and I nervously linked Chloe's arm as we made our entrance. Everyone looked great and had made an effort. There was lots of nice food and plenty of drink, and I began enjoying myself for the first time in ages. I chatted with old friends. I danced with a giant Dalmatian, Darth Vader and Father Ted. I queued for the toilet with Michael Jackson and Susan Boyle, and then I saw him, the big hairy gorilla, helping himself to crisps and hummus; his gorilla mask was pushed onto the top of his head, creating the illusion of being inhumanly tall, and he seemed to be staring straight at me. I wondered whether I was supposed to know who he was.

"Chloe," I whispered, "who is the gorilla?"

"That's James. He's Tom's triathlon mate, and underneath the hairy suit he is gorgeous," she 'whispered' back to me in her drunk, one volume voice. "Go and say hi," she said, prodding me in the back and trying to steer me in his direction.

"No," I said between gritted teeth, tensing my body, so I remained rooted to the spot. "I just can't."

"Okay," she said softly, "I understand. Let's drink more."

"Good plan," I agreed hurriedly, as we made our way to the fridge and topped up our wine glasses.

****

The following day I relaxed with Chloe enjoying a lazy Sunday morning; slightly hung over, with an endless pot of coffee and a mountain of toast (although I think that Chloe secretly wanted her staple of Coco Pops and sweet milky tea). I logged onto my email while Chloe dished up, there were two unread messages:

JAMES GREEN SENT YOU A MESSAGE ON FACEBOOK.

Hi Anna,

I hope you don't mind me messaging you? I was at Tom's party last night; I was the sweaty gorilla with the hummus habit......

Anyway, I just wanted to tell you that I thought your outfit was great, by far the most original there, and it was a really nice touch to bring a living horse with you ;-) (Sorry Chloe!)

Hope the hangover isn't too bad!

J x

JAMES GREEN HAS ADDED YOU AS A FRIEND ON FACEBOOK.

I felt a big grin spread across my face.

"I knew he was staring at you!" Chloe said smugly. "You did look hot in that outfit; you have to admit it."

"Shut up!" I retorted.

"Let's check him out," Chloe urged, snatching the laptop from me. "What's your password?"

"DylanWatts1982," I replied, taking a sip of my coffee. "Jeez Chloe, how much bloody sugar did you put in here?" I asked, trying to ignore the look I'd just seen flash across her face at the mention of Dylan.

"Four. I was distracted by your message, thought it was mine."

"How do you have any teeth left, at all?" She didn't hear me; she was already in James' photo albums. There was no denying that he was very attractive, he was tall with dusky blond hair and a boyish grin. There were pictures of him competing in a triathlon.

"Oooooh, that Lycra doesn't leave much to the imagination does it?" she winked at me mischievously and zoomed in on the photo. "It obviously wasn't cold that day!"

"Chlo!" I protested. It was true though, the tri-suit didn't leave much to the imagination, and there was no denying that James was gorgeous, even in Lycra.

* * * *

I've got an itchy foot. I can't believe how much for granted I took the ability to scratch an itch! It's my left foot; it's been itchy for ages. I've been concentrating for what feels like hours on trying to get my foot to move so I can rub it on the sheet. The frustration is unbearable; why don't I work anymore? Mum has gone to let me get some rest. I didn't want her to go. I can hear Viv rustling about nearby. I think she is getting ready to wash me. I wonder what I look like? I wonder what my hair is doing? I bet my eyebrows are huge! I like to get busy with the tweezers at least every other day. Mum's pa, Franco, was Italian and I have inherited his incredible monobrow. My skin is olive, and my hair is light brown and very thick and wavy. I know for sure that when the nurses wash my hair, they do not put hair serum in it, or even any conditioner. I bet it is a frizzy, wiry mess. I am tall, around 5' 9", and I am also fairly slim. My feet stick out the end of the sheets, and it gets on my nerves. I like to have my feet tucked in. Oh God, imagine how hairy my legs must be now! I must look like a lanky, sallow-skinned gorilla with giant eyebrows and shocking hair.

"Okay sweetie, just going to give you a little freshen up, alright darling?"

I want to say no, it's not okay for you to wipe me with tepid water and then rub me with a rough towel, but of course, I say nothing and the 'freshen up' commences.

"Just washing your face sweetie."

A wet cloth is rubbed gently across my face and around my mouth, around my ears, under my chin. Then there is a gentle patting of my face with the towel.

"Now your hands my darling."

My face feels horrible now. Viv doesn't use moisturiser, and it feels tight and dry.

"Okay sweetie, just going to wash your upper body."

Viv washes both of my arms, she lifts them and washes my armpits. I dread to think how hairy they are too.

"Just going to give you a little freshen up downstairs sweetie. Oh deary, you've got your period. I'll just get you a pad."

This is so humiliating. I feel the crying begin again. Nothing, no tears, no sobs, no sign to the outside world of my inner turmoil. Why can't I work this out? What if I'm left like this forever?

"There you are sweetie, all sorted. I'm just going to roll you and wash your back and bottom, deary, okay?"

Argh, no it's not okay, I'd much rather just go for a shower! There is another nurse in with Viv now, helping her to roll me and change the sheets. Together they slide me up and down the bed and get me cleaned up and into a fresh hospital gown. The other nurse isn't as nice as Viv, her name is Pam, and she is brisk and businesslike, for some reason I imagine her to look like Pat Butcher from *Eastenders*.

****

"Right," I announced to Chloe, pouring most of the super sweet coffee down the sink, "I'm off for a shower."

"Okay hun," she replied from behind the laptop.

"What are you up to?" I asked her, noticing a look of mischief in her eyes.

"Nothing," she replied, trying to look innocent.

"Give me the laptop," I ordered, laughing at her futile attempt to keep a straight face.

"Okay bossy, I was giving your profile a little revamp."

"What? Let me see!"

Chloe had changed my profile picture to an old holiday snap.

"No way, I can't use that picture."

"Why not?"

"Well, it's out of date, and I'm in a bikini, so it's indecent."

"What's indecent is that rabbit you have as your profile picture; makes you seem boring."

"I love that picture."

"Yes, but it's your pet rabbit!"

"Okay you can change it, but not to one of me semi-naked."

"Deal."

"Right, I am going for a shower. Don't do anything else to my profile!"

"Okay, when you're all clean and fresh we can reply to James," Chloe added, choosing a picture of her and me together at the previous night's party.

"Can we now?" I asked. "I'm sure that message was for me!"

Chloe looked up from her handy work and smiled.

"Hmmm, we're a team though, remember?"

Later that afternoon, Chloe and I replied to James, and although I am perfectly literate, I found it surprisingly difficult not to sound either desperate, stupid or both. In the end, Chloe composed a message, I okayed it and off it went:

Hi James,

Thanks for your message. It was a good night. Tom seemed to enjoy himself.

Chloe made my outfit; she says thanks for the compliment!

My hangover s fine, I have fed it well today. I hope you didn t suffer too much. Good to hear from you. Have you been doing anything nice today?

Anna x

* * * *

I don't know what the date is today. I know the date that I had the accident. That was on the 17th March 2011, but now I have a very limited concept of time. I feel like I have been trapped here for years, but I think it has been about three weeks, maybe less, maybe more. As I lie here, I think about how much I had taken my health and my life for granted. Things that I believed were important mean nothing to me now and things that I had never even noticed before are more important than ever. The large deep cleansing sigh, a yawn, licking my lips, scratching an itch, blinking, taking sips of water, the taste of food, these are all the things that I miss. Before the accident, I would stress about my weight, my hair and other trivial things. I didn't appreciate my body, my working, functioning body. I wish so hard that I will have another chance to count my blessings.

At the moment, I feel determined to wake up. Sometimes I feel hopeful, other times I feel hopeless. When I feel hopeful, I concentrate hard on moving. I start at the top and work my way down. I try blinking, moving my head, lifting my arms, opening and closing my hands, wiggling my legs, moving my feet, then I go from the bottom all the way up to the top again. Nothing happens. It feels like I am moving, but I am not. Usually, at this point, my hope begins to wane, but then I'll desperately begin praying.

Please God, please help me. Please, please help me to get back to normal. I will never take a single thing for granted again. Please God, please. Amen.

I will then become angry, and that is when the

beeping of the heart monitor picks up the pace. This gives me hope, something works. When I feel hopeless, I just allow myself to drift in and out of consciousness. I flit between a twilight world of drug-induced nightmares and wakeful paralysis. I pray for death, and an end to this imprisonment.

****

Hi Anna,

Not done much today. I went for a swim when I woke up but didn't do too well. I think I over-indulged last night!

Now I am going to watch a DVD, then hit the hay. I've got to be in London for 8 am, boring meetings all day long.

Are you working tomorrow? What is it you do, by the way?

J x

"Don't reply yet," Chloe warned.

"Why?"

"It will look like you have been waiting for a response."

"But we were!"

"Yes, I know, but we don't want you to look desperate. Trust me, reply tomorrow." "Okay," I said, "I've got some marking to do anyway."

The next day at work, I thought about James quite a few times. It seemed strange to me; I hadn't even had a real conversation with him. *This is weird*, I thought, but I knew I would end up sending him a message after work.

Later that evening Chloe called me, as she often did. "I've just been to Tom's and got all the goss on James." She hardly stopped for breath. "He's been single for two years and get this: his ex-girlfriend is a total psycho. She went to prison for assault. He is scarred for life; he was in hospital because she attacked him with an iron doorstop. Tom says that James is a great guy, they have been doing triathlons together for about ten years now. He was pleased when I told him that James got in touch with you. Tom sends you a big squeeze." I smiled, Tom was like a brother to me too.

Tom and Chloe's mum Jess, and my mum Rosa had been friends for years. They'd gone to secretarial school together and got married in the same year. Tom was four months older than my sister Eve, and I was six months younger than Chloe. We had spent summer holidays camping together, gone through school from playgroup to secondary school together. When Jess had died of breast cancer at thirty-eight years old, the devastation in all our lives was huge. Chloe and Tom stayed with us a lot. Their dad Trevor was like a lost soul. Suddenly a widower and a single parent to a ten and eight-year old, he did his best, but was a lousy cook and useless at doing

Chloe's hair. She used to call on me in the morning, and my mum would redo her messy, bumpy ponytail into a nice tidy French plait for school. Poor Trevor couldn't bear to see his children upset, and whenever they cried for mummy, he would give them sweeties, the result of that is that they both have the most unbelievable sweet tooth. Chloe is forever eating sweets, they both take three to four sugars in tea and coffee, yet they both have the most beautiful white shiny teeth and no fillings.

I ate my dinner; then I settled down to make some lesson plans for the rest of the week. I love planning lessons; I love my job. I miss the children at my school. I miss all their funny ways. A lot of people dislike teenagers, society generally seems to be terrified of them, but I love them. They are so funny and idealistic. I love their enthusiasm and passion, and they get on well with me too. I have the odd problem, but on the whole, most of the students behave in my lessons.

It was quite near the beginning of the school year, and I was busy planning lessons for my new year sevens. *Oh, bugger.* I thought as I logged on to my computer. *Why can't I stop thinking about him? He's a stranger!*

Hi James,

I'm an English teacher. Yes, I was at work today, I had a nice day. Hope your meetings weren't too

boring. What is it you do?
Anna x

He's broken like me, I mused. I felt like I had been through so much, too much to move on to a relationship anyway. Maybe someone like James, who had suffered too would be the perfect person to find some happiness with. *What are you thinking?* I ask myself. *It's just a few emails, slow down!*

****

Lying here paralysed and frozen, reliving my life so far, takes up the majority of my time. I feel sorry for the naïve Anna, who just over eighteen months ago, let this wolf in sheep's clothing into her life. I want to warn her, to tell her what he is, but instead, I am forced to watch the story unfold again as I replay my experiences from the viewpoint of a silent and helpless spectator. How I miss Dylan.

DYLANWATTS1982

Apparently, we all have a tragic love story to tell, one of unrequited love, or forbidden trysts with the 'one who got away' or who could never be. Maybe this love of ours never actually becomes our lover, or maybe we spend years with them in our lives, loving them from a distance, in secret, or perhaps we are lucky enough to be with them for a time and love them fully and in every way only to lose them. There are plenty of stories to tell the tale too; *Romeo and Juliette, Wuthering Heights, Tess of the D Urbervilles, Like Water for Chocolate*, to name but a few. My point is that it's a rite of passage, a coming of age and a teacher of many lessons when love hurts.

Let me introduce you to Dylan.

As a teenager, I'd fantasise about meeting the love of my life. Always I'd be wearing my nicest clothes, my hair would be perfect. We'd meet by chance. Perhaps he'd be sitting in my seat on a crowded train, and as our hands brushed in passing, the electricity would surge through our bodies, and we'd fall madly in love. Or maybe we'd crash into one another at traffic lights and fall passionately in love during a heated row over liability? Usually, in my mind, the love of my life would look a lot like Ewan McGregor. In fact, usually it was Ewan McGregor, and I had given it a lot of thought!

However, the reality of my love story is far more beautiful, well to me it is anyway.

19th October 2001

I was eighteen years old, and three weeks into my first year at university, I was beginning to overcome my shyness and finally knew my way around the university campus. I was determined to do well in my English degree and already knew that I'd probably like to go into teaching. I'd noticed a strange one-off session on my timetable. It was called IEL and was timetabled for one whole day, it was in a building right at the edge of campus, and no one in my usual lectures knew what it was about.

Nervously, I arrived at the building. I looked around at the other students, small groups were forming around the outside of the large building, and nobody looked happy. *I don't know anyone.* I thought, panicking. We began making our way into the building, signing in at a desk at the entrance.

"Name?" the lady at the desk barked at me. "Anna Bright," I whispered to her nervously. *What is this all about?* I wondered silently to myself, feeling anxious as I made my way to room c12 as directed by the ogre at the desk. From what I could gather, the whole of the first year was to attend this day, and we'd been split into random groups. I arrived at room c12 and nervously stepped inside. I scanned the room quickly. There were no desks, only chairs, which had been arranged in a large circle. I took a seat next to a girl who looked as though she was only twelve years old. I glanced at her and smiled; she looked as terrified as I felt. The room began to fill, and people muttered uncertainly. I watched as the seats in the circle became occupied, and I felt as though I was part of some bizarre psychological experiment. Most people tried to sit as far away as possible from any other human, but this became more difficult as the majority of the group arrived at this mysterious IEL session.

"Right, ladies and gentlemen!" the lecturer announced. "You are probably all wondering what this session is about!" No one spoke. I looked at my feet. "Well, this is a bit of an experiment," she added. *Great!* I thought. "IEL stands for Inter Educational Learning. This university is committed to promoting and enhancing great interpersonal and interprofessional relationships, and we have devised today's session as a way of bringing students together and enabling you to build bonds through teamwork and problem-solving."

"Isn't that what the student union is for?" the twelve-year-old whispered to me. I smiled at her observation. Today was going to be about bullshit.

Great.

"You will not be formally assessed on today's session, but it can form part of your portfolio, which you will use when looking for employment or further study, so please treat today as a learning opportunity, a networking opportunity and a fun way of enhancing your skills," she added smiling. "My name is Mandy. First, we need some ground rules."

Just then, the door was pushed open, and a latecomer tried to sidle in unnoticed. "Hello," Mandy announced, "sleep in?"

"Got lost actually," he said, looking quickly around the room for an empty seat. "Sorry, I'm late."

"Don't worry,' Mandy said to him, "find a seat, you haven't missed too much." I watched him make his way carefully across the room and sit in a seat directly opposite mine. He was tall and skinny, with messy, curly red hair. He seemed to be at that stage where he was tall like a grown man, but with a boyish face, almost like a child in adults clothing. Our eyes met, and he flashed me a lovely big grin. I smiled back at him, and Mandy continued talking about the session.

"All phones on silent please," she said, as people began rummaging in their bags and pockets. "The toilets are along the corridor to the left, and we will have refreshments in an hour and a half."

Then came my worst nightmare.

"Let's all introduce ourselves first of all. I want each person, in turn, to stand up, tell the group their name, where they are from, what they are studying and an interesting fact about themselves. I'll go first to get you all started." *NOOOO*, I screamed in my head, *no, no, no.* I felt my palms become clammy. *Something interesting? There is nothing interesting about me. What can I say? Oh God no.* I wanted to disappear.

"My name's Mandy; I'm a senior lecturer in textile design. I've lived here in Nottingham all my life, and my interesting fact is that I once appeared as an extra in Coronation Street."

One by one each person in the circle stood and made an awkward little speech about themselves. Of course, I was going to be last. Just my luck. At least I could try and think of something interesting to say. I trawled through my mind desperately. No, I couldn't think of anything at all. The latecomer stood up.

"My name is Dylan," he began, his facing flushing red, "I'm studying Music and Philosophy. I'm from Leicestershire, and my interesting fact is that I have a secret motorbike." He sat down quickly, looking relieved. How can it be secret? I thought, he's just told everyone. Eventually, my turn came around.

My hands were shiny with sweat by now. *Get over it, Anna*, I told myself. *This is what teaching is going to be like. Everyone looking at you, talking to lots of people, come on.*

"Hi, I'm Anna. I'm studying English, I'm from Shepshed, and my interesting fact is too boring to tell you," I said, far more loudly than I had intended, almost knocking my chair backwards as I sat back down quickly breathing a sigh of relief.

"Okay," Mandy said, "Thank you, everyone. Now, I'd like you to split into five groups of three, and we will begin today's first task." I ended up with Dylan and the twelve-year-old, who was an archaeology student called Sophie. We all stared at the cardboard box that Mandy had placed in front of us.

"Right guys, inside your box you will find some objects. The aim of this morning's session is to work as a team to build a vessel, which will enable you to drop an egg from a height of around two metres without it breaking." Sophie looked at me with an expression of utter horror on her face. People began muttering under their breath.

"Brilliant!" Dylan said enthusiastically, opening the box and examining the contents. There were a couple of balloons, some feathers, strips of cardboard two packets of toffees, a ball of string, sticky tape, glue and scissors. Dylan laid the contents out and pushed the empty box out of the way. I looked across at the other groups, they were slowly and reluctantly emptying their boxes, which contained the same items.

"What do you think the sweets are for?" Sophie asked, squeezing one of the packets of toffee.

"I know!" Dylan said, picking the other packet up and tearing it open. "We could use the wrappers as shock absorbers." I glanced again at the other groups, who seemed to despise this morning, and looked at Dylan unwrapping toffees and Sophie busily trying to make a basket from cardboard strips. It suddenly occurred to me that I was having fun. I knew if I'd gone in one of the other groups I too would be reluctant to enjoy myself, but I'd just experienced the 'Dylan Effect' for the first time. His enthusiasm and optimism were contagious, and I was soon to learn that this was his generic approach to life. As we worked, we chatted and learned about one another. Sophie was from Edinburgh. "I love it," she said. "It's my home. It's gorgeous, and there's loads to do."

"Why'd ya come to Notts then?" Dylan asked curiously.

"It's just a big village!" she explained. "I wanted to spread my wings you see! But like all Scots, my heart belongs at home," she added, looking for a second like she might cry.

"Yeah, I feel like that about Fleckney," Dylan said,

grinning. "I'm going back there tomorrow."

During coffee break, Dylan, Sophie and I continued chatting easily together. Sophie generously bought the three of us coffee and cake in the student coffee shop. Sophie was very pretty. She was small and slim, with shiny straight shoulder length hair, big blue eyes and fair skin. Dylan and I towered over her; he was at least 6' 2", Sophie was lucky if she'd even reached 5' tall! I felt protective of her, and I didn't know why. Was it the big eyes, baby blue like my beautiful Chloe's? Was it the expressive face, which seemed to show her deepest emotions without her consent? Perhaps it was simply her stature; she was tiny. I felt compelled to look after her anyway.

"Who do you keep your bike a secret from?" I asked Dylan.

"My folks, of course," he told us, grinning his big contagious grin. "They'd never stop worrying about me if they knew about it."

"Where do you keep it?"

"In my uncle's garage."

"How did you afford it?" I asked nosily. "Aren't you about the same age as me?"

"I've got this amazing uncle," Dylan began, "he's invented loads of gadgets. He also had his own business, something to do with medical gas supply and transit. Anyway, he had a heart attack two years ago, and he decided that he was going to give his fortune away before he died so that he could see us enjoying it. Mum and dad think that the £12000 is in a savings account. I am nineteen; it's my birthday today, that's why I'm going home tomorrow."

"Happy birthday," Sophie and I chimed in unison. "Are you out tonight then?"

"Yeah, I'm going for a drink or two, come and join us if you like."

Back in room c12, it was time to test our egg carrying creations. The three of us enjoyed the unwrapped toffees as we watched group one's attempt smash onto the ground in an eggy, feathery mess.

"Using the sweets as weights was a big mistake," Dylan whispered to me.

"They obviously weren't taking it as seriously as us," I whispered back to him. Three of the groups managed successfully to get their egg to the ground without breaking it, but we were the only ones who had managed to incorporate the sweets into the design. "Well done everyone," Mandy said. "I hope you all found this morning enjoyable. You have an hour and a half for lunch. Meet back here at one thirty for the afternoon session."

The afternoon session involved more team building activities. Dylan's influence meant that Sophie and I attempted every task with vigour and enthusiasm. That day was the best day I had experienced at university yet, and my cheeks ached from smiling by the time it was through.

Sophie and I arranged to meet Dylan in the student bar at seven-thirty that evening.

"Come and get ready with me," Sophie had offered. Her room wasn't too far from mine. "I've a wee bottle of voddy under here," Sophie said, reaching underneath her bed and pulling out a huge bottle.

"Wee?" I asked.

"Aye, it's Scottish for small," she said smiling.

"I know that Sophie. It's just that's not wee!"

"Ah," she said, laughing, as she poured us both a generous serving and topped it up with Fanta. "I've found that some people here don't understand me. When I say Scottish words, they look at me like I'm talking Chinese."

We got to the bar, Dylan was standing with a small group of friends. "Sophie! Anna!" he exclaimed, "Come and meet everyone." The night was brilliant. We went out in the city, and it was buzzing everywhere. Kylie's *'Can't Get You Out Of My Head'* was playing wherever we went. It was a secret pleasure of mine, although I pretended not to like it. That song evokes happy memories of being at university, meeting Dylan and Sophie and spreading my wings, swapping small-town life for city adventure. Why are happy memories so painful when framed by the presence of loss, pain and uncertainty? Surely happy memories should fill my heart with hope and joy? Instead, they shine a blinding light on my loss and hurt, illuminating every excruciating aspect of the here and now, forcing me to experience it sharply, deeply and painfully.

* * * *

Mum is back now; dad is with her. I think it is evening time, the pace of the hospital has slowed and quietened. The doctors' rounds are in the morning, then visiting time, then a freshen up and a rest, then physiotherapy. This is where my arms and legs are manipulated by Jeff or Kate, the hospital's physiotherapists. They are both kind and gentle, and I appreciate their efforts to stop my muscles from wasting away and to keep my chest clear and strong. I hate the fact that I can't thank them for their help. After physio, it's visiting time again, and visitors can stay for as long into the night as they wish. At first, someone was with me all the time, but as days and weeks have gone on, I've been left alone gradually more and more. This saddens me, but also gives me hope that people mustn't think I'm about to die at any given second, I'm sure that if that were the case, they'd never leave my side.

"Alright Anna," dad says, "how are you love?'

Bless him; he's even more awkward than mum is at talking to the mute, unresponsive daughter. Dad is nice. He's nice, but a bit of a waste of space. I'm under no illusions about him, although mum has always tried to hide the fact that he is a functioning alcoholic, and he's only managing the functioning bit because of mum. I strongly suspect that if he didn't have mum, he'd have no job, no house, just drink. She's amazing my mum. She's kept everything together and stood by a husband whose first love is whisky. He is never any different though, dad. When he has a drink, he is always funny, happy, endearing. Only mum, Eve and I know that funny, happy, endearing dad is not real. To the outside world, we present the perfect family unit, but the reality is very different. "Dad was speaking to John at work darling; he reckons that there is no way they will grant that monster bail when his crime is so hideous, he will be held in custody for sure."

"They ought to throw away the key," dad added, his voice sounding small and strained. Oh, my poor parents, the hell of thinking that a violent assault had left me in this state. The horror that they must be imagining, I guess that images of James smashing my head against the bidet, the look of fear and pain in my eyes, me pleading for mercy, are what play through their minds taunting them constantly. I bet they are imagining James turning away from me heartlessly and leaving me lying unconscious and broken on the hard, cold tiles of the bathroom. I know that I was very close to death when I was found. I know that my lips were blue, my breathing shallow and slow, my pulse barely palpable; I could hear the medical team discussing me as they worked to save me. I could hear the sobs of the hotel worker who had found me. My poor parents; tormented by horrors that are not real. I wish I could just tell them the truth. I slipped, it was an accident, and James wasn't even there. Poor James, he must be so scared too, and with all the hatred and scorn that is now being heaped upon him, his life must be intolerable. The initial hearing is tomorrow.

* * * *

By the time Christmas 2001 arrived, Dylan, Sophie and I had forged a friendship. I'd never had a male friend before, unless you count Tom of course, but he was as much of a big brother to me as he ever was to Chloe and I'm quite sure that I managed to irritate him to a level at least equal to that of his real little sister. He used to stomp off to hang around with Eve, who thought that Chloe and I were silly and immature. We caught Tom and Eve kissing once. They deny it to this day, but Chlo and I saw them with our own eyes. Being friends with Dylan and

Sophie was brilliant. The other girls in my halls of residence were nice enough; I just didn't seem to gel with them and the same with the others in my lectures. Dylan, Sophie and I just *got* each other. It was effortless, comfortable and fun to be around them both.

I was the last to know that I was in love with Dylan. It was the last day of our first year at university, and the celebrations had culminated in a huge piss up at the student union bar. One of Dylan's friends, Simon, was having a house party and, of course Dylan, Sophie and I went along. It was a late spring evening, the sky was clear, and the air felt soft and warm. Simon lived about half a mile away from the university campus, and we made our way there on foot. Sophie was really drunk, and Dylan and I walked on either side of her, holding her up as she wobbled along the road telling us both over and over that she loved us and that she couldn't wait to have a burger because she was sooo hungry. She was asleep within ten minutes of arriving at the house. Dylan and I made sure she had water, a sick bowl and some covers, then we went to join the others, who were all celebrating the end of their first year and saying goodbye for the summer. Everyone seemed to be smoking, and someone had put some terrible drum and bass music on.

"Anna," Dylan said to me, putting his hand on

the small of my back and steering me towards the door, "come with me to the shop, we need more beer." I grabbed my jacket, and we set out into the fragrant spring evening.

"Let's go for a walk down by the river," I suggested, glad to escape the hot, smoky house. My back tingled where Dylan's hand had been only seconds before, and I suddenly wanted to be alone with him more than anything. We had spent very little time alone. Usually Sophie was with us, and it had never seemed to matter before, but right now I just wanted him to myself. We walked along the river, the air was cooling, and the bright blue of the sky was fading.

"Let's hang out here for a bit," Dylan suggested. We lay down on some grass and chatted about our plans for the summer. "I can't wait to go out on my bike; it's brilliant. I'll take you riding if you want? You'd look good in leathers." Dylan lay back looking up at the sky while he chatted. I lay on my side watching him. Why had I never noticed how beautiful he was before? His hair was messy, curly and dark red. It framed his lovely open, friendly face. His nose was quite large and straight, and his lips were full, and his eyes were dark, maybe green, maybe grey, it was hard to tell in the fading light. I reached over and took one of his hands in mine.

"I'll miss you in the holidays," I told him.

"We can meet up," he offered, "it's not like we live far from each other, it'll be no time on my bike to get to yours."

"And we'll be visiting Sophie in August," I added. We had arranged to go up to Edinburgh for the festival. Sophie was excited about showing us her beautiful Edinburgh.

"But I'll still miss you."

"Softie," he murmured, his eyes closing. I lay back on the grass and looked up at the sky, Dylan's hand still in mine. I stroked his thumb, and he did the same back to me. I'd never held his hand before; it felt lovely. We lay side by side, holding hands for a few minutes, I slowly edged my leg towards him, and he did the same to me. Now we were lying with our legs touching and our fingers entwined. My heart was racing with anticipation. I knew I couldn't keep it in much longer. Nervous butterflies fluttered in my belly.

"Dylan," I whispered.

"Yeah?" he whispered back.

I took a deep breath, "I love you."

WHO IS JAMES GREEN?

Chloe is here; she visits me often. I always hear her chatting with the nurses before she makes her way into my room. I presume it's a room; it may be a bay. I don't know who can see me. I don't know what the place I am in looks like, save for a strip-light and a couple of ceiling tiles that are directly above me. Chloe is lovely; everyone likes her. She is incredibly friendly and bubbly, and she always gets people talking. Everyone who meets her warms to her.

"Hi gorgeous," she says to me. I bet I'm far from gorgeous. "Do you remember when we made a solemn promise to one another?" she asks me, knowing full well that I cannot answer her. *Which one?* I wonder to myself. We've made hundreds of promises over the years, Chlo and I. When we were little, we promised that we would get married to one another. Then when we developed a joint crush on the driver of the school bus, we promised that we'd both become bus drivers. I can hear Chloe rummaging in her bag. I wish so much that I could watch her, she carries so much crap around in her oversized handbag. I guess that she's pulling out random items; a clothes peg, maybe a couple of receipts, an odd glove, lipsticks, batteries, battered apples... "Ah, here we are. Right, Anna, a promise is a promise. I'm sorry if this is the wrong thing to do..." Ow! Chloe is plucking the three thick dark hairs that sprout from my chin. I made her promise if ever I was in a coma she would pull them out; I'd forgotten all about them and had never really believed that it was a promise that she would have to keep. "I can't do your eyebrows because it'd take too long, I think we'd need to wax them really." My worst fears are confirmed! They must be huge. "I'll just do the bridge of your nose; I don't want the nurse to see me. She scares me, that Pam woman." She scares me too. "Hmm, your face looks blotchy now. Sorry. But at least you've got two eyebrows again."

I can hear my mum and dad talking to Pam. Mum sounds upset.

"Yes, there are conditions, but I can't believe they aren't locking him away. He's a monster, a fucking monster." Mum never swears, preferring to use words such as 'blooming' 'flipping' or in extreme cases, she might stretch to a 'bloody', and that's when you know she is really upset! She is sobbing now; my dad is trying to comfort her in his awkward way. I wish I could have seen his face when she swore; I wouldn't be surprised if that were the first time he has ever heard her curse in their thirty-three years of marriage.

"I'll be right back," Chloe says to me, patting my arm and joining in their conversation. I listen to their discussion. It's hard to hear them properly, but from what I can gather, James has been granted bail and is free until his trial.

Mum and dad are devastated, and Chloe is shocked. I want to scream at them 'HE DIDN'T DO IT. IT WAS MY OWN FAULT!' But I am frozen. Rage and frustration course though my body, why can't I break this spell? What is wrong with me? *MOVE. MOVE. MOVE. FOR FUCK'S SAKE MOVE!* But I am broken, and I can do nothing about it. Inside I have collapsed into a sobbing heap, but outside I am lying serenely on a hospital bed. Surely there must be a way to fix this? I can't even move my eyelids, and right now I am completely hopeless. I just want to die.

* * * *

James was incredibly charming. When I received his reply, I couldn't help but let in a little glimmer of hope that something good was going to happen to me after everything I had just been through.

Hi Anna,

I'm an architect.

You know, it'd be nice to get to know you a little better. Would you like to come out for a meal with me this weekend?

Jx

My heart skipped a beat. Would I? Yes, I think I would. Was I ready? I wasn't sure, but what was there to lose? I couldn't spend the rest of my life wishing that I could change the past. I had to get over Dylan and move on. I rang Chloe. "Go for it!" she told me, and I needed little persuasion.

Hi James,

I am free this weekend. Yes, a meal would be nice. Where would you like to go?

Anna x

My heart raced as I pressed send.

His reply came within minutes:

How about the King's Arms? The food there is meant to be rather special. Is Saturday okay? I can pick you up around 7ish.

J x

I typed a brief reply:

Yes, Saturday is fine. I've never been to the King's Arms. X

Saturday raced around, and I was a nervous wreck as I tried to decide what to wear. I chose skinny black jeans, a long black and white stripy top and my favourite boots. I had nervous butterflies in my belly but resisted the urge to pour myself a gin and tonic. No point in getting drunk and embarrassing myself! I allowed myself a moment to think about

Dylan: a sick guilt mingling in with the butterflies, and then I made a promise to myself not to make any comparisons between the two men. Maybe a tiny little gin and tonic would help? I poured myself a micro-measure of gin and topped it up with flat tonic water that had been sitting in the fridge for weeks and gulped it down. Just then my phone rang.

"Hi Anna, is it left or right at the school?"

"Left," I replied. Oh God, he was less than two minutes away. I swigged a mouthful from the gin bottle and allowed the relaxing warmth to dampen the butterflies, I glanced in the mirror, smoothed my hair, took a deep breath and then the doorbell rang.

* * * *

Mum is crying again. She's had her head on my arm for the past hour, and I have pins and needles where she has been leaning on me. I want to lift my arm and wiggle my fingers to get the blood circulating. Instead, mum's head becomes heavier and heavier, and the wet of her tears on my sheets begins to sting uncomfortably. This is so miserable. I know that the thought of someone deliberately hurting me is destroying my mum. I hold the key to easing her heartache, the thoughts in my mind are here, so close to her. The truth that would soothe her is locked away inside me, and I cannot help her. Dad is sitting somewhere close by; he is reading the paper. I can imagine how he is sitting, leaning slightly back, with his legs crossed and his paper held up high in front of his face. I know he is reading the paper because he always makes a funny little 'ahem' noise as he turns the page. I also know that he has just finished a cup of coffee, after each sip he always says 'ahh'. He's quite irritating actually, and if we were at home I'd chuck something at him; maybe a scrunched up piece of paper, or if he was really irritating me, something harder, like a boiled sweet. Mum doesn't even hear his annoying noises anymore; she has become deaf to him. Soon dad will begin the crossword. I'm good at crosswords and mum and dad are both useless, this is going to be excruciating! Sure enough:

"One across; nine letters, hush money?" *BLACKMAIL!* I shout at him silently. "Mmmm, hush money?" Mum muses, lifting her head from my arm, causing a painful tingling as the nerves are bathed with blood again, "No, I can't think. What about the next one?"

"Slimy invertebrate with a long thin body, four letters."

"Snake," mum says enthusiastically.

"Well done love. Oh actually, no, that doesn't fit." *WORM*, I tell them, but they can't hear me.

SILENCING ANNA

* * * *

I opened the door to James, my heart racing away and my hands slightly shaky. He was only a person, why was I so nervous?

"Hi!" he said, as we briefly embraced and kissed one another on the cheek.

"Come in," I said to him. He was gorgeous; I did a quick scan from head to toe. His shirt was nice, his jeans were nice, just the right fit, not too tight like the indie kids', and to my relief, he was wearing decent shoes. God, was I shallow enough to have to check? Yes, apparently I was. I imagined what my reaction would have been if he'd been wearing a pair of hideous white trainers, or worse, sandals with socks!

"Would you like a drink?" I asked him.

"Yes okay, what do you have?"

"Gin and flat tonic? Or there's a bottle of Rioja open."

"Rioja please," he answered. I poured us both a glass, and we walked from my little kitchen into my living room. James wandered around looking at my photographs and ornaments. "It's lovely in here," he said.

"Thanks," I replied.

"What's this?" he asked, picking up a large wooden picture frame. "It's song lyrics," I told him. "They are cut to into a picture of a tree." He squinted at it, turned it to one side and began reading them.

"Mirrorball? Who's that by then?" he asked, as I tried to stifle the sadness that had just flooded my chest.

"Elbow," I told him.

"Oh yeah, they're alright they are." I quickly gulped my wine down, feeling it burn my throat and chest. James looked at his watch.

"You ready?" he asked smiling.

"Yep," I answered, pulling on my jacket.

James's car was parked behind mine on the road. My battered ten-year-old VW Polo looked very sorry next to his silver Audi. "Nice car," I said, as he opened the passenger door for me.

"It's a little treat to myself," he told me. "It was either the RS4 or a 911, but I think Porches are just a little too… *poncey."* I laughed. *A little treat?* I thought it must have been £30,000 plus worth of car. My idea of a little treat was a bubble bath, a bar of chocolate, or some new makeup, not a high-performance car!

We arrived at the King's Arms and made our way inside. It was an ancient inn, with exposed beams and a roaring open fire. The interior was beautiful; oak flooring, sturdy solid wooden tables, comfortable upholstered chairs and Farrow and Ball colours on the walls. Our table was close to the fire. It was a mild late September evening, and I could feel my cheeks beginning to flush pink, with a combination of the wine, gin and heat from the fire.

"You look lovely," James told me, placing his hand on top of mine. "Your cheeks are rosy; you look really sweet."

"It's the heat!" I said, putting my other hand on my face and feeling my burning cheeks. As James studied the menu, I studied his face. Dusky blond hair, slightly messy; high cheekbones and straight white teeth, but it was his eyes that were the most beautiful. His eyelashes were long and thick, and his eyes were huge, dark brown almost black. Even when he smiled, his huge brown eyes made him look sad and vulnerable. I think they are the kind of eyes that my mum would describe as 'puppy dog'. We ordered our food, ate and chatted. There was a bottle of wine on the table, and my glass was topped up again and again. I was beginning to feel very drunk and nipped to the ladies to try and pull myself together. I stared at myself in the mirror. My cheeks were red still, but my hair and make-up looked okay. My lips were stained burgundy from the bottle of Merlot on the table, and my teeth had become a kind of blue-purple colour. I rinsed my mouth in the wash hand basin and tried to rub the red wine from my teeth with a paper towel.

When I got back to the table, James was studying the dessert menu. "You got room for something sweet?" he asked.

"No chance," I replied, "I'll have a coffee though."

"Good choice, I think my eyes are bigger than my belly." James had ordered a large, rare steak, and I had felt very sick at the sight of the bloody juices swimming around on his plate. I could never understand the appeal of a plate full of blood and pink flesh. My chicken pie had been delicious though, and even with the hideous sight of the bloodbath opposite me, I'd managed to polish every last morsel off easily. James handed me the menu, leant back in his chair and ran his fingers through his hair, lifting it. He had a small bald patch and what looked like an indent on the left-hand side of his head. The shock must have shown on my face momentarily, "You looking at my war wound?" he asked.

"Sorry James," I said, embarrassed.

"Don't worry," he reassured me, "I know it looks horrible, luckily it's hidden by my hair, and it could have been worse. I could have been killed, but I am still here to tell the tale."

"What is the tale?" I asked cautiously. "Don't tell me if you don't want to," I added hurriedly.

"No, it's fine. I don't mind talking about it," James leant in close to me, just as we were interrupted,

"Ready to order?" the waitress asked.

"I'll have a double espresso," James told her.

Yuck. I thought.

"I'll have the cappuccino, please," I added, handing her the menu back and then leant towards James to hear his tale. Of course, I knew that it had been his ex-girlfriend who had injured him, but I didn't want him to know that I knew anything about him. I'd have been mortified if he had known that Chlo and I had been discussing him and that she had been trying to extract information from Tom to pass on to me. It'd make me look like a stalker!

"My ex-attacked me," he said quietly.

"Why?" I asked, expecting to hear that he'd cheated on her.

"Because she didn't like me leaving her to compete in triathlons."

"Really?" I said, surprised.

"Yes, she used to make it into a huge deal and then when there was an argument about it, she would become violent. She used to bite and scratch like an animal. She is crazy Anna; I've never known anything like it."

"That sounds horrendous," I said, squeezing his hand.

"She went to prison for GBH for this," he said, lifting his hair and showing his scar again.

"How did she do that?" I asked.

"She'd kicked off about me going away to

compete. We were arguing, and she began to hit and kick out at me. I grabbed her and wrestled her to the floor. I know I shouldn't have, I should just have walked away, but I was so sick of the attacks," he said, his incredible brown eyes full of sadness. "She picked up an iron weight that we used as a doorstop and crashed it onto my skull."

I listened in horror.

"I don't remember her doing it. She rang an ambulance and then fled through the back garden when they arrived."

"What is her name?" I asked.

"Daniella," he spat. "Daniella Frost."

"I'm so sorry to hear you have been through something this horrible James," I said to him. "Did you live together?"

"Yes, for a year. The thing is, I'd given her so much. She's a lot younger than me. Twelve years younger in fact, and she was only eighteen when we started seeing one another. I paid for everything because she was at university. I gave her everything Anna, and she has left me like this." He gestured to his head again. "I still suffer terrible headaches, but the mood swings are under control now. There was a time when I felt like I couldn't leave the house."

I thought back over the previous eighteen months of my life. I had experienced such hurt and sorrow, and I too had felt unable to face the world. James was damaged like me. Both of us had experienced pain and suffering. Maybe this was meant to be?

James drove us back to my house after our meal, and we polished off the rest of the Rioja, then we got stuck into the gin. I had a nice time with him, and he was playful and funny. We lay on the floor together going through my CD collection. "So Anna,' James said, "when am I going to get a kiss from you?"

"Erm, how about now?" I answered grabbing his face with both hands. It was good to get the first kiss out of the way. I hadn't kissed another man since Dylan, and it felt more like a hurdle to get over than a pleasant thing to do. *Fuck it!* I thought. *I may as well sleep with him too and get it all out the way in one fell swoop.* Not very romantic really! I was very, very drunk. James didn't need much persuading to stay over, and we fell asleep at around four am after some pretty disappointing, drunk sex. Nausea woke me at around seven, and I spent the rest of the morning vomiting. It was so embarrassing. James brought me some water, then left me to recover, I couldn't believe how perky he was when I was so violently ill. He could obviously just handle his drink better than I could.

I crawled out of bed at around midday and ran myself a bath, filled a jug with ice, water, lemon and mint leaves (this was my friend from work, Hattie's failsafe hangover cure) then checked my phone. There were three messages from Chloe, one from one am:

Hi, hope you are having fun, I've thought about you all night. Xxx There was another from ten-thirty am: *Hi hun, can't wait to hear all about your night. Hope you had a nice time. Love you xxx* and another from about ten minutes previously: *Hi Anna, let me know that you're okay. Love you xxx.* I pressed reply:

Hi, I'm so hungover. Think I might be dying! Xxx There was a message from James too, from around eight am; he must have sent it just after he left me: *Thanks for a great night. Call me when you feel better. J x*

I stepped into the warm bath, poured myself a glass of the iced water and tried to work out what it was that I was feeling. Apart from the churning in my belly and the headache, I felt flat, sad, empty and guilty. I felt disappointed with myself for getting drunk and cheapening the first experience of intimacy since saying goodbye to Dylan for the final time almost eighteen months ago. Maybe eighteen months wasn't long enough; maybe I needed longer, perhaps I wasn't ready yet after all?

I sipped my water and tried to talk myself into feeling better, but all I could think about was Dylan. I had promised myself that I wouldn't compare Dylan and James, but that promise was broken now, and I indulged heavily, comparing everything about them and immersing myself in my memories of the biggest love I had ever experienced. Like picking a healing scab and watching the blood flow red again, I let the memories of happy times break my fragile heart into a million pieces once more. The salty tears ran down my cheeks and into my mouth, my pounding head hurt more with each wracking sob and my chest ached with a suffocating longing for the man that I truly, deeply loved.

THAT LOVE AFFAIR

When I had told Dylan that I loved him on the last day of our first year at university, our hands entwined, and our bodies touching, I had been surprised by my sudden realisation, by the awakening of my feelings.

"I love you too Anna," he had murmured, turning onto his side to face me and stroking my hair with his free hand. "I've loved you since we met." We lay in the grass, looking at one another and talking quietly, the air cooling and the light fading rapidly. "We should go, you've got goosebumps," he said, stroking my face gently.

"You can keep me warm," I told him, snuggling up to him. He put his arms around me and pulled me close. "Your hair smells beautiful," he told me, burying his face into my neck and inhaling deeply. I loved the way he felt to me. I loved his gentle touch and his warm, soft skin. I gently stroked the back of his neck; I wanted to stay lying in the grass next to him forever, but I was shivering now.

"Come on, Anna. You're freezing. Let's start walking back." He helped me up to my feet, and we stood facing one another grinning.

"I love you, Dylan," I told him again.

"I love you too Anna," he said, smiling. He put his arms around my waist, and I wrapped mine around him tightly. I looked up at him, his beautiful dark eyes fixed on mine, and the world around us evaporated away as we kissed for the very first time.

"Shall we keep this to ourselves?" I asked as we approached the house.

"Yeah, definitely," Dylan answered. "We need to tell Sophie before anyone else."

I suddenly felt worried. What if this shift in dynamic changed our friendship? What if we upset Sophie with our new closeness? "It's okay," Dylan reassured me. "I have already confessed my feelings to Sophie!"

"What! When?" I asked him.

"It was one of her vodka nights. You'd passed out on her chair, and we were just talking. I was pretty drunk, and she asked me if I'd ever been in love and I told her then that I was in love with you."

"What did she say?" I asked.

"She said she didn't blame me because you are lovely. Then she said she didn't think you felt the same yet, and that it was probably only a matter of time."

"How on earth could she know that?" I asked.

"I have no idea," Dylan said, "but she was right.

Maybe it was just a lucky guess?"

Sophie's vodka nights usually happened after either she had been home to Scotland, or one of her friends from Edinburgh had been down to visit. Invariably, she would end up with yet another huge bottle of vodka and Dylan and I would provide the mixers and the snacks, and we'd all get stupidly drunk. I wasn't very keen on Fanta anymore, but like most eighteen-year-olds, I wasn't very fussy and drank practically anything! Although I can never drink Dr Pepper again, after my two-day vodka and Dr Pepper hangover, even now the smell of it makes me want to hurl.

Sophie was still asleep when we got back to Simon's. "Where's the beer?" someone had asked as we made our way back through the kitchen.

"We didn't have any ID," Dylan lied quickly.

"You were ages."

"Yeah we tried a couple of places, but they are really strict." I looked at the floor, embarrassed. Dylan disappeared to talk to Simon, and I went to check on Sophie. She had woken up on the sofa, eaten some crisps and then gone to bed in one of the rooms in the house. She was fast asleep, and I didn't disturb her. More than anything, I wanted to be with Dylan. I sat on the end of Sophie's bed and thought about the night's events. Only a few hours before, I had seen Dylan as a friend. Why hadn't I realised how I felt about him? Just then my phone vibrated in my pocket; it was a message from Dylan.

I just want to be alone with you xxx

I feel the same xxx, I replied.

I made my way back down to the party, feeling paranoid that everyone could guess what I was thinking. Dylan met me at the bottom of the stairs. "Let's go," he whispered and the thought of us sneaking off and spending the rest of the evening alone together made my belly do a little flip of excitement.

"What about Sophie?" I asked him.

"Oh come on, she's gonna be asleep at least until morning. We'll come back and get her first thing." We crept away without saying goodbye to anyone. The night was quite cold now, and Dylan put his arm around me warmly.

"Where shall we go?" he asked.

"My room, it's cleaner!" Back in my room, we listened to music and lay together on my single bed. I took Dylan's hand in mine again and turned onto my side to look at him.

"Gorgeous," I told him, planting a kiss on his lips.

"You're beautiful," he replied, kissing me back. I stroked his belly, and he did the same to me, edging his hand slowly under my top, finger by finger, my heart racing faster and faster with each touch of his skin upon mine.

"Your skin feels lovely," he whispered to me, pulling me closer to him.

"You feel lovely," I whispered back to him, my whole body alive with this tender experience. I put my hand inside his top and felt his heart beating, fast like mine. Slowly, he unbuttoned my shirt.

"You truly are beautiful," he sighed, pulling it down past my shoulders and letting it drop onto the floor behind me. I had never experienced intimacy like this before. It was delicious. I helped him pull his tee-shirt over his head, and he unfastened my bra. "Beautiful," he said again, looking at me and shaking his head. We lay on the bed, slowly inching our way toward 'the point of no return' as Chlo called it, eventually falling asleep, a tangle of limbs, in my tiny single bed, as the sun began to rise.

* * * *

There is a student nurse looking after me today. She is quiet and gentle. She reminds me of one of the students in my school. I miss school, I miss my friend Hattie, she is also an English teacher, and she is the most super-organised woman I have ever met. She's in her early forties, and she is wise and astute. She has everything anyone could ever need in her multi-compartmental bag: every type of painkiller, lip balm, Vaseline, chewing gum, Tampax, makeup, moisturiser, a first aid kit. If you think of something that you need, no matter how random, Hattie usually has it in one of her compartments! She doesn't suffer fools, but she is kind, loyal and strong. I admire Hattie. I wish she would come in and visit me.

The student caring for me is called Lauren, and I hear the nurse she is with explaining all the equipment and machinery to her.

"Always assume that a patient can hear you," she advises Lauren. "Never say anything that could make them feel afraid." After the doctors' rounds, the physiotherapy session and the inevitable freshen up, Lauren comes and sits next to me. I can tell she is a lovely person. She gently holds my hand and tells me that I am doing well. She describes the room that I am in to me and tells me what she looks like. I try so very hard to squeeze her hand, to thank her for the attention, but of course, nothing happens. I'm amazed at her insight. It is almost as if she has put herself in my place and imagined exactly what it is like to be unable to open your eyes and look around.

"Would you like me to read to you?" she asks me tentatively. "Yes please!" I respond silently. "I know this is a young person's book, but I think it is brilliant, I hope you like it!" *I am a young person!* I say to her in my head, as she begins to read the opening paragraph of the first Twilight book. "I'm here for ten weeks," Lauren tells me. "I hope you get better in that time."

Oh God, so do I, I think, terror engulfing me at the thought of being locked inside my broken body indefinitely, the endless, boring days and nights stretching ahead of me. Lauren's soft voice is lovely, and I really enjoy the story that she begins to read to me. I had always meant to read these books, so many of my students love them, and any book that gets children into reading is a good book in my opinion. I become engrossed in the gathering mystery of the characters in the story and their unfolding love affair. Is this another story of love that can never be? I wonder, my heart aching for Dylan again. When my parents arrive, I listen to my mum chatting to Lauren and hear the appreciation in her voice when she realises that she has been reading to me. "Anna will love you for that," she tells her, and it's the truth.

* * * *

Sophie was undaunted by our announcement. We walked back to Simon's house at around eight in the morning, hand in hand and grinning from ear to ear. Sophie was nowhere to be seen. "Shit!" Dylan said. "Where's she gone?"

"Hi guys!" she shouted, pushing the front door

open a moment or two later. "I've bought a wee bit of breakfast," she announced, plonking two bulging carrier bags onto the worktop. "Everyone is still asleep, but if you give me a hand with the dishes, then we can get this lot going." She gestured first to the piles of glasses, plates, bowls and ashtrays and then to the food that she was unpacking. "They'll soon be down when they smell this lot."

I helped her unpack the goodies: bacon, sausages, eggs, hash browns, black pudding, mushrooms, tomatoes, potato scones, beans and crusty bread.

"Sophie!" I exclaimed. 'You must have spent an absolute fortune.' She was always so generous; on the first day we met her she bought us coffee and cake, she always shared her huge bottles of vodka, and would regularly turn up at my room with chocolate for us both.

"Sophie," Dylan said.

"Dylan," she replied, placing the eggs carefully next to the hob. "Anna and I have something to tell you." She turned around and looked at us expectantly.

"Go on," she said encouragingly.

"Well, we are...you know...*together,*" I ventured cautiously. She launched herself at us both, landing between us and hugging us both tight.

"At last!" she said, squeezing us again.

"Sophie?" Dylan asked, "are you crying?"

"Might be," she answered, her voice choked, "with joy of course," she said squeezing us both again and sniffing loudly.

The summer of 2002 was amazing. Dylan and I saw one another often. He would ride from Fleckney to Shepshed on his secret motorbike. I discovered a love of motorbikes, the speed, the freedom, the thrill of sitting behind Dylan, with my arms around his waist, with the countryside whizzing past us. Of course, my family warmed to Dylan right away, even Eve, who had strongly disliked my previous boyfriends and treated them with disdain and disapproval, thought that Dylan was perfect.

"It's only because they're not good enough for you," she would tell me when I complained to her about her attitude toward my previous love interests. "You are too lovely to go out with some toad!" She did have a point; they had been toads. "He's so lovely!" she had gushed about Dylan, "Funny and clever and *nice!*"

"You two seem perfect together," Chloe had told me. Mum and dad both thought he was great. Polite, charming, interesting and interested in them too.

"How did you two meet?" he'd asked them, and we'd all been surprised to hear that dad had stolen mum from his best friend and that Mike Fisher still hadn't forgiven either of them for betraying him!

"Well, he didn't deserve her," dad informed us. "He was more interested in football," he added, "didn't realise what a wonderful woman he was about to lose," he concluded, kissing my mum on the top of her head.

Eve and I had looked on astounded at the rare show of affection and appreciation. The irony of what dad had said was not lost on either of us. We both knew that his first love was drink. I felt sad that their relationship could have evolved into this mundane routine and that they both just accepted their lot. It had never occurred to me that at the beginning, theirs was a passionate love affair too. Parents are just always parents to their children, aren't they? This was all part of the 'Dylan Effect'. He always got people talking about their lives, loves and passions and I learned so much about my parents just from spending time with them in his company.

August came around quickly, and we took the train up to Edinburgh to stay with Sophie. She had paced the platform at Waverley Station excitedly waiting for us. "I've missed you guys so much!" she said squeezing us tightly. "It's about a twenty-minute walk to our flat," Sophie told us. "Are you happy to walk it or do you want a cab?"

"Let's walk," Dylan said. "We've been sitting for hours." We set off along Princes Street. "What do you think?" she asked proudly, gesturing to the incredible imposing castle, standing proudly on Castle Rock.

"It's beautiful," I said, trying to carefully negotiate my way along the bustling street. It was a beautiful day, and there were crowds of people everywhere. The atmosphere was brilliant, and there were street performers with crowds gathered around them and raucous laughter and applause coming from every direction.

"I love it here already!" Dylan decided.

"It's not usually this busy of course," Sophie told us. "It's festival madness at the moment." I admired the beautiful Georgian buildings, with their copper roofs and tall windows.

"It's so gorgeous here Sophie."

"I know," she said proudly. "Only problem is the weather. If the weather was better, I think it would be perfect!" We crossed a bridge over a fast flowing reddish-coloured river. "That's the Water of Leith," Sophie told us. "It's that colour because of the peat."

"What's that smell?" Dylan asked. "It's making me hungry."

"The distilleries," Sophie replied. "It's lovely, isn't it? I live near the Galleries," she told us. "We can go there later; it's beautiful." Sophie's home was on the top floor of a large detached house, with a round turret on one side. The house had been converted into flats. "Please tell me that the turret is part of your flat," I said to her. "Yes, it is. It's lovely in there, you can see over to the castle. We can watch the fireworks from there later if you like? Mum has gone out shopping. She can't wait to meet you two; I've told her all about you."

Sophie lived with her mum. Her mum and dad had split when she was a baby, and she had only had sporadic contact with him, describing him as a "Lazy, selfish prick," and her mum as, "an incredible, strong, determined woman."

* * * *

Lauren is looking after me again today. "I do short shifts," she tells me, "five per week, but I have to wait an hour for my lift home at the end of each day, so I will read to you at the end of each shift." I want to hug her so much. I am enjoying the book and look forward to her reading to me. If she is on shift, but not looking after me, she pops in first thing to let me know that she will be in later to read to me.

"I don't want you to wonder endlessly whether you'll get your Twilight fix," she tells me insightfully. I can hear my sister chatting to Pam. I've learned that the other members of staff are not keen on her, and they call her Frosty behind her back. I wonder whether this is because she is so cold and emotionless.

"No, no change," Pam tells my poor hormonal

sister.

"Can she listen to this radio though?" I hear Eve ask.

"Yes, but not until it has been tested by our electrician. Pass it here; I'll put one of her name stickers on it so that it doesn't get lost." I listen to Eve's heavy footsteps as she makes her way over. She sounds a bit breathless. I wish so much that I could open my eyes and look at her growing bump. Pregnant with her first child, Eve has become the most emotional woman in the world and every time she visits me, the first ten minutes or so is spent with her crying desperately until she eventually composes herself enough to begin to talk.

"This baby is such a wriggler," she tells me, taking my hand and placing on her tummy. "It has hiccups. Wait until you feel it, it is so cute Auntie Anna."

I feel Eve's bump jerk gently. I am amazed, and I want to tell her how much this means to me. "I have turned into such an idiot," she tells me. "I didn't used to believe it when people said that pregnancy affected the brain, but I am doing such stupid things. I went into town yesterday, and when I tried to find the car in the car park, I couldn't remember where I'd left it. I got really upset, because it was nowhere to be seen and I felt like I was going mad, then I remembered that I'd gone into town on the bus because Liam had used my car for work while his was in the garage. I felt so stupid, waddling around the car park looking for a car that wasn't even there."

Poor Eve, she is usually so on the ball. "I also took that faulty DVD player back to the shop, and after explaining in detail what was wrong with it, announcing I'd like a refund and handing the receipt over, I realised that the DVD player was still at home." I laugh inwardly. Eve is so easily embarrassed, I would love to have seen her face.

"Everyone says it only gets worse once the baby is born, so they may as well lock me up now." I know that Eve is scared of becoming a mum, I think she will be incredible, but she worries too much. I wish that I could reassure her, and I also wish I could laugh about her mishaps.

Sophie's flat was as lovely on the inside as it was on the outside. It had high ceilings, tall sash windows and wooden floors. The kitchen was tiny, but the other rooms were large, there were two bedrooms, a living room and a large dining room which lead on to the turret room. The turret was a large hexagon, made up mainly of windows, there were large comfortable bean bags in there and a low battered wooden box that was used as a coffee table. The view from the turret seemed to stretch for miles and Sophie, Dylan and I stood drinking our coffee looking out at the roofs and treetops.

"There's mum," Sophie announced. "I'm just going to give her a hand, back in a sec." A few moments later, Sophie and her mum Claire were back in the turret. "Mum, meet Dylan and Anna. Guys, meet my mum, Claire," Sophie said happily.

"Hello, you two," Claire greeted us both with a warm hug. "Sophie has told me lots about you."

"Hello, and thank you for letting us stay," I said.

"Yes, we really appreciate it," Dylan added.

"No bother at all," Claire replied. "I hope you have a brilliant time. I'll just go and unpack my groceries, Soph, would you mind making me a cup of tea darling?"

"Back in a minute," Sophie told us. "Do you want another drink?"

"No thanks, I'm fine," I told her.

"Me too," Dylan added. Sophie disappeared into the kitchen with Claire.

"Come and sit with me," Dylan gestured to one of the bean bags. "What I really mean is come and sit on me," he said pulling me onto his lap.

"How gorgeous is Claire?" I asked him.

"She's stunning," he answered. "She is not old enough to be Sophie's mum. She doesn't look like she's even out of her twenties."

"I know," I said to him. "She must have been young when she had Sophie." Claire was just like Sophie; small, slim, pale skin, shiny straight hair, although Claire's hair was in a shorter style. They had the same large blue expressive eyes and looked more like sisters than mother and daughter.

"How old is your mum?" I asked Sophie, moving from Dylan's lap to the beanbag beside him as Sophie returned to the turret.

"She's only thirty-four," Sophie told us.

"She looks much younger," I reply.

"I know, she got asked for ID at the supermarket a few weeks ago, I've never seen anyone so excited in all my life. She didn't have any, but I did. It was really funny. I thought she was going to kiss the checkout lady!"

"I haven't booked anything for tonight," Sophie told us. "I thought we could just have a wander around then come back here for dinner. Is that okay with you two?"

"Yeah, that's great," I said looking at Dylan, who was nodding approvingly.

Sophie, Dylan and I took a walk into the city. The sun was shining, and there was something or someone interesting everywhere we looked. On the walk back to Sophie's, she told us a little bit about Claire.

"She was sixteen when she had me and still at school. Everyone told her she was stupid and believed that she would languish on benefits."

"I'm guessing that she didn't?" Dylan ventured.

"No, she worked, studied, scrimped and saved. She went without so that I could have what I needed, and she never gave up. Now she runs a successful marketing agency, she earns a decent wage, and is well respected. I am so proud of her."

"What about your dad?" I asked.

"He is a waste of time. In and out of my life when it suited him. He's four years older than my mum. He is a user, and I don't bother with him at all now. I haven't seen him since I was fifteen.

"What are your parents like?" Sophie asked.

"My mum and dad are just average people," I said, not wishing to betray my family's perfect image by mentioning my dad and his drinking. It didn't seem all that significant. Not really, I mean mum had just always kept everything together, and dad wasn't horrible. I suppose he was just a bit like an extra child to her, but he still worked, brought in money and supported his family financially.

"My parents are perfect," Dylan said. "Anna is coming to meet them next week, aren't you?"

"I'm nervous," I said.

"Don't be silly," Dylan reassured me. "They'll love you; you just have to remember not to mention the bike that's all. No pressure!" he said grinning.

That evening, back at the flat, we all sat around the large dining table. Dylan and I had bought wine and lilies for Claire, and she had placed the flowers in the centre of the table and immediately opened the wine, pouring four large glasses and draining the bottle in one go.

"Cheers everyone," she said smiling broadly and raising her glass. "Here's to beginning a new festival tradition, you are welcome here every year to celebrate Edinburgh's finest hour."

"Cheers!" we all said loudly. "Although I think that Hogmanay is Edinburgh's finest hour," Sophie said.

"Yes, you are welcome to stay for Hogmanay too," Claire told us, playfully nudging her daughter's arm. Claire had made a huge feast; there was so much food; tacos, rice, jacket potatoes, fajitas, chilli, guacamole, salad, garlic bread.

"Sophie, I can see where you get your generosity from," Dylan said. "This is so kind. Thank you very much," he added to Claire.

"It's my pleasure," Claire told us topping up our wine glasses again.

Claire was a real joy to be around, and her relationship with Sophie was lovely. They were almost like friends or sisters, laughing together and obviously enjoying one another's company, but Claire had just managed to keep a parental edge.

"We grew up together," Claire told us, leaning on the table, looking a little worse for wear after a lot of wine. "She gave me all the strength that I needed to make a success of my business. I did it for her, for us," she continued.

Sophie had begun to take the leftovers into the kitchen and Dylan and I were helping pile up the remaining bowls and plates. "You see, people will let you down in life, but you have to take responsibility for yourself. This is what I always tell Sophie. People will do whatever they feel they have to do and sometimes it's shit, but if you take responsibility for yourself, then you will always be okay."

"I think that's good advice," I said politely.

"Good," Claire added, hiccupping a little. "I think I need a cup of tea. I feel a bit wonky."

"Kettle's on," Sophie called from the kitchen, bringing in a tray, with mugs, a milk jug and a sugar bowl. "Mum gets drunk then tries to fix herself with tea," Sophie told us.

Dylan and I slept on a double air mattress in the dining room. "Luxury!" Dylan said, lying spread-eagled on top of the covers. We'd only ever shared a single bed before, and that was only twice: once on our last night at university and once when my parents were away. Mum and dad 'weren't keen' on him staying over and as annoying and frustrating as it was, we had to respect their wishes, sneaking moments together alone in my room while my parents were at work.

"Come here gorgeous," Dylan said, holding his

arms out to me, and we tumbled into bed together, a little drunk, very full and extremely happy.

The next day, Dylan, Sophie and I took a picnic and climbed Arthur's Seat. "It's worth it," Sophie told us. "The views are fantastic."

She was right, and we enjoyed our picnic right at the top, with the stunning far reaching views, eastwards out to the sea and westwards across Scotland towards Glasgow. "I love it up here," Sophie told us. "Mum and I often walk up on a Saturday morning after a big breakfast to blow the cobwebs away."

"Your mum is lovely," I told her.

"I know," she said, "she really likes you guys."

We said goodbye to Sophie and Claire on platform nineteen of Waverley Station. We had found out where Sophie got her generosity from, and we had left with a huge bottle of vodka, courtesy of Sophie's Gran, who ran a grocery store and was, like Sophie and Claire, extremely generous.

"That's where the vodka comes from," Dylan had said to Sophie.

"Yes, I told her that I liked a wee voddy and orange now and again," Sophie had told us, "and she always brings me a bottle when she comes to visit. I'm not sure that she realises its strength though. She's never touched drink in her life."

We found our seats on the train. Dylan sat by the

window, and I took the aisle seat next to him and rested my head on his shoulder. We chatted quietly about what a great time we'd had with Sophie and Claire, making plans for our next visit up to our new favourite place as the choppy North Sea whizzed past the window to our left. There was an elderly lady in the opposite seat mine, she was small, with white hair and a floral-patterned skirt, a clashing patterned blouse and lots of rows of coloured beads around her neck. I noticed that she was staring intently at Dylan and me. I smiled tentatively at her, and she raised her hand slightly and nodded at me. She had beautiful long, pale, elegant fingers and I noticed a fine gold wedding band sitting loosely on her wedding finger. I felt a stab of sadness, imagining her marrying her love many years before. I don't know why, but I presumed that she was a widow, and for a moment our eyes met, and I felt a strange connection with her.

Before long, the motion of the train had sent me off to sleep, and as our station approached, Dylan gently nudged me awake. "Come on gorgeous!" he said. "Wake up." We made our way to the vestibule of the train, and I leant against him as the train began to slow.

"Forgive me, dear," it was the lady who had been staring at us. She took my hand in hers. Her skin felt beautifully soft. "Know this," she said. I stared at her, taken aback by this sudden contact. She took Dylan's hand and put it on top of mine. "Yours is a love that will never die," she looked at me. "When the light is gone, and all is dark, this love will always protect you." She had tears in her eyes as she turned away from us and stepped off the now stationary train. Dylan and I stared at one another for a moment. Then we too stepped off the train as she disappeared into the crowds on the platform.

DEATH BY RADIO

"I'm getting your radio sorted," Lauren tells me. "Fro.. I mean Pam didn't think it was important, but your sister wanted you to have it on, so I have given it to the electrician, and he will have tested it by tomorrow morning."

I am so impressed with Lauren. She speaks to me as though I can hear her, which of course I can, and she sounds so natural. She is caring and thoughtful, and I believe that she has grasped the concept of me being aware, but unable to respond, which of course is what I am. It is how all the people involved in my care are supposed to treat me, but I get the impression that most believe that I am just a lump of living tissue, a biological shell that once housed a person, and although they are not cruel, they do not tend to my emotional needs in the way that Lauren does. As she sits next to my bed at the end of her shift and begins to read to me, I try so hard to respond to her, to move my eyelids, or wiggle a finger. It's impossible though, like one of those nightmares, where you know if you could just shout that you would wake up and everything would be okay. Instead, I struggle in a futile attempt to move, paralysed and helpless.

"I've got to go now," Lauren tells me. "I'm not in over the weekend, so I will see you on Monday. You've got a friend coming in soon; she rang earlier to see whether she was allowed to visit." I wonder who is coming. Chloe knows when she can visit so she wouldn't need to ring. Sophie? Mum had said she was trying to get a long weekend so that she could visit. I don't have to wonder for long.

"Anna Bright?" I hear Hattie enquire. "Just through here," the nurse tells her. "You can sit on that seat over there, bring it closer to her. Don't worry about the machinery, all the beeping and noise is normal, and we are just out here at the desk," she says kindly. Hattie is not good with hospitals. I know this because she broke her ankle on a school trip and had tried to convince us all that she was fine, even attempting to walk on it rather than go to the hospital. I'm really grateful that she has faced her fear and made the effort to visit.

"Anna," she says, her voice choked, "you look so vulnerable." She gently takes my hand and sits in silence for a few moments. I feel sorry for people when they first see me. I hear the shock in their voices. I wonder how bad I actually look? "I've brought you something," she tells me eventually. "It's a book. I'll read it to you." *Oh good.* I think. More stimulation, I usually have at least two books on the go at a time, and I feel lost without my usual form of escapism. "It's a one-off," Hattie tells me. "And you will have to excuse me because I am not sure that I can read it without crying. It's called Reasons to Get Well Soon, and it has been written by pupils that you teach." Hattie's voice is wobbling dangerously.

"Dear Miss Bright, you must get well soon, because we really miss having you for English. You are the best English teacher we have ever had. Love from Hannah Stevens." Hattie pauses to compose herself. "The pupils came up with this idea themselves and every child that you teach, from year seven right through to year twelve, has written you a message." I am so touched.

"Dear Miss Bright, please get well soon, because I miss you making the lessons interesting and we have to put up with Mr Harrison for most of our lessons! Please get well. From Samuel Wilkinson." Hattie continues, reading message after message, and I cry silent, dry tears, so touched by the effort that the children have gone to in their quest to let me know that they miss me. Mum and dad arrive just as Hattie is getting ready to leave and she shows them the book proudly.

"Aw look at it,' Mum says. "What a wonderful, thoughtful thing to do," she adds, her voice cracking. "Hattie please can you pass on our thanks to these thoughtful children. This will mean so much to Anna; I just know it will." I agree, but of course, no one can hear me.

Mum and dad stay for an hour or so, looking through the book and reading out the occasional quote to one another. "Ah listen to this one," mum says, "Miss Bright, please get well soon. I miss your passion for literature and your interesting and absorbing ways of teaching and inspiring us all. Love from Gemma." I can guess which Gemma the message is from. She is an amazing student with a flair for creative writing and a grasp of the English Language that far outweighs mine. I can't wait to get back to school. As always when I think about my life pre-bidet, I am filled with fear. What if I never get better? Why hasn't anyone managed to fix me yet? Mum and dad leave me to 'get some rest'. This statement always makes me laugh as if I have been sitting up chatting with them and wearing myself out playing hostess. I don't even do my own breathing, that is how rested I am right now!

It's morning now. I listen to the nurse that has looked after me overnight hand over my care to Pam, or Frosty, as I get to hear her called more and more often. She seems to be here all the time, and I don't like her, my heart sinks when I hear her whiny voice. I want to know what she looks like. Short and stocky, with a square head and short hair, is how I have begun to imagine her.

"Hi Pam, really sorry I'm late. Joy says that it's okay for me to work with you today, do you mind? I'm only here until three." Lauren is here. Thank God. "That's fine," Pam says dully. "You can take care of the obs chart then, I've got to go and make a phone call."

"Morning Anna," Lauren says brightly. "What is this?" she asks. "'Reasons to get well soon.' Oh, this is lovely, the children at your school must really care about you to do this. I can't imagine going to this effort for my old English teacher. I am going to see if your radio is back when I have filled in the obs chart. I think that you need a little bit of stimulation and you will know what is going on in the world." If I could, I would jump up and hug Lauren; she is delightful. What an amazingly thoughtful person.

"Good news!" Lauren tells me. "It's passed, let's put it on." I feel so excited. "Hmmm, which station?" *Something good, please!* I plead silently. "Oh, it's a digital radio, very nice. I think we should have this one." Lauren says, tuning the radio in and turning it up so that I can hear it, my heart sinking again. I don't want this station, the adverts and playlist will drive me crazy.

I'm not sure if I am hearing things right, there is a song on the radio that has just mentioned constipation in the lyrics. Perhaps I am more affected by the drugs than I thought? Why would anyone sing about constipation? I feel so ungrateful. The radio seems to become louder and louder, drowning out my thoughts intrusively. I feel so miserable and helpless, the radio presenters' light-hearted chatter drilling into my brain. God, I wish I could throw something at it.

Lauren comes to read to me again at the end of her shift. *Turn the radio off.* I plead, unable to concentrate on her lovely voice. I try to listen to the story and drown out the terrible song that has begun to play, but again, I find the lyrics just too distracting. I don't think I have ever heard such a disturbing song and I wish I could laugh about it with someone. Perhaps it's a parody? In fact, a feel a bit violated listening to the lyrics, plus the singer is mixing tenses. The English teacher in me is appalled!

"Hi there! What we listening to?" It's Chloe. She will know that I can't bear to listen to this shite.

"I got Anna's radio sorted," Lauren says happily.

I realise with horror that Lauren will feel terrible if she finds out that today was my idea of torture. *Chloe, please don't tell her, please.* I want to save Lauren's feelings; I don't want her to be embarrassed.

"That's brilliant Lauren," Chloe says tactfully. "She needs a link to the outside world. Would you mind if I put it on to her favourite station?"

If I could breathe, I would breathe a huge sigh of relief right now, because Lauren's feelings have been spared by Chloe's tact and I am now listening to my favourite music. No more double-glazing adverts or horrendous jingles.

GROWING UP

Dylan and I were so happy. I was almost smug about our love and believed it would be forever. There was no way that Dylan would ever hurt or betray me, of that I was sure.

Soon after our first trip to Edinburgh, he took me to meet his parents. "Don't mention the bike," he reminded me, as we walked along the road towards the house that he had grown up in. The house was a large red brick Victorian building.

"Wow, this is massive."

"Mum and dad were pretty well established in their careers by the time they had me," he told me. "They worked very hard for all of this," he said, gesturing to the garden and house.

I felt nervous as we approached the front door and I gripped Dylan's hand tightly. "Don't worry," he reassured me. "They will love you." We stepped inside into the cool house, a welcome relief from the hot, dry sun. "Hi!" he called loudly.

"In the kitchen," a woman's voice called back. I don't know what I had expected his parents to be like. He had told me that they were established in their careers when he had been born, so I imagined them to be in their late thirties by the time Dylan came along, making them in their mid-fifties now. We walked toward the kitchen, my nerves increasing as we approached the door.

"Mum, I've brought Anna to meet you," Dylan announced as we walked through the door, my heart pounding loudly.

"How lovely to meet you," Nell told me, hugging me and kissing me on the cheek. "Would you like a drink?" she asked.

"I'll sort it, mum, you sit with Anna, and I'll put the kettle on. Where's dad?"

"He's playing golf," Nell replied, turning to me. "It's so nice to meet you, Anna," she told me.

She was nothing like I had imagined. She was so old! She looked like she was in her late sixties. She was wearing old lady clothes too, a high-necked blouse and a mid-calf length skirt. 'Sensible length,' my Gran used to call it. 'Not too long, not too short.' Her hair was in a kind of cottage-loaf style, and she was wearing large spectacles.

Dylan placed my cup of coffee down on the dark, mahogany table and handed his mum a cup of tea.

"There are biscuits in the tin, son," she told him, and he reached up into one of the cupboards and brought down a vintage Cadbury's Roses Tin.

"Ah look at your tin!" I exclaimed. "It's lovely, how old is it?"

"Gosh, it must be thirty years old," Nell told me. "And I hadn't even noticed until you pointed it out. We've always used it for homemade biscuits."

Dylan picked up the tin again and studied it, before taking three biscuits and putting them on his plate.

"These are my favourite, thank you. You'll need to make some more though."

Nell smiled at him. "He's always had a good appetite but is as skinny as ever. I worry about him away at college. Does he eat properly Anna? Or is it all junk food?"

I reassured her that Dylan ate well while he was away from home, and we all sat around the table chatting and enjoying Nell's home baking.

"I worry too much about Dylan," Nell confessed. "Sometimes I still can't believe he's here, and he's going to be twenty soon! We waited a long time for our boy."

"I used to pretend that mum and dad were my gran and grandad," Dylan told me. "They were embarrassing!"

"That's right," Nell continued. "We didn't mind though; we were just so happy to have him, we knew he'd probably be embarrassed by us."

Nell went on to tell me that she and Edward had tried for a baby for years after they had married, eventually accepting that their much-desired child would never be.

"I was only eighteen when we married," Nell told me. "And in those days, you were expected to have a honeymoon baby. I was eventually told that I was 'barren' and that we should adopt a child, but we didn't want to. We just accepted that it would only be the two of us and enjoyed our lives together. When I went to the doctor with weight gain, bloating and fatigue, the last thing that I expected to be told was that I was six months pregnant. Especially not at forty-eight years old, I thought it was my thyroid or the change of life."

"Wow, six months! Didn't you feel him moving?" I asked.

"No, I thought I had wind!"

We went into the sitting room, and I wandered around looking at the pictures of Dylan that adorned every surface.

Dylan as a tiny baby in Nell's arms, her smile huge and proud. Dylan as toddler on a little wooden trike, his gorgeous red curls as messy as ever and his unmistakable grin as infectious as always. Dylan in his first school uniform, rows of school pictures through the years with toothless grins and badly combed hair. My favourite school picture was one of him aged around nine, his teeth far too big for his mouth and his beautiful red curls flattened into a terrible centre parting.

"Mrs Meade did that to me," Dylan told me. "My hair always annoyed her."

"I know it's a bit of a Dylan gallery in here," Nell said. "But we wanted to remember every precious minute of his childhood. When he was born, and I held him for the first time, I just knew that every moment with him would be precious. He was so beautiful and perfect, and I remember saying to the midwife that all I wanted for him was a life full of joy. The thought of my child ever suffering, well that was unbearable to me."

"Mum's so soppy," Dylan teased.

"I know I am," Nell agreed, "but I'm the first to admit it."

Later on, when Nell had gone to pick Edward up from golf, Dylan and I cuddled up on the sofa chatting about his parents and his childhood.

"Your mum totally dotes on you doesn't she?"

"Yep, and so does my dad."

"Why'd they call you Dylan? It seems like a young parents' name."

"Come on, I'll show you," he told me, jumping up and taking me by the hand. We walked back out into the hallway and through another door that led us toward the back of the house. I was amazed at the room that I found myself in. It was large with tall windows on one side and a grand piano on the other, on the nearside, from floor to ceiling and wall to wall were shelves upon shelves of CDs. There was a stereo system next to the piano and large guitar-shaped case that I guessed held a cello. There were three different kinds of acoustic guitar and two electric guitars and a large oak bookcase filled with music books.

"This room is incredible," I told Dylan. "But it doesn't explain your name."

"Mum and dad were obsessed with Bob Dylan!" He told me. "Dad more so than mum and mum was sure she'd have a girl, so she told dad that he could call me whatever he liked if I was a boy, but she'd choose the girl's name, plus my dad is half Welsh. Look over here." He gestured, showing me a large wooden box. He opened the lid to reveal a Bob Dylan treasure trove. It was filled with original vinyl: *Bringing it All Back Home, Highway 61, Blonde on Blonde, Blood on the Tracks* and others that I hadn't even heard of. Posters, gig tickets, a signed photograph, tee-shirts and magazine articles.

"This is amazing," I said to him. "Do *you* like Bob Dylan?" I asked.

"I wasn't too impressed with him when I was little, but I certainly appreciate him now. I don't mind being named after him. It could have been a whole lot worse! They could have been Elvis fans."

I thought about the music that my parents were into. Born into our family, Dylan could have been called Elton or Gene, but would most likely have been a Neil, Phil or Paul.

Nell and Edward's music collection was vast and diverse. Classical music, ballets, opera, brass band music, and every genre of popular music that I could think of filled the shelves. The room was like an Aladdin's cave.

"What did your parents do?" I asked, picking up a picture of Dylan wearing a lime green blazer, holding a trombone.

"They ran their own business before I was born," he replied. "I was eleven in that picture," he told me, gesturing to the image in my hand. "They sold the business when I was a baby, and then both worked from home. Mum teaches music, mainly piano, and dad teaches guitar, and he also tunes and repairs pianos. It just keeps a bit of money coming in, although they are pretty comfortable."

Dylan went on to tell me that his parents had worked extremely hard building up their business and had sold it when he was three months old, making them a very nice profit and meaning that they could buy their lovely house and work from home spending as much time as possible with their precious son and of course teaching him to play and love music just as much as they did.

Dylan's dad was just as warm and friendly as Nell. He was tall like Dylan, and also shared the same mischievous grin. I felt comfortable and welcome in their home and best of all; they didn't mind at all that Dylan wanted me to stay, telling us that we should take the spare room with the double bed.

"We were married at your age!" Nell told us. "It was a long time ago, but yes, we were young once, and actually I remember it like it was yesterday," she continued winking at Edward, who winked back and grinned like a schoolboy.

"Your mum and dad are ace!" I told Dylan later that night as we lay on the double bed in the spare room watching *I'm a Celebrity, Get Me Out of Here.*

"I told you they were perfect," he reminded me. I practically moved in with them for the summer holidays, only returning home when my mum nagged at me to "Remind me who my youngest daughter is?" She worried that I'd be outstaying my welcome there, but Nell and Edward made it perfectly clear that I was more than welcome, and why would Dylan and I want to go and stay at my parent's house where we had to have separate beds when we could sleep together every night and enjoy Nell's amazing cooked breakfasts every morning?

* * * *

Dylan and I did our growing up together, and during the following two years at university, our relationship strengthened and flourished. The vodka nights with Sophie continued, only now we all shared a student house in Nottingham with three other students, two from my course and one from Sophie's. Our New Year and festival traditions continued as Claire had suggested, with us falling in love with Edinburgh a little bit more each time we visited.

"Let's move up here," Dylan suggested as we sat at the very highest point of Arthur's Seat watching the fireworks. It was August 2004, a week before my twenty-first birthday and we were getting ready to go travelling together for six months. "We'll be back in March. Let's apply to do our PGCE here. What have we got to lose?"

It was a great idea. Dylan and I had both decided to go into teaching, at least for the time being. Dylan taught cello, piano and guitar privately and brought in a little extra cash and I had begun working in a soul-destroying call centre for a company near Shepshed. I hated it so much, but it was only temporary, and in four weeks I would be getting on a plane with Dylan and experiencing what Eve had described as, "The best thing I have ever, ever done."

****

Lying here, still and silent, I grieve deeply for my life. Dylan gave me strength and an eagerness for living that I had not quite achieved before. My parents' cautious approach had made me wary of new experiences, but Dylan's way of treating everything as an adventure, as something exciting to embrace, gradually changed my outlook and my approach to the world. I try desperately to muster up some of that optimism and belief. *Come on Anna*, I tell myself, *you can do it, you can move.* The radio is playing quietly in the background, and just as I begin to feel the despair creeping in, a song that I love begins to play. I quiet my thoughts and listen. It's a song by Elbow. I feel the emotion stir in my chest, the lump in my throat. I yearn for Dylan. The song is called *One Day Like This* and we had listened to it together many times. The sob is in my throat now, a huge wracking sob that would make my shoulders shake if my body was working. The tears would be running down my face by now if I wasn't broken, it feels as though they are, but I know it's an illusion.

"Anna?" It's Lauren, she takes my hand gently in hers. "You have tears. Oh, Anna, can you hear the music? Do you have sad memories?" She wipes my face gently with a soft tissue, and then she squeezes my hand. "Pam, Anna had tears," she says, her voice slightly choked.

"I doubt it," Pam says abruptly, "it was just secretions. The pollen count is high. That girl is not responsive."

YES, I AM. I shout happily to myself. *I CRIED REAL TEARS! THANK YOU ELBOW.*

"Anna was crying earlier," Lauren whispers to Chloe, who has popped in to visit me.

"You sure?" Chloe whispers back.

"Yes, I think so, there was a song on the radio, and it was quite a moving kind of song, and when I looked at her, she had tears running down her face. Pam reckons it's the pollen count, but I really think they were genuine tears."

They were! I tell her in my head. Chloe takes my hand and asks me to squeeze hers if I can hear her. I try so very hard but nothing happens, and I hear the despondency in her voice.

"What song was it?" she asks Lauren.

"Not sure."

"Sing it," Chloe suggests.

"No, I can't remember the words."

"Can you hum it?" Lauren hums something that resembles the song, and Chloe pauses for a second.

"Yes!" she says excitedly. "Elbow, yes that would definitely have her in tears. Anna, you can hear us?" she exclaims, as she begins to cry, setting me off again.

"See!" Lauren tells her. "She's crying again!"

I laugh inwardly at the irony of it all. Chloe has worked so hard to help me stop crying in the past and now here she is celebrating my tears. She is lovely. I think back to all the times that she has been there for me, and realise that it equates to every time I have ever needed a friend. Chloe knows when to be bossy and forthright and when to back off and let me have a good cry. She knows when I need to spend time with her, despite what I tell her, and she knows when to leave me to wallow.

FACING FORWARDS

Do you want a hangover buddy? xxx

It was a text message from Chloe. I had been lying in the bath for an hour, turning the hot tap on and off with my foot and lazily sipping the iced water with the mint leaves and lemon slices. Yes, I did want a hangover buddy, I wanted someone to talk to about all the thoughts that were buzzing around my mind.

Yes please! xxx I replied.

Give me 20 mins xxx came Chloe's response.

I stepped out of the bath, dried myself quickly and pulled on some comfy jogging bottoms and a hoody. I wanted to feel safe and cosy. I washed up the wine glasses and put the empty bottles in the recycling. *Where did all the gin go?* I wondered. I was sure we hadn't had that many gin and tonics, but the bottle was empty, and I was incredibly hungover, so maybe we had. *Ugh, my head hurts.* I thought as I sat down on the sofa and waited for Chloe.

"I come bearing gifts!" Chloe announced letting herself in and waking me up from my uneasy dose on the sofa.

"That was a long twenty minutes," I told her, looking at the clock. An hour and a half had passed.

"I popped to Tom's. He sent you these," she told me holding up a massive packet of cheese and onion crisps. "And I've brought you these," she added, handing me a litre bottle of cola and some Alkaseltzer.

"Thanks," I said, smiling. Chloe fixed me some Alkaseltzer, tipped the crisps into a bowl, poured us each a large glass of cola and sat down next to me on the sofa.

"Thanks," I said to her.

"No worries gorgeous. Soooo, how are you feeling? How did last night go?"

"Oh Chlo," I began, "he's lovely, and I had a nice time, but I have felt so rubbish today."

"I thought you might," she reassured me. I went on to tell her my train of thought while I was in the bath and she reminded me that it was normal considering the circumstances.

"It's time to start facing forwards Anna," she told me. "If you keep looking back, you will be stuck forever."

"Yeah, I think you are right. I just feel so cheap. I mean I got so drunk, and I can hardly remember having sex with him. In fact, I am slightly worried that I fell asleep during the sex."

Chloe laughed.

"Oh Anna, sorry, but how drunk were you to do that?"

"I was wrecked! I could hardly stand."

"Tom says James was fine today. He saw him at the pool."

"What? Am I just really bad at holding a drink?" I asked her.

"Well yes, you are really bad at holding your drink and don't forget, James is a big lad and pretty muscular, so he's got to be able to handle his drink better than you," Chloe reasoned. "You heard from him today?"

"Yeah, I had a text this morning, but I haven't got back to him yet, I felt too negative," I answered, pulling my phone from my pocket and looking at the message from James again. "I'll text him now." I typed a reply into my phone.

Hi James, I had a good night, thank you. X

Chloe managed to cheer me up and help me to think positively about the future. It was natural to feel strange. I had been with Dylan for six years, and before that, I had only had two short relationships, one for three months and one for four months. I was bound to feel a little bit different starting over with someone new. "James is really into you," Chloe told me.

"Tom said that he couldn't stop grinning at swimming today and that he kept talking about you.

Tom says he's going to blackmail you to keep him quiet about all the stuff he knows about you from your childhood."

"Really? Well, I've got plenty to tell about Tom if he does that!"

James replied to my message later that evening. *Hi Anna, glad you had a nice time. Do you fancy going to the cinema midweek? I'm free Tues and Wed evening. X*

And so began my relationship with James Green. He was charming, good-looking, funny and generous. He had a well-respected, interesting job. There was nothing that was not right about James, or so it seemed.

"You are so wonderful," he'd tell me. "You make me so happy," he'd say. "You are so different to Daniella. After everything I have been through with her, you are like a breath of fresh air."

Slowly I warmed to this new relationship. It wasn't like my relationship with Dylan. I took longer to let down my guard, but day by day, week by week. I let James in a little more until after three months or so, I began to have stirrings of what felt like love. *Am I in love with him?* I asked myself thinking about him; his big searching brown eyes, his sense of humour, his gorgeous body. The way he treated me like a princess, handled me with kid gloves, paid for everything, (actually a bit annoying) told me over and over again how happy I made him. *Yes, I think I am.* I answered my own question, and what was more, I had begun to recognise a nice fuzzy feeling in the pit of my stomach. Were they the seeds of happiness growing in my belly? I hoped so.

"My parents are having a party in a few weeks," James told me. "They'd like us to come; they can't wait to meet you."

I was nervous about meeting James's parents. His dad, Clive, was also an architect and his mum, June, took care of the admin side of the family run business. I was so worried about what they would think of me. They were a big part of James's life, and he visited them often, worked alongside them and seemed to value them highly.

"My parents have supported me through so much," he would tell me. "I used to ring mum in tears about Daniella, when I didn't know what to do about her, mum would always give me great advice."

"How do they feel about Daniella now?" I asked.

"They hate her!"

"I don't blame them," I said, stroking his scar.

When we arrived at James's parent's house it was already dark. It was a large town house in an affluent suburb. There were people milling about outside smoking and James took me through the house and into the garden, which had been kitted out with heaters.

June was a slim woman, in her early sixties. Her hair was perfectly done, she was wearing lots of jewellery, and her clothes were glamorous. She smelled of Chanel No. 5 and wore bright red lipstick.

"Mum, I'd like you to meet Anna," James announced.

"Hello dear," she said, taking my hand. "It's wonderful to meet the girl who has put the smile back on my boy's face."

June and Clive seemed to like me, and I was relieved to hear that I had passed the parent test. The party had been interesting; it was in aid of their wedding anniversary, and there were lots of members of James's family there. Everybody that I met told me that they were glad he had met a nice girl and was away from Daniella now. I heard how she was immature, selfish, only after his money, lazy and even ugly. I wondered why he had ever bothered having a relationship with her if she was all that bad.

"Honestly?" he'd said when I asked him later in the evening. "You want to know?"

"Yeah," I said. "Well she certainly wasn't ugly," he told me. "She was this gorgeous, petite little thing with a great body, I just really wanted to fuck her. Nothing more."

I felt my stomach churn with a horrible sickness. Why would anyone base an entire relationship on lust alone? If James was to be believed, he had embarked on a relationship with someone horrible and shallow, who he didn't even like, simply because he wanted to have sex with her.

"Oh," I said quietly. But what I was really thinking was; *You deserved everything you got for thinking with your cock.*

James's comment played on my mind and the following day I asked him about it again.

"Did you really only go out with Daniella because she was good looking?" I ventured.

He shrugged.

"Don't really know what I saw in her to be honest. I suppose she was pretty fit, but she's a complete state now. She got fat." He shuddered and I assumed that it was because of his unhappy memories.

"So, what is it you see in me then?" I asked cautiously.

"Are you kidding Anna?" he asked incredulously.

"No! What if you just want to fuck me? How would I know?"

"You are just the most wonderful woman I have ever met. You're vibrant, funny, and beautiful and your body is incredible. You make me laugh, I am so comfortable with you. You make me so happy. Anna, please don't ever doubt that. The only similarity between you and Daniella is that you are both female."

James had succeeded in making me feel better. Of course, he was going to be unkind about Daniella; I imagined that it would be difficult for him to admit to having once loved someone who had attacked him as brutally as she had.

How I wish now that I had listened to the alarm bells that had begun to ring in my mind. Why didn't I hear them? Which part of my brain thought it was a good idea to ignore what I was sensing about James? Now I am lying here, still, silent and voiceless, looking back at our relationship with the all-illuminating glare of hindsight. Every tiny warning sign that I remember seems blindingly obvious now. In fact, the relationship as I remember it now seems to be one long series of ignored warnings. How did I end up so deeply enmeshed in something so obviously toxic? I thought that was something that only happened to other people. An experience saved for women who came from broken homes, or who had low self-esteem, vulnerable women. *Had I been a vulnerable woman?* I ask myself. Perhaps? My heart was broken after all.

Eve is here to see me again. She tells me more stories of life with pregnancy brain.

"Earlier on, when I got back from mum and dad's, I tried to unlock the front door by pointing the car key at it and pressing the button," she told me. I laugh silently. "Luckily no one was about; I did a sly glance over my shoulder to check that no one was looking."

Poor Eve, I wonder how much more dizzy she will become with the imminent arrival of my niece or nephew.

"Anna, please wake up," she begs, beginning to cry. "I can't do this without you. Liam is really worried about the birth; he's going to be useless, I know he is."

Eve had asked me to be her birth partner, and I had jumped at the chance of being with my sister at the arrival of this much wanted little bundle. Liam planned to be there too, but as the kind of person who fainted at the dentist, none of us held out much hope of him managing to see the entire birth through. I feel so helpless; I should be there for her. I feel myself beginning to cry again. This time I know that the sensation of tears running down my face is real, but Eve doesn't notice, and I hear her sniffing and clearing her throat in an attempt to pull herself together. She tries to compose herself.

"I'm so scared," she whispers, "and everyone is worried that I am going to go mental. The midwife has written across the top of my antenatal notes: *High risk for depression, sister in coma.*"

Eve stifles a sob.

I blame James for putting me here. He didn't

push me. Not physically anyway, not that day, not on the 17th March when I cracked my skull onto the hard enamel and severed the connection from me to the world. James charmed me, he flattered me, and he swept me off my feet. On the surface he appeared perfect, but underneath, behind the scenes and in secret, James was working to unravel me, to destroy my very person, to dismantle me piece by piece until he had what he was after: a puppet.

Suddenly he was in my life constantly.

"I love you, Anna," he'd tell me. "I've never been in love before."

"I love you too," I'd tell him, always with a stab of guilt about Dylan. I just didn't feel the way I had felt about him with James.

"I want to give you everything," he'd tell me, buying me expensive gifts, and taking me away for surprise weekends to stay in boutique hotels. My work began to suffer, and I'd find myself staying up until two or three in the morning marking work, or planning lessons. Somehow James managed to fill my time in a way that Dylan never had. I can list the small yet significant warning signs that James was not all that he seemed now. At the time, they either seemed like positives, or completely insignificant.

The first and most telling sign was that nothing was ever James's fault. Nothing. In the car with him, this became so obvious, as he blamed others for his own bad driving. I thought this funny most of the time, annoying at other times, but believed it was of no significance at all.

James had worked on a large project in the south of England that had failed spectacularly, but apparently, this was not his fault. He cited his colleagues, his client and even Daniella as the ones to blame for his misfortune.

"I blame that useless bint," he told me. "She was so unsupportive. I was going through hell, and she didn't give a toss, just sat on her fat arse stuffing her face, letting me pay for everything." He shuddered. "You make me so happy," he'd tell me over and over again. I didn't realise at the time, but by making me responsible for his happiness, James was also making me equally responsible for any unhappiness that he experienced. James could not take responsibility for his own emotions, behaviour, driving, diet, in fact, James took no responsibility for himself at all, appearing to believe that he was entitled to whatever he wished by any means he saw fit.

James sounds so horrible that even I am wondering why I bothered with him. He had some very persuasive redeeming features. He was charming, generous, softly spoken and funny. He would plan brilliant surprises for me, and he didn't do things by halves.

"Let's go down to London, and do some Christmas shopping at the weekend," he had said to me one Wednesday in December. "We can go for a drink in the evening and stop over somewhere."

I had packed my overnight bag, and we had caught the train to London St. Pancras early on the following Saturday morning. All the way down to London, James kept grinning in a sneaky, up-to-no-good manner.

"What *are* you grinning at?" I asked him.

"Nothing," he'd said, trying to act innocent.

We arrived at St Pancras for eight a.m. "Let's have a coffee," he suggested, steering me into one of the eateries in the station.

"Good plan," I agreed, my head still fuzzy from the early start and the inevitable late night that I had with him the previous evening. I sat at a table and James queued for our drinks.

"This is for you," he said handing me a cappuccino, "and so is this," he added, placing an envelope onto the table next to my cup of coffee. I tore open the envelope, and inside it was two first class tickets to Paris on the Eurostar. "We board in half an hour," he told me, as I stared at the tickets in surprise. "I hope you don't mind, but your mum got your passport for me, I didn't know where you kept it. I wanted to treat you, you have been working so hard."

"Thank you so so much!" I said, jumping to my feet and planting a huge kiss on his lips. I felt so special. James had booked a five-star hotel just a five minute walk from The Pantheon, and he had booked a table at a beautiful restaurant on the banks of the Seine. He even managed to persuade me to try *escargot,* leaving me feeling both pleasantly surprised and absolutely disgusted simultaneously and in equal measures.

* * * *

Things began to move quickly with James, and in hindsight (that all illuminating glare!) I can see that I didn't know him well. Not really. When he sold his house, which had been on the market for two years, we had been together for just over eight months, and he had begun to spend most nights staying at my flat.

"You can move in here if you like," I told him, as he tried to decide where he was going to live.

"Thanks," he said, "but I don't think I could handle living here, it holds so many memories for you."

He was right; my flat did hold many memories for me. Dylan and I had rented it together and bought most of the furniture in there between us too. I did understand why he felt like that, Dylan and I had shared so much, and it was understandable that James would perhaps feel a little insecure. I made allowances for him, handed the notice in on my flat and distributed my furniture between my friends and family and moved with James into a beautiful barn conversion in a nearby village. The rent was three times that of my modest flat, and when I had broached my worries about the financial commitment, James had reassured me in his gentle and convincing way. "Don't worry, we are okay for money, we'll work something out that suits us both."

The keys to my old flat were handed in, my possessions were gone, and my signature was on the tenancy agreement. I felt happy and free, as though I had finally let go of Dylan, and faced the future without him. *This is what I need to do.* I told myself. *It's the right thing; I'm facing forwards.*

THE BUBBLE

Dylan was accepted to do his PGCE at Edinburgh, and I wasn't. "I'm not going without Anna," he'd told his proud parents. We just couldn't bear the thought of living so far apart. "We can move up there when we are both qualified," Dylan had suggested, and so that was our plan, to get our teaching qualification, and then head, "up the road," as Sophie called it, to live in our favourite city. Our course was due to start in the September of 2005, and we found ourselves a small flat to rent together. When we did our festival trip that year, life felt brilliant. Sophie was incredibly happy too. She had met and fallen in love with a fellow archaeologist. Dylan and I couldn't wait to meet Hamish, who despite his name wasn't actually Scottish, but from Manchester.

"There's an age gap," Sophie had told me on the phone. "I think we may have caused a bit of a stir."

We boarded the train, found our seats and settled down for the journey. Dylan had brought his MP3 player and a headphone splitter so that we could both listen. He sat opposite me and chose to be the one who travelled backwards because he knew it made me feel sick. We held hands across the table and listened to the music that was playing. With my other hand, I absentmindedly flicked through a magazine, and Dylan read his book. I put the magazine down and looked out of the window at the changing scenery. I thought about how little of this country I'd experienced and imagined Dylan and I exploring the UK during our long summer holidays when we qualified as teachers. Maybe we could buy a VW Camper? I'd always wanted one of those. Was that just like being in the caravan club though? My parents had owned a caravan, and we had been to Wales every year until I was fourteen. The caravan then spent years on the drive, acting as a spare room until eventually, mum decided to admit that it was an eyesore and got rid of it. I missed the old caravan though, with its cream and beige exterior and its chintzy curtains.

"We should get a camper van," I said to Dylan, removing one of the earphones from my ear so that I didn't shout too loud.

"Eh?" he responded, doing the same.

"We should get a VW Camper, and go exploring," I repeated.

"Yeah," he said smiling. "Yeah, I'd love to do that."

He popped the earphone back in his ear and returned to his book, I did the same and looked back out of the window. I felt so content. The future before us felt so inviting. I smiled a little-contented smile as the music played.

I stared at Dylan; he continued to read his book, oblivious to my gaze. He was moving his fingers in time to the music and nodding slightly. I smiled again as a lovely warm rush of love filled my chest.

Dylan looked up from his book and took one earphone out. I followed suit.

"Can I have a kiss?" he asked.

I leant over and kissed him.

"Anna, I'll always love you," he said, looking into my eyes for a moment. "You're beautiful," he murmured, then he popped his earphone back in, and went back to his book as the Kaiser Chief's *I Predict a Riot* began to play, altering the mood completely.

Sophie and Claire were waiting for us at Waverley Station, and we all hugged tightly like the old friends that we now were. We walked along Princes Street excitedly exchanging news.

"I hope you like Hamish. He's quite nervous about meeting you both," Sophie told us.

We had tickets to a show that evening and would be meeting Hamish for the first time there. Back at Claire and Sophie's we drank coffee and ate the delicious cakes that Claire had baked that morning. She always made us feel very welcome in her beautiful home. '

"So what's new with you guys?" Claire asked.

We told Claire and Sophie about our upcoming courses and our new flat.

"Wow, things are on the up for you two!" Claire said, happily.

"Come and stay when we're all settled," I suggested. "And we can look after you for a change!"

"I've told you before; it's no bother having you here," she reiterated.

"Oh yeah!" Dylan said excitedly. "I almost forgot to mention my new bike!"

"Yeah, he's finally told his mum and dad about his little hobby," I explained, "and now he is getting a bigger bike to celebrate!"

"Well I had to wait two years after getting my license to be allowed to ride a bigger bike, so I just made do with the small one until I finally confessed to mum and dad, but now that they know. I'm really giving them something to worry about," he said grinning, his eyes sparkling.

I couldn't wait for his new bike either. I loved going riding with Dylan and was even toying with the idea of getting my bike license. A thought that made me laugh, as I had never believed that I would ever be interested, and the thought of me, the world's most cautious driver who took four attempts to pass my driving test, racing around on two wheels seemed pretty absurd! It was almost as absurd as Dylan, the gentle, thoughtful, almost nerdy, musician riding around the countryside on a 1100cc Ducati. It amused me that the Dylan at a concert, playing his cello, beautifully, elegantly, perfectly, was the same person who passionately loved all things superbike, subscribed both to *Performance Bikes* and *Classical Music Magazine* and never missed the Festival of Speed. This was Dylan though, passionate about life and finding enjoyment everywhere.

That evening, we made our way into town on foot. The weather was surprisingly nice, and we chatted easily. Hamish was going to meet us at the venue because he was coming from the other side of town and had some things to do before he got there. Sophie kept grinning a funny little grin whenever his name was mentioned. I recognised it as the "cheesy grin" that she had teased me about having when Dylan and I had first got together. I wondered if I still grinned like that at the mere mention of his name, I wasn't sure that I did, but I did know that I adored him. The previous three years had seen us grow up, make plans, begin to build our future together, and now we were going to be living together properly at last. It wasn't going to be easy, but we had lots of support. I was going to be working evenings back at the hellish call centre, and

Dylan was planning to continue teaching music alongside his studying. Nell and Edward had given us £10,000 to "start out with" and Dylan still had £4000 of his uncle's money in a savings account. We knew that we were luckier than most people our age.

"There's Hamish," Sophie said, flushing red.

"Hamish!" she called, and a very attractive man in his early forties turned to her voice, then smiled a smile every bit as cheesy as Sophie's at the sight of her. They embraced in greeting, both of them smiling from ear to ear. "These are my friends, Dylan and Anna. This is Hamish."

We all said hello to one another and began to chat. Unsurprisingly, Hamish was incredibly nice. He was about 5' 8" tall, with dark hair that had more than a little sprinkling of grey through it. He had twinkly blue eyes and a lovely smile that lit up his entire face, revealing a gorgeous set of dimples. He had a soft northern accent, and he couldn't take his eyes off Sophie. I could see the appreciation in his gaze as they began to tell us how they had met seven months previously when they had first worked together. Sophie had managed to secure a job where Hamish already worked, and they had hit it off immediately, finding themselves laughing their way through each day, until after three weeks, Sophie had taken "the bull by the horns so to speak" and asked him out to dinner, they had seen one another every day since and were going to be moving in together in the very near future. Sophie's family had not been phased at all by the age gap, or if they had, they had kept their thoughts and opinions to themselves, but Hamish's family were unimpressed, particularly his daughter, who was one month older than Sophie. Hamish was forty-three years old, making him twenty-one years Sophie's senior and five years older than Claire.

"My family will have to get over it," he said simply. "I won't be emotionally blackmailed by them."

We had a great evening, and back at Claire and Sophie's Dylan and Hamish were getting on well, talking about football and things with engines. Hamish also liked bikes, and he and Dylan began to plan a bike trip across France for the following summer. Unusually, Sophie curled up on the sofa and fell asleep, while Claire and I got outrageously drunk, first on Prosecco, and then Bloody Mary's.

"You guys…" Claire told me, "are like my lost friends… I had friends like you… I would have gone to uni… I'd have had the life you are having…. but nobody wanted to know…don't get me wrong, I don't regret or resent it, I just feel…" she hiccupped, "sad…sad for the Claire that wanted to be young and carefree, but Sophie, Sophie is my reward, and she is so happy, and I am so proud, so I wouldn't change a thing....apart from maybe having some fun first," she concluded, hiccupping again.

I'd never heard Claire talk like this before; I knew it had been difficult for her financially and that she had worked incredibly hard to make her business successful. I knew that she had gone without so that Sophie could have what she needed, but I hadn't realised that Claire had sacrificed so much of herself. I hugged her and told her what an amazing mum, woman and friend I thought she was; then I put the kettle on so she could fix herself with tea before bed.

In the morning, Sophie was the last up. This was unusual as she had been the first to bed. I had been sick during the night and woken Dylan in a panic because I thought I had internal bleeding, but it was just the tomato juice. Dylan, Claire and I were sat at the big table with a pot of coffee and a pile of toast when Sophie and Hamish finally surfaced. Sophie refused her usual cup of coffee and sipped from a glass of water.

"You okay Soph?" Dylan asked.

"Aye, just feel a wee bit fragile today," she responded.

"Let's climb Arthur's Seat then," Claire suggested. "It always clears the cobwebs away."

We all agreed that was our plan; Claire immediately began making a picnic while we all got showered and dressed. I could hear her singing along to her radio in her tiny kitchen as she worked. Now I felt a new sadness for Claire, I thought she was like a little bird with clipped wings, and I hoped that she would find her freedom and her fun now that Sophie was all grown up.

We climbed the hill together, the weather becoming progressively windier as we got higher. I walked in front of Dylan, who took every opportunity to pinch my bum.

"Lovely view!" he told me, eye level to the back pockets of my jeans. "I love your bum," he said again and again. We got to the top and set up our picnic.

"Okay...." Sophie said tentatively. "I wonder if you have guessed, but Hamish and I have something to tell you." I stared at them blankly. I certainly hadn't guessed. Were they going to get married?

"We're having a baby," she announced, as Claire began to choke on a sausage roll.

"Oh my God! When?" Claire managed, jumping up and rushing over to her daughter to hug her.

"March," Sophie said, beginning to cry.

"I thought you'd be mad."

"What? How could I be mad? A baby is never a bad thing Soph, you'll see," she said, cuddling Hamish too.

The rest of our picnic was spent with Claire saying, "I can't believe it," quite a lot, and the rest of us trying to guess what the baby would look like.

"Sophie you were a gorgeous wee thing. Oh you were so cute, you used to have this mop of dark hair," Claire reminisced.

"I was bald until I was two, then it was only the back of my hair that grew, my fringe stayed short," I told them as we all began discussing ourselves as babies.

"I had loads of hair," Dylan told us. "I've had this same hairstyle since I was a baby," he said, gesturing to his mop of messy curls. "When we have a baby, I hope it doesn't inherit your mullet Anna," he said cheekily.

"I hope it doesn't inherit your hairbrush phobia," I retorted, an excited little flutter forming in my belly at the thought of having a baby with Dylan one day.

"I can't believe it," Claire said for the hundredth time.

****

The months sped past and Dylan and I settled into our new life of living together, working and studying. Although it could be very stressful at times, we got on brilliantly, and I loved cuddling up in bed with him every single night and waking up with him every morning. We spent our first Christmas morning alone together in our little flat, with a champagne breakfast and only the gifts that we had bought for one another to open. We had lunched at

Nell and Edward's, then cuddled up on the sofa to watch *It's a Wonderful Life* at my parents'. We said goodbye to 2005 in Edinburgh with Claire, Hamish and a very round Sophie, this time choosing to watch the midnight fireworks from our favourite spot in the city. Sophie breathlessly, but determinedly leading the way on our ascent of Arthur's Seat. This year Chloe had joined us too, and she and Claire chatted like old friends. As the midnight fireworks lit up the skyline and illuminated the incredible imposing castle and Auld Lang Syne rang out through the street party below, we made a circle, sang and linked arms, all of us happy to be in the company of this special group of friends. I hoped that 2006 held more of the same for us.

Sophie's pregnancy progressed uneventfully, and she moved with Hamish into his beautiful flat, just a ten-minute stroll along the river from her mum's. On the 28th February 2006, Dylan and I were woken at four am with an emotional phone call from Claire.

"Sophie's had a wee girl," she told us through the tears. "They haven't named her yet, but she is beautiful, Sophie's image, 6lb 6oz, the new family are over the moon. I'll send you a picture from my mobile." Dylan and I pored over the tiny grainy picture of Sophie and her little bundle. We could just make out the baby's mop of dark hair. Sophie had a look of complete satisfaction on her face.

Two weeks later, we travelled up to Edinburgh on the train, to meet this new little person. We made our way to Claire's where Sophie and Hamish were going to be meeting us.

"She's feeding at the moment," Claire told us as we walked up the stairs to her flat. Sophie was sitting on the sofa breastfeeding the baby.

"She'll be finished in a minute then you can have a hold," Sophie told us, as we greeted and congratulated her and Hamish. "There we go," Sophie said, as the baby's head lolled back slightly, "milk coma!" Sophie wrapped her tiny daughter in a shawl and then passed her to me to hold. "Meet Rose," she said as Dylan, and I gazed in awe at the prettiest baby I had ever seen.

"She looks like a doll Sophie," I said.

"She's beautiful," Dylan told her. She had lots of dark hair, long dark eyelashes and a tiny rosebud mouth. "I thought newborns were supposed to look like Winston Churchill."

"She looked funny when she was born, she had a cone head and a squashed nose," Hamish said.

"She did not!" Sophie scolded.

"She did!" Hamish continued.

We stayed with Claire for a couple of nights. There was the usual abundance of great food and conversation, but now Sophie was in a different place to Dylan and me. I felt like she knew something that we didn't, now that she was a mother. Baby Rose was delightful, and although it seemed that as a new mum, all you do is feed, change and cuddle your baby, I began to feel broody for the first time in my life.

"When shall we have a baby?" I asked Dylan lying in Sophie's old bed on the last night of our visit.

"Hmm, how about 2010?" he suggested, kissing my head. "Let's get a few more years of practice in first."

"Good plan," I answered, smiling through the darkness.

That spring was warm and dry, and Dylan and I went riding as often as we could, taking advantage of the weather. We were both tired, but enjoying our courses, excited at the prospect of qualifying as teachers and finally earning some good money. It was during this time that I met Hattie, who was a teacher at the school that I was placed at for my training. She helped me to stay organised and became a good friend of both Dylan's and mine.

"You two enjoy each other," she'd advise us often, particularly after a glass of wine. "You're very lucky to have found each other."

"I'm the lucky one," Dylan would say.

Our trip to the festival that year was going to be a

little different. Sophie now had baby Rose to think about and would only be coming to one show with us, while Claire was going to be away with work, but had very kindly allowed us to stay at her flat. Sophie's gran was going to babysit for Rose, and as Sophie had never left her with anyone before, she spent the evening fretting and looking at her phone, eventually relaxing when her gran called her to say that Rose was asleep and had taken the bottle of breast milk without any fuss.

"I'll have a wee drink then," Sophie had said relaxing, and we all drank a toast to Rose, to Sophie and Hamish. "I feel drunk," Sophie said after just two drinks. "I haven't had any alcohol for over a year."

We all went back to Claire's after the show, and Sophie and I chatted in the kitchen while she expressed milk into a bottle and then chucked it down the sink. "Breaks my heart chucking it away, but it's tainted with vodka," she explained. "My boobs were killing me all night; they were so full."

On the last morning of our visit, Dylan got up early and prepared a picnic while I slept, then he brought me coffee and toast in bed. "Come on sleepy head," he said gently. "Let's get up that hill before the weather changes."

"It's seven o'clock!" I said surprised.

"I know, but it's going to rain later, come on, let's

go," he said. I ate my breakfast, showered and dressed, and we set off for our favourite spot.

"Are you okay?" I asked him; he was acting a little strange, talking more than usual.

"Yes, I'm fine, just excited," he answered.

We reached the top of Arthur's Seat, and for the first time, we were the only people there. Dylan laid his jacket on the ground and opened up Claire's picnic basket. He poured us both a cup of coffee from the thermos and put his arm around me.

"Look at the clouds," I said, gesturing eastwards towards the coast, where dark clouds were forming in the distance.

"It's sunny here though. We'll worry about the rain later," he said, moving so that he was kneeling in front of me.

"Are you okay?" I asked again.

"Anna, I love you. Will you marry me?" he asked, taking my hands in his, I could feel him quivering with nerves.

"Oh my God, YES!" I answered, throwing my arms around him as he reached into his pocket and handed me a tiny jewellery box.

"Thank God for that, I was shitting myself!" he said, pulling a bottle of champagne from the picnic basket and pouring us both a glass.

"To the future Mr. and Mrs Watts," he said holding up his glass.

"To us!" I said smiling. "Although we'll have to double barrel our names. Bright-Watts? It sounds like a light bulb."

We both giggled. I let Dylan put the engagement ring on my finger, and we enjoyed our champagne together as the rainclouds grew ever nearer.

* * * *

Back home, we set about arranging our wedding. We would marry in a registry office on the 21st June 2008 and then have a garden party back at Nell and Edward's; their large garden was perfect for a marquee, and we were really happy that our wedding was going to be on the summer solstice. Dylan's friends were in a band, and they offered to play, and Nell and Edward also wanted to provide some of the music. Everyone was happy for us, and lots of people were offering to help us out with arrangements. I asked Eve, Sophie and Chloe to be bridesmaids.

"I'll try not to be pregnant then!" Sophie told me.

"Are you likely to be?" I asked.

"Well I'm pregnant now," she announced casually. "And I blame you and Dylan!"

"What have we got to do with it? Surely it was Hamish?"

"You got us drunk," she said laughing. The baby that Dylan and I were responsible for was due in

May, big sister Rose would be fifteen months old.

Sophie and Hamish took it all in their stride though and were excited about their second little bundle of joy.

WAKING UP

I'm making good progress. Slowly my body seems to be beginning to listen to my mind, and apparently I am now initiating some of my own breaths. This is the best thing ever because if I carry on this way, I will be able to come off the ventilator. I regularly cry real tears, and even Pam now believes that I am becoming responsive, to my surprise occasionally sitting and talking to me. Today is one of those occasions. I hear Pam pull up a chair and take my hand.

"You're doing well sweetie," she tells me. "I'm going to be away for a week, but Lauren is still here. Keep working hard, and we'll get you better. You don't deserve what that monster has put you through."

I struggle to communicate. *He didn't do this!* I think as loudly as I can, and I hear the ventilator picking up speed as my frustration builds at my enforced silence.

"People like him deserve to be locked away forever." Pam takes my speeding heart rate and sudden increase in breaths as a sign of my fear of James. "Don't worry; you're safe here. He can't hurt you anymore." Argh, he didn't do it! I fell, IT WAS MY FAULT. "He is going to get what he deserves darling; he won't be able to hurt you from prison."

I think it is nice that Pam is being a bit softer and more human, but I wish she would stop talking about James constantly. It's all she ever talks about to me. How he is a monster, how he deserves to go to prison, how he'll never be able to hurt me again. I'm beginning to believe she has a personal vendetta! Perhaps she has been in a bad relationship; maybe she has her own issues?

"Anna Bright?" I hear the familiar voice enquire.

"Through here," Viv answers. "And you are?"

"Her brother." I don't have a brother, and my mind takes a few seconds to process the information.

"Anna, you've got to help me. What happened? You were fine…. I went to calm down….What happened? I didn't do it, Anna help me, please. No one believes me. Wake up, wake up and help me or I am going to prison."

James pleads desperately in my ear.

"What happened? Did you fall? Did someone attack you? Anna, you know I didn't do this to you."

He is crying like a child now, and I feel a mixture of pity and responsibility, I want to wake up and help him, I can't bear the sound of desperation in his voice. Nothing that he has put me through seems to matter at this moment. He needs me to help him, and the complex emotions that stir in my chest make my breaths come quicker and my heart rate increase. I feel responsible for James, as he pushes my buttons just like he did when we were together and makes me want to rescue him, but it is me who is helpless and broken and although he is tearful and desperate to know the truth, he only really seems concerned about himself. It seems that as always, James is the only person who James truly gives a shit about. I know that if I were awake, I'd be shouting at him in a confusing mixture of angry tears and protective worry. I imagine his big brown eyes full of fear and feel the pull of sadness at his childlike vulnerability. I wish he would go.

"Is this the first time you have seen your sister since it happened?" Viv enquires, sounding concerned.

"Er yeah, I've got to go," James says, hastily kissing me as he leaves.

Viv is sitting next to me now and talking soothingly. I feel so upset and confused. My feelings for James, swinging from pity to love to hatred to anger, swirling in my chest in a raging storm with nowhere to go. I am trapped with my emotions bubbling away inside me; I feel like I will explode and I know that angry tears of frustration are running down my face, cool wetness gathering around my ears.

"It's okay," Viv soothes. "I think your brother was just shocked when he saw you, but we know that you are better each day Anna." She gently strokes my hair, assuming that my tears are for my 'brother's' shock.

I hear mum, dad and Eve arrive. "How is she doing today?" mum asks Viv. "Very well, but she was upset when your son came in to visit her earlier."

"My son?" I hear mum ask.

"Yes, he visited earlier, he was very distressed."

"I don't have a son."

"He said he was Anna's brother; I'm sure he did. Perhaps I have made a mistake. No, he definitely said he was her brother. Tall chap, dirty blond hair."

"I don't have a son," mum repeats. "You say she was upset?"

"Oh mum, you don't think it was him, do you?" Eve says, her voice full of trepidation.

"I'm calling the police," Mum says.

"Is this him?" Eve asks. I wonder which picture she is showing Viv.

"Yes, that's him," she confirms.

"The fucking bastard," dad says. "Terrorising her in here."

I hear mum on the phone to the police and Eve trying to comfort Viv who sounds heartbroken. "I let him in," she says sadly, "I told him where she was, I comforted him. Anna I'm so very sorry," she adds, as everyone's attention is turned back to me. Viv tells us that she will have to speak to her manager about what has happened.

The police are on the way to interview her. I realise with a terrible wrench that James has broken his bail conditions, and he'll be going to prison for sure. I feel sad, frustrated and so sorry for him.

Eve is holding my hand as everybody around me discusses what has happened. My mum keeps calling James a shameless fucking bastard, and I can't get used to hearing her swear, the absurdity of my mum saying the word 'fucking' makes me want to laugh, and although I am emotional and angry about James, my reaction begins to teeter on that fine line between laughter and tears. I try to get Eve's attention by squeezing her hand. I miss our 'in' jokes about our parents; Eve and I can communicate a million things with just a look or a glance, and I desperately wish I could share mum's newfound potty mouth with her.

"The cheek of the shameless fucking bastard," mum says again, and I try again to squeeze Eve's hand, which is now sitting limply in mine. Eve squeezes my hand back and whispers in my ear.

"You don't know how happy you have just made me. Can you do that again?" I squeeze her hand again, and she squeezes mine back. I wonder why she isn't jumping around telling everyone about it, but I guess that it is because she wants to keep a little bit of me to herself, I can't be sure though. I decide to squeeze her hand every time mum swears, and Eve soon catches on.

"It's so weird isn't?" I squeeze her hand again. "You should see dad's face when she does it. I can't wait for you to wake up." Her voice cracks and she begins to cry. "I miss you so much." All I can do is squeeze her hand again and again as I begin to cry too.

My hand squeezing soon becomes a system; once for yes and twice for no, all Lauren's idea. I am so overjoyed that I can now manage some simple communication! Conversations are still a little one-sided, but at least I can be involved, and each day that passes, I am gaining more movement and control of my body, there is talk of a trial without the ventilator too. Oh, and I can open my eyes, Pam is actually quite attractive, and her head is round, not square! Everyone is excited about my progress, and the first thing that I am going to do once I can talk is clear James's name. I can't bear the thought of him locked in a cell. I hate that he is being punished for something he did not do.

Pam is back from her holiday, and when she is on shift, she sits with me each morning, chatting and asking me questions. Today she is asking me about

James, a particular favourite subject of hers.

"You must be relieved that he is in prison now," Pam tells me. I squeeze her hand twice for no. "You aren't relieved?" she asks, sounding perplexed. "But he attacked you!" Two more squeezes.

"Are you saying that he didn't attack you?" Pam asks, sounding annoyed. I squeeze once for yes.

"What happened then?" she asks. I do nothing, irritated that she has asked an open question when she knows that I can't answer. "Did James Green attack you, and leave you for dead? One squeeze for yes and two for no," Pam says in a slow and deliberate voice. I squeeze her hand twice.

"I don't believe this," she says as she gets up and walks away. I am so relieved that I have finally managed to tell someone that it wasn't James. I wonder how long it will take before he is released from prison. I wonder how my parents will take it. I think they will be relieved that it was an accident and that I wasn't attacked, I think that they will find some peace once they know that their images of me afraid and pleading for mercy are nothing but imagined events.

PHONE CALL

January 2008 came and now Dylan and I were qualified and both working as teachers at the schools we had trained in. I felt slightly disappointed that we hadn't managed to move up to Edinburgh yet, but Dylan would reassure me that we had plenty of time.

"We can go anywhere, we'll do it, baby," he'd say, in his optimistic way. The impending wedding took up most of my thoughts; there was so much to arrange: dresses, food, music, a theme? In the end, we had decided to keep everything as simple as possible.

Sophie had managed to be pregnant again; baby number three was due in September, making both Rose and Iris big sisters, and somehow, Dylan and I were to blame again! We had bought Soph and Hamish the bottle of whisky for Christmas, so I suppose we could be indirectly responsible.

"Every time we drink we get pregnant!" Sophie had told me on the phone.

"Let's get them a fondue set next Christmas!" I'd joked to Dylan later that evening when I told him their exciting news. Sophie's dress fitting would have to be as close to the wedding as possible; she'd be about six months pregnant.

Eve and Chloe arranged my hen party. We were going away for three nights to a mystery destination over the first bank holiday in May, and they teased me mercilessly about it, making me believe it was either going to be incredibly dull or unbelievably trashy. Everything in my life was exciting and good. I had no idea that my world was about to be shattered, no idea whatsoever and the shock of the unfolding events still makes my belly lurch painfully.

27th March 2008

"Just going for a shower and shave, baby." Dylan had been using the laptop while I straightened my hair in front of the mirror in our small living room. It was a Thursday evening, and we had both been working that day. There was lasagna in the oven, and we were looking forward to sitting down together to eat.

"You look gorgeous," he told me, running his fingers through my now smooth hair, on his way to the bathroom. *Messy bugger*, I thought as I looked at the place he'd been sitting. A yogurt pot, banana skin, two magazines and a little pile of cherry stones lay on the coffee table. His untidiness drove me crazy. I scooped the food remnants into the yogurt pot and shoved his magazines under the cushion on the sofa, then I picked up the laptop and did my usual browsing of wedding sites, followed by a look for reviews of our honeymoon hotel in Mexico, a familiar panic rising in my chest as I spotted the occasional bad one.

Loved it!
Wonderful
Stinking hellhole I wouldn't send my dog there
Friendly, clean and well run!
Amazing pool, beautiful rooms
Staff will bend over backwards to help
Incredible service, amazing views, fantastic beach!
Good if you want food poisoning!

Just then I heard the pop of a chat message and realised that Dylan was logged in. Glad of the distraction from the food poisoning comment, I clicked the open tab intending to shut it down. A message caught my eye.

Hi, you looked and sounded great today. Can't wait for a repeat performance tomorrow! ;-)

My skin prickled hot; my belly flipped over. The message was from a woman called Kate Bradshaw. I felt jealous and suspicious; there was something about her over-familiar tone that I didn't like. I pulled myself together. Dylan was not interested in anyone else; he was too into me. I would ask him who Kate Bradshaw was when he got out of the shower, I knew when he was lying, so my mind would soon be at rest, and I could stop being so silly.

I started to set the table for dinner as I heard the shower stop. A few moments later, Dylan came through to the kitchen.

"Who is Kate Bradshaw?" I asked, staring straight at him. He looked surprised.

"Why?" he responded, in a confused tone.

"Who is she?" I repeated.

"She's a drama teacher at school." His brow was furrowed. "Why?"

"So why would she be sending you messages?" I asked, feeling more and more foolish by the second, Dylan's innocent confusion soothing my misplaced suspicions.

"Because we are in the middle of rehearsals for the Easter show. You know that! You have been listening to my fascinating work anecdotes, haven't you?" By now I felt completely stupid. What was wrong with me?

"I'm sorry!" I said sheepishly, burying my face into his t-shirt.

"Numpty," he whispered, kissing my head.

We spent the rest of the evening cuddled up on the sofa chatting and listening to our new favourite album: *The Seldom Seen Kid* by Elbow. Dylan was always full of trivia about musicians, and I called him a nerd as he told me that the album was a tribute to their friend who had died.

"They're love songs," I said to him. "Let's have this album at our wedding."

28th March 2008

Dylan pulled me close as I turned our alarm clock off for the third time; we were both rubbish at getting up in the morning. It was seven am and time to get ready.

"Five more minutes," Dylan uttered, pulling me tighter towards him.

"Just five minutes of my gorgeous girl, then I'll get up."

"You're already up," I teased.

"Don't waste it, Anna, when we're old; you'll miss me poking you in the back every morning!"

I wriggled from his grasp and headed to the bathroom. Friday at last, it had been a long week. I was looking forward to a glass or four of wine later, then a lie in on Saturday morning. I put my shower cap on and stepped into the shower. Dylan came into the bathroom and started having a pee.

"Charming!" I shouted above the water. He stuck his hands around the shower curtain to wash them, squeezed my bum then disappeared into the kitchen. I could hear him singing above the kettle, and true to routine, he put the stereo on, Elbow's album filling our flat. I knew when I went back into the bedroom there would be a cup of coffee sitting on the windowsill for me. I stepped out of the shower and reached for the towel; it'd gone! He'd walked off with it.

"Dylan!" I yelled, shivering. I didn't want to walk across the flat naked; I knew he would have opened the curtains. "Dylan!" I shouted again, becoming annoyed, I could hear him singing away, oblivious to the fact he'd nicked my towel. It wasn't a big deal, but I felt really pissed off. I stomped out of the bathroom into the kitchen and spotted the offending towel draped over a chair.

Dylan was leaning on the counter, eating cornflakes, a trail of sugar and a puddle of milk next to his cereal bowl. "Thanks a fucking lot," I snapped, adding, "you're so messy," as I picked up the towel.

"Anna!" he called, as I marched into the bedroom. "Sorry!"

I got dried and dressed and put on my make-up as Dylan showered, and by the time he came into our bedroom to say goodbye, I was feeling completely head over heels in love with my messy, irritating, thoughtful, gorgeous, lovely fiancé. Of course, I had to act a little bit moody still, so when he kissed me goodbye, I tried not to smile, and as soon as he had ridden off on his motorbike, I wished that I'd given him a bigger squeeze, or maybe a snog. *Moody Cow.* I scolded to myself in the car on my drive to work.

As I sat in the staff room, drinking another coffee before the teenage onslaught, I felt my phone vibrate in my bag.

I keep getting excited, thinking of you naked in that floral shower cap.....

I giggled.

Pervert! I responded to him.

Seriously... you looked gorgeous. Can't wait to get my hands on you later. Xx

I would stop off on my way home and get him a lemon meringue pie. I knew that was the best way to make it up to him after my over the top moody reaction. A lemon meringue pie and sausage and mash and Dylan would be over the moon. The way to his heart was definitely through his stomach.

The day dragged, and when I finally got through my front door that evening and started to peel potatoes, I was looking forward to the Pinot Grigio that had been chilling nicely in the fridge. I toyed with the idea of opening it and having a small glass before Dylan got in but decided that drinking alone was the first step onto a slippery slope. I didn't want to go skidding into my father's footsteps. I checked my phone, becoming agitated. Quarter to six, Dylan was usually home by now. He could have let me know he was going to be late.

Hurry up! I want wine xx I texted him.

I became more irritated as the minutes ticked by.

I set the table, opened the wine, cursed Dylan, poured a small glass and took a sip as my phone began to vibrate. I answered it without checking who was calling, assuming that it would be him.

"Where are you?" I demanded.

"Anna." It was Nell.

"Nell?" She sounded strange.

"Anna, go to the hospital, Dylan's been injured. We'll meet you there." Then she hung up. *Been injured?* I thought, doesn't sound too bad, but Nell was usually more talkative than that.

I rushed to my car and drove badly, ignoring red lights, other drivers and all rules of the road. Maybe he had a broken leg? Two broken legs? Broken arms and broken legs? I could cope with that, but nothing could have prepared me for what I was met with.

Nell and Edward met me at the entrance. They were ashen-faced, with a look of agony that I am sure is reserved only for a parent who endures what they were enduring.

"Where is he?" I asked rushing into Nell's arms. She didn't speak, she couldn't speak and neither could Edward. A nurse came and took us into a room.

"I'm sorry," she said, bowing her head. Dylan lay on a bed, his face white, the red of his hair, more vibrant than ever, seemed to be the only colour in the room. His body was covered with a sheet. I dread to think what had happened to his beautiful body.

"He's still with us," the nurse told us. We sat around his bed; I took his left hand, Nell put her cheek to his and Edward took his right hand. None of us could speak. I had a million things that I wanted to tell him, but not one word crossed my lips as my lover, my best friend, my 'one', breathed his last, shallow rasping breath.

"He's gone," the nurse told us after a few minutes. And I turned and fled, running through the hospital car park to my car.

"He'll go cold; he'll go cold," I could hear myself repeating as though I wasn't even part of my own body. As I drove, I screamed a blood curdling, primal scream. I screamed "NO" over and over again. Then I went to my parents' house and screamed and sobbed in mum's arms until I fell asleep in the early hours of the morning. Dylan was dead. My heart was broken.

AFTERWARDS

In the days that followed Dylan's death, there was a flurry of activity. Our focus was, of course, his funeral. Where only a few days before, we had been planning our wedding, now all focus was on how best to pay tribute to Dylan, a life ended so suddenly and cruelly.

The morning after Dylan's death, I had awoken in my mum's bed, disoriented and groggy and for a blissful moment, I had forgotten. The realisation that dawned within a second or two crushing my chest like a ton of concrete, rendering me unable to breathe. Everything moved so quickly in those days, and arranging the funeral acted like a buffer. I was focused on making this day right for Dylan, so focused that when the crushing grief settled in my heart, I could distract myself in this final act of love. Family bustled around me. Nell and Edward were either at my parent's home, or we were all at their house. I couldn't bear to go to my flat and dressed in my mum's and Eve's clothes. Our whole world revolved around Dylan keeping him alive and part of us and buffered us from the reality of our loss.

The service took place on Thursday 3rd April at the

crematorium. I couldn't allow myself to accept what this meant. That Dylan's beautiful face, his body, every last scrap of his DNA, was going to be turned into a pile of ash and dust. Nell and Edward had visited him every day since his death, allowing themselves to drink in every last detail of their son's lifeless face. I had chosen instead not to view the body, a decision that I was warned by well-meaning friends and relatives that I'd regret, but one that to this day, I am still sure was the right choice. I wanted to remember Dylan with life in his eyes, colour in his cheeks, and warmth and a beating heart in his body. His body was dressed in his wedding suit. I chose not to see him in it. After all, I would never wear the wedding dress that hung in the wardrobe in my parent's spare room, like a ghost of the life that was never to be.

During the service I felt numb, I felt nothing when I stared at the coffin that would soon disappear behind the red velvet curtains. People around me sobbed, but I stared straight ahead, glassy-eyed and unfeeling. I drifted in and out of a strange trance-like state as I listened to a stranger, who had never met Dylan, talk about his life, slipping in passages from the Bible and urging us to turn to Jesus like an opportunist salesman for God and Christianity. I stood before the congregation and read the words that I had written about Dylan, and was aware of loud sniffs and sobs from those gathered. People were crammed into the tiny chapel, face after face swam before my eyes and I returned to my seat quickly, sure that I was about to lose consciousness at any second.

The wake that followed was better. People who really knew Dylan talked about him, told real stories about his life. I actually found myself laughing as members of his family told me funny stories about him from his childhood. I truly didn't want it to end. After all, what would I do afterwards?

In the days and weeks that followed the funeral, people gradually slipped away as their lives returned to normal. I couldn't believe that the world could be so cruel as to carry on as normal without Dylan in it, but it did and the initial bustle that surrounded me eased. Chloe carried on visiting me daily, and for a few weeks, I stayed with my mum, unable to face going into the flat. Eventually, after two weeks or so, I plucked up the courage to go home for a few hours.

As soon as I unlocked my front door, a horrible smell of rotten food and unemptied bins hit me. I bent down and picked up the pile of mail that had accumulated behind the front door, and placed it onto the kitchen table, then I slowly walked from room to room, concentrating on my breathing as intense crushing grief filled my heart. It was just as I had left it on that fateful Friday, the open bottle of wine, the table set for two. Mouldy sludge lay in the sink, the remains of the potatoes that I had been peeling, the lemon meringue pie sat on the table in its box. I felt the familiar stab of guilt as I remembered how I had been with Dylan the very last time I had ever seen him. Why hadn't I kissed him and told him how much I loved him? I went into the bathroom, Dylan's razor lay next to the sink, I picked it up, and tapped it onto the side. Tiny hairs fell out onto the white enamel, and I scooped them onto my finger and looked at them. I thought about how those tiny hair fragments contained Dylan's genetic code, now useless, extinct. I rinsed the hairs away angrily and wandered into our bedroom. Dylan's boxer shorts lay on the floor, typically messy of him. I opened our wardrobe, looked at all of his clothes, hanging, redundant, then I lay on our bed, buried my face into his pillow and cried myself to sleep.

When I woke up, it had gone dark. I checked the time. It was nine-thirty. I went back into the kitchen and made myself a black coffee; then I began to clean up the mess that I had left the day that Dylan had died, crying bitterly as I worked. I flicked through the pile of letters. Wedding brochures and RSVPs that had been arriving in a steady stream from friends dominated the pile. Of course, they all knew now that there would be no wedding, but each acceptance card acted like a knife twisting deeper into my heart. There was a red Royal Mail parcel slip, telling me that there was a parcel in the bin cupboard at the bottom of the stairs. It was addressed to Dylan; I wondered if it would still be there, the date on the slip was from two weeks ago. Eventually, I tired of pottering around and decided to go back to my mum's. I checked the bin cupboard on the way out, and to my surprise, the parcel was still there. I put it into my bag, hurried to my car and headed to my temporary home, emotionally exhausted.

Mum looked worried when I arrived home.

"Where have you been?" she asked, obviously trying to hide the hysteria in her voice. I felt annoyance at her over concern, swiftly followed by guilt. I was putting her through so much. I went to my room and pulled the parcel from my bag. *Should I open it?* I wondered. It was about A4 size, and the address was handwritten. I turned it over in my hands a few times; then I began to unpick the tape. Inside there was a wooden frame wrapped in bubble wrap and brown tape. There was a handwritten note attached to the outside.

Hi Dylan,
Thank you for the cheque.
I hope this is what you were after.
If there are any problems, let me know.

Enjoy your big day. I hope your new wife likes her gift.
Steve Aldwell

So it was a gift for me. I slowly peeled away the tape and turned the parcel over and over as the layers of bubble wrap became thinner and more translucent. Eventually, I got to the end. I stared at the frame. Inside it was a paper tree with the lyrics from the Elbow song *Mirrorball* cut into it. I turned the frame over; there was a small plaque attached to the back.

To my gorgeous girl. You make me so happy. Love always. Dylan xxx

"Love always," I said aloud. Then I remembered the lady on the train and what she had told us. "A love that will never die," I repeated, and then an image flashed into my mind of Dylan sitting opposite me on the train to Edinburgh, leaning forward to kiss me. "I'll always love you," he had told me, as we had listened to music together, dreaming of our future. Dylan had died, but our love hadn't, and it wouldn't, of that I was reassured. The next day, I moved back into the flat.

On my darkest days, I only got out of bed to use the toilet. The doctor had prescribed me sleeping pills, and I allowed myself a respite in the groggy oblivion of drug-induced sleep. On better days, I made myself get up, visit family or friends, try and be part of the world, eat, walk, talk.

At the beginning, the majority of my days were bad. Chloe visited me every day. She had a key to the flat, and even when I was in my drug-induced sleep, she would let herself in, sometimes tidying up, washing dishes or putting a load of washing in the machine. She would always leave me a little note, with something sweet, a lollypop or a piece of chocolate or cake, on my kitchen table.

Popped in today. Washed up - you messy bugger! Love you xxx

Hi hun, I know it's hard, but please believe you'll feel better. The Murray Mints are from my dad. Love you xxx

Hey beautiful, brought you some milk and bread. I baked the cake. I hope you don't get food poisoning from it.... Love you xxx

Popped in. I'll come for breakfast tomorrow, 10 am. I checked in your fridge, so don't worry I'll pop to the shop first. Love you. See you tomorrow. Xxx

Even though I became the worst friend in the world, ignoring all her efforts, barely even mentioning that I'd noticed what Chloe was doing for me, she never stopped, she never wavered. She is truly an incredible friend.

"Dad says you need something to focus on," she told me one day. "He had Tom and me; we were his reason for going on, for not giving in when he felt like lying down and dying."

I had wondered how Trevor had got through it. I was young, only eight years old when Chloe's mum had died, but remember the atmosphere of grief and shock. My mum always seemed to be worried about Trevor, and I remember her cooking them casseroles and stews and taking them to their home, returning with baskets of dirty laundry. She would wash all of their stuff and determinedly work first through their clothes and then through ours as she did her Sunday ironing, while Chlo, Tom, Eve and I played and dad and Trevor visited the pub, or played golf or went fishing. Chloe had seen and experienced grief first hand. Hers was a deep understanding; she had no expectations, she just knew. I don't think I'd have got through it without her.

Slowly, I began to accept my loss and return to my life, but of course, there was a huge Dylan-shaped hole in everything I did. Dates suddenly held horror for me. I dreaded the 21st June, the date of the wedding. I was so afraid of that day, the day that only a few months before I had been looking forward to more than anything. It approached steadily; I had to find something to occupy myself. The night before, I took a double dose of sleeping pills. When I awoke, I took strong codeine tablets that were Dylan's from an old back injury and more sleeping pills. I lay on the sofa underneath my quilt and slept through the day that should have been the most memorable of my life.

I went back to work in September, part-time initially, gradually building back up to full-time by Christmas. It was work that kept me going; I put everything that I had into my job; my students and their hurdles and achievements guiding me through the fog of my grief. Sophie gave birth to her third daughter, Poppy, exactly nine months after Christmas on the 25th September, and Chloe and I drove up to Edinburgh to meet her in the October half-term holidays. Everything was different without Dylan, and a heavy sadness hung in the air as I tearfully cradled tiny Poppy, wishing that she and Dylan could have met.

In the year that followed, I took baby steps forward and the occasional giant leap backwards, and with the help the incredible people around me, I found myself functioning at a level of almost normality. By the time Tom turned thirty and threw his fateful fancy dress party, my existence had almost begun to resemble a life. I slowly emerged into the light - blinking and wobbling - straight into the arms of James Green.

A WOLF

I vaguely knew of abusive relationships, women who hid bruises under long sleeves and sunglasses, and who made up stories of falling down the stairs. I never in my wildest dreams believed that I would tread in the footsteps of those women. I thought that if someone hurt me, I would stop loving them and walk away. I did not realise the power that existed within those toxic relationships, but I do now. And every minute that I spend lying in this bed, I become more enlightened. All I can do is go over my life, analyse my experiences and come up with a better way of living for when I am freed from my prison, and the light that I am holding up to my past is illuminating every dark corner and clearing away all the mist and fog. I allowed James to hurt me. I didn't ask him to do it, and I am not responsible for his behaviour, but every second that I spent with him after the first time he crossed the line from friend to abuser was another second in danger and I should have got out of the way, but I didn't and here is why......

"I am so happy for you!" Sophie told me on the phone when I told her the news that James and I were going to move in together. Mum kept telling her friends about this lovely new man in my life, and my beautiful Chloe took a small step back, obviously relieved that I had someone to care for me and love me. Chloe had given so much of her time to me, and I was so grateful to her; she certainly needed a break from worrying about me! There was a collective sense of relief surrounding my relationship with James. People around me had worried that I would spend the rest of my life pining for Dylan, unable to move on, and when everyone around you believes that your relationship is perfect, it's difficult to disappoint them, especially when they have been through what my friends and family had been through with me. It did seem perfect though. Indeed, the first eight months were perfect, but when I handed my keys back to the letting agent, James became a different person.

My subconscious was way ahead of the rest of me. On the first night in our new home, I awoke screaming at the top of my lungs. "I'M TRAPPED!" I screamed, panicking and sweating. The nightmare had been about being locked in a stone staircase, damp and dark, with no light to show me the way out, and only the oppression of the dark, damp walls surrounding me. As I fumbled for the light switch in my new and unfamiliar bedroom, James began to speak, but instead of the sympathy that I would have offered someone who had just had a terrifying nightmare, he began to chastise me.

"Well thank you very much. You do realise I'm working tomorrow? I'm going to be tired, you know I struggle to sleep. It's alright for you. You can just go straight back off." I lay in silence, stunned at his reaction. He was acting as though I had deliberately woken him up. He went quiet, and I tried to get back to sleep, but my mind was swimming. Maybe he was reacting normally? I mean everyone could be grumpy if they were woken up, couldn't they? I tried to avoid imagining what Dylan's reaction would have been in the same situation, but it was impossible not to, because without even having to think about it, I knew what he would have done. He would have given me a cuddle, asked me what the nightmare was about and offered to sleep with the light on. I tried not to think about Dylan, but all I could see in my mind's eye, was him looking sad and disappointed at how James had just treated me.

I lay awake for most of the night, listening to James snore; he'd had no trouble getting back to sleep after all. I eventually dosed off about an hour before James's alarm clock was due to wake him. I didn't need to get up for another couple of hours. He was getting the train into central London as he did once each week and as his alarm woke him, he turned to me and pulled me close.

"Morning gorgeous," he whispered.

"Morning," I said, wondering whether he'd apologise for his reaction during the night. He took my hand and pushed it inside his boxer shorts.

"I need you to sort me out baby," he told me, kissing the back of my neck and holding my wrist so I couldn't pull my hand away.

"I feel a bit upset at how you spoke to me in the night," I ventured. James said nothing. "I had a nightmare, it was horrible," I continued.

"It's all about *Anna*," he sniped nastily, still trying to get me to move my hand the way he wanted it to move. I resisted his attempts, clenching my fist.

"How?" I asked. "How is it all about me?"

"You just don't give a fuck about anyone else Anna, that's your problem."

"My problem?" I repeated. "I don't have a problem!"

"Yes, you do. You're a fucking twat. Take some responsibility."

With that, he got up and went into the shower, and I lay on the bed stunned. What had just happened? Were we arguing? Why did James think that I only cared about myself? And what kind of adult calls their girlfriend a twat? I went over it all in my mind. He was the one acting like I didn't matter. He didn't care about my nightmare, hadn't seemed bothered when I told him that I'd felt upset, but somehow, he thought I didn't care about him. The whole altercation didn't make any sense at all. James left for work and unable to go back to sleep, I showered, dressed and arrived at school super early, my mind racing with confusing thoughts. I spent the day distracted and not my usual self.

"Anna's tired," my colleagues quipped. "Too much fun on your first night in your new house eh?"

I laughed along with them, a fake uneasy laugh.

That night when James got home, he acted as nothing had happened. I decided to do the same, and we cuddled up in bed to watch a film, my heavy, tired eyes closing within seconds of it starting.

"Aren't you even going to stay awake?" he asked accusingly.

"Sorry, I'm so tired."

He tutted and turned off the TV.

"You watch it," I said, "I don't mind, it's not disturbing me."

"It was supposed to be for us to watch together, but if you can't be bothered…."

By now I felt wide awake. I felt like telling him to fuck off, but somehow, already, he had managed to get the upper hand. I believed then and still believe now, that life is too short for stupid arguments, so while now I know I should have told him it was unacceptable to treat me how he was treating me and then leave him, back then I believed that if I just didn't make a big deal about it things would be okay. I guess that was the moment that I handed James the power in the relationship. He manipulated me, I gave in and bit by bit, slowly, insipidly, I gave myself away.

I stood up and put the TV back on.

"I'm awake now. Come on, let's watch it together as we planned."

"Okay," James said sullenly.

And I found myself making an effort to soothe him, cheer him up, jolly him along and make him happy. The film was boring, and James soon fell asleep. I turned it off and lay down, unhappy and confused. I'd just spent the last half hour desperately trying to keep my eyes open, fighting the tiredness that James had inflicted upon me and then criticised me for, and he had just nodded off. Really, I didn't care if he wanted to fall asleep, but I had felt unable to do the same without upsetting him. Two nights of living together, and I was already tiptoeing around on the eggshells that James so effortlessly created.

The following morning, my alarm went off first, and James pulled me close as he had the day before.

"Do you have time to help me out with this gorgeous?" he asked, again pushing my hand into his shorts and edging his way closer to me, kissing my shoulder gently. Time wasn't the issue, of course; it was his treatment of me, the way I was feeling about him and about myself, they were the issues here.

"I suppose I can make time," I said, disgusted with myself, but hoping that placating him in this way would somehow fix the situation, show him that I did care about his feelings and what he wanted. James lay back on the bed, put his hands behind head and closed his eyes. I could have been anyone. Afterwards, he said, "Thanks, baby, you're the best." And I began to get ready for work.

When I came out of the shower, there was a cup of coffee and some toast sitting on my bedside table, and James was sitting up in bed with his laptop on his knee grinning. "I love living with you," he told me as I ate the toast, dried my hair and drank my coffee.

****

"There's a surprise for you outside," he told me. We had been living together for ten days. There had been no further shouting, or arguments and I had convinced myself that what had happened was all something to with what he had been through with Daniella.

"Close your eyes!" James instructed as he guided me through the house. It was a Saturday morning, and he had been out for a couple of hours. I had thought he was training as he had a triathlon in two weeks' time. "Tah dah!" he exclaimed happily. On the driveway sat a brand-new VW Golf 2.0L GTI, *exactly* the car that I had been drooling over since my little Polo had begun to die a death a few months previously.

"Because I love you, because you are gorgeous and because I want you to be happy," he told me, handing me the keys. "It's yours, Anna, now where would you like to take me?"

"Oh my God James! Thank you so much."

I flung my arms around him and kissed him.

"I love it; it's beautiful! Let's go and show Eve and Liam; they will be so jealous!"

We spent the rest of the day driving around. I loved the car, and I couldn't stop smiling. It was easy to push my doubts to the back of my mind, the back of my waking mind anyway; my subconscious had other ideas. I was plagued with nightmares. Every night I would wake up screaming in terror, usually around half-an-hour after falling asleep.

My nightmares were recurring. There was the 'TRAPPED!' one, where I was either buried alive, stuck in a staircase or locked into a coffin about to be cremated. There was the one where I had to make a choice. I'd be handed two boxes, one would be empty, but one contained explosives that would blow up in my face if I opened it. In the dream, I had to choose one of the boxes to open. Always I'd have the box in my shaking hands, lift the lid and then wake up screaming and sweating before I found out what it contained. There was another nightmare where I was drowning in a murky, stagnant lake, littered with rubbish and filled with stinking brown water, while my friends and family waved from the shore happily, oblivious to the danger I was in.

The week after James had bought me the car, we went up to visit Sophie and Hamish in Edinburgh. James had never met them before, and we were going to stay at Claire's as Dylan and I had done many times previously. I worried about the trip and how I would feel going up there with James rather than Dylan. I tried to hide my worries, but James too was concerned about the trip.

"Maybe we should stay in a hotel?" he suggested. "It's not like we can't afford to." So that is what we did, and James booked us into a gorgeous five-star hotel.

Sophie's gran babysat for all of the children and Sophie, Hamish, Claire, James and I went for a meal and a few drinks. Everyone appeared to be getting on fine, and the wine, which was flowing freely, helped us all to relax. Back at the hotel, James and I giggled our way back to our room and jumped in the shower together, giddy and drunk.

"Let's get room service," James suggested after our joint shower, picking up the telephone. I lay on the huge bed in the hotel robe and slippers, giggling at him as he put on a stupid accent and ordered us a bottle of champagne.

"I love you," I told him, as we lay on the bed waiting for our bubbly. Our champagne was soon delivered, and we opened the bottle, giggling and drunk and drank a toast to the future. James downed his glass quickly, pouring himself a second glass as I slowly sipped mine, beginning to feel that more alcohol was maybe not the best idea.

"You drink quickly," I observed aloud.

James shot me a strange look, got up and walked into the bathroom. I felt my eyes begin to close, the room start to spin. When I opened them a few seconds later, he was standing over me with both champagne glasses in his hand.

"You ungrateful bitch," he slurred.

"What?" I sat up astounded.

"After everything I have done for you, you just throw it back in my face."

"What?" I asked again. "James, is this a joke?"

"You're the joke *Anna*. Perfect *Anna*. *Anna's* been through so much. *Anna* is so lovely. Well I know what you are. You're an ungrateful bitch."

"James, I don't know what your problem is, but I am going."

I stood up and started to get dressed. He snatched my clothes from me and threw them on top of the wardrobe.

"You're going nowhere until you have drunk this champagne. You said you wanted it, now drink it," he said thrusting the bottle into my face.

"No, give me my clothes. What is wrong with you?"

"You, you are what's wrong, you are nothing but an ungrateful little whore. Wanking me off so that I'll buy you a car. Sucking my cock so that you can live under my roof. Slut."

His face was contorted with rage.

"Drink the fucking champagne, you've earned it being a dirty fucking whore."

I tried to get past him. I didn't care that I was in a robe and slippers, I just wanted to get away from him and the disgusting onslaught that was pouring from his mouth.

"You are going nowhere until you have finished this champagne," he told me. "DRINK IT!"

I snatched the bottle from him and drank what was left, it was around half a bottle. Then I pushed past him to the door of the hotel room. He spun around and grabbed the belt of the robe.

"You are going nowhere with this on. I paid for this room, this belongs to me."

He undid the robe and pulled it off my body then pushed me towards the door.

"Go on then, out you go," he said sneering, as I tried to push my way back into the room, naked.

"Give me my clothes."

He stood in front of me. I pulled a chair over and tried to climb up for my clothes, but he effortlessly swiped them from the wardrobe before I could reach them and marched over to the balcony door, opening it quickly and throwing my clothes into the street below. I got some knickers from my overnight bag and put them on. By now I was crying with anger and frustration, and the champagne that I had just drunk was making my head spin and my belly churn.

"Why are you doing this?" I asked as he pulled my bag from my hand and flung it onto the wardrobe.

"Apologise," he demanded.

"For what James?"

"For being a cunt." He leered towards me, and I backed away.

"I'm not apologising, and I am not a cunt," I slurred, defiantly, the alcohol making me unsteady on my feet.

"You are a cunt, a whore and a piece of shit."

"Why are you so angry? I haven't done anything."

"If you hadn't done anything, I wouldn't *be* angry, you stupid little whore."

His face was inches from mine now, and he had managed to back me up against the wall, his hands on either side of me and my feet between his.

"You're an ungrateful little whore," he repeated, and that is when I slapped his face.

"So, this is how you want it? Violence is it?" He rubbed the side of his face where my hand had struck him.

"I just want you to leave me alone and let me go."

"Whore," he spat in my face. "Slut."

"Let me go," I repeated.

"You belong with that useless ginger twat. Dead."

I brought my knee up as hard as I could into his groin. He doubled over and I tried to run, but he grabbed my hair and pinned me to the wall again.

"How dare you kick me, you bitch?" He stood on my feet and pushed me against the wall, holding my arms tightly by my side so that I could hardly breathe.

"Because I mentioned perfect Dylan? Loverboy? Well it's not his cock you're sucking now, it's mine, and when I let go of you, you are going to get dressed, get out of this hotel and fuck off. I never want to see you again. You can fuck off back to the stinking drain that you came from." At that moment he let go of me, and I pushed him hard in the chest as I walked away.

"That is the final straw," he said menacingly grabbing my hair and ramming my head against the wall painfully.

"How dare you push me you, evil little bitch? You

lay one more finger on me, you piece of shit whore, and I will smash your ugly face to a pulp. Do you hear me? I am going to let go of you, and if you don't apologise for being the useless, ugly, stinking, cunt that you are, I am going to smash your teeth into your throat."

His grip tightened on my hair painfully, and my head was pulled up so that I was facing him. Hatred and rage coursed through my body. He tugged hard on my hair again, then let go of me.

"Cunt," he said. It was the last straw, and an angry mist descended in front of my eyes.

I punched him as hard as I could in the face, blood trickled from his nose. He threw me onto the bed, pulled his arm back and slammed his fist into my mouth, fleeing straight onto the balcony as I held my hand to my lips, crying with pain. The room was spinning, I felt sick, and I crawled to the toilet and began to vomit. Blood, tears, sick filled the toilet bowl as I retched and sobbed.

He came into the bathroom, poured me a glass of water and knelt beside me gently. I wanted to tell him to go away, but I was still retching. He gently stroked my hair away from my face, picking up a hair band from the sink and securing it up gently.

"Anna," he said tenderly, rubbing my back, tears running down his face, his brown eyes full of sorrow. I closed my eyes, and he continued to rub my back, then he helped me up and supported me as I wobbled to the bed, placing the glass of water next to me, then climbing beside me, putting his arms around me and gently telling me how sorry he was. I lay with my back to him, staring towards the bathroom door. My head was spinning; I felt sick, shocked and confused. He stroked my hip; I didn't know what to do. Part of me wanted to push him away, but a bigger and more influential part of me needed to feel some love and tenderness. He continued to stroke my hip, and I didn't stop him. He buried his face in my hair and began to kiss the back of my neck, pressing his body against mine. He stroked my belly and began to kiss his way along my arm. His breathing was shaky and he was crying.

"I love you," he told me, as he began to kiss my breast. I pushed him away, a moment of clarity.

"James, I can't do this," I told him.

"I need to show you how much I love you Anna. I need to be close to you," he told me, kissing my breast again. "You are so beautiful," he uttered, his touch was soft and gentle, and his eyes brimmed with tears as he looked at me tenderly. I couldn't help my body responding to his touch, his soft whispers and the look of utter love that was written on his face and I felt my heart begin to race with anticipation as I gently stroked his face. The sex we had was the most loving and intense that we had ever experienced together. I couldn't believe how alive my body could feel after such a terrible experience, but every pleasure was heightened, and by giving in to James at that moment, I had unknowingly allowed a cycle to complete itself, the cycle of abuse which was to become my life, spinning me around, confusing me and tearing me to pieces.

SINKING MUD

I am deteriorating. Nobody knows why, but I have become unresponsive, and all talks of trials without ventilators and getting me up and into a chair have ceased. Instead, I hear snippets of conversations involving 'low sats' 'septic screens' 'BMs' and the worst one 'last rites'. It's fair to say that I am terrified. Someone is with me pretty much constantly now. Family members and friends are taking it in turns to keep watch over me. When I try and respond to their words or touch, I feel as though I am trapped in sinking mud, flailing around helplessly and getting further and further away.

I no longer have any concept of time, whereas before I could work out roughly what time of day it was from the familiar routines surrounding my care, now I am aware for only fleeting moments. One second my mum is here sobbing and stroking my hair and the next it is Eve or Dylan. I don't know how Dylan has got here; I thought he was dead. I hear distorted voices; monsters lurk in shadows. James is going to kill me. My head pounds with a sickening pain. The monsters are hitting me on the head with a hammer beating my skull to a pulp with each beat of my heart. Someone is sitting on my chest, holding me down and someone else is forcing me to drink burning liquid. I manage to open my eyes, but I am not in hospital, I am lying across a railway track, shackled to the sleepers. How did I get here? I can hear the train in the distance, hurtling toward me. I am going to die. I don't want to die, not now that I know that Dylan isn't dead. The train becomes louder and louder, I try to scream for my mum, but I make no sound. Trapped, I try to wriggle free, but I am tightly bound to the tracks.

"Anna," mum is here. "Sweetheart, your pulse is racing."

I hear the beeping of the machines; the train has gone, I am in my bed, and I am safe. Dylan is dead after all. I wish the terrifying hallucinations would stop. They are like nightmares, but one hundred times as realistic and I have been plagued with them ever since I began to get sick. Mum is talking to me. I try and listen, but I can hear a whooshing noise, it sounds like it is inside my head. Mum's voice begins to slow down like a record playing at the wrong speed, slow, deep and distorted. Now I am sinking, through the bed, through the floor, descending further into the bowels of the hospital, intense heat surrounding me. I think I am going to hell. I don't want to go to hell; I am so scared. Wicked black creatures with red eyes stare out at me from the walls. I know they are going to tear my body to shreds. Fear fills every part of my being.

"You're so hot," Lauren tells me. "I'm just sponging you down to cool you off."

I am back in the bed again. Lauren is making me feel safe, but I know that it is only a matter of minutes before I am off on another terrifying trip courtesy of my subconscious.

"Come on Anna, keep fighting the fight," Lauren encourages me as she works to cool my burning body down. I focus on her voice, her gentle touch, the way she chats, so fluently and naturally to me, but despite my efforts to keep my mind engaged her voice begins to fade. I am spinning now, moving far away from Lauren. Spinning into a dark tunnel, so black that it's like the light has never existed. Terror engulfs me again. What if I never leave this dark place? I hear a rushing sound in the distance. It's water. The tunnel is filling up with water; I am going to drown. My heart races at one hundred miles per hour as the freezing water rushes over my body and splashes my face. Soon my lungs will fill with water. I try to move my arms and legs to swim, but they are like heavy lead weights. My face is submerged now, and I am holding my breath. I'll have to give in soon; I know I will. My lungs will fill with water; I am going to drown. My heart races in my chest, my lungs burn with the effort of holding the air inside them. My eyes are wide open, wild with terror, staring into the black void, the cold water stinging my eyeballs as bubbles begin to escape from my nose. I feel dizzy; I'm going to pass out. My chest heaves with the effort of holding it full of the stale hot air. I can't stand it any longer. I exhale slightly to take the pressure off, but lose control, breathing out fully then gasping desperately, water filling my nose mouth and lungs as I pass out.

My mum is back.

"You're going to beat this thing, Anna. My papa had a clot on his lung, and he fought it and won. You can do the same."

So that's what the pain in my lungs was, I wasn't drowning after all. I don't know how long has passed since I was last aware of anything around me, and I have just been existing inside my hallucinations. I am so frustrated. One minute I am getting better, the next I am deteriorating. I can't be bothered fighting anymore. I just wish I'd either wake up or die. At least if I die I can be with Dylan and my family can move on. Right now, everybody is trapped in this terrible limbo as I wobble precariously in the no man's land between life and death.

Why is Pam the only member of staff in this place? She seems to be the one looking after me the most. Lauren works alongside her the majority of the time. Pam has stopped speaking to me now, but Lauren is as lovely as ever. I get the feeling from Pam that I have upset her, which is really strange considering my position here! I'm mute, unresponsive, extremely sick and fully at her mercy, hardly in a position to do something to offend her. Still, I cannot shake this feeling off, and I am so cross with her for not passing on the information I gave her about James. She knows that he is innocent, but she has not done anything about it. Not to my knowledge anyway.

Mum and Eve are chatting at my bedside. "They are giving her all this clot-busting medication," mum tells Eve, "but they have had to increase the sedative because she was fighting the tube. She needs it because of the clot now you see?" she explains.

"She looks so thin," Eve says, touching my arm.

"I know," mum says, her voice wobbling. "She's got an infection; her temperature is up and down constantly."

I hear Eve's breathing become slow, loud and deep.

"Another one?" mum asks. "How often are they coming now?"

"Five minutes apart now," Eve says, breathlessly. "I don't want to leave her though," she says, and I feel her lean her head on my arm. "I wish you could come with me Anna, Liam is shitting himself." Eve must be in labour. I am going to be an auntie soon. I wonder if she will have a boy or a girl.

"It's a boy," Dylan tells me, kissing my head gently.

Eve stays until her contractions become three minutes apart and mum and Liam take her to the labour ward, practically by force! Chloe takes their place beside me.

"Sophie rang me today," she tells me. "She is going to try and come down within the next couple of days."

Sophie hasn't been to see me yet. It's really difficult for her with the three girls. I wonder if Sophie is coming because she's been told I might die. How shit for her: first Dylan and now me.

Chloe chats away about her day, and I enjoy a respite from the hallucinations, they seem to have slowed down. As Chloe continues to talk, I notice that I can hear another voice in the room, it's talking in a barely audible whisper, but I concentrate hard to listen to it.

"You are in danger," it tells me. "Keep fighting Anna, keep your wits about you. Keep listening." How can I keep my wits about me? I'm in a fucking coma. I can't even move! I feel chilled to the bone. What danger am I in? Is it another hallucination? I feel the bed begin to vibrate beneath me and I know what is coming next. The temperature drops and I can smell the most disgusting stench; my feet are cold and wet. I open my eyes and try to focus. It is almost dark, and I realise that I am in a deep ditch. The smell is that of rotten flesh, dead bodies surround me, soldiers in varying states of decay. Rats scurry around, gorging on the bodies, and beetles and maggots give the impression that the dead, eyeless men are squirming. I clasp my hand to my mouth in horror as I realise that I too am going to be shot. Do I try to escape, run and risk enemy fire? Or do I stay here, with these poor rotting corpses and the rats and disease and starve to death? I didn't know that being a soldier would be like this. I crouch down among the lice and vermin and begin to cry. I want to go home; I want my mum. This place is definitely hell. I want to get away, and I begin to pick my way through the bodies, trying desperately not to stand on anybody. *How will I get away from here?* I wonder, terrified as a huge brown rat scurries over my feet, making me scream with fright and with a sickening jolt I am back in my bed.

"You're an auntie," mum tells me. "It's a boy, Archie. He looks just like Liam."

Thank God I am back here again and away from the stench of death and fear of the trench. I can't believe how vivid my imagination is.

"He's totally bald," mum continues. "8lb 12oz. Eve was incredible, and Liam was fine. Eve says he is definitely going to be an only child! The midwife said that she's heard that one before."

Mum settles down for the night in the chair in my room, and I listen to her breathing change as she falls asleep. I follow suit, knowing that my night will be filled with terror and as I begin to doze, I hear the strange whispering voice remind me that I am in danger.

"Oh Anna, look at you." It's Sophie; she is here at last. I hear her gasp with shock when she sees me. I must look so hideous now. As with most people, it takes Sophie a little while to talk normally, but once she gets going, I get to hear all about her girls and their funny ways.

"Rose is a wee madam. She wants to wear make-up, but we won't let her. She's only five years old, for God's sake. Anyway, she took matters into her own hands and gave herself a felt-tip makeover. Lipstick, eyeliner, blusher and a wee flower on her forehead all done with a felt pen. Then when Hamish saw it and told her to wipe it off, after getting a photo though 'cause she looked so cute, she ran into the bathroom and tried to clean her face…….with toilet cleaning wipes. Anna, she's such a wee madam, and Iris just copies her all the time. Poppy is different, completely placid, she just sits and watches them. Anyway, you'll never guess what? Hamish had a vasectomy last month, but it was too late, I'm pregnant again. Due in September, I had no idea this time until a few weeks ago. I'm already nearly five months."

Pam asks Sophie to leave while she tends to my care, and my heart sinks as I realise that Lauren is not with her and she works silently as though I am an unfeeling piece of flesh.

"That nurse is a misery," Sophie says when she comes back in. "What's with her? She's got a face like a bulldog chewing on a wasp."

I laugh silently at Sophie's way with words. I decide that I am going to fight to get better. Two new babies, my amazing friends and family, I have so much to live for. "You are in danger," I hear the strange whispering voice in my ear as Sophie chats away next to me. *How?* I wonder again.

HANNAH

When James and I eventually fell asleep in our hotel room in Edinburgh, the light was already beginning to creep across the sky. I lay with my head in the crook of his arm. We were both breathing with shaky and jittery breaths. James kept telling me how much he loved me, how beautiful I was, how he couldn't bear his life without me.

"I think I'd die without you, Anna. I love you so much."

After the fighting, the shouting, the poison that he had filled me with, I was desperate for a loving and tender touch. His soothing words acted like a salve to my bruised and battered soul, repairing the damage that he had inflicted, and I hardly even noticed that he was replacing the original Anna with a weak and submissive woman, that he was stealing my very person from underneath my nose.

When I opened my eyes in the morning, the first thing that I noticed was the pain. My head thumped with a combination of hangover and trauma. My mouth was swollen and painful, and the scab that had begun to form in the corner of my lips broke painfully as I opened my mouth to yawn. I turned to look at James, and he began to stir. Both his eyes were bruised, and the bridge of his nose was slightly misshapen. Guilt flooded my chest. I had broken his nose; I felt disgusting. My whole body was aching, every muscle that I had strained in the fighting was tender.

"Ow ow ow," I winced as I tried to get up to walk to the toilet.

"Baby what's wrong?" James asked.

"Everywhere hurts," I answered.

"What was last night all about?" he asked sadly, putting his arms around me soothingly.

"I have no idea," I answered, gingerly standing up, my head banging with pain. He looked at me with a look of remorse, guilt and sadness.

"I'm going to nip out, I'll be back in ten," he told me, as he began to get dressed. He brushed his teeth quickly and then fumbled around for his sunglasses.

"I suppose I ought to wear these, don't want to give the wrong impression eh?" he said flippantly, softly kissing my cheek and heading out of the door.

I walked into the bathroom and turned on the shower. It was a huge walk-in affair with a showerhead the size of a dustbin lid. Expensive toiletries in glass bottles, made with essential oils sat on the side. I stood under the stream and closed my eyes, my tears mingling with the water. I looked down at my body: my feet were bruised where James had stood on them, my arms had purple finger marks around them where he had restrained me, and my chest was bruised where he had angrily jabbed his finger at me. My back hurt where he had pressed me against the wall, and my head and scalp were lumpy bruised and painful from the hair pulling and the slamming against the wall. I dried myself and climbed up to get my overnight bag from the wardrobe, humiliation washing over me at the thought of my clothes lying in the street below. I dressed gingerly, pulled my hair back into a bun and then stood in front of the mirror to apply some make-up. There were thumb marks on my forehead, and there was a scratch below my left eye. My lips were swollen and bruised. I applied my make-up and then dried my wet hair so that I could wear it down and use it to hide as much of my bruised face as possible.

By the time James came back into the room, I was looking just about presentable. He handed me a Boot's carrier bag. Inside it were some painkillers, some soothing body soak, and some arnica cream.

"To heal the bruises," he explained, gently putting his hand under my chin and tilting my head up to inspect my face. He handed me another bag; I peered inside, it was a glasses case. I opened it to find a pair of Oakley sunglasses.

"I thought they'd come in handy," he said,

pulling me into an embrace. "Oh Anna, what are we like?"

James had picked my clothes up from the street below, and he folded them carefully and put them into the carrier bag that I had brought for our dirty washing. We gathered our belongings together, put the empty champagne bottle and glasses on the tray, and I shuddered at the memory of the previous night. It didn't seem real. He was loving, attentive and gentle, and I wondered if I'd imagined the horror of it all. We didn't go for breakfast in the hotel. Neither of us wanted to. We made our way to the car, and I began to get in the driver's side door.

"I know you don't want to drive," he said to me, following me.

"I don't mind, honestly. You drove up, it's my turn," I told him.

He placed his hand on my shoulder and said, "It's a really long way. I'll drive, you clearly don't want to, it's best if I drive."

"If you want?" I said, perplexed, I didn't care whether I drove or not. I climbed gingerly into the passenger seat. Maybe I was a really bad driver and just didn't realise? I wracked my brain. Had I been complaining about driving? How had I managed to give the impression that I didn't want to drive without even knowing?

On the way home, James kept his hand on my

knee as much as he could. He put my favourite CD on in the car, and when we stopped off at a petrol station, he bought me a coffee and an egg and bacon roll.

"Don't worry, I'll go," he told me as I went to get out of the car and go with him to the garage, wincing again as my aching muscles protested. We sat in the car and ate our breakfast rolls, James constantly concerned for my welfare. When we arrived back at the house, we drew the curtains and James lit the fire, even though it wasn't cold or dark. We shut out the world and hid away. James put a DVD on, and we began to watch a box set. We sat for hours, cuddled up on the sofa watching the fire crackle, dance and spit. James stroked my hair tenderly, kissing me repeatedly.

"You're my beautiful girl. I'll never do anything to hurt you." I began to wonder whether he'd even been there the night before.

"I need a bath," I announced, stretching and yawning, we'd watched the entire series of DVDs, and I was feeling sleepy, but also pretty crusty from the journey and the heat of the fire.

"I'll sort it, baby," James said, leaping up and running to the bathroom. I fumbled in my bag for my phone. The battery had gone dead, so I plugged it in and waited for it to turn on. I could hear James in the bathroom, whistling. My phone came back to life and message after message appeared on the screen. There were three from Sophie that she had sent that morning.

Hi Anna, we can climb Arthur s seat after 11. You up for it? x

Hi, did you get my message? Meet us there if you like? x

Hi, we are here, I hope you are ok. x

Shit! Had we arranged to go? I couldn't remember, I had been pretty drunk. There was no way that we could have gone covered in bruises anyway.

I typed a quick reply into my phone.

Hi sorry, Soph, just got your messages, my phone was dead. We were too hungover to do anything. Back home now, see you soon. xx

"Bath's ready," James called from the bathroom. I climbed the stairs to the bathroom. He had filled the bath, there were bubbles overflowing, and the bathroom was full of lit candles. A glass of wine and a box of chocolates sat on the edge of the bath, and there was a basket of expensive looking toiletries with a card on the floor next to the towel rail.

"For you," he told me, handing me the card. I opened it.

Anna, you mean so much to me. You are the most amazing and beautiful woman that I have ever met. Let's be brilliant forever. Love you so so so much, James xxx

I put my arms around him. "Yes, let's be brilliant."

I got into the bath, and James handed me the wine.

"You're my princess," he said.

Life continued, and I found that James was loving and attentive, always trying to please me. I still walked on eggshells, aware of covert messages about his expectations of me, but only my subconscious noticed what was happening. I began to have a new recurring dream. In this dream, I was trying to tell someone about something that had happened to me, but as I said the words, they changed, and I spoke a completely different sentence to the one that I had formed in my mind. The more I tried to correct myself; the less control that I had over my mouth and I'd wake up angry and frustrated.

A couple of weeks after our trip to Edinburgh, I came home from work one day, to find James looking worried.

"Something's happened," he told me before I could even put my bag down and he came straight over to me and hugged me.

"What's wrong?" I asked.

"I have something to tell you," he said, grasping both of my hands and looking into my eyes, a worried expression on his face.

"I have a fourteen-year-old child."

I felt so relieved! I thought he was about to confess to an affair.

"Her name is Hannah. I have never seen her."

"Why?" I asked, shocked that he had never seen his daughter. "Didn't you know about her?"

"Her mum is a total weirdo; she only got pregnant to get her hands on my parents' money."

"Are you sure?"

"Of course I'm sure. Don't start on about stuff you know nothing about okay?"

He was obviously shaken by something.

"So what's happened then?" I asked tentatively.

"Hannah has found me on Facebook. She wants to be in touch with me."

"That's good isn't it?"

"Your way out hippy opinions are incredible. Good? Of course it's not good."

"Why?" I asked, annoyed at the things he was saying to me.

"Because it's shit. I don't want anything to do with that money grabbing bitch. Stop sticking your half-formed opinions in, you don't know what you are talking about."

"Explain to me then!" I said.

"Why do you have to make this all about you?"

"I'm not!"

"You are. It's all about *Anna*. In *Anna's* world,

everything is wonderful. Well, I'm from the real world."

"How am I making it about me?"

"Just drop it, will you? You're starting shit again."

With that, he pushed past me, grabbed his keys and slammed the front door behind him. I heard the engine of his car burst into life and the screech of his tyres on the gravel as he sped away.

I stared at the door, astounded and confused. I still had my bag on my shoulder and my keys in my hand. What had I said that made him think that I was making it all about me? Had I not listened properly? Did I butt in too quickly with my opinions? Why did he see bad where good was intended? I didn't need to think for long because within seconds, I heard his car come screeching back into the drive. He threw the door open and marched straight past me, up the stairs.

"I forgot this," he said brusquely, waving his toilet bag at me. "I need some space."

"Where are you going?" I asked, shocked.

"Mum and dad's."

"But why? What have I done that's so bad?"

"Stop playing the innocent. You're a twat, and you know you are."

"Don't call me names!" I shouted.

"Listen to you, shouting, hysterical, just because you can't take responsibility for your behaviour. Get out of my way," he retorted.

I was standing in front of him, my hand on his arm. "James please," I begged. "I don't know what I have done. I'm sorry if I was insensitive, but I honestly don't know what you are so angry about."

"GET OUT OF MY WAY," he shouted. I moved to one side to let him past, and he stood staring at me for a moment.

"I don't know what you are," he sneered, then he turned and left.

I stood rooted to the spot, my breathing fast and shallow, tears stinging my cheeks. What the fuck had just happened? Was I speaking another language? I paced the kitchen for a few moments, then I took my phone from my pocket and wrote a text message to him.

Hi, I'm not sure what just happened, but I want to be there for you. I don't know why you think I was attacking you; I wasn't. Come home. X

He replied quickly.

Get fucked.

I couldn't believe it. How could he be so mad at me? I had lots of work to do. I'd brought home some marking, so I made myself a cup of coffee, sat at the table and tried to concentrate, my head spinning with confusing thoughts. After an hour or so, his car pulled back into the driveway. My stomach lurched, I had no idea what he would be like when he walked through the door. I looked up expectantly as he appeared.

"Hi," he said, looking sheepish. "Can we sort this out?"

"I'd love to," I said. "It's just when you go jumping in with your opinions, well you have no idea what Hannah's mum is like."

I felt angry; I hadn't jumped in. Had I though? I tried to listen to what he had to say, while simultaneously running the previous conversation through my mind. Maybe I had jumped in? Obviously, that's what he thought I had done. He must have had a reason. I began to speak, "James I just…"

"Shh…" he said, kissing my mouth. "Come here." I began to speak again, and again he shushed me with tender kisses until I gave in and he led me to the bedroom.

The following morning, James told me about Hannah. I lay in bed and listened to him talk, careful not to interrupt at any point. He had dated her mum, Fiona when he was in his first year at university. She was also studying to become an architect.

"She was stunning," he told me, "but devious. Mum had taken an instant dislike to her, but I didn't listen to her warnings and carried on with the relationship. Three months down the line and she had got herself pregnant."

Got herself pregnant! I thought, but I said nothing for fear of starting a riot.

"I finished with her, because she became hysterical, trying to control me. Mum and dad have been so good to me. They have paid her £200 a month since Hannah was born. The last thing they wanted was for me to have to struggle through university."

"Are you going to get in touch with Hannah?" I asked tentatively.

"I don't know what to do for the best. I think I will have to discuss it with mum and dad and see what they think."

"Can I see her message? Don't worry if you don't want to show me." He reached for his phone and opened his Facebook page. I read the message.

Hi James, (dad!)

I have been wondering whether to get in touch with you for a while now. Mum told me to go for it if I wanted to.

Mum says I am like you. Apparently, we walk the same!

I hope you don't mind me getting in touch; there is so much that I'd like to ask you. Maybe we can meet up. We live in Newcastle. I could get a train down or something.

Love Hannah x

"She's gorgeous James," I told him, zooming in on her profile picture. "She looks so much like you!"

She had inherited James's beautiful eyes and just looked familiar. All day at work I imagined Hannah checking her Facebook account and her hopes being dashed that he still hadn't replied. I looked at the fourteen-year-old girls in my Year Ten English class. They were so vulnerable, just making their way into the world, finding their feet, searching for their identity. I really hoped that James wouldn't let his daughter down, but I didn't feel able to tell him that those were my thoughts for fear of making him angry with me. A sense of disappointment began to seep into my bones, disappointment in myself. I knew what was right in this situation, why was I too scared to say it?

THE STRINGS TIGHTEN

"What are you doing?" James asked me. I was staring out of the window into our garden watching a pair of woodpigeons.

"I'm watching these daft birds," I said.

He came and stood beside me and put his arm around me.

"They are funny," I told him. "I put some bread out for them. They chuck it up in the air before they eat it. One of them has just chucked it onto its own back then strutted about confused trying to find it."

"They are comical," James agreed.

We stood at the window watching them for a while, and after that, we seemed to notice them everywhere. They always seemed to be cooing and romantic.

"Aw, they're in love like us!" James told me. I came home from work one day to find a card on the table; it was a picture of two woodpigeons and James had labelled one Anna and one James. The message inside the card read:

Saw this card and had to buy you it. You're my woodpigeon! I love living in our nest. Lots of love
James xxx

"Thanks!" I said, displaying the card on top of the bookcase in the kitchen and giving James a big kiss.

* * * *

James and I were visiting his parents. James had broached the subject of Hannah with them, and I had been really surprised to hear June say that she thought he ought *not* to contact her.

"Do what you want James, I'm not trying to interfere, but if you do contact her, I'm warning you, you will be making a big mistake."

I tried to support James as he wrestled with his decision, eventually telling him that I thought she'd been really brave to contact him, and telling him how I imagined she would be feeling after not hearing back from him. James had begun a dialogue with Hannah, who came across as a funny and intelligent girl. We had decided that we would travel to Newcastle the following weekend and James and Hannah were to meet in a coffee shop. I would get some much wanted retail therapy for a few hours while they got to know one another.

James was nervous, really nervous, and whenever we talked about it, his hands would become clammy and his heart would race. I was proud that he had decided to do the right thing, even though it was clear that he was far from comfortable with it.

"What if she hates me?" he would ask. "What if

Fiona has poisoned her mind?"

"Don't worry," I'd soothe, "she obviously wants to meet you, so Fiona can't have said too much to her."

When we arrived at James's parents', Clive was at the local golf club, and June was getting ready to go and collect him.

"Is dad having a few after golf then?" James asked.

"I should expect so," June answered. "He's playing with Dave, and they usually have a couple of pints after the game."

While June was out, James turned on the laptop, and we began looking for a hotel in Newcastle.

"Let's just get a Travelodge," I said. "As long as we are together, we don't need all the trimmings!" I was sitting on his lap, and he was doing his usual, browsing boutique hotels, or grand five-star luxury places.

"I hate Travelodge. It's like an office block with beds," he answered.

"Up to you," I said, knowing that he would be paying anyway; I never seemed to pay for anything anymore. Everything ended up going on James's card, and when I tried to pay him back, he would say it didn't matter. It made me feel uneasy, and I didn't know why.

"This one looks nice," he said. "It's got a sunken

bath in the room."

"It does look lovely!" I said.

"Mmm, I can just see us in that bath. Champagne… bubbles… I'm booking it." And with that, he parted with £200 for one night in Newcastle.

We made our way to the kitchen, and I boiled the kettle and made us a pot of coffee. June and Clive returned, and June began preparing the dinner. I stayed in the kitchen to help her and James disappeared into the lounge to watch the horseracing with his dad. Clive soon came back into the kitchen; he picked his laptop up.

"The boy's asleep!" he announced to us. "You must be keeping him awake at night Anna."

I feigned a smile at his remark, a little uncomfortable with it, then went back to chopping the vegetables and chatting with June. After a moment or two, Clive called June over to him.

"What do you think of this June?" I peeled potatoes while June wiped her hands on her apron and began looking at the laptop with Clive. I tried not to listen as they muttered in a low tone, obviously trying not to let me hear. I put the potato peeler on the side and began to walk towards the lounge where James was sleeping.

"Anna, come here please," Clive said authoritatively. I swung around so that I was standing behind him and he gestured to the laptop.

"Why has James been looking at hotels in Newcastle? Is it something to do with Hannah?"

I felt incredibly uncomfortable; I knew that they disapproved of James seeing Hannah.

"We are going for a weekend away," I said.

"Why Newcastle?" Clive asked.

"Why not?" I said, feeling as though I had been caught doing something terrible. Just then James walked into the kitchen looking gorgeous. His hair was tousled, and his cheeks were flushed from sleep. Noticing my discomfort and the atmosphere in the kitchen, he placed a protective arm around me.

"James, why are you going to Newcastle? Are you meeting Hannah?"

"What?" James asked.

"You are, aren't you?" June scolded. "After everything I have done for you! You throw it all back in my face."

I stood with my mouth open, shocked at the way she was trying to make James feel guilty.

"We have paid thousands and thousands of pounds over the years so that you don't have to get involved and this is how you repay us. *We have bent over backwards to make your life better James."* On and on she went. "I have been so ill over the years, and your father has worked his fingers to the bone to protect you from *her.* I am warning you, James; you are making the biggest mistake of your life."

Clive stood next to June, a protective arm around her, and James stood next to me, his arm around me. I was holding tight to the back of his t-shirt, my fingers clenched tightly as I listened to the ludicrous ranting. I could feel James shaking with his mother's words. I wanted to protect him, to say something to stop the onslaught.

"Please don't shout," I managed, just before James exploded into a rage.

"I am sick of you trying to run my life!" he yelled at his mother. "I am a grown man. I don't need your permission to see my daughter."

"I knew it!" Clive butted in. "That is what they are doing. Sneaking around, *lying to us!*"

"We haven't lied!" James shouted.

"You didn't discuss any of this with us," June said. "All we ask is that you discuss things with us. After all we have done to support you. All that money we have paid to that money grabbing bitch."

"Well June, I'll be cancelling that direct debit first thing in the morning. He doesn't appreciate what we do for him."

It was horrible. Poor James couldn't get them to see that he wasn't trying to hurt them and they had absolutely no right to demand that he discuss his decisions with them.

"We're going," James said, grabbing my arm and pulling me towards the door. I didn't need much persuasion, and we quickly got into the car and began to drive away. "Oh my GOD!" I said as we pulled away. "What the fuck was that all about?"

"They are just worried about me. They've done a lot to help me over the years; they're getting old now."

"James, that was unreasonable behaviour. They had no right to say all that stuff to you."

"They just worry Anna."

"Well, I felt uncomfortable when your dad started to question me about why we were going to Newcastle. He didn't seem to care how bad he made me feel."

"SHIT!" he exclaimed suddenly. "I've left my wallet in their house; we'll have to go back."

We pulled back into the Green's street, and I waited in the car while James let himself in.

"Wish me luck," he said grimacing as he leapt out of the car. I waited for what seemed like an eternity, biting my nails and wondering what was being said behind the doors, nervous butterflies fluttering in my belly. After a few moments, June appeared in the doorway and made her way to my side of the car.

"Anna, can I have a word?"

I climbed out of the car, and she began to berate me.

"How dare you say you feel uncomfortable? *After everything, I've done for you!* I've bent over backwards to make you welcome in my home, and this is how you repay me?"

"June I…" she interrupted.

"I have a migraine coming on now. You have made me so ill."

I wanted to tell her to get a fucking grip but was careful not to spoil all chance of reconciliation. I began to take responsibility for the ridiculous way that June was treating me.

"I think there's been a misunderstanding," I soothed, taking her hand. "Can we sort it out, please? I hate arguing."

June sniffed a little and then said, "Come on inside dear, let's get a cup of tea or something."

She put her arm around me and steered me in the direction of the front door.

"I was just upset Anna that James hadn't even mentioned that he was going to meet his little girl. I mean this is a big thing for our family, and we always thought that he didn't want to be in her life. We've just tried to protect him for all of these years. We were hurt Anna; you can probably understand why. We felt pushed out."

She was talking in a soft voice, and I actually began to wonder if she had a point.

"How's the headache?" I asked.

"It's quite sore, but if I get an early night, it shouldn't take hold. It's very upsetting. Actually,

James has never shouted at me before; I feel heartbroken."

I thought about James's temper and was surprised that he had never shouted at his mum, I wasn't sure that I believed her.

"I'm afraid I was so upset that I tipped all the dinner into the bin, but I could make you a sandwich or something if you are still hungry?"

We were inside the house by now, and James was standing in the kitchen with his dad. They were talking about work.

"Are you two okay?" James asked.

"Yes we are fine," I answered as June boiled the kettle.

"Did you want a sandwich, Anna?" "

No thank you," I said, looking at James, hoping that we could leave as soon as possible.

We left after about half-an-hour or so, and James and I both sighed loudly as soon as the car was out of their street.

"That was weird," I said.

"Yes, I've never shouted at mum before, I feel really guilty."

We sat in silence for a few moments and then James turned on the radio.

"I love you; I'm sorry about all that." "I love you too," I said, a loud thud making us both jump.

"It's a woodpigeon!" I exclaimed. Blood ran

down the windscreen and feathers flew everywhere as the poor pigeon catapulted into the air then landed in a lifeless heap at the side of the road.

"Aw poor thing," I said as I began to cry, huge wracking sobs that just would not stop.

"Baby, are you okay?" James asked.

"Do you need me to pull over? What is it?"

I didn't know what it was. I felt like the poor dead woodpigeon was an omen. I felt upset and confused at how the day had gone. Everything felt bad and toxic and tainted, and I just could not understand it. I felt afraid, and I felt needy like a child. When we got home, I asked James to light the fire. I drew the curtains, pulled all the cushions onto the floor in front of the hearth, pulled a cosy throw from the back of the sofa and cuddled up to James, holding on to him tightly as though my life depended upon it.

NEAR MISS

My hallucinations continue, each one as terrifying as the last, and although I know that they are hallucinations once they are over, while they are happening, I live them as vividly and convincingly as any other experience. I hear my mum and dad nearby. They are trying to do a crossword. I have completed quite a few crosswords silently, in my mind now.

"Four across, five letters; vital sign also provides protein," dad reads slowly.

"Hmm," mum muses, in her usual confused manner. "That makes no sense," she says.

It's pulse! I say in my head. Suddenly I want to shout the word *pulse*; I have to get them to hear me. *Pulse, PULSE!* I scream in my head, nausea rising in my chest with a sense of desperation and impending doom.

"Keep fighting," I hear the whispering voice tell me. "Keep shouting, someone will hear you." *PULSE!* I scream again as a deafening ringing sound begins in my ears.

"Anna, ANNA!" mum screams.

The last thing I hear is the sound of an emergency

bell.

It's a hallucination. I tell myself, although I know that it's not because I never know a hallucination until it is over. I am in a sudden silence, a lull of everything. I am neither awake nor asleep, alive nor dead; I'm suspended in a warm nothing. *I don't want to fight*; I think for a second, *I'm too tired*. And in that instant, I begin to rush upwards, away from my mum, my dad, sister, new nephew and friends. I see the hospital become smaller, and then I see the surrounding countryside begin to shrink as my world starts to look like a model shrinking rapidly. Homesickness washes over me, a longing for my family, my friends, the simple pleasures in my life. An image of my parents with the same look of loss in their eyes as Nell and Edward now flashes before my eyes, and I change my mind. I do want to fight; I'm never going to give up, no matter how hard it is, no matter what, I am going to get better. Instantly, the world begins to grow again as I change direction and I move through the silence back towards the hospital and my bed. My body jolts and burning sears through my chest.

"She's back," I hear someone say as the steady beeping of the heart monitor begins. How do they know I was gone? I wonder if they saw me float through the ceiling.

"Well done," the whispering voice tells me.

SILENCING ANNA

After a few moments, my mum and dad return to my side, and I can almost feel their shock. I want to promise them that I will fight harder and better from now on, but of course, they can't hear me, and I can no longer squeeze their hands. I learn that I have just had a cardiac arrest and it probably won't be the last. The clot on my lung is not responding to the treatment, but now that I am in fighting mode, it will have to, because I don't want to die.

I hate Pam; she is here so much. Why does she have to work so many shifts? The only saving grace is that I am now on so much medication that sometimes I don't even think I exist.

I can't believe that my heart stopped beating, it took them four minutes to get it to start again. I had CPR, and then my heart was shocked back to life. It's terrifying. I find myself listening to the beeps of the monitor more closely now, thankful that I can still feel my battered and bruised heart pounding away in my chest.

Viv is looking after me today. She is nice, so gentle and caring. I listen to her conversation with a colleague. I presume she thinks that she is talking out of earshot, but I have developed a kind of supersonic hearing. It's amazing what you can do when you put your mind to it, especially when there is nothing else *to* do, other than try to think up ways to get better, and my options there are pretty limited.

"Yes, she is taking all of the shifts here," Viv tells her friend, in a hushed tone.

"I heard that everyone hated her at her last place too, I hope she doesn't get a permanent position here," the friend, who I think is called Gavin, tells Viv.

"The thing is Kevin, she gets twice as much as us working on the agency, so there is no incentive for her to apply for a permanent position, and while we have so many off sick and on maternity here, she will have plenty of shifts."

Okay, so it's Kevin, not Gavin.

"Hopefully she'll get bored and go somewhere else soon. Didn't she used to work at Leicester?"

"Yeah, but apparently she had some family problems. Her daughter got into a spot of bother, and she went a bit *doolally*. She basically left before she was pushed."

"Well I regularly feel like pushing her, she is so rude to everyone and the way she talks to the families. Well I think it is just disgusting."

Ooh, so Pam is not liked by her colleagues. I wish I could join in with this conversation, tell them how she has not passed my important information on to the police. That James is innocent and she has withheld the evidence! How unlucky that she was the only one I got the chance to tell, and now I am locked away again, with no form of communication.

"It has nothing to do with luck," my whispering voice tells me. *How do you know?* I think.

After twelve hours of Viv's tender care, I start to feel better. I wonder if this is perhaps my imagination, but I'm sure that my hallucinations slow down when she is here, or rather when Pam is not here. Pam has told Lauren that she needs to work with someone else because she is not getting enough of a variety of experiences with me, and she needs to put her training above her feelings for me. Lauren came and told me this yesterday. I am gutted, and I really do believe it's because Pam doesn't like anyone nice. I actually wonder whether Pam is deliberately punishing me by taking the nicest thing in this whole experience away from me. I still cannot shake the bizarre feeling that I have upset her somehow.

Chloe is here now, and I can hear her unwrapping sweets, she then chats away to me with whatever it is she is eating stuffed into one cheek like a hamster. I know she is doing this because as she chats to me, she sounds like she has a slight speech impediment. I imagine her doing it, and I want to laugh/cry/laugh, she is so funny. My mum used to tell her off for it when we were young and Chloe devised a way of eating a sweet in secret by hiding it under her tongue and managing to talk almost normally. I wonder what it is she has. Chocolate limes perhaps, or Murray Mints? I wonder what she is wearing? I want to open my eyes and look at her. I have to get better, I have to fight, but what can I do? Dylan used to say that you can do anything and the only tool you need is determination, so I need to work on determination. I decide to make a list of all the reasons to get better. Number one at the moment is to free James from prison. The thought of him alone, afraid and desperately trying to prove his innocence is torturing me.

THE WARNING

The weather was beautiful. The sun was shining, and the sky was blue as we set off for Newcastle.

"Shall I drive?" I asked.

"No, I know how you feel about driving Anna."

This perplexed me, and I had no idea how I had managed to give James this impression.

"Your car or mine?" I asked.

"What?" he said, looking at me as though I had just asked him if he wanted a shit sandwich.

"I think you'll find that both cars belong to me. *Your* car? I don't remember you shelling out £30,000."

It was true, both cars did belong to James, initially when the documents had arrived from the DVLA, I had been a bit surprised to see that James had registered himself as the keeper of *my* car, but at the time, he had said that he had been so stung by Daniella's financial exploitation of him that he was just really wary, I accepted this explanation without question, why shouldn't I have?

He was obviously in one of his 'moods'. I would have to tread very carefully if I didn't want him to blow up in the car on the way to Newcastle. My heart sank as I realised that we were potentially going to have three hours of cat and mouse on the journey, where I tried to decipher his mood, his meaning, and tread very carefully on the eggshells. I felt so tired, my mouth felt dry, my heart fluttered nervously in my chest. *This is shit.* I thought. I got into the passenger seat and waited for James. He'd gone back into the house to get changed for the second time. He was obviously very nervous, he had sweat patches forming on his t-shirt, and he kept opening and closing his hands and stretching his fingers, a habit that I had begun to recognise as stress induced.

"Why don't you bring a t-shirt to change into when we get there? You might feel better once we get going and then you may not be as sweaty."

"Shut up," he snapped. "Stop going on about stuff." He was in the car now and had started the engine. I stared at him astounded.

"I wasn't going on; I was trying to help you."

"No you weren't. You were trying to make me look stupid as usual."

"How?"

'How?' he mocked in a high-pitched voice, presumably an impression of me.

"Why are you mocking me?"

"Me, me, me, me, me. That's all I ever hear from you. It's all about Anna."

"No, it's not James! I can't understand why you think that."

"Oh, you understand alright. You understand very well."

"I'm not getting into this," I said, and I began to stare out of the window. Why did he have to do this? Why did he always get me wrong? Why did he seem to misunderstand my words?

"Are you going to stare out of the window for the entire journey?"

"I don't know James," I said quietly. "I just think that you misunderstand me and when I try to tell you what I mean, you tell me I'm lying. It's really frustrating."

"It's really frustrating," he said, mocking my voice again. "Grow up Anna."

I sighed and took my phone from my bag and began to play a game. It had annoying sound effects on it, and I quickly set it to mute. My heart was pounding; my head was spinning. No matter what I said, no matter how I tried, I could not get James to hear what I was saying. During this sort of argument, I would try and change the way I said things. I'd attempt to explain them more carefully, try and get him to see how much it hurt when he thought that I was behaving horribly to him, but nothing worked. It was like there was a soundproof barrier between us. James would look as though he was listening, and then say something like; "You over analyse. Analyse, analyse, analyse, that's all you do, and it's so fucking boring." Or, "Here you go, analysing again." And I'd feel so frustrated that he didn't seem to *get* me.

I continued to stare at the game on my phone, not really taking in what I was doing, trying to calm myself down. James put the radio on and turned it up loud. I suspected he was doing this to get at me.

"Put your phone down Anna."

"I beg your pardon?" I said, astounded.

"I said, put your phone down. You are only playing on it to annoy me."

"No, I'm not, stop telling me what I think," I retorted.

"You have two choices Anna, either you put the phone down, or you get in the back like the child you are, or I'll take the phone off you and throw it out of the fucking window."

"That's three choices James," I said sarcastically, rage swirling in my chest.

"That is it," James said menacingly, grabbing my hand and trying to get my phone. We were on the motorway by now, and the car was swerving dangerously across the lanes as we grappled with one another. James got hold of the skin on my arm and twisted it painfully with his nails.

"Give me the fucking phone!" he demanded,

opening the window of the car.

"No!" I shouted. "Stop it, you crazy bastard!"

"How dare you call me names, you evil cunt."

The car continued to swerve all over the road, and I began to feel scared.

"Get in the back then if you won't give me your phone."

"Watch the road!" I screamed.

"GET IN THE BACK! NOW!" he ordered.

"No! Stop it! Why are you doing this?"

"Because you are acting like a child Anna and children sit in the back. Get in the back," he said again, pulling the sleeve of my top roughly and unfastening my seatbelt.

"Stop it! STOP IT! WATCH THE ROAD!"

"GET. IN. THE. BACK," he ordered again. "The front seat is for adults."

I fastened my seatbelt again and stared back out of the window. My breathing was fast and jittery.

"Get in the back Anna, or I will take my hands off the wheel of this car and put my foot down."

He was playing on my fear of the road. I knew that accidents happened, that people were killed, and he knew that since losing Dylan, I had become more nervous, more vigilant when I drove and that was probably why he made such a big deal about doing all of the driving.

"Get in the back Anna," he ordered again, and so

I unfastened my seatbelt and began to climb through to the back, bitter humiliation choking me. He grabbed me roughly and pushed me through the two front seats and as I passed him I slapped the back of his head. I knew that I shouldn't have done it, but I felt so humiliated at submitting to his orders that I just lashed out at him.

We drove along in silence for a few minutes and then he began to speak.

"I'm getting sick of your violent outbursts. You are obviously totally fucked up. It's probably something to do with grief after lover boy died, but I swear if you take one more of your moods out on me I will knock your teeth into your throat."

I said nothing. I was so angry that I couldn't speak and all my concentration was going into controlling my breathing. James turned the radio off and then began to make a call. The phone was on hands-free so I could hear both sides of the conversation.

"Hello darling!" June said brightly.

"Mum," James said, his voice cracking slightly.

"James are you okay?" she asked, concerned.

"Not really, mum, Anna has just hit me, and it's not the first time that this has happened."

"Oh my goodness, are you okay? Oh my word, what on earth is going on?"

"We were arguing, and she just lashed out at me. I

just thought I'd let you know mum; I might have to come and stay with you and dad. I can't go through all this again."

"Okay darling, keep in touch, I hope you are okay. I am so shocked James; I was sure she was such a nice girl."

I sat with my mouth open in shock. Had James really just told a tale about me to his mum? Were we five years old again? I dialled June's number, and she answered quickly.

"Anna," she said coldly. "What is going on?"

"June I just want you to know that the story that James has just told you isn't strictly true."

"Why, what happened?"

"Look I am not going to start telling tales. You don't need to know what has just happened, but we didn't *only* have an argument where I lashed out."

"Anna, did you or did you not hit James?"

"I did June."

"Well, in that case, you are very much in the wrong. There is never any excuse for hitting another person, no matter what they have just said to you and I am afraid that I have lost all regard that I once held for you. Goodbye Anna."

And with that, she hung up.

This is shit. I thought again. *Really fucking shit.* I looked out of the window, wishing that I was somewhere else. What had happened to my life? I remembered the road trips that Dylan and I used to take: the car was usually filled with laughter, a nice atmosphere, good music that we both wanted to listen to. As though reading my thoughts, James flicked the radio back on and turned it up. I leant my forehead against the glass of the window and watched the countryside speeding by.

Clouds had begun to gather towards the west where I stared, and I remembered Dylan asking me to marry him on Arthur's Seat, the huge rolling clouds in the distance like a warning of our tragic future, I thought about us basking in the sunshine and the joy of our bright and brilliant dreams. The big fat tears rolled freely down my face now, gathering on my chin and plopping onto my top. I imagined Dylan putting his arm around me and comforting me. I tried to remember the smell of his skin, the sound of his voice, the feeling of complete and utter love and safety that I had when I was with him. I imagined how he would feel if he could hear the way that James spoke to me, and I knew that I was letting him down by staying. I was letting everyone who loved me down by staying with James and most of all I was letting myself down. I would leave him. I had decided. I would just get through this weekend, if I told him now that I was going to leave him, he might not meet Hannah and I couldn't risk him hurting her. No, I would wait until we were back home, then I would see if Chloe would let me stay with her until I got sorted.

James turned the radio off and turned briefly to me, "Why don't you get back in the front Anna?"

"No, I'll just stay here."

He tutted.

"You are unbelievable. Prove your point then," he said, turning the radio back up.

"Knob," I muttered quietly under my breath.

We continued to drive for ten minutes or so, and then he turned the radio back down again.

"Anna, are you going to sulk for the whole journey? I've spent a lot of money for us to have a nice time this weekend and you are ruining it with your mood."

I ignored him. What could I say? His double standards, the way he rewrote history, his blame shifting, were infuriating, but if I tried to defend myself, I knew that it would just descend into mayhem.

"Anna, I'm getting sick of you sulking like a child and ignoring me. Why don't you act like an adult for a change? Why don't you treat me like a *human being?*"

I couldn't help myself, and I snorted a loud, indignant snort at the 'human being' bit.

"When exactly was I treating you like anything other than a human being, James?"

"Hitting, the hitting! It's disgusting behaviour. You are disgusting."

I decided to ignore him again. He turned the music up loud and began to sing in a really irritating, exaggerated way. I wanted to push his head through the windscreen.

"Prick!" I muttered under my breath again.

"Anna, get in the front," he turned the music down again.

"No!" I said indignantly. "I don't want to sit next to you."

"Why do you have to ruin everything?"

I decided to ignore him again. He tapped his fingers on the dashboard for a few moments and then he began to make another call.

"Hello," June said tentatively. "Are you okay? Are you safe?"

I snorted again. *Safe?* What did she think I was going to do to him?

"Yes, I'm safe mum. I just don't know what to do. I'm trying to sort it out with her, but she's got into the back of the car, and she won't come and sit in the front with me to talk about things and sort them out."

"Oh, how pathetic of her."

"She can hear you mum; you're on loudspeaker."

"Anna, why don't you stop being so childish? You have a good man there, don't spoil it."

James looked smug for a second.

"I'm in the back because James ordered me to get in the back."

"No he didn't, Anna!"

"Yes he did, June."

"Did you do that, James?'

"No! Of course, I didn't," he lied.

"You liar!" I shouted at him. "You barefaced fucking liar!"

"Oh dear!" June said. "She sounds hysterical."

"See what I mean mum? She is totally crazy."

His voice was cracking again, with fake emotion, his acting skills were quite something else! Why did I have to be trapped in the car with this lunatic? My heart felt like it would pop at any second. I was so angry. So outraged! He was a complete liar, and the scary thing was that he seemed to believe his version of events more than he believed the truth.

He pulled into a service station for fuel and got out of the car, giving me a withering look and then slamming the door.

"Arsehole," I said, as soon as he was out of earshot. A man at the adjacent pump began to speak to him, and I opened the door slightly to hear the conversation.

"Yeah I think I do have some jump leads mate," James was saying. "Hold on a sec, and I'll check in the boot."

He leant into the car to release the boot catch.

"Ooh aren't you a kind and decent human being," I quipped at him, outraged at the way he could switch from bully to victim to friend in the blink of an eye and whenever it suited him.

"You are so bitter," he said to me quietly. I watched him hand the man the jump leads, and then he leant back in to open the bonnet of his car to charge up the man's battery, he was mid-conversation.

"Yeah, you are welcome to keep them, we've got another set in the boot anyway, take them, there's nothing worse than being stranded."

His compassion to this stranger after the way he had just treated me was too much for me to bear, and I opened the car door and began to walk across the car park. From the corner of my eye I could see James watching me, but of course, he was acting like a normal person in front of the stranger at the pump, and he said nothing to me. I made my way to the café area and ordered myself a coffee while I tried to decide what to do. It was three days until payday, and there was hardly any money in my account, I was at a service station in the middle of nowhere at least one hundred miles from home. I could ring my parents, but that would involve explaining to them about James and dragging them out on a Saturday afternoon. My dad would more than likely have been drinking by now, and I imagined how stressed the whole situation would make my mum. It didn't seem worth it to bother them. My phone began to ring; it was James, I rejected the call and went to the toilets to try and decide what to do. I hid in a cubicle with my cup of coffee and tried my hardest to work out what the best course of action was. My phone rang again, and again I rejected James's call. He sent me a text message: *Anna, where are you? I am so worried; please answer, let's talk.xx*

The phone began to ring again.

"Hello," I said.

"Where are you? Can we talk?"

"What's the point when you always tell me what I think and feel anyway? You may as well just have a conversation with yourself."

"Anna, don't be like that. I'm so stressed, please come and talk me. Please tell me where you are."

"I just want to go home James. Why is it that you can be nice to a total stranger, yet you speak to me like a piece of shit?"

"Anna, I am sorry, I didn't mean to hurt you, I am so stressed about meeting my daughter. Please tell me where you are."

"I'm in the ladies' toilet."

"Okay, so I will wait outside until you come out."

"Okay, bye," I said and then hung up. Was he

truly sorry, or did he just want to get me back into the car to carry on giving me a hard time? I wasn't sure but felt that my hands were tied. I decided to carry on to Newcastle with him, bury our problems in a shallow grave and deal with them when we got back home, after all, I didn't want Hannah to be let down.

I left the toilets and James was leaning on a wall opposite. Why did he have to be so damn good looking? He came over to me and held his arms out. His head was bowed, and his big brown eyes looked sad and sorry.

"You are my everything, Anna. Sometimes I am just a complete idiot."

I felt my anger, my resolve all melting away. He looked so lost and vulnerable that my heart softened and I let him take me in his arms. We got back into the car and continued our journey. I swallowed the disappointment that I felt about myself, pushed it deep down inside, as we began making small talk.

We arrived in Newcastle, found our hotel and checked in. The room was just as gorgeous as it had looked online, and there were some chocolates and a bottle of champagne waiting for us.

"For you, Anna, as a thank you for all your support through this Hannah business."

"Aw thank you," I said, "can't wait to drink that later." How could he be so thoughtful and generous, yet so cruel and manipulative? I was so confused.

James got changed, and we made our way to the coffee shop where he was to meet his daughter for the first time. He was so nervous, he kept opening and closing his hands and running his fingers through his hair, sighing loudly. We approached the door of the building, and he clasped my hand tightly, his palms were sweaty and cold. We stopped just short of the entrance, and he looked at me, sighed loudly and then said, "Here goes."

He opened the door and scanned the tables briefly. Hannah was waiting inside with Fiona, and we all introduced ourselves and one another. Hannah was beautiful, tall like James and slim, with the same large expressive brown eyes.

"Okay, give me a ring when you are done," I told James as I left them to it.

"Okay baby, see you later," he said, quickly kissing me.

I headed out into the shopping area. James had stuffed £200 into my bag, but I was reluctant to spend it on myself after what had just happened in the car, so I made my way towards a department store to find some stuff for the house. "Excuse me!" I heard footsteps behind me.

"Anna is it?" It was Fiona.

"Yes, hi Fiona. Are you okay?"

"I'm probably not supposed to say this, and it's

none of my business, but how well do you know James? Have you been together long?"

"Er, just coming up for a year," I said, taken aback by her forwardness.

"It's just, well, he used to have a temper that's all. That's why I wouldn't let him see Hannah when she was a baby, but people change don't they? I mean they can if they want to." Her voice began to falter, and she looked really uncomfortable and embarrassed.

"Er, thanks for the warning," I said. "I guess you mean well, but we're fine." We both felt uncomfortable, looking at one another for a second. "She's beautiful. Hannah is," I said, my words tumbling out in a nervous muddle.

"She is his double!" Fiona said, smiling. "Thankfully his looks were never the problem. Listen, Anna; I had better go. Hope I didn't offend you there, bye."

"Bye," I called as she rushed off into the crowd. I stood rooted to the spot. All the puzzle pieces were beginning to fit together, and the emerging picture was ugly and sinister. James had told me that he had chosen not to see Hannah because of Fiona, yet Fiona had just told me that she had never let him see her because of his temper. What kind of man was I sharing my life with? I tried to quell my worries, explain them away, but Fiona's warning rang in my ears, and a nagging, sinking doubt enveloped me. I knew what I was going to have to do.

THE POISON SPREADS

My body is weak. At the moment I am ravaged with infection. My blood is filled with bacteria; its poison is reaching every part of my body. My temperature soars and I feel dreadful. Every thump of my poor bruised heart is painful, it beats quickly, twice as fast as it is supposed to, and every surge of my poisoned blood causes me the most tremendous pain in my head. It feels as though someone with a sledgehammer is beating me on the skull with every heartbeat. If I could, I would cry out with pain. My skin feels tender and bruised; my entire body aches as though I have the worst dose of the flu imaginable. It's really difficult to remain determined in these circumstances. I am trying hard, mustering up every positive thought that I can, but the pain itself is draining me and knowing that my body is filled with poison is so disheartening. The doctors are pumping me full of antibiotics, and I overhear mum telling Eve that one of the medicines that I am on could leave me disabled. I can't understand how I have become so ill, I only fell and banged my head. Why do things keep going from bad to worse? What if I die? If I die, James will be charged with murder or manslaughter. I can't bear that thought. I have to get better; I have to.

This poison in my blood, the way it is travelling to every part of my body reminds of the poison that James filled me with. The vile toxic abuse would spout from his mouth, and fill my being, spreading to every part of my life.

Some of it was so subtle that I am only just beginning to see it for what it was now that I am stuck here, forcibly reliving every experience. If I were enthusiastic about something I had done, some achievement or accomplishment, James would find a way of removing the sheen, curtailing my happiness, or just out and out pissing on my fire. And if anything that I was doing were likely to infringe on my time with him, then James would give me a really hard time until eventually, I stopped having the energy to attempt to live a life that involved any activities without him.

I had been asked to help write and produce the school Christmas show, and although it meant a lot of work, I was flattered. The drama teacher at my school was known for being incredibly fussy about the yearly show, and she didn't let just anyone get involved! I got home from work and went to tell James, who was in his office doing some work.

"Hiya!" I said brightly. "Want a coffee?"

"Yes please baby," he replied. "Come here!" he

said grabbing me and pulling me onto his lap.

"Guess what?" I ventured

"What?" he asked.

"I'm going to be doing the school play."

"What will that involve?" he asked, narrowing his eyes.

"Thursday evenings I'll be at school until seven thirty," I answered.

"Anna," he sighed, "have you given this *any* thought? You aren't leaving very much time for yourself. I mean what about our time together as a couple? You haven't even discussed this with me."

"Why do I need to discuss it? I want to do the school play. Why do I need to discuss something that I want to do with my own time with you?"

"Anna, part of being in a relationship is to discuss things together. You act like a single person."

"No, I don't! What about all the things that take up your time? Training, for example, I don't recall you discussing how much time you spend training with me."

"Totally different!" James retorted. I could have carried on, tried to argue my point, but I knew how it would go if I did, it would descend into an argument. I went and made our cups of coffee feeling hurt and deflated and when I handed James his drink, he began to make digs at me.

"Stop sulking," he said. "You're sulking and

ruining our evening."

"I'm not sulking; I just wish you'd been a bit more happy for me."

"Grow up *Anna*," he snapped. "I've had enough of you," he got up and went upstairs. When he came back down again, he was in his cycling gear, and he left the house without saying goodbye to me.

As seemed to happen so often, I tried to continue with my evening, an uncomfortable knot in my stomach where there had once been an appetite. 'Fuck it,' I thought, beginning to stuff some clothes in a bag. 'I'm going to leave. I don't have to put up with this.'

I went to 'my' car, threw my overnight bag onto the front seat and began to drive, bitter tears stinging my cheeks. I put Elbow on and began to imagine that Dylan was with me. I wasn't sure where I could go. Not to my parents, I couldn't bear thought of worrying them; they were so relieved that I had met James that I wanted to be sorted before I told them. Chloe's? No, I felt the same about worrying Chloe. All of my friends and family had been through so much with me after Dylan's death that I didn't feel able to tell any of them that things weren't good with James. Not only that but for some reason, I felt ashamed. Why did I feel ashamed? It wasn't me who was behaving atrociously. I drove aimlessly for a while and then I parked the car in a local park.

Mirrorball was playing, and I remembered the brief time that Dylan and I had enjoyed this album together. I'd probably listened to it more times without him now. That thought pushed me over the edge, and I began to sob. *Why? Why did things have to go so wrong? Why did James have to be so nasty? Where could I go? Why did Dylan have to die? Stupid fucking motorbikes.* I hammered the steering wheel with my fists, rage and grief swirling like a powerful tornado in my chest. I pulled my phone from my bag, it was still set to silent from work, and there were seven missed calls from James and some voicemails. I began to look through my contacts to see if I could find someone to stay with, but I couldn't imagine telling anyone what was happening in my life. Perhaps I could stay in a Travelodge? I rang my bank to check my balance. I had less than £10 available. I decided to listen to the voicemails.

"Anna, I'm back home, where are you?"

"Are you ignoring me? Anna stop being so childish and let me know what you are doing."

"Anna, I'm getting worried now. Call me."

"If you don't call me I'm going to ring the police and report you as missing."

Oh for fuck's sake! Was he really worried or was he just trying to control me?

Just then my phone lit up again. It was a call

from my mum.

"Hi!" I answered, as normally as I could.

"Anna, where are you? James is worried sick; he says he has no idea where you are."

"Oh, I just nipped out for some groceries," I lied, her worried voice instantly grating on my nerves.

"Well call him darling, for some reason he's got it into his head that you've had an accident. Your dad and I were so worried when he called."

"Okay mum, bye, love you."

The sneaky bastard! I thought as I dialled his number.

"Anna, where are you?"

"I'm not coming back James, not tonight."

"Why?"

"I'm just sick of the double standards."

"Come back, Anna, I'll listen. I promise."

"I would, but I have had enough James. You never listen to me, you always give me a hard time, and you act like I am bad like I am deliberately trying to upset you and I am not, and I am sick of walking on eggshells."

"Anna, please come back, I won't be able to rest without you, I'll listen, I promise."

His voice was shaky; he sounded desperate. Was this the wake-up call he needed? I ignored my inner voice, I quashed the feeling of foreboding, and I nurtured the tiny glimmer of hope that James would genuinely stop being an arsehole, that all he had needed to do was see that his behaviour was upsetting me and he would stop, and I went home. I could see Dylan looking sad and disappointed in my mind's eye, and I said a silent apology for letting him down. Deep down inside I knew that I was doing the wrong thing, but I was becoming excellent at ignoring my feelings, or at least telling myself that they didn't matter. Why was I doing this? Why did I make James more important than me? Why did I aid him in his quest for domination?

When I got home, James and I had a conversation about what had happened. He said that now he could see how important doing the school show was to me he could understand why I was upset. After our discussion, I didn't feel that anything had been resolved, after all, why should something be justified as being important to me, just to ensure that James would not give me a hard time about doing it? Surely I should just do whatever I wished and not expect a hard time – ever?

A couple of days later a card and a book arrived in the post. The book was a guide on adapting stories for the stage, and the message in the card read: *I want to support you in everything you do. You are my world, love you baby xxx*

I was so confused! Which was it then? Did he want to support me or did he want to make me feel bad? I couldn't work it out, so I decided to believe that nice James was the real man and snappy, nasty, selfish James was just the result of a stressful life.

****

He would make remarks, which on the surface appeared benign, but were chipping away at me piece by piece. I was ordering some toiletries and make-up online, and he sat next to me and glanced at the laptop while I made the transaction.

"You getting that same make-up?" he asked.

"What makeup do you mean?"

"That cheek stuff that you use."

"Blusher?" I asked.

"Yeah, do you really like wearing it? Did someone tell you it looked good?"

"Yes, I do like wearing it!" I responded. "And no, no-one has ever mentioned it either way," I said, feeling insecure.

Did I look horrible when I used blusher? I thought it looked nice, my olive skin could look a little sallow at times, and I only used a little to brighten my cheeks. The next day when I got ready for work and went to apply my blusher, as usual, I felt uncomfortable. Maybe it didn't look nice? I applied a small amount and gazed at myself in the mirror. Did I look like a clown? I wiped it off with a cleansing wipe. Now I looked too pale. I reapplied it and went to work as usual, but all day I felt uncomfortable, as though my cheeks were flashing like cheap fairy lights. I worried about how I looked; I worried that the children were all laughing at me behind my back, that the staff all ridiculed me. It was horrible. Eventually, wearing blusher became such a source of stress for me that I ceased to use it at all.

As the season began to change from summer to autumn, I dusted off my warmer clothes and boots. Some of my stuff was a little tight for me this year, but most of my clothes fitted okay. James was competing in a triathlon, and I was going along to watch him. I quite liked spectating, and always felt proud of his achievements. He was a very good athlete. I showered and dressed quickly because we were running a little late, and when I came down the stairs, James was ready and waiting. He looked me up and down briefly and then said, "I knew we should have gone shoe shopping in Newcastle."

My heart sank. I mustn't look good. I glanced at my boots. Was there something wrong with them? They were a bit worn, but I quite liked them like that. I'd had them for a few years; maybe they were looking dated now? I hadn't noticed. I got into the car feeling self-conscious and unsure of myself. James had good taste in clothes and always looked very nice. For some reason, I now felt that he was better qualified to decide whether my choice of clothes was suitable or not. My feet felt huge, and I kept looking at my boots. *I look stupid.* I thought. *I can't even get dressed properly anymore.* We got to the event, and I went off alone to find a good spot to watch the race. My feet felt heavy and clumsy with my ridiculous boots on, and I felt as though they were painted bright fluorescent yellow, hideous and impossible to miss. Usually, at something like this, I would be energised by the surrounding crowd, but this time I had an uncomfortable knot in my stomach. I felt anxious and unsure of myself, as though I didn't belong with all these people who clearly knew how to choose suitable footwear and apply the right kind of make-up.

Now that I look back and see it for what I was, I am angry at myself for allowing it to happen. I can see now that I should have left him. I was running around like a headless chicken. My mind raced constantly, I worried about what I was saying, wearing, doing, thinking and eating. The result of being treated the way I was being treated by James was that I lost my spark. Hattie noticed, Chloe noticed and Sophie noticed. My mum asked me what was wrong whenever I saw her, but still no one made the connection between James and the change in my persona. I became oversensitive, under confident and snappy and defensive. Back then, I felt as though my energy was vanishing, but now, now that I am trapped here I have to find that energy and use it to get better. I have to or everything will be wrong for ever more.

'Keep trying,' I hear my whispering voice tell me. 'You can do this, just keep listening.'

FROM BAD TO WORSE

It was the middle of October and James, and I had been living together in the beautiful barn conversion for five months.

"Let's have a Halloween Party," he suggested. "It will be brilliant to have this house full of laughter."

"Yeah you're right," I agreed with him. "The last house party I went to was Tom's birthday. I like house parties; I used to go to lots of them when I was at university." As soon as the words had left my mouth, I regretted saying them.

"Who did you go with?" James asked his face flushing red.

"Sophie mainly," I lied, knowing that he was feeling jealous of Dylan.

"What you never used to go with *lover boy*?" he asked.

"His name was Dylan," I said, angry at the way he belittled my relationship with Dylan by calling him lover boy all the time.

"Thanks for that *Anna*. I'm well aware of what *lover boy's* name was. Did you go to house parties with him?" he asked, narrowing his eyes and staring at me.

"Yes, of course I did!" I said. "You know I did; I don't see what difference it makes to you though."

"So when you used to go to these house parties with *lover boy*, did you used to fuck him afterwards?"

"What? Why on earth would you ask that?"

"Well did you?" he asked, taking a step towards me.

"I don't want to have this conversation."

"Tough luck *Anna* because I do, now answer the fucking question."

"I'm going!" I said, and I grabbed 'my' car keys from the kitchen table. I'd just finished a large glass of wine, and it briefly crossed my mind that I would probably be over the limit, but I desperately wanted to be away from James who seemed hell-bent on making himself feel bad and attempting to cheapen what Dylan and I had once had together.

"You're going nowhere until you answer the fucking question."

"I'm not having this conversation James," I told him, heading towards the door. He stepped in front of me, swiftly locked it and stuffed the key in his back pocket.

"Why?" I asked him, as he stared at me triumphantly. "Why are you doing this?"

"It's not me; you are the one causing this. It's YOU. You blame me, blame, blame, blame, but it's

YOU. When I moved in here, it was supposed to be the start of my great new life. And do you know what? It's shit, it's a stinking shit life, and it's a stinking shit life because I am living with an ugly stinking shit. You. You are a stinking shit, and you have ruined my life, you selfish whore. Now answer my question, you dirty little cunt. Did you used to fuck *lover boy* at your stupid student parties?"

I stared at him, astounded at the foul torrent of bullshit. My mouth was opening and closing like a goldfish, but no words would come out. I just couldn't understand what was happening, why he was so angry about something that I might have done before I had ever even met him.

"James, please will you unlock the door so that I can leave?" I asked as calmly as I possibly could.

"Answer the question."

"No."

"Is that your answer?"

"I'm not answering your ridiculous question, now let me go."

I backed away from him towards the back door of the house. If I could get to the back door, I could get out of the garden and round to the car. I'd have to climb over the wall though. I was starting to feel panicky. Why wouldn't he let me go? I didn't want to submit to him and answer his question, it felt too much like a betrayal of Dylan.

"You are going nowhere. ANSWER. MY. QUESTION."

"NO!" I screamed at him.

"You hysterical bitch," he said, laughing in my face like a maniac.

"Piss off," I retorted. "Get out of my fucking way," I said, lunging toward the back the house.

He stood in front of me, his evil smile playing on his lips.

"Going somewhere?" he asked smarmily.

"Yes, I am actually. Away from YOU. Now get out of my fucking way, you PRICK."

"Ooh, temper temper little Miss Perfect." He took a step forwards, and I took a step back.

"You are going nowhere until you have answered my question. ANSWER THE FUCKING QUESTION."

"NO, I WILL NOT, NOW LET ME GO."

I clenched my fists tightly. I wanted to punch him. How dare he stop me from leaving? How dare he hold me prisoner.

"If you shout at me again I am going to have to shut you up. Go on, you ugly piece of shit. I dare you. Come on, shout at me again and see what happens."

He had managed to back me against the wall by now, and he was talking in a mocking and sinister soft voice, pressing his body against mine and breathing in my ear. I began to cry with frustration, the tears ran down my face, he had me trapped, but there was no way I was going to do what he told me this time, I would not sully what Dylan and I had done together, not ever. No matter what James said or did to me, I would not betray Dylan.

I tried to reason with him.

"Look, I can see that you're upset about this, but don't you think it will be better if we talk about it when we have both calmed down? I mean, we are both wound up right now, and it will probably just lead to a big row."

"I wouldn't be wound up if you would just simply answer the fucking question."

"Well, I'm not prepared to James."

"Why are you keeping secrets from me?"

"What? How is it a secret? I don't ask you stuff about your ex-girlfriends."

"Yes you do Anna, and I answer them honestly. All I want from you is a little bit of honesty and you, for some reason, are acting like a spoilt little child."

"I do not ask you about sex with your ex-girlfriends, James."

"Well I can tell you this, Daniella and I were at it all the time. She loved my cock."

"You *are* a fucking cock," I retorted.

"She was a better fuck than you. You frigid little bitch."

"Good James, I'm glad you've had a better time

with someone else because perhaps you won't miss me so much when I am gone. And by the way, either I'm a whore, or I am frigid, make your fucking mind up and stop contradicting yourself."

I was shaking with rage now, and I hated James more than I had ever hated anyone in my entire life. I tried again to get past him to the door, but he stepped in front of me and wouldn't allow me past.

"You have no right to keep me prisoner."

"Stop being so fucking dramatic and answer my fucking question."

"NO!" I shouted, trying to pass him. Again he blocked my way and my frustration was reaching boiling point, I was ready to explode. I decided to try and go upstairs, away from him, but he began to follow me.

"Why are you doing this?" I asked again.

"Because you are being a cunt."

"How?"

"Because you have no respect for me. I have asked you a simple question, now FUCKING WELL ANSWER IT."

"James, I am not answering your question. Why don't you respect my wishes?"

"Why the fuck should I when you won't respect mine? I have asked you a simple question Anna, and you are being pathetic by not answering it."

I had gone upstairs and into our bedroom. He

had followed me and insisted on standing inches away from me, I could feel his breath, smell his aftershave and I wanted so much to push him away from me. I pulled my suitcase from inside my wardrobe and began to pack some clothes. 'My' car keys were stuffed tightly into the pocket of my jeans, and I could feel them digging painfully into me as I moved to pack. James watched me, and for a few seconds, neither of us spoke.

"What do you think you are you are doing?" he asked, condescendingly.

"I'm packing a few bits and going to stay with a friend."

"Oh *really?* You are, are you?"

"Yes I am. I don't need to put up with this."

"Actually, I think you'll find that you do need to put up with this because you are going nowhere until you have answered my question."

"I am going James," I said, stuffing a pile of underwear into the suitcase.

"We'll see about that." he retorted, swiftly grabbing the suitcase and holding it above his head so that I couldn't reach it.

"Give me it!"

"Answer my question."

"NO!" he marched across the room and put the filled suitcase back into the wardrobe then stood in front of it, blocking my way.

"Why?" I asked, beginning to sob again. "Why are you trying to hurt me?"

For a brief second, something that resembled remorse flashed across James's face, followed almost immediately by a sneer.

"You're pathetic Anna, always feeling sorry for yourself, you think you have been through so much, you expect special treatment. You're a selfish, stupid little whore, a nothing from a drain who expects others to provide for her."

"How? How do I expect others to provide for me? I work full time!"

"You never pay a penny for anything; you just expect me to pay for everything."

"You insist on paying for everything! I always offer," I responded. Why were we now arguing about this?

"Give me my clothes, James."

"No."

"Give me them!"

"No. You're not having them 'cause you're a stinking cunt." I tried to push him away from the wardrobe to get my bag.

"Move!" I said, pushing him. It was futile; he was very strong and stood fast.

"Stop pushing me."

"Move then!" I said, determined to get my clothes from inside the wardrobe.

"I'm warning you," he said. I pushed at him again, trying to get him to move, I don't know why I didn't just give up there and then, I suppose it was the anger, the adrenaline pumping through my veins.

"I warned you!" he said through gritted teeth, grabbing my arms and pushing me onto the bed. He lay on top of me, holding both of my arms by my side, I could hardly breathe and had my face turned away from his. "If you weren't so disgustingly ugly, I could fuck you right now," he whispered into my ear, his breath warm on my face.

"I hate you," I said to him, tears running down my face. I could taste blood in my mouth where I had bitten my lip.

"Now, are you going to answer my question you piece of shit whore?"

"Don't call me names."

'Don't call me names,' he mocked.

Huge sobs were wracking my body now, and I imagined poor Daniella in this situation reaching out for the nearest thing to hit him with so that she could escape. I was glad that there was nothing within reach because if I could have done at that point, *I'd* have hit him on the head with an iron doorstop, or worse. I imagined if I were in the kitchen preparing dinner, I could easily see myself stabbing him with a paring knife. Poor Daniella, she must have been pushed and pushed, and now she had been made to look like the villain, exactly what James was trying to do with me. I decided to say nothing more to him.

"This is cosy," he said, pushing one of his knees between mine. "Perhaps I *can* get over the fact that you're so ugly." Did he mean what I thought he meant? No, no way, surely he wasn't capable of *that*? He let go of one of my arms and began to fumble with the button of my jeans.

"Stop it!" I screamed, thumping him on the back with my free arm. My jeans were a bit too tight for me now, and he was finding it difficult to unfasten the button as I wriggled and squirmed. I grabbed his hair with my free hand and began to pull it as hard as I could, sinking my teeth into his shoulder and biting down with all my might.

"Ow, ow, ow, you crazy little bitch," he shouted, pushing his thumbs into my eyes forcing me to let go of him. He sat up, and I went to run, but he stuck his foot out in front of me, and I tripped and fell to the floor. I scrambled to my feet, and again I made to run, but he grabbed me and flung me against the wall.

"I have had just about enough of you," he seethed. "Stop trying to make a fool out of me."

By this point I was hysterical, and I sobbed and hyperventilated. I just wanted him to stop. I looked at his face, searching for the tender and gentle man that I had seen in there behind those eyes before.

"You have ruined my life," he spat, coldly.

"Pig, pig, pig, pig," I repeated, sobbing and trying to gain control of my mouth. I recognised this place, this depth of dark despair where words tumbled from my mouth without my consent. The last time I had been here was when Dylan had died, and I had screamed, "He'll go cold," over and over again. This time though, I repeated the word 'pig' at James. He let go of me and stared at me, a strange smile playing on his lips. Then he took his phone from his pocket and for a second I thought that he was about to call his mum again, this time though, he began to film me.

I turned and began to run, the realisation of what he was doing bringing me back to reality. I just had the edge on James, who was still fumbling with his phone and I got down the stairs and out into the back garden before he could catch me. I could hear him behind me, and I dived into the bushes next to the wall that I'd have to scale to escape from him. I crouched quietly, trying not to breathe, and he came out into the garden and began to look for me. *Please don't find me, please don't find me,* I begged in my mind. He walked up and down the garden and then must have concluded that I was back inside. He turned back into the house, and I took my chance, clambering over the wall and running to the driveway, getting into the Golf and starting the engine. James came running out onto the driveway just as I got away. Now all I had to do was drive as fast as I could and go somewhere to get away from him, somewhere safe. This time I would definitely go to my mum and dad's, they were the nearest people to me, and I could go the back route that James didn't know.

Predictably, my phone began to ring, as he frantically tried to get hold of me. I stopped at traffic lights as a text message from him flashed onto my screen: *Anna, you have ten minutes from now to get back home. If you are not home within ten minutes, I am going to call the police and tell them that you have stolen my car (it is registered in my name). By the way, it may have escaped your attention that you are drink driving. Ten minutes.*

It would take me at least twenty minutes to get to my parents' house on the route that I was on. What if James called the police? What would I say to them? I knew that I was probably over the drink drive limit. I had just sunk a huge glass of Merlot; it was one of those wine glasses that holds almost half a bottle. Shit, what could I do? I wracked my brain. I *could* go back; maybe he would have calmed down by now? And did I want to bring my parents into this? Was it just a silly domestic? Was this kind of thing normal in a relationship? Dylan and I had never rowed like that, but we had rowed. Maybe Dylan and I had been the exception to the rule; people had told us all the time how amazing our relationship was. Maybe I just had my expectations set too high? By the time I had processed these thoughts, I had already turned the car around and was on my way back to James. Looking back now I want to scream at myself, "WHAT ARE YOU DOING? STOP!" But it is too late. Back I went, back to James, back to the beautiful barn, the gilded cage that I was becoming a prisoner in, with a little bit less of my self-worth intact.

I pulled onto the driveway, my hands trembling. James was sitting on the doorstep. I got out of the car, and for a second I changed my mind, and almost got back in.

"Anna," he said, leaping to his feet and running over to me. He fell to his knees. "I am so sorry, so so sorry."

Tears streamed down his face; his big sad eyes looked sadder than ever. "For a few minutes there, I thought I had lost you. Baby, I don't know how I'd live without you."

He was still kneeling on the gravel at my feet. He had his arms around my legs and pressed his face against my thighs. He was sobbing like a baby.

"I keep thinking about you crying," he said. "I

just don't know when I have gone too far. I think that I need to go back to the counsellor that I saw after Daniella assaulted me. I think that I am too angry sometimes, old anger that is really about her and what I went through at her hands."

Did I believe this show? Did I think that this performance of an apology was enough? I'm not sure; I can't honestly remember now. Looking back, I can see it for what it was: A Big Fat Lie. Back then, I swallowed it, tried to see the best in him, and I walked back into our home arm in arm with the man who had just threatened me, ordered me about, verbally and physically abused me and, if I was honest with myself, had attempted to rape me. Where did he get his power from? Why was I putting myself back into the path of danger?

BEST BEHAVIOUR

Shakily, we went back into the house. I sat at our table while James boiled the kettle, he was sniffing loudly, and his shoulders shook with each breath. Every evil word he had spoken to me, each disgusting insult he had thrown my way had bruised my heart, and I yearned for some love and tenderness. I quashed the nagging voice that told me that none of this was good enough, and I let James cover my face with tender kisses, hold me in his arms and tell me how much he loved me. How he would do whatever it took to sort out our problems, to make it better. When he held me, I let his loving touch soothe my aching heart and damaged soul. I did not realise that every loving word that he spoke was filled with the same bitter poison as the disgusting insults, the sugar-coated, sickly sweet display of tenderness was all part of the campaign of domination, it was just one more tactic, but one that I craved and responded to. This was the cycle: hurt me, then heal me, then hurt me again and I was trapped, unable to see my way out, relying on his mood, his whim for my sense of wellbeing. How could I have allowed this to happen?

James handed me a cup of coffee, then sat opposite me while I drank it. He gazed at me with so much love in his eyes, and the sorrow that was written on his face was enough to melt the steeliest of hearts. Both of us were breathing the odd, shaky breath and my tears kept on falling. I felt so hurt, so violated, but instead of needing to be away from James, I felt an almost irresistible desire for his love, for his approval. I felt like I *needed* him, something that I had never experienced before in my life.

"Anna, I am the luckiest man alive. I am so lucky that you are standing by me. I will sort my temper out; I know it is unacceptable."

"I'm proud of you," I told him.

Proud? Proud of someone who had just treated me the way James had. Proud of the man who had just screamed and shouted at me, called me the vilest names, restrained me and held me prisoner! My thinking was seriously skewed! I sipped my coffee, and James kept kissing me and stroking my hair. The atmosphere between us was charged, and now gentle and tender, in contrast to the filthy and disgusting abuse. It created intense chemistry.

James pressed his lips against mine, and I didn't stop him, I kissed him back, a tingling running down my spine. He gently cupped my face in his hands and gazed into my eyes. I thought I heard my subconscious screaming at me to stop, to run, to leave, but I ignored it, this felt right. James had finally realised, of that I was sure, and his promises of change anchored themselves deeply in my heart.

He gently stroked my neck, his searching brown eyes brimming with tears.

"I love you so much, that I don't think I can stop crying," he told me. He punctuated his words with kisses. He knelt on the floor at my feet, and I put my arms around his neck. He unfastened my boots and kissed my feet.

I laughed. "You're brave!" I quipped.

"Everything about you is beautiful, Anna, everything," he told me, slowly unfastening my shirt. How could I ignore what had happened less than an hour ago? It was as though the words that he was now saying to me were the truth and somehow had the power to erase the other stuff.

"I love you," he whispered in my ear, sliding my bra strap from my shoulder so that it hung loosely over my arm. He remained kneeling on the floor between my knees, I leant my head on his shoulder, and he put his arms around me, unfastening my bra and letting it fall to the floor.

"I need to be close to you, I need to show you how much I love you, how much I need you," he told me, pulling me up to my feet and placing my hand on the buckle of his belt, gesturing for me to unfasten it, I did as he wished and he pushed my free hand inside his t-shirt, I could feel his heart beating fast like mine. Again he fumbled with the button of my jeans, but this time I wasn't trying to get away, and before very long we were both standing naked in our kitchen. He turned me towards the hallway and walked behind me, his hands in mine as we made our way up to our bedroom.

Of course, this was just part of the cycle, the endless cycle that I could not see beyond to break, the cycle that distorted my clarity and left me craving more of the same. This bit, this delicious, sensuous adoration, the tenderness, the affection, the approval, this was what I desperately craved from James, and when he hurt me with his abuse, instead of making me want to run from him, I craved him more than ever. I was like some crazed junkie, unable to see the damage and toxic filth around me, accepting of every piece of crap that came my way in search of the delicious nirvana of my next hit.

James and I spent the rest of the evening in bed. Instead of having dinner, we ate a big pile of toast and James made us both hot chocolate. We watched repeats of comedy shows on the TV while James insisted on rubbing my feet with lavender oil.

"You work so hard, you're on your feet all day," he told me. The evening was cosy and I felt safe and loved. We eventually fell asleep in one another's arms and when my alarm clock woke us in the morning, James was still clinging to me tightly.

Like the aftermath of all the other fights, the pain was the first thing that I noticed in the morning. Each and every muscle ached and moving was very painful. This time though, James anticipated this and brought me some painkillers and a glass of water. When he looked at me in the day light, his face crumpled with grief.

"How could I?" he asked. "I am ringing the counsellor today. I know that I was only restraining you so that you didn't attack me, but still, it's no excuse, just because I'm so afraid after what happened with *her.*"

His voice tailed off into a remorseful sob and I stroked his hair and told him again that I was proud of him, even though an angry shudder had just coursed through me at his denial of what had actually happened. I was sure though, that when he discussed it with his counsellor, she would be able to make him see that he had in fact attacked me, and not '*only restrained*' me as he seemed to believe. He had angry teeth marks on his shoulder where I had bitten him, and I ran my fingers across it, it felt disgusting and lumpy.

"It hurts," he told me, looking sorry for himself. I got up and showered and looked down at my body. Of course, I was covered in bruises. Angry purple finger marks had appeared on my upper arms where James had restrained me, there were lumps and bumps on my head, and there was a bruise in the corner of one of my eyes. My legs were covered in bruises, and my knees were black from landing on them when he had tripped me up. I stared at my back in the mirror, there was a huge bruise on my left shoulder blade, and the base of my spine was black and blue too. Even my buttocks were bruised, and I had scratches on my arms and on my face from hiding in the bushes. I dressed in the most comfortable clothes I could find. I wore a long-sleeved top, pulled my hair over my face, even though it drove me mad to wear it loose at work. I piled on lots of make-up in an attempt to disguise my bruised eye.

James made me breakfast, he made me coffee, and he fussed around me like an overprotective parent. That day at work, I was distracted, I worried whether James would contact his counsellor. I felt that his going to see her held the key to making him realise that he had been hurting me; it seemed as though my whole existence depended upon him making that phone call. I was in pain, and I was paranoid that someone would notice a bruise and question me. Every time anyone looked at me or spoke to me, I felt embarrassed, ashamed and uncomfortable. James sent me message after message, and I was relieved to hear that he had made an appointment with his old counsellor Lizzie, who he had seen for a few months after his relationship with Daniella. When I finally got home that evening, relieved to have finally escaped the scrutiny of others, James had prepared a delicious meal.

"You had better get used this, because I am never going to let you go, I am never going to lose you," he told me when I thanked him for his efforts.

After dinner, I went into our room to get changed and there was a card and a small gift on the bed for me.

I opened the card.

The message inside read: *Anna, my beautiful girl, I want you to know that I love you with all of my heart. I will do whatever it takes to make everything perfect for us. Please believe in me baby, because I will never give you up. Love always, J xxx*

I reread the message. A bitter gall was rising in my throat.

"It's beautiful, thank you, baby," I told him, but a strange flatness had settled in my heart, and I couldn't put my finger on the reason why.

I opened the gift. It was a handmade silver necklace, and it was beautiful.

"It's bespoke," he told me, tenderly lifting my hair and fastening it gently around my neck.

"It's beautiful, thank you," I told him. But when it settled against my skin, I felt like it was burning into my flesh and when I looked in the mirror, it seemed to be the only thing that I could see clearly as it glinted and flashed in in the light against my blurry silhouette.

James became the most super attentive, loving, caring and considerate man. Every morning he would bring me a cup of coffee. Each evening when I came home from work, there would be a delicious meal on the table. When I worked at home, planning my lessons, he would bring me treats, cups of tea, slices of cake. It was almost as though he had dedicated his entire life to serving me and it became suffocating.

"I think I am going to cut down on the booze," he had announced to me. Although drink hadn't been involved in every abusive episode it seemed to make an outburst from James more likely. I had noticed more and more that James drank heavily, far more than he admitted to drinking.

"I just like a nice glass of wine with a meal," he would justify, but we were getting through at least a bottle and a half each night, and I was only having one large glass and usually drank it slowly, making it last the amount of time it took James to finish just over a full bottle. Of course, James being James, the wine that he bought was expensive and he seemed to believe that this was somehow better than getting drunk on cheap alcopops or spirits. Inevitably, the result was the same, and I was beginning to strongly suspect that he was an alcoholic.

He had been for his first session with Lizzie, and when he walked back in through the door, he looked like a new person.

"I should never have stopped," he announced. "I was far from ready to stop going, but we are going to pick up right where we left off, I need help to recover from what Daniella put me through."

"I'm so pleased," I told him, putting my arms around him. I was sure it was only a matter of time until he was all sorted. With Lizzie's help, he'd be able to see what effect his behaviour was having, and I was sure that would be enough to get him to change.

"Oh, one thing that Lizzie mentioned," he began, as we loaded the dishwasher after our meal, "I told her how you react so violently during a row, and she's suggested that you go for some therapy too. She says it sounds like repressed anger."

My skin prickled hotly.

"Really?" I asked, trying to keep my voice steady.

"Yeah, you have been through a lot too Anna."

Put like that; I thought that maybe there was some truth in what he had to say. After all, I had been through a lot, and I *was* angry that my fiancé had been killed. Who wouldn't be affected by the experience that I had endured?

"She's given me the number of her colleague," he continued, rummaging in his pocket then handing me a piece of paper with the name Dee and a mobile number written on it carefully in fountain pen.

"Thanks," I replied, stuffing the phone number into my bag. "I'll give her a call tomorrow."

The next day I gathered all of my courage, and during my lunch break I called Dee. When she answered I was relieved to discover that she was pleasant and easy to talk to. I briefly explained that I had been violent during arguments and that I had felt extremely angry at times. Dee reassured me that she was very experienced at dealing with these sorts of issues and I made an appointment to go and see her before the week was over. In the meantime, James continued to be super attentive, super loving and extra keen to please me.

When I came in from work on the day that I was going to see Dee for the first time, he was grinning like a kid in a sweet shop.

"I've got you a brilliant surprise!" he told me, pacing about as I took off my coat and shoes. "Come and look at this email."

I followed him to his office and he opened up an email from Ticketmaster. It was confirmation of two tickets to see Elbow live the following March at

Nottingham Arena.

"Happy?" he asked, putting his arm around me.

"Of course I am! Thank you baby. Thank you. That is so thoughtful of you." Really, I wasn't happy at all. How could he think that this gift wouldn't make me yearn for Dylan? Watching our favourite band in the city that we met and lived in for three years and on the week before the anniversary of his death too! I couldn't believe how wrong he had got it, but of course, I couldn't tell him this, so I pretended.

That was all I seemed to do anymore, pretend. Pretend that I was happy, pretend that my life was good, pretend that when James hurt or disappointed me that I hadn't noticed or it didn't matter. Pretend that he wasn't lying to me when he minimised and denied that he had attacked me. Pretend that I wanted to have sex when I wanted to sleep. Pretend that I loved everything that James did so that he wouldn't change back into the abusive monster that I had met before. Was anything in my life real at all? Was James pretending too? Was he pretending that he wanted to do whatever I wished, that all he cared about was making me happy? Was anything he said or did genuine? I was sure that sometimes I noticed him grimacing when I chose something: what to listen to, what to watch on TV, where to go for dinner. Just a momentary grimace that would always swiftly be replaced by a smile, a smiling mask that didn't quite reach James's eyes. Was there any point to this strange relationship that was built entirely on a shaky foundation of pretence?

James had prepared a stir fry, and I ate nervously, worried about my upcoming appointment with Dee.

"Don't you like the dinner?" he asked, a slightly accusing tone in his voice.

"It's lovely; I just don't feel as hungry as usual, bit nervous."

"Glass of wine?" he offered, pushing his chair back slightly.

"No, I'd best not! I don't want to drink drive."

"How about just a tiny little one? You'll be okay to drive with just a small glass, especially with food."

"Oh, okay then…" I caved in easily. One small glass of wine might ease my nerves. He leapt up from the table and pulled a bottle of Shiraz from the wine rack.

"This one is lovely," he told me, his eyes lighting up. "I think I'll join you, I haven't had a drink since Sunday," he poured us both a glass, then made a toast to the future.

I took a small sip, it was lovely, and I drank it quite quickly, its warmth spreading through my chest and easing my nerves. James poured himself a second glass while I was still only halfway through my first, and a small flutter of dread began to play in my chest. I hoped that he would stop after a couple of glasses. The minutes ticked by quickly and soon it was time to leave for my first appointment with Dee. I hastily kissed James on the cheek.

"Just leave the kitchen," I suggested, "I will clear up when I get home, you cooked."

"Good luck baby." He kissed me back and walked me to the front door.

I got into the car and started the engine. My head was swimming, and I wondered whether Dee would be able to help me at all as I pulled off the driveway and out into the darkness of the country lanes.

LOOKING WITHIN

Dee was younger than I had expected, and for a moment I felt disappointed. I had imagined her to be in her late fifties, maybe early sixties, when I had spoken to her on the telephone, but Dee was thirty years old maximum, and for some reason, I thought that this would mean she wouldn't be suited to the job in hand.

"Hello Anna, come in, have a seat," she said, gesturing toward a small comfy looking leather chair. I sat down nervously and clasped my hands together on my knees. The room was cosy; it had a large pine bookcase filled with books about relationships and different types of therapy. There was a colourful well-worn rug on the wooden floor and a miss-match of armchairs. It was a small room on the back of Dee's tiny home a few miles away from mine and James's place.

"Would you like a cup of tea or coffee?" Dee asked.

"Yes please, a coffee please," I answered nervously, my heart pounding.

Dee went into another room and came back in with a tray with our drinks on it and placed it on the coffee table that sat between us. There was a box of tissues on the table ready for any tears that might fall, but I didn't feel like crying, I was just keen to get sorted and get out of there. Dee settled into the seat opposite me, looked at me and smiled.

"Well!" she said. "It's very nice to meet you, Anna. Usually I start by taking a few details and learning a little about you and your background and then when I know a bit more about you we can begin to work on the issues that have brought you to see me."

"Okay," I said, taking a sip of my coffee.

"I'll just briefly tell you a little about me. I'm very experienced, I worked for the NHS for five years, but have been working mainly independently for the last two and a half. I still do a little bit of work through the NHS, but most of my clients are private now." I nodded and took another sip of my coffee; it was already almost finished!

"So Anna, I'll just start by asking you some questions. First of all, how old are you?"

"I'm twenty-seven," I answered

"Do you have any children?"

"No," I told her.

"Okay, and do you work?"

"Yes, I am an English teacher at a secondary school."

"That's a good job," Dee told me, smiling. "Do

you enjoy it?"

"I love it!" I told her, and I felt myself become more animated.

"Are you married? Or in a relationship?"

"I'm not married, but I live with my partner," I answered, relaxing a little more.

"Okay and how long have you been with your partner?"

"We met just over a year ago, and we have lived together for about four or five months."

"What is your partner's name?"

"James."

"Tell me a little about James."

"He's thirty-four, he's an architect. He has a business with his parents."

"Does he have any children?"

"He has one daughter who he has only just met; she is fourteen."

Dee was writing some notes, and she looked up at me and raised her eyebrows.

"So, what is it you want to achieve by coming to see me? What brought you here?"

"I get quite angry at times, and I have lashed out at James during rows."

"What do you mean by lashed out?"

"I've hit him; I've done it a couple of times," I told Dee, bowing my head.

"Well don't worry Anna, because I'm sure that we

can get to the bottom of this behaviour. You have made a really brave choice to talk to me."

Dee was nice, and I found it easy to talk to her. I had a few surreal moments where I felt it absurd that I was telling this stranger all about myself, but on the whole, my nerves disappeared, and I began to enjoy the session.

Dee began to ask me about my family.

"Tell me about your mum," she said.

"My mum's amazing," I told her. "She's really amazing; she keeps everything together for everyone."

"How do you mean?" she asked.

"Well, she just makes sure that everyone is okay, she always puts herself last. She has a lot to deal with, my dad is..." My voice tailed off; a lump had formed in my throat.

"Go on Anna," Dee encouraged gently. "Your dad is?"

"An alcoholic," I blurted, reaching for the tissues as tears began to run down my face. Why was I crying? I'd always known that dad was an alcoholic. I'd never said it aloud before, but I had always known it. Suddenly, it seemed so unfair that mum kept everything together and put herself last because of my dad's alcoholism. Suddenly, I had seen clearly how sad my mum's life was, and I didn't like it. I had spoken it aloud to Dee, and in doing so, a spell had been broken, and I had instant clarity.

Dee waited for a moment. "I'm sorry!" I apologised, "I don't know where that came from."

"No need to apologise Anna, you are perfectly entitled to your feelings."

"I've never said it aloud before. I've always known it, but none of us says it. The word is almost taboo!" I laughed a little, a spluttery, snotty, laugh.

"We just say things like, *What about dad?* Or, *Dad's going to start.* Don't get me wrong, he's never horrible. He's just useless and at times embarrassing and my mum has to plan and execute everything carefully, all around my dad's likelihood of being drunk. It's like he has surrendered all responsibility for himself to mum. I think that I have only just allowed myself to see how unfair that is." I couldn't believe how much clarity I was getting, just from talking to Dee, and she hadn't even said anything much yet.

"We can look a little deeper into your relationship with your dad, that's something that we can work on. It certainly seems like it is something that has affected you. How long have you known about his drinking?"

"I think I have always known. There was always an atmosphere of dread around certain situations, and I used to think that mum was boring and dad was exciting and fun, but when I look back now, I can see that she was trying to keep us safe.

He'd say he was going to take us out somewhere, and mum would put her foot down and say we couldn't go and it would just seem unfair, but looking back, she didn't want us to get in the car with him. My sister and I would blame her, and I can see now she was just probably stuck, trying to do the right thing and being the one who made everyone unhappy."

I began to cry again. Poor mama, she was so responsible, I didn't think that I appreciated her enough.

"Okay, I think it will benefit you if we have a look into your upbringing more in-depth. Do you think it would be helpful if today we had a brief chat about what happens when you row with James? We might be able to sort out some strategies to help you before your next session."

"Yes please. I hate it when the rows escalate, I just don't seem to be able to stop them from getting worse no matter what I try."

"Have you had a relationship like this before? Were you violent towards any previous partners?"

"No, oh my God no." At the thought of Dylan, my tears began to fall again. "I'm sorry," I apologised to Dee once more. "I'm really sorry."

I sobbed and spluttered into a handful of tissues and tried desperately to compose myself so that I could explain to Dee why I was so upset.

"It's okay Anna, just take your time," she soothed gently.

"It's just...it's just....that...." I was finding it difficult to get my words out. "....everything was wonderful with him.....Dylan......I miss him so much, and I feel like this is shit with James, but it's only because..... because I miss him....I can't.....I can't get over him......nothing.....nothing will ever be the same...... no one else will ever be......no one." I was sobbing, and the words poured out in a jumbled mess.

"Why did your relationship with Dylan end?" Dee asked gently.

"He was killed. Killed on his motorbike." I was staring straight ahead now, concentrating on my breathing, trying to pull myself together.

"Oh Anna, I'm so sorry to hear that, when?"

"Just over two and a half years ago now. I still can't believe it sometimes."

"How long were you together for?"

"Six years, we met at university."

I began to tell Dee all about Dylan and how wonderful he was. It felt nice to talk about him, and I felt stronger by remembering his loving words, and the way I felt when I was around him.

"The last time I saw him I was horrible to him," I confessed to Dee, beginning to cry again. I told her about that morning, when Dylan had walked off with my towel, and how I'd been snappy with him. I told her about his text messages saying that he was thinking about me in my shower cap and how I'd bought his favourite food, but had never been able to make it up to him for my morning moodiness. I told her how the last time I had heard his voice, or seen his face I had been in a stupid mood. I used handfuls of Dee's tissues as I sobbed and sobbed.

"Anna, I'm not surprised you have been left with some angry feelings after everything that you have been through," she said gently. "Have you noticed that our hour is almost up?" I looked at my watch, surprised! It felt like ten minutes, not fifty.

"Shall we think about some strategies for keeping safe? Ways of dealing with situations to minimise the chance of you lashing out?"

"Yes please," I answered.

"Okay, first of all, let's take a brief look at your triggers. What is it that makes you angry?"

I thought for a moment about the times that I had been angry enough to lash out at James. What was it about those times that made me so mad? Unbelievably, I couldn't answer. I wasn't sure what it was about those rows that made me mad enough to hit. It was as though I couldn't focus properly on my memories, as though when I looked back and tried to remember the facts, everything was shrouded in a strange mist.

"I don't know," I answered unhelpfully. "Sorry," I added shrugging my shoulders.

"Don't worry, we can work on your triggers in another session. If you remember them, then write them down and we can work on them later. How about before you are angry enough to lash out? Do you notice any warning signs that you are becoming so angry?"

"I clench my fists!" I told her.

"Okay good, what else?"

"My heart races, I breathe quickly, I repeat myself, I pace up and down!" I listed the warning signs quickly and easily.

"Right Anna, this might seem a little bit extreme, but as soon as you notice *any* of these warning signs, you must go somewhere to cool off. So, for example, go for a walk, to a friend's, sit in the car with music on, the important thing is that you go away and calm down."

"Okay," I said. This seemed simple enough.

"What should I say to James?" I asked.

"I suggest that you explain to him when you are both calm what you intend to do the next time you feel angry and that you are doing it because you don't want to continue lashing out in an argument."

"Okay, I will try it," I said.

"When you have calmed down, you need to call

James and tell him you are going to come back. Should you need to leave again to calm down, please do. It isn't the best solution, but it is a temporary measure until we can work through your issues and find some permanent solutions."

"Thank you," I said to Dee. Our hour was finished, I couldn't believe how quickly the time had passed. I thanked her and gave her a cheque, and then I drove back home feeling a strange mixture of relief, anticipation, hope and sadness.

On the way home, I called my mum and told her that I loved her and thought that she was amazing. It felt really important to let her know. I wanted to thank her for all the support she had given me when Dylan died, but I could feel my voice beginning to wobble, so I quickly made my excuses and ended the call.

When I walked back through the door, James was lying on the sofa watching the TV.

"Hi baby," he said happily. "How'd it go?"

"It was brilliant!" I told him, sweeping a glance to the coffee table. James's wine glass was half full and there was an open bottle of Rioja and a huge bowl of crisps next to it.

"Get a glass baby, come have a drink with me and tell me all about it." He patted the sofa next to him, gesturing for me to sit with him. I walked into the kitchen to get a glass and remembered that I told him to leave the dishes. He'd done as I had suggested and it was a complete mess. I piled up the plates and quickly started to load the dishwasher.

"Baby, come sit with me," he shouted from the sofa.

"Just loading the dishwasher, two minutes!" I shouted back.

"Just leave them," he called.

"No, they'll only annoy me."

I was almost finished anyway. I picked up the empty bottle of Shiraz and placed it into the recycling bin. He must have drunk it all, I'd only been out for an hour and a half and he was already on his second bottle of wine. A nasty feeling began to seep through my body.

"Anna!" James shouted. "I said leave them."

"I know you did, but they will annoy me so I want to sort it," I called back, spraying some surface cleaner on the table and wiping it. He appeared in the door way.

"Are you going to be doing this all night?" he asked accusingly.

"No. I'm finished now," I told him, spraying the surface cleaner onto the worktop and giving it a quick wipe. He marched over to me and snatched the bottle out of my hand and threw it across the room.

"I told you to leave it," he hissed. "Why do you

insist on winding me up?"

"What?" I asked, incredulously. "How?"

"You know that I have been waiting to see you all night and you can't even be bothered to talk to me when you come in. *It's all about Anna!*"

"No, it's not! I just wanted to get these dishes out of the way so that I could relax with you. Look I have even got a glass out of the cupboard. I *want* to come and sit with you. It's just that I don't like to get up to a pile of dishes in the morning."

"It's all about *you,*" he said again. "Stop being a cunt, Anna."

"What?" I said again. "Why do you think it's okay to call me names?"

"Because you are a cunt and a twat and you fucking well know that you are. You've walked into this house with the intention of making me feel bad about not loading your precious dishwasher."

"What? No, I haven't! I don't care whether you do it or not! I suggested that you didn't do it!"

"Whatever. Twat," he snapped. "Now are you going to come and sit down or are you going to sulk like you usually do and spoil our evening?"

He had his wine glass in his hand, and he drained the remainder of the wine with one long swig. I paced up and down the kitchen. I looked down at my clenched fists, felt my heart pounding in my chest and realised that my breathing was fast and shallow. It was time to leave the house before it got nasty.

"James," I said, as calmly as I could, "I'm going to go out and calm down. I don't want this to turn into a nasty row."

"I don't fucking think so!" he said. "Where do you think you are going to go at this time?"

"I am just going to go for a drive and calm down."

"No, you are not."

"It's important. I need to calm down." I could feel the anger rising in my chest.

"I said no," he reminded me.

"It's not up to you!" I told him.

"If you drive away from this house I will call the police and tell them that you have stolen my car."

"Why are you doing this?" I asked him. "I am trying to help us, trying to do the right thing."

"Try to stop being a twat," he suggested, reaching across to the garden door, locking it and putting the key in his pocket. "You are going nowhere."

The anger was choking me now. How was I supposed to do the right thing when James wouldn't even let me leave the house? How was I supposed to remain calm?

I climbed the stairs and lay on the bed, I took deep slow breaths and tried to relax and calm down. I could hear James in the kitchen pouring himself another glass of wine. He was muttering away to himself. I had the feeling that no matter what I did, it would be the wrong thing. He was in a bad mood, and somehow it was my fault, and I was going to pay the price. I crawled under the duvet and pulled it up to my chin. I heard his footsteps on the stairs. I gripped the covers tightly and closed my eyes. I felt like my heart was going to jump out of my chest. He pulled the door of the bedroom open and marched over to the bed.

"Right!" he said menacingly, pulling at the covers. "This is the final straw."

THE DOMINATOR

I've decided to stop bothering to pray. I don't believe in God anyway, and I have a sneaking suspicion that if by some chance there is a Supreme Being who is listening to the desperate pleas of us mere mortals, they are going to be more likely to help the ones who believe in His or Her existence. Instead of praying, I have decided to believe that I will get better and to use this belief to feed my determination and positive thinking. If I were going to pray though, it would be for Pam to fuck off because I hate her.

She must have some serious financial problems, either that or no life, because she seems to be here ninety percent of the time. Apparently, according to Kevin and Viv, who gossip about her regularly within earshot, she works five twelve-hour shifts per week. The reason she can work so many hours is that an agency employs her and this also means that she earns approximately twice that of the permanent staff. Pam has not endeared herself to anyone in this department, least of all me, but for some reason, I seem to be the person she looks after the most. I get continuity of care, and I don't want it!

The thing that I find most unforgivable is that she has not told anyone about James being innocent. Surely she can see how wrong it is to let somebody go to prison for something that they did not do? I know that James has done some really terrible things, but he didn't attack me and leave me for dead. He didn't break me in the way that I am now broken.

Mum is here. She is chatting away, and I listen. She pauses in the places that I would be reasonably expected to provide an answer, and I answer her silently in the pauses. She is full of news today: James is still in custody awaiting trial, and although everyone was upset that he had broken his bail conditions by coming into the hospital to see me, they all seem pretty happy that he is now behind bars.

"He still denies the attack," she tells me in a low, hushed tone. Of course, he does! It didn't happen. Archie has had his first weigh in since the birth, and he has not put on any weight, he still weighs the same. Eve had cried for forty-five minutes, even though the midwife told her that it was a great sign because most babies lose a little in the first few days.

"Between you and me, I'm a bit worried about Eve; she seems so anxious about everything," mum whispers. I seem to have become a bit of a worry doll for mum, and she has taken to pouring out her concerns to me always starting with the line 'between you and me' which amuses me because I can't speak to tell anyone what she tells me anyway! Maybe this is the best way to be there for somebody? Just to be silent while they tell you their worries and fears? Right now I am desperate for the toilet. Not for a wee, because I have a catheter and all of my urine is collected in a bag. I am trying to clench my buttocks, but of course, it is futile, I have no control over my body whatsoever. Mum carries on chatting with me.

"When I had Eve, I was the same I suppose. You know, I was anxious, I was so scared that I would hurt her, that I'd get it all wrong. Oh, sweetheart, I'll just get the nurse."

I hear mum push her chair back; then I listen to her talking to Pam.

"Anna's just had her bowels open."

It doesn't matter how many times I have been through this already, I simply cannot bear the humiliation of it, especially when the person who is cleaning me up is Pam. I hear her tut and sigh. I've obviously inconvenienced her somehow. She gets a colleague to help her, and between them, they wipe, wash and change me. My heart is breaking, I feel crushed and humiliated. If I ever get better, I mean when I get better, control of my bowels is something that I am going to add on to my list of things to be thankful for. Sitting on a toilet will never again be taken for granted!

Because I cannot eat there is a tube that goes in through my nose and into my stomach and I think that they feed me some kind of disgusting slop through it, of course, the fact that I am on a liquid diet means that I often need to be cleaned up in this way. It is one of the more hideous aspects of my condition. In fact, I cannot think of one aspect of my condition that is not hideous. This lack of control is hell, and when I get better I am going to cherish every single tiny bit of autonomy that I have, because right now I have none, and when I was with James it was under attack....

****

James threw the covers onto the floor.

"Get up!" he demanded.

I leant over, picked them back up and wrapped them around myself tightly. I closed my eyes and clung on to the covers. He pulled them again, trying to remove them, but I clung on to them as though my life depended on it.

"Get up you lazy bitch," he demanded once more.

I made a silent vow not to respond to him, and I continued to hold on to the covers. James was very strong, and as he pulled the covers, trying to get them from me, he lifted me up from the bed. I didn't know what to do for the best. I had learned from experience that there was nothing that I could say to James in this situation that would stop him from behaving like this. If I tried to tell him that I hadn't been trying to make him feel bad for not clearing up the kitchen, he would just tell me that I was. I had tried to do what Dee had suggested, but it hadn't worked. He wanted me to apologise.

"Apologise, for being a cunt." That's what he would shout at me in these arguments. How could I? What would I be apologising for? What had I done that had made him think that I was trying to upset him?

I wracked my brain, trying to come up with an explanation. I couldn't bring myself to say sorry, I hadn't done anything wrong and the thought of apologising to him and grovelling, well that just felt completely humiliating.

Meanwhile, he pulled at the covers, throwing me about, trying to get me to let go of them.

"You ignorant bitch!" he seethed. "Stop ignoring me."

He picked me up again and then threw me on to the floor. I kept the covers wrapped around me tightly and still did not speak.

"Okay, if this is how you want it," he told me, and he picked up a picture of Eve and me that I had in a frame. It was an old picture, and we were little in it, aged around seven and nine years old. James lifted the picture high into the air and then smashed it onto the floor, the frame breaking into hundreds of pieces. I leapt up to get to the photograph before he could, but I was tangled in the duvet, and he got there before me. He picked the picture up and held it as though he was about to tear it up.

"Don't James, please don't," I pleaded with him. The bastard, why did he always have to find a way to get me to do what he wanted?

"Oh, you are speaking to me now are you?" he said smugly, putting the picture back onto the drawers. There was glass all over the bedroom floor from the frame, and it crunched underneath his feet as he took a few steps towards me.

"Come on, let's sort it out," I said, afraid of what he would do to my belongings. I couldn't bear the thought of him spoiling that picture. It was my mum's favourite picture of us and Eve had framed it for me for my eighteenth birthday, and she had painted little flowers around the edge of the frame.

"I'm sorry James. I didn't mean to make you feel bad; I didn't realise you were so upset when I didn't come and sit with you." I spoke in a calm and soothing voice, but underneath I was furious. I swallowed the bitter gall and put my hand on his arm, humiliation burning my heart.

"You know Anna when you have been out all evening, I just want you to come and spend some time with me. And you just had to get your digs in about the kitchen being a mess. I am so tired. I have been working so hard lately, you know I have. Sometimes I think that you just imagine that I am sitting on my arse all day doing nothing and I am *not.*

I am working my fingers to the bone for you. I am bending over backwards to make you happy, to spoil you with all the things that you love."

Something about his little speech was very familiar, and it took a few minutes for me to realise where I had heard it all before. Of course, he sounded just like his parents had when they had exploded at us for looking at hotels in Newcastle. While James was talking, I briefly imagined that I saw the word 'bullshit' flash before my eyes. I knew from experience that he probably only worked for around three hours each day. Unless he was down in London, which was only once each week anyway, he either went for a run, swim, or cycle during the working day and he also found time to read a newspaper, and as he used a clean cup for each cup of coffee, I knew that he went through around seven or eight cups per day. Of course, all of this was up to him, but it hardly portrayed the message that he was working his fingers to the bone.

I bent down and picked up some of the larger shards of glass and the splinters of wood from my picture frame. I was trying not to cry and kept swallowing hard. I was so angry with James but afraid that he would go on a rampage, destroying my belongings. I had to keep him calm so that I could get all of the things that meant anything to me out of the house and somewhere safe. I had the framed *Mirrorball* lyrics that Dylan had bought me, I didn't display them because of the way they made James feel, but they were in the house, and I was pretty sure that James knew where.

"Let me sort that," he said gently, and he went down the stairs and came back with the brush and dustpan.

I sat on the bed and watched him sweep the glass up, then he went back down the stairs and reappeared with the vacuum cleaner, he got rid of all the debris and then came and sat next to me on the bed. He pulled me towards him and began to kiss me, his breath smelt of stale wine, and I wanted to push him away, but I was too afraid to do anything that might set him off again, so I kissed him back, and let myself go through the motions of it all as he started to tug at my clothes. Somewhere in the back of my mind, I think that I heard my inner voice trying to tell me that I was rewarding James for his disgusting tantrum, and I think that I made a little vow to my inner voice that I was going to start listening soon, just as soon as all of my belongings were safe and out of harm's way.

When I awoke the following morning, James was still asleep, and I tried to get out of bed without waking him. I had stuffed the picture of Eve and me into my bedside drawer, and I wanted to get it somewhere safe as soon as possible. I sat up slowly, but it was too late, and James reached over and took my hand.

"Sort me out," he said, pushing my hand into his boxer shorts. I didn't want to. Not one part of me wanted to 'sort him out', but I pretended. I pretended that it wasn't a problem and that it was exactly what I wanted to do when I had just opened my eyes.

Afterwards, he said, "I meant to say last night, my mum and dad have invited us to theirs on Saturday for dinner. I said we'd be there. You'll be alright, I'm sure they've forgotten all about before. They've been fine with me the last few weeks."

Great! I thought. As if I wanted to go there and be around them after the last time we had visited them.

Saturday came along all too soon. I hadn't had the opportunity to get my precious belongings out of the house, and I was walking on eggshells around James constantly. I was jumpy and uncomfortable.

I vetted every sentence that I spoke in my mind before daring to open my mouth. I worried about what I did, what impression I was giving him. I worried that I was in the wrong room in the house. I began to crave his approval, feeling uneasy and anxious if he seemed unhappy or annoyed. What had I turned into? I didn't recognise myself.

"Who's driving?" I asked him, feeling unable to even make a simple suggestion any more. Instead of having ideas of my own, I had begun to ask him for suggestions, and this would even be the case for the most mundane things. I was rapidly disappearing; James was erasing me bit by bit.

"I'll drive, we'll take the Audi," he said.

I was nervous; I didn't want to see June and Clive after what had happened the last time. We popped to the supermarket on the way for some wine and James bought his mum some flowers. By the time we pulled up at the house, my hands were shaking, and my mouth was dry. What was going to happen this time?

We walked to the front door, my nerves jangling and I clung to James's hand like a nervous child on their first day at school. He kissed me on the head and told me that it would be fine. We let ourselves in, and June was in the kitchen clearing up, she was wearing a green cashmere sweater, and her hair was perfect. She had her trademark red lipstick on and lots of jewellery.

"Hello, my favourite couple!" she said kissing us both. James handed her the wine and the flowers.

"For the best mum!" he told her. I wanted to stick my fingers down my throat and pretend to vomit, but instead, I smiled sweetly. I wondered if my smile reached my eyes. I didn't think that it did.

Clive was watching the TV and James went to sit with him.

"Do you need a hand?" I asked.

"Yes please, just with the table and the drinks Anna."

I wondered how this happened? How James automatically went off to relax with his dad, while I ended up helping with the dinner. I imagined us going to my parents for dinner, and I was pretty sure that James would be affronted if he was expected to help when he was a guest in someone else's home. June poured us all some wine, and I set the table.

We sat down to our meal, and as the wine started to flow, the conversation began to improve, and I felt less uncomfortable.

"How's work, Anna?" Clive asked me.

"It's good thanks!" I told him. "It's pretty full on, but I love it."

"I bet you are the type of woman who thinks she knows it all at work."

"Dad!" James said, sounding annoyed.

"Clive!" June scolded. "Just ignore him, dear. He's been drinking all day."

I said nothing. I couldn't understand why he had said it and began to worry that I appeared conceited. Did I?

"Sorry, Anna," Clive said. "I'm sure you are very good at your job. It's a nice *little job*. June was thinking of getting herself a *little job* when the children were young. Didn't you apply at the primary school?" He turned to June.

"Yes, I used to have the little ones read to me in school when the children were young. It was a way of checking up on them really!" she told me, smiling.

I wanted to tell Clive that June's school job was hardly the same as teaching English to secondary school children, but I felt that there was probably no point. He had just dismissed my career as a *little job*, in the process he had belittled me and my entire profession and also devalued the people that I taught. What a cock!

June asked James how he had got along in his last race and I told her that I had some pictures on my phone. James was talking to Clive, or rather Clive was talking at James, and I reached into my bag to get my phone to show some pictures of James at the last triathlon.

"Ooh isn't he handsome!" she said. I agreed, he

did look good in the pictures.

"Some people can't wear Lycra," I giggled, flicking on to a rather unfortunate picture of another runner.

June laughed.

"Anna! Put your phone away!" I looked up, astounded. It was Clive, and everyone was staring at him with their mouths wide open in shock.

"Pardon?" I said.

"You heard me, Anna. Put your bloody phone down."

"Dad! Don't talk to Anna like that!"

"It's my house; I'll say what I like. She's rude, looking at her phone all the time. She's ignorant. Put it away woman."

I kept my phone in my hand; there was no way I was going to put it away.

"Well done Clive, you have spoiled dinner," June said, pushing out her chair and leaving the table. "After all the effort I made," she said to him.

"She's spoiled dinner," Clive said gesturing to me.

"I don't have to listen to this!" I said, and I got up and made my way to the front door.

"Well done dad," James said, following me to the door.

We got into the car, and I began to cry.

"What the fuck?" I asked James. "What was that all about?"

"Dad just likes to be the centre of attention," he

told me. "He couldn't handle it that you were laughing with mum and he wasn't involved. He's so domineering, he continued. "Always has to be in charge of every situation."

Like father like son! I thought. Then I began to wonder: *Is it me? Do I cause these situations? Am I attracting the arguments? What is wrong with me?*

JAMES REALLY CHANGES....

James and I travelled in silence for a few moments. I brooded over the evening's events. How dare Clive be so rude to me? I couldn't imagine ever going back to their house again. I couldn't imagine ever feeling comfortable in their company.

"I don't think that I can ever go there again," I told him.

"I don't blame you. I am fucking furious at my dad," he said to me, putting his hand on my knee.

James's phone began to ring; it was a call from his parents' home number. I looked at him and said nothing, wondering what his course of action would be. He swiftly rejected the call, and I put my hand on his leg and squeezed his knee.

"Did he ever speak to any of your other girlfriends like that?" I asked him.

"Well there was one evening when he laid into Daniella, but she deserved it, she was such a spoilt little cow." I shuddered. I was beginning to have my doubts about James's version of Daniella.

"What did you do when your dad laid in to her?" I ventured cautiously.

"I just left him to it. She never mentioned it

anyway, because she knew it was true."

I thought about what I knew of Daniella. I knew she was young and she was very pretty. I had seen a picture of her at June and Clive's. It had been in a packet of photographs that June had been showing me.

"This was only a week or so before they split up," June explained, screwing the picture up and tossing it in the bin. I hadn't imagined that she would be attractive because James had described her as someone awful. She looked very petite, with long dark curly hair.

"I thought that you said she was fat?" I had questioned James later on.

"No, she was just greedy and lazy," he told me.

Strange, I was sure he had said she was a 'state' and 'had got fat.'

I imagined Daniella on the receiving end of Clive's put-downs and wondered if James had supported her. It didn't sound like he had. Poor Daniella, I wondered what had become of her. I knew that there was a good chance that I would have done what she did with the door stop in the same situation, and that thought was enough to make my blood run cold.

"I don't think that your dad had the right to do that to Daniella," I said, my annoyance at Clive spilling out.

"Anna, she was a selfish, lazy bitch. You have no idea what it was like for me when I was with her. I used to call mum in tears; my life was so shit with her. She was like a stranger to me by the time she was arrested. You have no idea what that is like."

James sounded annoyed, and I didn't want to provoke him further, but I strongly suspected that he wasn't telling the story quite how it happened.

We got home, and James lit the fire. I felt upset about what had happened, and I hoped that he would defend me to his parents. We lay down in front of the fire, and I cuddled up to him while he began to talk about his parents and his childhood.

"Dad's always been the domineering one, he has to be king of the castle all the time and if he's not the centre of attention he spits his dummy if you know what I mean?" James was stroking the back of my neck.

"Yeah, I think I saw that today. I've noticed that he likes to appear very knowledgeable about everything," I said.

James stopped stroking my neck and turned toward the fire, he had a piece of kindling in his hand, and he broke tiny splinters of wood off and threw them into the flames.

"When we were kids he was just never there. I don't have many memories of him. Mum did everything for us; dad was always either working, playing golf or at the pub."

"Sounds like a stereotypical seventies dad," I said.

James began to tear a newspaper into pieces and throw those into the fire too.

"Mum used to do everything you know. She never shouted at me; I don't think that we have ever fallen out. It's weird this stuff that's happening now. I mean they're old, and I feel like I ought to be helping them more."

"Helping them with what?" I asked.

"I dunno," James shrugged, "I just always feel like I am indebted to them."

"That's strange. Why would you be indebted to them?" I asked.

"Well, there's the Hannah stuff. The money that they paid to Fiona. I told them to stop years ago and that I'd take over the payments, but they insisted on carrying on paying for her. I only let them do it because I was at university and I couldn't afford it."

"Well if they choose to do that then it is up to them, it doesn't make you indebted to them."

I felt irritated by Clive and June and their manipulative ways.

"All parents do things for their children. Isn't that just part of being a parent?"

"I don't know; it is just a feeling I suppose, it probably doesn't mean anything."

"What made you decide to follow in your dad's

footsteps and become an architect?" I asked him.

"I don't know really, I just kind of always knew that I would. They've worked hard to build the business up and I just always assumed that I'd be part of it," he was on to his second newspaper now, and the fire danced and crackled, with flames that burned briefly brighter with each piece of paper that it was fed.

"It's just that you don't seem to enjoy working with your parents," I ventured.

"I don't. I hate it, but I feel like I can't leave. I mean they are getting on a bit now, and I don't think that they could cope if I left." James had finished all the newspapers, and he stood up and stretched.

"Want a glass of wine baby?" he asked.

"Yeah go on then, may as well."

He went to the kitchen then reappeared with a bottle of red wine.

"Chateauneuf-du-pape," he said. "It's a delicious red," he added, beginning to work the corkscrew into the cork.

"Lovely," I told him, kneeling up and opening the big bag of kettle chips that he had brought in too. I wanted to say that I had drunk it before but didn't want to risk him asking where - it had been at Dylan's parents' - and I could imagine how the evening may go if I brought up my life with Dylan.

SILENCING ANNA

"I love you, Anna," James told me, pouring some wine into my glass. "Nobody has ever cared about me the way that you do. No one else has ever noticed that my job makes me unhappy."

"I will support you with any changes you want to make in your life. If you don't want to keep working with your parents, I will support you to do something different. Money isn't a problem; we can always live a bit a cheaper if we need to."

"You're brilliant baby," James said kissing me.

"To us!" he added, raising his glass, then taking a massive gulp of wine.

"You're supposed to savour it!" I scolded, slowly sipping mine. It was nice, but I certainly couldn't have guzzled it down the way James did.

"Tomorrow I am going to ring my dad and tell him that he has to apologise to you."

"Don't bother," I said, "I'm not interested in empty apologies, I'd rather just avoid your parents as much as possible."

"Fair enough," he said, picking up one of my feet and massaging it.

"You know I am mad at my dad," he said again.

"He just does and says what he likes and expects everyone to pamper to his wishes."

"He expects *what*?" I asked.

"He expects his wishes to be pampered too," James said again.

"Do you mean *pandered* to?" I asked.

"Er, yeah probably," James said, an impish smile on his face. "So, Miss English teacher. Can I have a kiss?"

"Of course you can!"

This was the James that I loved. He was playful, sweet, gentle and just a little bit vulnerable.

We chatted for hours and he told me some more about his childhood. He had been settled in his secondary school, happy with a nice circle of friends when one evening his parents had told him that they were going to be moving house the following day. James hadn't even had the chance to tell his friends.

"I hated it," he told me. "And I was bullied for having a different accent."

"Why didn't they tell you that you were going to move?"

"I don't know," he answered, his gorgeous brown eyes looking sad and lost.

"They deny doing it that way. They say that we had a family meeting about it, but I have no memory of that happening, and I doubt I'd forget something like that."

That night I felt like I was close to James, I felt that I had a genuine intimacy with him, and it was lovely. I felt happy.

The following day, we went for a walk in the country.

"Get a bike Anna; then we can go riding together."

"I'll give it a go!" I said. "I just don't think that I'll like it."

The day was lovely, and James and I went for Sunday lunch in the country pub that we had been to on our first date.

"To us!" we toasted again.

Suddenly, life felt nice. I wasn't sure that I needed to get all my belongings out of the house. Maybe I could just see how things went and if he started again, I could take them to my mum and dads.

Monday came and it was already time for my second session with Dee. I felt far less nervous as I pulled up outside her home. I wondered what the hour would bring.

"Hello again Anna," Dee greeted me, smiling.

"Coffee?" she asked.

"Yes please," I said, settling myself into the comfy leather armchair. Dee quickly made a coffee and settled herself opposite me once more.

"So how are things?" she asked. "How has your week been?" She was rummaging through a pile of papers as she spoke.

"It was mixed really," I said.

"Did you need to use the tactics that we spoke about?" Dee asked.

"Well yes I did, and I tried, but they weren't particularly successful. I'm not sure that I was doing it right."

Dee handed me a piece of paper.

"I know this refers to the man being the abuser, but I was wondering if you recognised any of these behaviours in yourself."

I stared at the piece of paper. It was entitled The Dominator. It had a picture of an angry-looking man, and there were eight boxes each with a different title and a list of related behaviours. I read each box, a sinking realisation in my heart.

The first box was The Sexual Controller. And the behaviours listed were:

- He rapes you
- Won't accept no for an answer
- Keeps you pregnant or
- Rejects your advances

An image of James on top of me, holding me down and trying to unfasten my jeans during a row flashed into my mind, followed by thoughts of his regular morning demands for attention. I felt sick.

The second box was entitled The Bully and the behaviours listed were:

- Glares
- Shouts
- Smashes things

- Sulks

Again, images of James flew through my mind. He had smashed my picture, he regularly shouted at me and he had perfected the most evil glare. My whole body was burning now; I felt my cheeks flushing red.

The third box was called King of the Castle, as I read the title, I thought about Clive saying, "It's my house, I'll do what I like." The behaviours listed were:

- Treats you as a servant
- Says women are for sex, cooking and housework
- Expects sex on demand
- Controls all the money

The last two on the list rung true. James had a way of making me feel as though I had a duty to satisfy all his sexual needs, whether I felt like it or not and he was very controlling with money.

The fourth box was the Bad Father and although none of the behaviours related to me, I thought about James's reluctance to parent Hannah, although I wasn't sure how much of that had come from Fiona's obvious mistrust of him.

- Says you are a bad mother.
- Turns the children against you.
- Uses access to harass you.

- Threatens to take the children away.
- Persuades you to have 'his' baby, and then refuses to help you care for it.

The fifth box was entitled The Liar, and by now I was shaking angrily.

- Denies any abuse.
- Says it was 'only' a slap.
- Blames drink, drugs, stress, over-work, you, unemployment etc.

James always denied what had happened, shushing me, or changing the subject when I tried to explain why his behaviour was so upsetting. He had said that he had 'only' restrained me, when in fact he had thrown me about, and also had no right to restrain me anyway! He always blamed everything but himself for his behaviour.

The sixth box was The Persuader, and I was beginning to wonder whether the person who had written this stuff actually knew James.

- Threatens to hurt or kill you or the children.
- Cries.
- Says he loves you.
- Threatens to kill himself.
- Threatens to report you to Social Services, DSS etc.

James did all of these things: he cried, he said he couldn't live without me, he said he loved me, and he also threatened to report me, not to social services, but to the police for driving his car. By now I felt like I was just discovering that I was the victim of a cruel hoax, and Dee was waiting patiently as I studied the sheet of paper.

The next box was called The Headworker.
- Puts you down.
- Tells you that you're too fat, too thin, ugly, stupid, useless etc.

Again I ticked the boxes, and I remembered James mentioning my make-up and my boots. Had he deliberately been trying to erode my confidence?

The eighth box was called The Jailer, and I already knew that James's behaviour would be featuring in it.
- Stops you from working and seeing friends.
- Tells you what to wear.
- Keeps you in the house.
- Seduces your friends/family.

Very subtly James had managed to reduce the time that I spent with friends, and I thought about the big deal he had made about me helping with the school production. Yes, he had definitely affected the amount of time that I spent at work or with other people. And of course, there was the obvious stuff where he had blocked a doorway or taken a key to stop me from leaving.

I had to face facts: James was a dominator. I wasn't quite sure what this meant, but I guessed that it wasn't a good thing. I felt foolish, angry and hurt.

I looked up at Dee.

"No, I don't recognise any of these behaviours in myself. I don't behave like this."

She looked surprised. I didn't tell her immediately that I saw James there, I just needed a minute or two to digest the horrible revelation.

"Tell me about what happened when you tried to use the tactics that we discussed last week," Dee suggested. "Then maybe we can work out what is going wrong."

I told Dee about what had happened when I had got in from her session the previous week, and she listened with a horrified look on her face. I finished my story by telling her that I now recognised that James was a dominator, and said that he displayed all of the traits listed on the piece of paper that I still clutched on my lap.

"Well this is a very different situation to the one that I thought we were dealing with," she told me. "Anna do you recognise that you are in an abusive relationship?" she asked.

"I think so," I answered, "but what can I do?"

"I don't like to give advice in this way, but my knowledge and experience tell me that without specialist help, James will never stop being abusive, and even with specialist help, he may never stop. Him changing would have to begin with recognising that his behaviour is abusive and denial is a huge problem in abusive people."

I clutched at my coffee cup.

"I would recommend that you leave him, Anna. Go somewhere safe. I don't usually instruct people in this way, but that would be my honest advice to you."

I was stunned, was it really that bad with James? I knew that he had been wrong when he had pushed me about and shouted at me, but I wasn't convinced that I was in any real danger.

Dee continued, as though reading my mind.

"In my experience, domestic abuse usually escalates, meaning what is a push and a shove now, in a year or so will be a punch and a kick. And it will be more frequent, more regular."

"But he has been so lovely this week," I told her, my voice sounding as pathetic as the phrase that I had just uttered. "I can't believe that it is really that bad with James, I think that I would rather just see how it goes with him," I told her.

"Of course, Anna," Dee told me. "As I said, I am not in the habit of giving instructions to clients and you must do whatever you wish to do."

Our session continued, and we touched briefly again on my relationship with my parents. I didn't take anything much in and didn't feel fully engaged with Dee this time. I was still trying to process the fact that James was there, on that piece of paper. At the end of the session, I folded the paper up and put it in my bag.

When I got back home, James ran us a bath, and we chatted about the counselling. I didn't mention what I had learned and told him that I had talked mainly about my parents. We went to bed as normal, and he continued to be the model boyfriend.

In the morning he made me breakfast, ironed my clothes for work and made me a packed lunch. Perhaps I had imagined all the other stuff? How could this kind considerate, thoughtful person be the same man who treated me so disgustingly?

THE ADMISSION

That day at work, I mused over what to do. One minute I was convinced that James was an abusive person, the next minute I was convinced that I had over reacted and that he was a perfectly normal boyfriend. In my lunch break, I tried to discreetly research abusive relationships and what I read confirmed the truth, my worst fears, that James was, in fact, an abusive person and I was a victim.

I read about the cycle of abuse and the wheel of control. I learned about the different types of abuse, about the denial that abusers live in. I even learned how to spot an abusive person right at the beginning of a relationship. Why was this stuff not common knowledge? Why hadn't I read about this before? Why didn't we teach it in our schools? James was there, written in those web pages and so was I. Our relationship was the stuff of nightmares and the sinking realisation that I was 'one of those women' made me feel physically sick. If I had known about this stuff right at the beginning of our relationship, I think I'd have worked him out straight away. I'd have run a mile in the other direction, but I hadn't known, and the warning signs had seemed like good things back then. Now I was in deep, what could I do?

Foolishly, I decided to wait. Despite the glaring evidence, I still wasn't fully convinced that James was an abusive person and sheltering in denial seemed easier than braving the truth. I went home after work and said nothing to him about the things that I had read. He continued to be super attentive; there was a bath ready for me when I walked through the door, and he was in the kitchen preparing a meal.

"Hi baby!" he said, turning to me with a big smile on his face. He planted a huge kiss on my lips.

"You're lovely!" he told me.

I enjoyed my bath while James finished preparing our meal and by the time I came back down the stairs, the food was on the table. James gestured to the meal proudly.

"Risotto," he said. "It's really good," he added, removing a cork from a bottle of wine.

"Thank you, it looks delicious," I told him, plonking myself in one of the chairs. "Just a small glass of wine for me, I get so tired at work."

"Yeah I'm not going to drink too much tonight. I've got that meeting in London tomorrow," he replied, shuddering a little at the mention of his meeting.

I didn't know the reason, but James seemed very anxious about his upcoming meeting in London. I knew that he wasn't keen on seeing his dad after what had happened at the weekend, but he had already seemed uncomfortable with it way before anything had happened between his parents and us.

"Spoken to your mum and dad yet?" I asked him.

"Yeah, I called my dad this morning. He just went on about work like he always does and didn't mention anything about what happened."

"Weird," I said, tucking into the tasty risotto.

I slowly sipped my one glass of wine and made it last me the through the entire evening, and I was disappointed, but not surprised when James drained the last few drops from the bottle into his glass an hour-and-a-half later. We went to bed early, at around ten and I began to fall asleep pretty much as soon as my head hit the pillow.

"Aren't you even going to give me cuddle?" he asked accusingly, shaking me out of my sleep a little.

"Sure, come here," I said, holding my arms out to him.

"I'm going to get some water," he told me, and I must have dozed back off while he was out of the room.

When he came back in, he turned the main light on and began to pack an overnight bag noisily.

"What are you doing?" I asked. I had the distinct impression that I had upset him somehow, but I was not quite sure what I had done wrong.

"I need an overnight bag in case I end up staying in London. My dad is staying, I wasn't going to, but I think I might now," he told me, glaring at me. "Why? Am I disturbing you?"

He sounded sarcastic. He looked angry, and I felt worried and unsettled.

"No, do whatever you've got to do," I said, closing my eyes and pulling the covers over my head.

I could hear him muttering to himself, but I tried to ignore him. Of course, I no longer felt sleepy, and my heart was racing, and my hands were clammy. He banged around for a few minutes then he climbed into bed. I pretended to be asleep, and he fidgeted around for ages once he had turned the lamp out, eventually cuddling up to me and starting to put his hands all over me, trying to take my underwear off. It was the last thing I felt like doing, but I found myself responding to him, playing along with his little game. Why did I do this? Was it to stop his behaviour from getting any worse? Probably. Whatever the reason for my actions, by giving in to him every time, I was giving him the green light to keep on treating me badly.

In the morning, James's alarm clock woke us early. I still felt on edge and got up with him to make breakfast while he got ready. Looking back now, I think that I was trying to show him that I cared mainly to stop him from blowing up at me again. I felt as though I was balanced on a tightrope, wobbling precariously and each thing I said or did was a dangerous wobbly step – I never knew whether I was about to go toppling to the ground.

When he left for London, I sat at the table to drink a cup of coffee. I felt relieved that he had gone, and I even noticed myself breathing a sigh of relief when his car finally disappeared off the driveway. I sipped my coffee and began to look on the laptop. It wasn't even six yet, and I had plenty of spare time before I would have to leave for work. I typed 'abusive relationships' into the search engine and began to read again. I was looking at a site called Hidden Hurt UK and what I read again confirmed my fears.

There was a page on the website with a list of questions relating to abusive relationships, and I answered a resounding yes to each question. I worked my way through the site, my cup of coffee becoming colder and colder on the table next to me. I began to read about power and control in an abusive relationship, again, the page could have been written about James, and I couldn't believe that

I had been so blind. I learnt that abusers believe that they have the right to control their partners. They expect compliance and have an arsenal of tactics that they utilise to maintain control.

With a sick gall in my stomach, I began to read about the warning signs of the abusive personality. It also seemed to be written about James. In fact, the list read as though it were a list of his personality traits. I was shocked to the core.

I got ready and went to work. All day I was distracted; I knew that I was going to have to talk to James about what I had read. Either that or say nothing and let it carry on the way it was going. Was it possible to do that? I didn't think so. By the time I got home, I was ready to confront him. I'd made my decision, and I was nervous yet determined. I knew this was going to be the only way to sort things out. I decided to wait until after dinner when we were both settled for the evening.

When I got home, he was still in London, and I made us some bolognese to reheat when he finally arrived back. I felt so nervous. How would he react? I decided to go for a bath. I needed to do something to stop myself from pacing up and down nervously. I sat on the edge of the bath, watching the water rise and I rehearsed in my mind what I needed to say to James. Should I show him the website? The handout that Dee had given me? I knew that I'd have to back up what I was saying to him or he would just dismiss it. I climbed into the bath and lay back so that my hair was immersed and my ears filled with water. I lay like that for quite a long time, thinking about what to do. I decided that if James wasn't willing to listen, then I would go to my parents. I didn't want my life to be one endless cycle of abuse, and I understood that there was only a chance James would change and only if he accepted that he had been in the wrong.

When the water started to feel a little cool, I got out of the bath and dried myself. I tied my damp hair up into a bun and got dressed. I went down the stairs intending to call him and see how long he was likely to be. It was beginning to get dark, and I switched on a couple of lamps and noticed his bag on the floor next to the door. *That's strange*, I thought, where is he?

I wandered through the house looking for him. His car was in the driveway, but I couldn't find him. I dialled his number, and his phone began to ring from his inside his jacket which was hanging on the back of the chair. He must have popped to the shop or something. I began to heat the pasta up and waited for him to come in. After ten minutes or so, I turned the gas back off, there was still no sign of him, and I was beginning to worry. I put the plates under the grill to warm them and opened the front door to peer down the lane. There wasn't much going on in this little village, so where was he? I stepped outside and walked down to the shop; it was closed by now. The only other place I could think of was the pub, but why would he come in then go to the pub without even saying hello to me? I began to have a nagging, worried doubt; it was eating away at me. Since losing Dylan, situations like this were stressful for me, and I struggled not to imagine the worst case scenario.

It was around six-thirty. I decided that I would give him until seven and then I would go to the pub and look for him. I paced up and down the kitchen, watching the clock. Where could he be? I was full of nervous energy, and I felt sick and worried. On the one hand I worried that something terrible had happened to James, but on the other I had a sneaking suspicion that I had somehow upset him and that he had gone off to the pub to punish me, that he hadn't said hello to me because he was, for some reason, annoyed with me.

I began to empty the tumble drier. I sorted the clothes out, piled them up into two piles, one to iron and one to put away. I got the iron and ironing board out of the cupboard and found that my nervous energy helped me to speed through the pile of clothes quickly. I folded them all neatly and put them on the edge of the table. All the time I worked,

I wondered where James was and why he hadn't been up to speak to me when he had got home.

I didn't need to wonder for much longer. I heard the crunch of his shoes on the gravel, and the outdoor security light flashed on. My heart began to race even more, I felt lightheaded, and my breath came rapidly. Why did I feel so anxious? This was my partner, the person who was supposed to be in love with me, *my sanctuary*. I certainly didn't feel safe. He opened the door. I felt so anxious I didn't even know what to do with my hands. Should I say hello? How could I act normal?

"Hi!" I said as he stepped through the door. "I was worried."

"Yeah right, as if," he responded, pushing past me, taking a mug from the cupboard and flicking the kettle on.

"Is there a problem?" I asked.

"Why would you care anyway, Anna? You knew I was worried about today and you couldn't even be bothered to make me feel welcome in my own home."

"What are you talking about?" I asked. He was busy making himself a cup of coffee. I knew he was upset with me if he didn't offer me a drink too, pathetic really.

"You. I'm talking about *you* and how you can't be bothered to make me welcome in my own home."

"I made us dinner."

"Big deal. I made dinner all week."

"I was in the bath; I didn't know you were even here. Why didn't you come up the stairs and say hello to me?"

"Why should I have to?"

"Because I didn't know you were in. How am I supposed to greet you and make you feel welcome if you don't even let me know you are back?"

"Yes, you did know I was in. You haven't even bothered to contact me today."

"You said you'd be busy and that you'd ring me if you were free at all, and no I didn't know."

"That doesn't stop you from letting me know that you were thinking about me does it? You did know."

"Why do you even bother with me, James? You know if I am so awful that I can't get anything right, why do you want to be with me?"

"I'm not sure that I do," he said, a sneer on his face.

"Fine, I will go then," I told him.

"Not in my car you won't."

"Oh, not this again James. Fine, I will call a cab."

James snatched my phone from where it sat on the table.

"No, you won't," he said, shoving it into his pocket, and looking at me triumphantly.

"Oh James, I don't know what you want from me. I can't keep doing this."

"I want you to stop being a cunt, Anna."

I sat at the table. What could I do? I wanted to go, but he was clearly hell bent on stopping me. I'd have to stay and listen to him. Where would it end this time? I wondered my heart sinking.

"So, you are just going to sit there and pretend there is nothing wrong?" he asked accusingly.

"I just don't know what you want from me," I said again.

"I want you to stop being a cunt," he repeated.

"Stop calling me that."

"Stop calling me that," he mocked.

I sighed and put my head in my hands. I wracked my brain for a way out of this. It was impossible.

"Did you do this?" he asked, gesturing to the pile of clothes on the table.

"Yes, I did some ironing while you were out."

"You can't have been that worried then."

"How do you know?"

"How do you know?" he mocked me once more.

I felt my anger levels rising dangerously. I knew that he was trying to provoke me. I took some deep breaths.

"I know because you are a cunt. A stupid ugly cunt."

"Stop it," I said.

"Stop it, he mocked.

"James, just tell me what it is you want from me."

"An apology."

"I have nothing to apologise for."

"Well that's where we differ."

"That's not the only way we differ," I retorted.

"Apologise for being a lazy self-centred cunt."

I stood up and faced him.

"I'm sorry," I said. "I'm sorry for being a lazy self-centred cunt."

He banged his coffee cup down on the side and strode towards me. I took a couple of steps back.

"You sarcastic bitch," he said, his face inches from mine, contorted with rage.

"Proof that I cannot get it right for you James. I've just done exactly what you asked, and it was still fucking wrong."

He leant closer, and I could smell a disgusting mixture of alcohol, coffee and cigarettes on his breath. I didn't even know that he smoked.

"You are nothing but a selfish little cunt."

"Shut up James," I snapped.

"What? What was that?"

"I said shut up."

He picked up the clothes that I had ironed and folded, and he flung them at the wall, scattering them all onto the floor. I began to pick them up, but he snatched them from me and threw them onto the floor again.

"How dare you tell me to shut up?" he seethed.

He stepped towards me, and I backed away.

"Who do you think you are Anna?"

"Leave me alone. Stop it!" I screamed.

"Getting hysterical, are you?" he said in his soft, sinister voice.

Frustration was building inside me. I felt so angry with him. I went to the door, but he did his usual trick and dived in front of me, locking it and shoving the key into his pocket. I felt like he was toying with me, like a cat with a mouse. He had me trapped, and he knew it. There was no way he was going to stop; no way was I going to get away from him unscathed tonight.

"I am sick of you. You have ruined my life. You have taken everything from me," he shouted.

"What? No, I haven't. What are you talking about?"

"You know what I am talking about."

"No, I don't, but I am sure that I am about to hear all about it."

"You are selfish, lazy and greedy. You take, take, take. Who bought you the car that you drive?"

"You."

"Who pays for every weekend away?"

"You."

"Who bought you that top you are wearing?"

"You did James."

"Take it off."

"What?"

"I said take it off. You don't deserve it."

He began to pull at the top, trying to get it from me. I slapped his hands away.

"How dare you hit me?" he screamed.

"I didn't hit you! You were trying to take my clothes off."

"You hit me and I don't need to put up with this."

He grabbed my car keys from the table and picked up the house phone and stuffed it into his jacket pocket, then he went out the door, locking it behind him. I heard his car start and he drove off. Great. Now I was trapped in the house with no phone and no car keys, James still had my mobile in his pocket. I could climb out of a window and try and walk somewhere, but it was miles to the nearest town. I was completely isolated. I could walk to the pub and ask to use their phone, but that would be so humiliating and who would I call? Mum and dad? Chloe? I still couldn't bring myself to worry them.

No, I would have to sit tight and hope that he would come back in a better mood.

I went up to the bedroom and changed my top for one that I had bought myself. I threw the one that I had been wearing onto the floor angrily and stamped on it. James was an abuser alright. Now I was sure beyond any doubt.

I lay on the bed and waited for the inevitable, the sound of his car, the crunching footsteps. Before long he was back. I hoped that he would have calmed down, but I hoped in vain. I heard him ending a call as he began to make his way up the stairs.

"Yeah love you too mum. Yeah I know, I will do. Bye."

Great, so he was involving June in this one. He came into the bedroom and stood in the doorway, which was lit with the light from the hall. His silhouette was menacing and my stomach lurched horribly at the sight of him.

"Get out of my house," he demanded.

I could smell the alcohol from where I was. He had obviously had a lot to drink.

"No!" I said.

Then I tried to reason with him.

"How about I sleep in the guest room tonight and tomorrow I will leave. It's late, I have nowhere to go, and you aren't letting me take the car so if we can leave it until tomorrow that would be great."

"I said get out," he repeated, taking a few steps toward me. "I am not sharing my house with someone who thinks it is okay to hit me, now get the fuck out of my house."

"Can I have my phone and the car keys then please."

He took my phone from his pocket and threw it at me. I didn't manage to catch it, and it fell to the floor. I bent down to pick it up, and that's when he hit me. I think that he hit me, whatever he did, he did it with force, and I fell to the floor, clutching the side of my head in agony trying to catch my breath.

"Cunt," he said, walking away from me and leaving me there, on the floor, crying in pain and shock.

I heard him go downstairs, he was muttering to himself, and he reappeared in the doorway a few seconds later with the pile of clothes in his arms. He walked towards me, and for a moment I thought he was going to strike me again, and I felt myself cower. Instead, he threw the clothes at me and marched out of the room.

"You're so ugly to me. I don't even know what you are," he said as he left me cowering and crying on the floor and went back down the stairs.

I could hear him boiling the kettle and banging around noisily in the kitchen. I looked down at the clothes. There was a hoodie of mine that Dylan had bought me. It was a few sizes too big, it was navy blue, and I loved wearing it. He had bought it for me to stop me from stealing his and making them 'smell girly' although I knew that he didn't mind. The hoodie had landed right next to me, and all of the other clothes were strewn across the room. I picked it up and put it next to my face. I remembered Dylan giving it to me. I remembered his happy face as I had unwrapped my impromptu gift and then flung my arms around him. I put it on and pulled the hood up; then I tightened the strings in the hood so that it was tight around my head. I pulled my hands into the sleeves and wrapped my arms around my knees and began to sob.

Why? Why did it have to be like this? Why did James have to hurt me? My head hurt where he had hit me. He had caught me with his nail, and I noticed blood on my hand from the scratch. I let myself think about Dylan. He was here in this hoodie, loving me, holding me. How could I stay with James when Dylan had loved me as much as he had? How could I let Dylan down this way? I imagined Dylan's arms around me. I imagined that I was leaning against him and I began to slow my breathing and calm down. I was worth more than this. I had to leave James. It didn't matter what it took; I had to get away from him.

I heard him climbing back up the stairs. I pulled my knees to my chest and kept my thoughts of Dylan and his protective love with me. James could never take that away.

"Anna," he said, his voice soft and shaky, "I've made you a coffee."

I stayed perfectly still. I just wanted him to go away. He sat opposite me on the floor, his legs crossed.

"Anna, I think I overreacted."

I looked up at him.

"It is never okay to do what you just did, no matter what."

At the sight of my face, he gasped, leapt up and into the bathroom and brought me some tissue.

"You're bleeding," he said, his bottom lip quivering.

"You made me bleed," I said angrily.

"I'm sorry," he said, bowing his head.

"Yeah, until the next time."

"There won't be a next time Anna, I promise there won't."

"And how are you going to achieve that?" I asked scathingly, holding the tissue to my bleeding cheek.

"I'm just going to remember that it's wrong."

"Look, James; I think I can help you. If you are serious, there is a way you can sort yourself out, but you have to work really hard."

"I'll do anything Anna," he promised.

I went down to the kitchen and got the laptop. I opened up the webpages that I had been looking at, and I showed him the dominator hand-out. He read every thing with tears running down his face then he looked up at me, his brown eyes full of sorrow, and said, "This is me. I am this person, and I don't want to be. I need your help."

TIME OUT

Sucked in by James's sorrow, I pledged to help him. Why couldn't I see how ludicrous this was? If someone had assaulted me in the street and then told me that they needed my help to change I would tell them to fuck off, yet here I was promising to support my attacker while he tried to learn to behave like a decent human being. I pored over web pages with him and encouraged him to call the Respect Phoneline, which supports the perpetrators of domestic abuse to change their behaviour and provides links to programs for abusers. I could tell that James was nervous about making the call, and I gently encouraged him to go ahead and do it. He went to his car with a cup of coffee and made the call. I busied myself in the house, waiting for him to come back in and tell me what had been said. I was worried that it would transpire that I was somehow to blame for the abuse, and by the time he finally came back into the house I was a nervous wreck.

He had his head bowed, and he took my hands in his. He tried to speak but was choked with tears.

"Take your time," I told him gently. Being choked with tears was something that I was all too familiar with.

"Anna I….I…..can't…..can't believe what I am……I'm so sorry…..It is all me." He began to sob, and I held him. "I don't deserve you. I have hurt you so much. I had no idea how much of a cunt I was being, no idea whatsoever. That woman on the phone, she has just told me what I have been doing to you and how my behaviour has been affecting you, and I am sorry, I am so so sorry. You have my word; I am going to sort this out. I don't deserve you."

He collapsed against my chest a sobbing wreck. "I will make this up to you Anna; I will make you happy, I have been such a pig to you. I am going to do everything it takes to sort this out, believe me."

"I do believe you. What advice did they give you? How do you go about changing your behaviour?"

"Well, first of all, I have to recognise when I am starting to become abusive and then I have to take a time out. It should be at least one hour, and I must not drink alcohol in that time."

"Sounds similar to what Dee suggested that I do when I talked about lashing out at you."

"Really?"

"Yes, only when I tried to do it, you wouldn't let me leave the house."

James bowed his head.

"I told the woman on the phone all about that, and she made me realise how wrong that is. How disgustingly I have behaved. Anna, I cannot apologise enough for what I have put you through, I really can't."

James continued to tell me about his conversation with the woman from the helpline, and I felt hopeful that he really had experienced a realisation. They were going to send him some literature to back up what they had discussed.

"She recommended that you ring them too."

"Why is that?" I asked, a little suspiciously.

"Well, you have also lashed out at me, and that is just as unacceptable as me lashing out at you."

"Fair enough," I said, although I felt that this was a little unjust. There was no way I'd ever have lashed out at James just because we were arguing; it was always in response to his abuse. Not that I thought that made it okay to lash out, just that he seemed to deliberately push me to the point of doing it, and I didn't for a second believe that he was afraid of me or my behaviour.

"I didn't realise how damaging my behaviour was," James continued. "I thought that everyone argued like that. I thought it was normal."

"I did try and tell you."

"I know you did, and I couldn't hear what you were saying. I'm so sorry Anna; I will never stop listening to you now. I can hear you now, and I am so, so sorry."

"So how else do you change your behaviour?" I asked.

"Well there are these perpetrator programs, but the nearest one to us is in Coventry, so I think I will just try and work with Lizzie. I can't wait to see her again."

"When do you next go?" I felt worried that this enthusiastic fervour would waver over time, I felt that it was important that he saw Lizzie sooner rather than later.

"The day after tomorrow," he told me, looking at me again with tears in his eyes.

This felt hopeful. Dee had told me that abusive people rarely accept responsibility for their abusive behaviour, and usually continue to blame others, yet here was James admitting openly that he was at fault and promising to change. Not only was he promising that he was going to change, but he was backing up his promises with actions. I was seeing Dee the next day, and I couldn't wait.

James made all the extra effort that he had made previously, but this time I knew that it was different, because James had rung Respect and now he accepted responsibility. He had read and related to all the information that I had read, and he was determined to change. We were a team, and I supported him as much as I could. When I went to see Dee the next day I told her all about James's admission. She listened carefully, and I was surprised by what she said when she finally spoke.

"Anna, I get the impression that you feel responsible for helping James to change."

"Really? I'm not sure that I feel responsible, I…"

My voice tailed off as I processed what she had said.

"Maybe I do feel responsible. I'm not sure. He seems so vulnerable and lost and hurt by his own behaviour. I just want to help him."

"Of course you do because you care about him, but what about how you have felt when he has been abusing you? Who is looking after you?"

"No one," I answered.

"I thought that for this session we could work on your relationship with your parents. Is that okay with you?"

"Yeah, I suppose," I said. Really I had wanted her to tell me how to help James, but that was not what Dee was there for, she was my counsellor, and she was there for me. We spoke about my childhood at length, and I told her more and more about my dad and how he had handed responsibility for his drinking to my mum and how that responsibility was felt by both me and Eve. One of us always 'kept an eye on him'. Whenever we were at a family function or if friends came around we would all automatically remove temptation from his path. The more I spoke about it to Dee, the madder I felt with both my dad and my mum. How could a grown man expect his family to take responsibility for him?

"I remember one day," I told Dee, "we had gone to a barbeque at a neighbour's house. I was about thirteen years old; Eve would have been about fifteen; everyone was drinking, and the wine was flowing. Mum had to nip home because she had forgotten her bag, and the phone went while she was in the house. Anyway, she ended up being gone ages. Eve and I were just messing about with the other kids there, and no one was taking any notice of dad. Anyway, he took his opportunity, God knows how much he had drunk, but he started to do a really stupid dance. I am cringing now just thinking about it. He fell onto the table and knocked all the food everywhere, there was smashed glass and food and drink all over the floor, then he started trying to clear it up, and he cut his hand. There was blood everywhere. Mum came back to carnage, and I'll never forget how disappointed she looked, embarrassed and disappointed."

"Who do you think she was disappointed with?" Dee asked. I noticed that I was tearing a tissue up into tiny pieces.

"Well at the time, I thought she was disappointed with Eve and me, but she was probably disappointed with dad. I felt responsible though, and so did Eve. I remember us both apologising to mum, and she didn't say it wasn't our fault which made me feel even worse."

"Whose fault do you think it was?" Dee asked.

"His. It was his fault for drinking so much."

"Yes, of course, it was. Do you see any parallels with this situation and your relationship with James?" Dee asked me. I thought about it for a second. It seemed so obvious.

"Yes, I feel responsible. I guess I've always felt like that."

By the time I left Dee that day, my head was whirling. Incidents from my childhood presented themselves in my mind one after the other, and I was astounded to see that I had been taught to be responsible for others' behaviour in a completely unacceptable way. I felt angry with my dad, but surprisingly I felt angrier with my mum for doing it and involving Eve and me. I kept telling myself that she would only have done what she had thought was the right thing to do, but still, I was annoyed at her for accepting and perpetrating dad's pathetic behaviour. The worst thing of all was seeing how I had carried this conditioning into my relationship and now I was some soft touch, easily manipulated into taking responsibility where it wasn't mine to take. Where my mum had once seemed strong and admirable, she now appeared weak and stupid. It was a horrible realisation, and I had more than a sneaking suspicion that I was acting a lot like her.

When I got home that evening, James was waiting in the kitchen for me. He fussed around me, making me a drink and staring at me with a look of adoration in his eyes.

"I've run you a bath," he said. And when I went up to the bathroom, there was a bath full of bubbles and a gift and card for me too. I opened the card. It was a pretty little handmade one with two tiny birds on the front. Across the top were the words, you *are my happily ever after,* and inside James had written: *Dear Anna, Thank you for everything. You are my happily ever after and I am never going to let you go. Love from James xxx*

I opened the gift; it was some pyjamas that I had been eyeing up in La Senza, they were lovely.

"You'll look gorgeous in those," he told me, and I got into the bath, my head in a crazy spin.

"Thank you for my gift," I told him.

I suddenly felt very tired from all the thinking.

"You're welcome. I just want you to know what you mean to me."

"Is it tomorrow you see Lizzie?" I asked.

"Yeah, six-thirty, I can't wait."

The next day, I got in from work at around six, just as James was leaving to go and see Lizzie.

"Good luck," I told him as he left.

I cooked us a meal while he was out and at ten to eight he walked back through the door. His cheeks were flushed, and his eyes were red, and the first thing that he did was come over and cuddle me. He seemed to be too choked to talk, and I waited for him to regain his composure. He leant past me to the wine rack and pulled a bottle out.

"I'm sorry," he said. "I know it's probably not helpful, but I feel like I need it right now."

He poured us both a large glass and gestured for me to sit next to him at the table. He told me what he could about his session with Lizzie. It sounded like she had been supportive and agreed that James's behaviour had been wrong. "One thing she did say though, was that every argument has two sides and that I shouldn't take responsibility for everything because it takes two."

My blood ran cold. That was not the case in an abusive relationship. Surely a counsellor should know that? Perhaps she hadn't said that?

"She agrees that you should also ring the Respect Phoneline because of your hitting."

Anger prickled through me. *My hitting?* Of course, hitting was wrong, but all the stuff that happened before the hitting. All the provoking that James did to get me to hit, surely that was at least as bad. My behaviour was always a reaction to his treatment of me, and whether it was the right or wrong reaction, it would never have happened without the prior provocation. I decided to say nothing. I felt like things were too shaky at the moment and that if I voiced my opinions, I would spoil this opportunity to have everything sorted.

Nothing had changed, because if it had, I wouldn't have been afraid to voice my concerns, to say what I thought, but the smokescreen of James's admission was working, and that was all that I could focus on.

****

Things have become strange in the hospital. I feel as though I am suspended a couple of centimetres above my body. It is quite a pleasant sensation, but extremely surreal and I am not sure whether my soul is actually outside my body or whether I am just really out of it on the drugs. I have not made any improvements, and my friends and family gather around me, I feel a sense of inevitability in the air, and I have caught one or two people discussing me in past tense. "She would have loved that." Or, "Do you know what her favourite song was?" This doesn't bode well does it? I still have a favourite song. I'm not dead yet!

I have not responded to the antibiotics, and there is another blood clot, in my leg this time. It is difficult to treat me because the doctors suspect that there is still a bleed in my brain and if they interrupt my blood clotting too much, this could worsen. I don't envy them. The decisions they make could mean the difference between life and death for me. I wonder what that is like? I wonder how it feels to have that much responsibility? Pam continues to be my main carer, but because my family are with me for the vast majority of the time, it's not so bad. They protect me from her coldness, although she seems to have warmed to me a little again. I can't work her out.

****

James was to ring the Respect Phoneline again. The woman he had spoken to had told him to give her a call in a few days when he had read the literature and spoken to Lizzie. He was being adorable. The only thing that I was worried about was that he seemed to believe that I was also abusive because I had lashed out at him. I hoped that the more work that he did with Lizzie, the more likely he was to see that I only reacted to his behaviour and that I never instigated any of it.

Chloe and I were invited to an old friend's birthday party. She was having a girly night in and then carrying on into town. It had been a long time since I had been out and I had accepted the invitation. As it approached, James began to ask more and more questions about the people I was going to be out with.

"Chloe is single, isn't she?" he asked.

"Yes, she is at the moment," I answered, wondering what he was angling at.

"So do you think she is the best influence on you?"

"What do you mean *influence?*" I asked, narrowing my eyes a little.

'Well, I know what single girls are like out on the town."

"I still don't know what you mean," I told him.

"Well if she's out on the prowl, you will probably be tempted too."

"Tempted by what?" I asked, annoyed. "I am not a single person, and Chloe is entitled to do whatever she wishes, but she tends to stay with the crowd and chat and have fun with the people she is with, not prowl around looking for men."

"Where are you going?" James asked.

"I don't know, just out on the town."

"Your old haunts? There will probably be ex-boyfriends there."

"So?" I retorted.

"Well, how would you like it if I did that?"

"James, it wouldn't bother me. Don't you trust me?"

"No, I don't. I know what Chloe is like."

"She's not *like* anything," I said, exasperatedly.

"And I have never cheated on anyone. Have you?"

"Not exactly cheated," he said, smirking a little.

"What does that mean?"

"Well, there was a woman at one of the sites. She just used to suck me off occasionally."

"What? That's cheating!"

"Not really, and it was when I was with Daniella. I was just glad of the affection."

"So if I gave someone a blowjob, you wouldn't class it as cheating?" I was astounded and angry at James.

"Well yes, that would be cheating on me."

"I don't understand!"

"Well *she* was sucking *me* off. It wasn't like I was doing anything for her, so it wasn't technically cheating. Anyway, it was only Daniella, and you know how awful it was for me with her."

I stood with my mouth wide open in shock. I couldn't believe how vile James was and how dismissive of his behaviour he could be. Why I couldn't believe this, despite the way he treated me, I do not know. James was capable of some pretty disgusting acts, yet there remained a part of me that could not fully accept this. I still believed that he was a good person who had somehow lost his way a little, and not a selfish, abusive monster who could play at Mr Nice Guy when it suited him.

"So if someone at work was just getting me off, and I wasn't doing anything for him, you wouldn't class that as me cheating on you?" I asked once I had regained control of my mouth.

"That's different," he said.

"*How?!*" I asked

"Because we are great together, Anna, we have a wonderful relationship, Daniella and I were shit. We should have been finished long before the attack," he argued.

Great together! Just how deluded was he? My mind began to race with horrible images of James and some unknown woman.

"Do you still see her?"

"Who?"

"Blow job woman?"

"Trish? Nah, I ended it with her when I started seeing you."

"What so you had a relationship with her?"

"Yeah, but it wasn't serious, it was just a bit of fucking here and there. She was married."

Again, I stood with my mouth wide open.

"James that's outrageous behaviour," I managed, "I have never behaved like that."

"Of course you have. Everyone does it at least once in their life."

"Are you serious James?"

"Err, yep," he said, looking at me with his eyes narrowed. "Come on Anna; you are only human, you must have done it at some point."

"I can honestly say I have never cheated on anyone before. I am not interested in anyone else, so you are just going to have to trust me on this one James. I am not going to cheat on you; I am going to go out with my friends and have a good time with them. You are going to have to deal with it."

As I said the words, I felt uneasy. I said them because I knew I should say them, but part of me just wanted to take the easy way out, to tell him that I would stay in to make him feel better. I think if it hadn't been for the fact that Chloe wanted me to go, and I felt as though I owed such a huge debt of gratitude to my beautiful friend, I'd have cancelled just for a quiet life.

James looked angry, and for a moment I felt afraid. I knew that if there were another abusive episode, I would have to leave him. I knew that I couldn't give him one more chance and I felt like my whole world hinged on his next move. His nostrils flared, and he began to breathe deeply and open and close his hands. Our gaze locked for a moment, and then he spoke.

"Now is the time for me to go for a time out. I want to do the right thing."

He quickly walked away, and within seconds he was gone. I peered out of the window, and I could see him sitting in the car. He was smoking a cigarette. I had only just discovered that he smoked, and it seemed strange, he was so into sport and fitness. I was relieved that he was doing something other than winding himself up and becoming abusive, and when he called me from the garden forty-five minutes later to see if I minded him coming back in, I could have punched the air with happiness. It was a success, James could work the time out, and we had a proper chance of actually, really having something good.

That night in bed, the conversation turned to James's parents.

"I've told mum about going to Lizzie and ringing that helpline. I thought she would like the chance to support me and I wanted to keep her informed because she seems to have a paranoia about being shut out of my life."

"What did she say?" I asked, turning on my side to look at him. He was lying on his back, and he kept his eyes closed while he spoke.

"She says that you are manipulating me."

"What?!" I said, sitting up, astounded. "How?"

"She says that you are trying to blame me for your behaviour and that you are trying to make me feel bad so that you can blame me for your problems."

"What did you say to her?" I asked, my heart pounding with rage and my palms clammy.

"I told her that I disagree, and she said that while I am being manipulated by you, she is not willing to talk to me, so now dad isn't talking to me either, and work has become a bit of a nightmare."

"I cannot believe this."

I stood up and paced across the bedroom floor to the other side of the room. I was so angry. Why did they think that I was trying to manipulate James? All I wanted was for him to stop being abusive so that we could get on with being happy together. It wasn't much to ask.

"Mum said that you are obviously trying to control me and that I haven't been myself since I moved in with you."

I was outraged by now.

"What?" I screeched. "How the hell do I try and control you? What have you been telling her?"

"Anna you know what they are like. They get something in their heads and make a big fucking deal about it."

He had joined me on the other side of the room, and he put his arm around me gently and led me to the bed where we sat together. He kissed my cheek.

"I love you Anna, and if they want to make my life hard, that's up to them. They will soon see how happy we are."

"I know, but I haven't done anything wrong. It's the other way round and I am so fucking angry."

"I don't blame you," he said, kissing my neck and pulling me towards him. "Why don't you turn that anger into passion and we can have some fun with it?" he suggested, stroking my back.

In the morning, after a restless night, James continued with his super attentive routine, and he brought me coffee and toast. He sat next to me in bed while I ate, and he watched me with a soppy grin on his face.

"You know Anna, we are great." I looked at him and smiled. "You know, I did that time-out thing. It works. We can sort the issues and be happy. I don't want to lose you. I know you are upset about my parents, and it is up to you what you decide to do. I will support you if you never speak to them again, and I will support you if you want to try and sort it. It's up to you."

"I can't see myself ever talking to them again. I'm too angry."

"Fair enough beautiful, it's your choice," he told me soothingly.

Buoyed by James's determination and the single successful time-out attempt, I allowed myself to believe that things were okay between us. I felt like James and I were a team and the step away from his parents cemented that belief further. Naively, I was building all my hopes on a shaky foundation, and I continued to ignore the blatant warning signs: the infidelity, James's flippant dismissal of another person's marriage and him selfishly satisfying his own desires at the expense of other people's feelings. As ridiculous as it seems now, I still believed that he was a good person – a misguided, but essentially good person. What had happened to my judgement? Was I ignoring my inner voice, or was I blind to reality?

PRETZELS

The night out with Chloe came and went. James was obviously unhappy about it, but he tolerated it, and I tried to enjoy myself, but it was difficult with the knot in my stomach and his reaction on my mind. The next day Chloe sent me a text message that simply read, *I miss you xxx,* and I felt sad and torn. I missed her too and felt unable to be close to her the way I had been before. I was no longer honest with Chloe; she didn't know my real life anymore, nobody did.

James needed to drop some documents off to a colleague who lived a couple of hours away. It was a Saturday morning, a few weeks before Christmas and he asked me to go along with him to keep him company. We set off in the car together. He had been stressed about the work he'd been doing and kept saying how much he needed a break from it all.

"Let's just fuck off on a plane somewhere," he kept saying. He knew that I couldn't go away in term time and he had begun to tell me repeatedly that he despised my job. It was getting on my nerves. He'd say, "Let's just book something." I'd say, "You know that I can't because of work." And then he would tell me, "I hate your job." I would then feel hurt and offended.

I loved my job, I was proud of being a teacher, and I felt that he was criticising part of my life that meant so much to me. I felt that by him saying the things he was saying he was actually insulting me as a person, and that he couldn't possibly know how much teaching meant to me, because if he did, he wouldn't keep making negative comments about it. In turn, I would feel disappointed that he didn't seem to know me very well at all.

I got into the passenger's side of the car, and he jumped into the driver's seat and started the engine.

"I thought we could go for something to eat and do some Christmas shopping after I've dropped these papers off, what do you reckon?"

"Yeah that sounds lovely," I replied, trying to sort my hair out in the wing mirror. "My hair is getting on my nerves; it's so frizzy in this damp weather."

He tutted. I pretended I hadn't noticed. I was sure I had somehow upset him, but I couldn't face trying to find out what it was that I had done this time.

I found myself adjusting my behaviour, trying to lift his mood, thinking of topics of conversation that he might approve of. I chattered away like an idiot, hating myself a little bit more with each sentence that I spoke and by the time we were shopping I just felt plain miserable. Of course, I attempted to hide my feelings, to force a smile. Nothing had changed because if it had, I wouldn't have been afraid to be myself.

We ate lunch in a nice hotel and James ordered us a bottle of Rioja.

"Let's just get a room here tonight," he suggested.

"Yeah if you want to," I said.

As we ate our lunch and drank the wine, I began to chat with James about Chloe. I was reminiscing about our holidays. I was starting to feel a little bit drunk, and I told him that I would like to go away for a weekend with her soon as I didn't seem to see her anymore and I missed her.

"Do you think you'd have chosen Chloe as a friend if your parents weren't all friends?" James asked.

"Yes, of course, I would! Why?" I answered, taken aback.

"Well it's just…… you know, she's a bit…..oh I suppose I shouldn't really say, I mean you obviously like her a lot."

"James, I love Chlo. You may not, but I do."

"Yeah, I know that I just don't see how you two are suited as friends. I mean she's a bit in your face, isn't she? I don't think she has much depth. She'd stab you in the back that one, I've always thought that."

He poured himself another glass of wine.

"What?! No she wouldn't, she's so loyal. Are you joking?!"

"You only see what you want to see Anna. Men get to see the other side of a woman and believe me; she would stab you in the back."

He leant back in his chair and took a long swig from his glass.

"I don't believe you."

"I knew you wouldn't believe me, that's why I never said anything before, but it's the truth Anna, Chloe isn't as perfect and trustworthy as you might believe."

"You can't say that and not tell me what you are talking about."

"Look, it's best that I don't say, I can't say, just be careful that's all. I'd hate to see you getting hurt."

"I don't know what you mean, but I am more certain that Chloe would never do anything to hurt me than I am about anything else," I told him, but a tiny nagging seed of doubt about my best friend had lodged itself inside me. I shuddered and tried to ignore it as it began to swell, sprouted roots and shoots and grew. Chloe wouldn't hurt me. Would she?

I changed the subject as quickly as I could, but the unease stayed with me. Surely Chlo wouldn't do anything to hurt me? But then why would James try and make me believe that she would? It just didn't make any sense. He must have had his reasons. I still believed that the things that James did were logical and honourable. I had no idea how far he would go to manipulate me and keep me under his control.

We had a nice day and night, but my feeling of unease dominated. I didn't feel able to talk to James about it any further, so I avoided the subject of Chloe. We bought some Christmas presents and hoped that we wouldn't regret buying gifts after a bottle of wine.

That evening over dinner, James asked me how I had met Dylan. It was really strange because Dylan was a subject that I tried to avoid with him, because of his jealousy.

"Are you sure you want to know about this stuff James?" I asked. "Maybe it's better to leave some things in the past."

"I'm just interested Anna because it is part of your life, part of who you are."

He sounded so sincere that I relaxed a little and told him the story of meeting Dylan in the strange Inter Education Learning session. My face must have lit up a little, because he said, "I can see you must have really enjoyed that time in your life."

"Yes, I did, it was brilliant," I said, smiling. I was just about to ask him a question about his time at university when he interrupted me. A dark look had flashed across his face.

"What about this?" he asked, gesturing from himself to me, to the dinner on our plates.

"What? The food?" I asked, confused.

"No, us, this, what we have and do. Is this brilliant?" He leant back in his chair and folded his arms across his chest.

"Well if I'm honest James, no, it's not brilliant all of the time, as you know, but I think it will be brilliant if we are successful with the counselling and stuff. It certainly has the potential to be brilliant." I was a little drunk, and the alcohol was acting like truth serum. I didn't feel able to lie and tell him how wonderful things were when they quite clearly weren't.

"So after everything I do for you, I still can't be as wonderful as lover boy. Things were brilliant with lover boy. Brilliant lover boy."

"James, I didn't say that you are twisting my words. Do you think you need to take a time out or something?"

He was already pushing his chair back. I was going to be left alone in the hotel restaurant; I felt humiliated. James went to the toilet, and I sat in my chair, my head spinning. Why did he have to be so unpredictable? A couple of minutes later, he came back.

"I'm sorry baby. Let's forget that conversation. Let's go up to bed."

"Okay," I said, and we made our back up to our room and climbed into bed.

James was quiet and brooding, and I felt as though I was treading on the eggshells again. Eventually, we fell asleep, and in the morning, when we travelled back in the car, he made little digs about me.

"I'll drive, shall I?" he said as we approached the car.

"I don't mind driving," I told him, but he ignored me and got in the driver's side.

"Some things are just too much effort for you aren't they?"

I ignored him. I felt like he was spoiling for a fight and I couldn't be bothered. When we got home, there was a handwritten letter addressed to me. James strode past me, through the house carrying the bags and I tore the envelope open. It looked like a nice letter, and I was intrigued. Inside there was a tiny card it was made from thick textured paper, and it had a lovely print of a butterfly on the front the message inside read:

Dear Anna, I thought I caught a glimpse of sadness in your eyes today. I hope it was my imagination. Remember I am here for you always. Hattie x

I had noticed Hattie staring rather intently at me in the staff room during my lunch break one day last week; she'd obviously read my mood. I suddenly felt a need to tell her everything, and I sent her a text message thanking her for the card and asking her if she was free later that evening. I was sure that James would be unhappy with me going out, but he would just have to deal with it. Hattie responded quickly, and we made our arrangements. I went into the bedroom where James was lying on the bed.

"Are you okay?" I asked. He was frowning and looked as though he had a headache.

"Oh you care do you?" he asked, without even opening his eyes.

"Err yes.." I said, pulling a face at him. "I'm going to Hattie's later, I think we are going to get a takeaway, so I won't be having any dinner here tonight."

"*Hattie's?*" he said as if I just told him that I was going to poke my own eyes out with a blunt stick.

"Yes, what's so strange about that?"

"Nothing.... I mean you obviously think she's good company. I find her a bit stuck up; I got the impression that she was looking down on you all the time."

I thought about Hattie for a second. She didn't seem stuck up to me, and I had never got the impression that she was looking down on me. She was just straightforward as far as I was concerned, and she mothered me, but in a very good way. I had learnt a lot from Hattie.

"She's a man-hater," he said.

"No she's not!" I said, surprised. "Why would you say that?"

"Well, a woman of her age living on her own. That says it all."

"Yeah, it says that she is happy in her own company," I said, turning away from James and going back down the stairs. He was getting to me, everything he said was negative, but I couldn't pinpoint anything particularly abusive about his behaviour. Nonetheless, I felt uneasy, as though he was about to erupt at any moment.

He continued to be prickly and cold towards me until I left for Hattie's later that evening. On the drive to her house, I found myself wondering why I didn't just leave him. I thought about the financial implications of leaving him. I'd have to pay half of the remaining rent, that was certain, and I had nothing of my own left. My furniture had all gone and been replaced with James's. If I left him, I would struggle financially. What had I done? Why had I trusted him? Maybe I should just stay, give him a chance with the counselling and decide what to do nearer the end of our rental contract?

I arrived at Hattie's, and she welcomed me with a

big hug. We settled down in her kitchen, and she boiled the kettle to make us a drink. She handed me a cup of steaming coffee then sat herself down opposite me and smiled.

"Are you okay Anna?" she asked. "You haven't seemed yourself lately."

With that, I burst into tears, and the whole sorry tale of James's behaviour came pouring out.

"Anna, please stay here. I have room; no one is worth putting yourself in danger for."

"No, I am going to give him a chance," I said. "He's trying to change now, he's admitted it, and that's a big step isn't it?" I asked, looking at Hattie's concerned and sad expression.

"Well yes it is, but these men don't change. Honestly, you would be doing yourself a big favour if you left him."

"I can't, not without giving him a chance."

"Well it's up to you, of course, you always know where I am."

The rest of our evening was spent with us chatting over our takeaway.

"You know Anna; I had no idea. He acts as though he dotes on you. I'm afraid of how wrong I had it. I loved the way his gaze seemed to follow you around the room, I thought it was because he couldn't get enough of you, but now it seems so sinister. My God, he is so charming. He seems like the perfect gentleman, he's so intelligent and good looking, and he seems so nice. I can't believe it. I am in shock."

"He *is* nice," I told her. Although I felt pathetic saying it. He was only nice when it suited him.

Hattie just looked at me with her sad, worried expression. It was obvious she wasn't convinced.

"You know that day when I noticed those bruises on your arm, and you said they were from falling over?"

I looked at the floor, ashamed and embarrassed.

"I'm sorry for lying," I said quietly.

"The evil bastard. Anna, please don't go back, please."

"I'm sorry, I am going to give him one more chance, but I promise I won't hide anything else from you. I promise."

"Okay," she said. "Just please leave at the first hint of danger. You are too precious; you do not deserve any of this."

"I promise."

Back home, James was watching a DVD in bed. I climbed into bed next to him, and he asked me if I'd had a nice evening. I watched the end of the film and James fell asleep. My head was spinning. I watched him for a few minutes; his breathing was loud and rhythmical. He lay with his arms above his head. I watched his bare chest rise and fall. His skin was tanned, and his body was lean and toned. His full lips looked fuller and more kissable than ever, and his long dark lashes curled beautifully. I stared at him, and I tried to work out how I felt about him.

Physically, James was beautiful, I don't think I had ever seen a more physically attractive man, and I'd certainly never had a relationship with anyone as good looking as him. But underneath his skin, hidden beneath the exquisite exterior, lurked an unpredictable, controlling monster, and that monster was who stared back at me from the incredible brown eyes when they were open, it was that monster who spoke to me from those soft full lips. James's beauty was nothing but an illusion. It was shallow and meaningless. I needed to go, regardless of the cost, I had to leave him, I was certain. I turned out the light and lay on my side and stared into the darkness, eventually drifting into an uneasy sleep.

When I opened my eyes, I couldn't see anything. The darkness was complete, and I couldn't even make out the slight light of my bedroom window. I tried to move but realised that I was tightly bound. My hands were tied together at the wrists and my legs at the ankles. I began to struggle, and that's when I realised that I was inside some kind of box. A coffin perhaps? I began to scream and scream. "Help! HELP ME! I'M TRAPPED!" I screamed at the top of my lungs. James turned on the light, and I realised with huge relief that it was only a nightmare. James soothed me and held me as I shook with fear. He brought me some water and then we slept the rest of the night with the lamp on and him holding my hand protectively. In the morning, he asked me about my dream, and he was sympathetic and loving. My resolve to leave him that had been so strong only a few hours before was rapidly melting away and in its place, hope that he *was* all I wanted him to be began to sprout. I left for work feeling confused, feeding the hope and starving the resolve to leave. I made excuses for James's previous behaviour in my head, and I let another part of my self-worth fall away.

James and I fell back into a lovely honeymoon period, where he doted on me and fussed around me and couldn't do enough to make me happy, couldn't say enough to let me know how much he needed and wanted me and how much I meant to him and that honeymoon period lasted for a good few weeks. During that time James *was* everything that I wanted him to be. I was lulled into a false sense of security. Christmas was difficult because I didn't want to have anything to do with James's parents. He accepted that and respected my wishes and we decided to spend Christmas day together and then Boxing Day at my sister and Liam's house. My parents had gone to stay with friends in Spain so it was just Eve, who was around four months pregnant, Liam, James and me.

Eve sent me a text message at seven-thirty on Boxing Day morning. My phone was next to my pillow and I leapt up in fright as it vibrated loudly.

"Who the fuck is texting you at this time?" James growled from underneath the duvet.

"It's my sister. She wants to know what time we will be there."

"For fuck's sake, what time is it?" he asked, flinging the covers back so roughly that they fell off the bed completely. He went into the bathroom, and I could hear him having a pee. My heart sunk. He was obviously in one of his moods.

"It's half-past seven," I told him. "Eve probably assumes that my phone is on silent like it usually is during the night."

"Well, she's assumed wrong, hasn't she?" He popped two painkillers into his mouth and took a swig of water. I guessed he was hung-over.

"Come back to bed," I said soothingly. "I've told her mid-afternoon so we can get a bit more sleep."

James got back into bed, and I tried to snuggle up to him. I could feel his heart beating. It seemed to be going very fast, and I knew that this was a sign that he was stressed and about to blow up. I realised with dread that I would have to tread very carefully today. I closed my eyes and tried to get back to sleep. James was restless next to me, and he kept sighing. I felt tense but kept my eyes closed so that he would think that I was asleep and maybe go back to sleep again himself. I hoped that he would doze off and then wake up happy, but I hoped in vain. He placed his hand on mine, and I gave his fingers a little squeeze. He pulled my hand to his crotch. *Not this again,* I thought, but it was a way of cheering him up, so I went along with it, and he pushed my hand into his shorts. I wondered how he could find it enjoyable. It didn't even seem to need to be me, just a hand moving the way he wanted it to move, a disembodied hand going through the motions. Afterwards, he went back to sleep, and I lay awake feeling used, dirty, unhappy and small.

I got up and showered and dressed. I sat downstairs quietly, alone, waiting for James to get up. When eleven-thirty came I knew I'd have to wake him, it took at least an hour to get to Eve's house, and I guessed that he'd want to take his time getting ready if he felt unwell. I climbed the stairs, feeling apprehensive. I could just leave him to sleep, but then we'd be late, and I'd be letting Eve down. Also, he might not want to sleep, he might want me to wake him up, but on the other hand, he might be annoyed if I tried to wake him. I felt so stressed. I was afraid to do the wrong thing, and I hated myself for giving James the power to tie me up in knots like a pretzel. When I ventured into the bedroom, James was already awake. He was sitting in bed looking at his laptop.

"We need to leave soon," I told him. "I said mid-afternoon to Eve."

"I'm not gonna come."

"What? Why not?"

"I feel grumpy, tired and hung-over. I just want to curl up on the sofa and read."

"Oh James, please come. Eve has bought food for you, and she is expecting both of us." He leapt out of bed and strode into the bathroom. I heard him turn the shower on and then he reappeared in the doorway.

"Okay, I'll come, but I really am not in the mood."

"Thanks, I appreciate it," I told him. My heart sinking even further at the thought of him spending the day feeling miserable. Our shaky foundations were beginning to give way.

I drove us to Eve's house, a sure sign that James was feeling unwell. I kept putting my hand on his leg and asking him if he was okay. By the time we arrived, he seemed to be feeling better, he slung our overnight bag over his shoulder, and we walked up Eve and Liam's front steps hand in hand. Inside, James and Liam began chatting about the best road bike to buy, and we all sat in the dining room together.

"Are you okay?" Eve asked me.

"Yeah, James and I just had a bit of a fall out this morning, but we're fine now," I said quietly.

"Must be a day for it, Liam and I had a row this morning too. I think it's my hormones." I smiled at Eve. Maybe James and I weren't so bad after all. Every couple falls out sometimes.

"I think we should have a Buck's Fizz," Eve suggested, pushing her chair back and heading to the fridge. I went with her, and we opened a bottle of champagne. Eve filled her glass with orange juice and poured the tiniest bit of champagne and topped it up with sparkling water.

"Next year I am going to get rat-arsed," she told me, rubbing her tiny bump.

We all held up our glasses and wished one another a very merry Christmas. I sipped my drink and let the bubbles relax me. I glanced over at James just as he put his empty glass on the table.

"Whoa, James!" Eve said. "Thirsty?"

"Yeah, sorry Eve, it's just so nice and refreshing, it's impossible to sip it."

I looked down at my glass. It was practically full, as were Liam's and Eve's. Eve topped James up, and he did the same again. I felt a prickle of embarrassment. Why couldn't he just drink slowly?

He must have noticed the expression on my face because he narrowed his eyes at me momentarily, but he was deep in conversation with Liam, so I carried on talking to Eve.

We sat around the dining table drinking and talking. Of course, Eve wasn't drinking alcohol, and I began to feel quite drunk.

"I feel shitfaced," I told her.

"Haha, you look it too," she said. "You've got a festive nose." I put my hand to my nose. It did feel hot.

"I'm going to put make-up on before Liam starts with the camera, I don't want a red nose in all the pictures."

When I came back downstairs, Liam and Eve were dishing up lunch. There was loads of food, and I noticed that James had opened one of the bottles of red wine that we had brought with us. We all sat around the table and began to enjoy the delicious roast. Eve and Liam had roasted a chicken, because Eve didn't like turkey very much, and there were roast potatoes, mashed potatoes, Yorkshire puddings and lots of vegetables and gravy. We ate and enjoyed each other's company. We pulled crackers and told rubbish jokes. After an hour or so, I noticed James draining the last of the bottle of red wine into his glass, and Liam got up and brought another bottle to the table. We chatted about perhaps going on holiday in the summer after the baby was born and I noticed Liam slurring his words a little. He seemed drunk like me, but James still appeared sober. Only I could tell from the expression on his face that he had been drinking and, of course, I knew that he had drunk at least a bottle of red and two glasses of Buck's Fizz.

We ate dessert and chatted about the usual topics of conversation. Liam had one glass of red wine from the new bottle, and I was still drinking the fizzy stuff. James poured the last of the new bottle into his glass, and I tried to work out what he must have had to drink so far, almost two bottles of red wine and two glasses of Buck's Fizz. I looked at the time; it was only six o'clock. Liam opened a bottle of rum and poured three measures. James knocked his back quickly, but I felt too full to drink mine. He poured James and himself another, and then we all began to help clear up, loading the dishwasher and scraping the leftovers into the bin. We sat back around the table and Eve put the kettle on. I had a coffee, and she had a cup of tea. By now the boys were on to their third measure of rum.

"I refuse to clear up vomit Liam," Eve warned.

"I'm not going to be sick," Liam slurred. "In fact I'm hungry," he added, going to the kitchen and pouring himself a bowl of pretzels. He sat back at the table and began to crunch on them loudly. Eve tutted and gave him a dirty look.

Our conversation continued, and Liam refilled his bowl of pretzels. Eve gave him another dirty look. James told us some funny stories about one of his colleagues. It was nice to see him animated and enjoying himself. We began to look on the internet for places to go on holiday in the late summer.

"Once Christmas is over, it's nice to have something to look forward to," Liam said.

The bottle of rum was taking a hammering and Eve had to stop Liam from booking us a villa in Mexico on his credit card.

"Maybe wait until you are sober?" she suggested.

James seemed to have relaxed and appeared to be enjoying himself, so I relaxed too.

Liam refilled his bowl of pretzels again. "I don't know why you bothered with the bowl," Eve jibed at him. "You know you'll end up eating the whole bag to yourself anyway."

Liam looked at her with mock indignation. "Want one squirt?" he said, pushing the bowl toward me.

"No thanks, I can't eat another thing," I said, lifting my top and pointing at the undone top button on my jeans.

"Alright squirt, we wouldn't want you popping," he told me, poking me in the arm.

James had moved around the table and was now

sitting next to me.

"Put it away," he whispered, gesturing to my belly.

"What?" I said, looking down at my top which had caught on my button, leaving my undone jeans and bulging belly exposed.

"I said, put it away. You are so vulgar."

"No I'm not!" I retorted, anger rising in my chest at being called vulgar.

"Yes, you are, encouraging another man to look at your naked flesh."

"I'm not doing this James," I whispered, and I got up and went back to the bathroom. I locked the door, put the toilet seat down and sat on it. I felt angry, but I couldn't risk an argument. James was drunk, it was Christmas, and we were guests in someone else's house. I'd have to go back down and do my best to diffuse the whole thing. I gave it a few minutes, and then I went back down to join the others. Liam had gone into the living room and turned the TV on. I went into the dining room where Eve was chatting with James.

"Hi hun," she said brightly. I sat down next to James and put my hand on his knee. He didn't respond.

"Are you okay?" I asked.

"As if you care," he whispered back to me.

Eve had got up to put the kettle back on and was

leaning against the counter in the kitchen waiting while it boiled noisily.

"Of course I care," I said.

"Why did you show another man your body?"

"I didn't!" I said, exasperatedly.

"Yes you did. You lifted your top and showed Liam your body. I bet he is thinking about your vagina right now."

I couldn't help but laugh.

"Are you joking?" I asked, hoping that he would say yes.

"No, I'm not joking. It's no joke when your girlfriend is a slut. I bet he is thinking about fucking you right now."

I looked into the living room where Liam was lying on the sofa. He had his bowl of pretzels balanced on his belly, and he had a bottle of beer clasped in his hand. He was watching the *Top Gear Christmas* special and emitted the occasional raucous belly laugh. He reminded me of a young Homer Simpson.

"Well if he is, he doesn't look particularly aroused James," I said, unable to take what he was saying seriously.

"Oh believe me, *Anna,* he'll be storing it all up. He'll have that image of his slut sister-in-law stored in the *wank bank."* I stifled a laugh. On the one hand, being called a slut was not in the slightest bit funny, but what James was saying was so ridiculous that laughter was the only appropriate response. I was certain that Liam did not find me attractive in the slightest. He had been with Eve since they were sixteen, so I had known him for almost half of my life, and he called me Squirt. Even if there was the slightest bit of attraction there, I am sure the sight of my food filled belly, spilling over my unfastened top button would not be an image fast tracking its way to the *wank bank*. And even if Liam did decide to think about me in that way, what did that have to do with James? Liam is perfectly entitled to think about whatever he likes! James was a tosser. One hundred percent. A ridiculous, jealous, possessive, alcoholic tosser. I was certain.

"Are you okay?" Eve asked James, coming back in from the kitchen and noticing his unhappy expression.

"It's just cold in here Eve." He was such an actor. Of course, he was referring to me being cold toward him, but Eve was oblivious to this and tried to think of ways to warm him up.

"Oh, I'll get you a blanket if you like? Or shall I turn the heating up?"

"No, I think I will go to bed thank you Eve."

I breathed a sigh of relief. He went up to bed and Eve, and I sat chatting. It was only about nine-thirty, but already Liam was snoring, his bowl of pretzels rising and falling on his belly with each breath.

"He always does this," Eve said, sounding annoyed.

"He's harmless though," I said.

We chatted for around an hour, and I thought I had given James enough time to fall asleep, sure that when he awoke in the morning he would be in a different mood altogether and we could get home without any arguing. I brushed my teeth, washed my face and crept into the bedroom as quietly as I could. The stench of alcohol hit me as soon as I opened the door. I got undressed as quietly as I could and gingerly pulled the covers back so not to disturb the sleeping James. I lay my head on the pillow and relaxed onto the bed.

"Why?" James whispered, sitting up suddenly and pulling the covers from me.

"Why what?" I said.

"Why didn't you give me a cuddle when you climbed into bed?"

"I didn't want to wake you up."

"Bullshit, it's because you hate me."

"What? No, I don't."

"Why did you ask me what was wrong and then ignore me when I told you what it was?"

"I didn't ignore you, James; I just don't think you've got a point."

"Of course I fucking well have. You humiliated

me down there, now tell me why?"

"James, I don't think now is the time to have this discussion. I can see that you want to talk about it, and it's obviously important to you, but we're both drunk, and I don't think that we will see things rationally tonight."

"I said why?" he said, pulling the covers from me again.

"And I said I would discuss it tomorrow; please keep your voice down."

"Anna if you don't tell me why then I am going to shout as loud as I can. I don't care who hears me. TELL ME WHY."

"No," I answered, pulling the covers back onto my naked body. James pulled them off again.

"I am not going to let you rest until you do as I say, now tell me why."

"Tell you why what?"

"Tell me why you pretended to give a shit about me."

"No, we can talk tomorrow."

My mind was racing; if things carried on like this, my decision would be made for me. If James didn't stop and take a time out I would definitely be leaving him; there was not going to be another chance. I tried hard to get him to see.

"Look, baby; we are both drunk, we are both tired, we can talk about it tomorrow."

"We are talking about it now."

"I don't want to. I think it's a bad idea," I said, trying to hold his hand and get him to calm down.

"Well, I do. Why should we do what you want?"

"Oh James. I am going to sleep in Eve's bed."

I stood up to get my clothes. He grabbed them from me and threw them across the room.

"Fine I will go naked if that's what you want," I said, heading for the door. Of course, he stepped in front of it.

"Move," I said.

"No! You are staying here until you tell me why."

"Just move James."

"Or?"

"Okay, fine. Don't move." I sat on the bed and put my head in my hands. I felt tired and drunk and angry and sick. I just wanted to lie down and go to sleep. He stood in front of me.

"Answer," he demanded.

I ignored him and lay down on the bed, pulling the covers up to my chin. He whisked them away and then turned on the light.

"Answer," he said again. I ignored him and pulled the covers back over myself and wrapped them around my body. James stood over me.

"Answer. The. Question."

Again I ignored him, and he began to pull the covers. I clung tightly to them, and he shook me angrily.

"Let me get back into bed."

I let go of the covers slightly so that there was enough for him to put over himself. Maybe he would lie down and go to sleep? He lay next to me and moved up close so that he was touching me. His rancid alcoholic breath felt warm on the back of my neck, and my skin crawled.

"Answer," he said again, and I tried to get up to leave, but he quickly wrapped his arms around me so that he was holding me tightly with my arms at my side.

"You will stay here until you answer."

"Let me go," I said, feeling the rage gathering in my chest. My breathing was rapid, and my heart was racing.

"You are going nowhere, you ugly little slut, until you have answered my question."

He squeezed tighter on my body, and I responded by kicking backwards so that my heel caught his shin.

"How fucking dare you kick me? You violent little cunt."

He picked me up and threw me back down onto the bed.

"James be quiet," I pleaded, I still didn't want Eve or Liam to hear. I may as well have said, 'Can you abuse me quietly please so that no one will find out?' Because if they had heard him, they would have called the police and that is what he deserved for his disgusting behaviour.

"I don't care who knows that you are a dirty little slut. Everybody who thinks that you are nice will find out eventually that you are nothing but a filthy little whore, a nothing, from a drain, who wants all men to fancy her. Flaunting your flesh at your brother-in-law because you want him to think about fucking you. You're nothing but a filthy, dirty, ugly pig and I never want to see you again."

"Good! Good, because I never want to see you again. Go away, go away and leave me alone."

I was crying. I was astounded at the rotten, toxic filth that was ever-present in James's psyche. I couldn't have thought of half of the things that he accused me of and called me. Where did it come from? I certainly didn't deserve it. I certainly hadn't caused it, even though he appeared to believe that he was justified in his treatment of me.

"Fine, I will go away. I will go away, and you will never have me to take the piss out of again. Do you hear me? Do you? You filthy, ugly, stinking little cunt. I have given you everything, and this is how you repay me, you selfish little bitch."

He was on top of me now. His nose was touching mine, and I struggled to breathe with his weight on my chest.

"I hope you die. If I could get away with it, I would smash every one of your teeth into your throat right now. That's what you deserve you evil little SLUT."

He pushed me hard into the bed and then got up and walked over to the window; his breathing was fast and shallow. I took my chance and ran from the room, down the stairs, down into Liam and Eve's basement. I didn't dare put the light on because I didn't want him to know where I had gone. I tried to be as quiet as possible. The basement was used as a games room, and I knew there was a pool table pushed almost against the wall. I knew it wasn't quite flush with the wall and I knew there was just enough room for me to squeeze into the gap, so that is what I did. I crouched uncomfortably, naked, between a pool table and a wall, in a dark, cold basement, in the middle of the night on Boxing Day. I knew that my life had reached a turning point. This was the final straw; it had to be.

THE ESCAPE

I crouched there, in the cold and dark, for what seemed like an eternity. I could hear James moving about upstairs and I could hear Liam's snores directly above me. I was cold and I had pins and needles. Eventually, all became silent, apart from the snores, and I began to hope that James had fallen asleep. I crouched and listened, like a frightened animal, with my bladder fit to burst. I was going to have to venture back up the stairs to the toilet; I couldn't hold it in much longer.

Slowly and quietly I crawled out from behind the table. I crept across the basement room and then began to climb the stairs, slowly, a painful tingling in my legs as the feeling began to return. I glanced at Liam, he was still asleep, the room was lit with the lights from the Christmas tree, and it occurred to me that I should turn them off, but as I was naked and bursting for the loo, it wasn't a priority. I padded up the stairs and into the bathroom and finally flopped onto the toilet. As I peed, I noticed that James's toilet bag was no longer on the shelf. Perhaps he had gone? I partly hoped he had, but I also knew that this would mean he was drink driving. I washed my hands and wrapped a towel around myself then I crept along the hallway to the bedroom that we were supposed to be sleeping in. The door was wide open, and I poked my head around it nervously. The bed was empty, the covers were on the floor, and there was no sign of James. My clothes that had been in our shared bag were on the floor in a pile. I crept to the window and looked out. The car was gone. I thought about ringing the police and reporting him for drink driving, but I didn't quite have the guts to do it. I lay on the bed and pulled the covers up over myself. My phone was under the pillow, and there were twenty-seven missed calls from James. I couldn't bring myself to listen to the messages, and my battery was low, I'd left my charger in the car. I turned my phone off and closed my eyes and waited for the morning.

I must have fallen asleep because when I opened my eyes, it was light. At first, I thought that everything was alright, but almost immediately horrible memories of the night before began to trickle into my mind. I lay quietly and listened for Eve or Liam; I didn't know if they were up or not yet. I didn't know what the time was. I was thirsty, and I had a headache. I lay for a few more minutes then I heard footsteps and low voices. After a moment or two more, there was a knock on the bedroom door.

"Come in," I said, and Eve pushed the bedroom

door open.

"Anna, James, I don't know if you realise…..oh….where's James?"

"Oh Eve," I said, and I began to cry. She sat on the edge of the bed and listened astounded as I told her everything.

"Look at your arms," she said. I looked to where her gaze fell; there were fingermarks around my upper arms. Those finger marks seemed to be a permanent part of me, they changed colour as the days and weeks passed, until they were just faint yellow spots, ready to be replaced by fresh, angry, black and red painful bruises. I couldn't recall a time when I had lived with James where there hadn't been at least one bruise on my body, one bruise that he had put there. Sometimes the bruise would be a faint tinge of colour, at others, it would be a lumpy, raised painful mass. And the bruises were just the physical signs, there were all the other injuries too, from the verbal insults and the mental game playing. Eve held my hand as I spoke, and then she said, "I feel sick. I'm going to be sick." Then she got up and went to the bathroom.

I heard the toilet flush and the sound of Eve brushing her teeth, then she came back in to talk to me.

"I can't believe that he was doing that to you here, in my house. I can't believe I didn't hear him.

Anna. I thought he was the bee's knees, I thought he was perfect for you, after everything you have been through. This is the last thing that I would have expected. I am so shocked."

I just lay on the bed with my eyes half closed as she spoke.

"I thought he was all of those things too," I said. "Eve, do you mind telling Liam while I have a shower? I don't think I can face telling him."

"Of course I don't mind."

I went for a shower and gave Eve enough time to tell Liam what had happened. I stood in the stream of water, trying to work out what I would do. Go and pack up my things and camp out at my parents' until they got back from Spain. Then what? Hattie's? My place? I knew that I couldn't live with my mum and dad, as much as I loved them, it would drive me insane.

I dried and dressed, put on some make-up and then I switched on my phone, my stomach churning nervously as it began to vibrate with text messages from James.

Why won't you talk to me?

Anna I am so sorry. How can I make it up to you?

What can I do to prove that I love you? I'm sorry for everything I am nothing without you. Please forgive me.

I know that I have acted like a complete pig; I will

do whatever it takes. Tell me how to make this better.

I turned my phone back off and went downstairs. Eve was making a pot of coffee.

"Where's Liam?" I asked.

"He's gone for a walk. I have never seen him so angry; I thought he was gonna take the car and go looking for him."

I was surprised, Liam was usually so laid back.

"I've been thinking about his ex. You know, the one who went to prison?"

"Yeah," I said.

"What do you think really went on there?"

"I know she definitely went to prison," I said, "but I'm pretty sure she was subjected to some strong provocation. I could have easily stabbed him on more than one occasion, and that knowledge terrifies me."

"Well you didn't Anna, and you can leave him and get on with your life now. A lucky escape before he can do you any lasting damage." She shuddered as she spoke. Just then Liam came back in.

"Squirt," he said, putting his arms around me. "I can't believe it. Are you okay?"

"I'll be fine," I told him.

"I can't believe that he thought I was perving over you," he said. "It's made me feel weird."

"Don't worry about it," I told him. "He talks

nonsense."

"What's your plan?"

"I don't know, probably go back and pack a bag then stay at mum and dads' for a while."

"I'll take you back whenever you want," Eve told me.

"Thanks, I'm going to be stuck for a car, because I am certain that he won't let me drive the Golf."

"Borrow my car," Eve said. "I won't need it for a few days at least."

"That would be helpful actually. Thank you."

I finished my coffee and replied to James's messages.

You can't do anything to put it right. I will be back in about an hour to pick up some stuff. I'd appreciate it if you weren't in while I am there. Thanks.

I put my phone on the table. It flashed up a low battery message. Eve poured me another coffee, and I drank it quickly, twisting my hair around my finger nervously. Eve and Liam both stared at me with worried expressions on their faces.

"Do you want me to come with you?" Liam asked.

"If he won't go out while I get my stuff it will probably be a good idea if you are there."

My phone vibrated with James's reply.

I will go out if that's what you want. I'm sorry for

everything

"It's fine,' I told Liam, 'He isn't going to be there."

I just wanted to get packing and leaving over with, so I set off alone in Eve's car to the house that I shared with James.

My phone finally gave up and switched itself off. I pressed play on Eve's CD player. She had been listening to Elbow; it was a live CD. I quickly turned it back off, I didn't feel able to cope with the emotions that those songs stirred in me. I drove for ten minutes or so, making a mental list of all the things that I would need for the next few days. I thought it would take me about half-an-hour to get everything together and then once I was out of there I could think about what my next step was.

I turned the music back on and allowed myself to think about Dylan. Thinking about Dylan had become a guilty past-time; I felt as though I was betraying James when I thought about him, but now that didn't matter. James was never going to be able to fill Dylan's shoes, and although I hadn't been looking for a replacement for Dylan, James's character measured up so poorly against Dylan's that it was almost laughable.

I thought about all the times that Dylan and I had spent with Eve and Liam. I thought about the way that Dylan always only saw the good in me. He knew that I wasn't perfect, but he focused on what he loved about me, and I always felt safe and loved when I was with him. I could be myself one hundred percent, and I hadn't even realised that it was possible to become so afraid of saying or doing the wrong thing. I thought about how James had managed to make me begin to believe that I was somehow a bad person, that he could see something in me that others couldn't that he knew my true, bad motives. It was all bullshit, and I realised that I had Dylan to thank for giving me so much protective love and helping me grow in confidence. I think that if I hadn't had my six years with Dylan, James's bullshit would have taken a stronger and more dangerous hold of me. I drove with tears running down my face, I wished so much that I could see Dylan. I wanted to feel his arms around me; I wanted to hear his voice, smell his skin. I did what I always did when I felt like that and I began to imagine him. I tried to recall every detail of his face, the sound of his voice, the smell of his skin, the way he walked. I was so afraid that those memories would begin to fade. I tried to remember his hands, but all I could see in my mind's eye were James's hands. I couldn't believe it; I felt so angry with him for intruding on my memories.

I pulled into the driveway of the house, and I took a few deep breaths. James' Audi wasn't there; he had respected my wishes and gone out. The front door was unlocked, I was glad because I realised at the last minute that I didn't have a key. I went inside and looked around. The dishes from Christmas Day were piled up next to the dishwasher, and the kitchen was very cold. I picked up the house phone and rang Eve to tell her that James wasn't in, she breathed a sigh of relief and so did Liam. I searched for a spare charger for my phone, but there wasn't one. I climbed the stairs to the bedroom. The bed was unmade, and the clothes that James had been wearing were lying on the floor. I began to pack my clothes, I couldn't think straight, so I got a bin liner and just tipped everything into it. It was easier than trying to work out what I would need for a few days. I dragged the bag down the stairs and put into the boot of Eve's car, then I got the laundry basket and began to put pictures and trinkets into it, wrapping them in newspaper as I went along. I looked in the bottom of my wardrobe and found the Elbow lyrics that Dylan had bought for me. I wrapped them up in a couple of layers of newspaper and put them into the basket. I heard the crunch of James's car pulling up into the gravel driveway, and my heart sank. I hadn't been there for very long. He walked into the house. I looked up and said hello, his eyes were red and his lip was quivering.

"I'm not quite finished, sorry," I said.

"Anna, please, please don't go," James begged, he

walked towards me, and I backed away.

"I have to go. It was the last chance; you did it again."

"Anna, please, please, we can work through this, we can. I love you." He had walked over to me; tears were running down his face. "I'm sorry, I'm so sorry," he said, holding his arms out to me.

"James, I can't. I can't stay. I'm sorry it has come to this."

His face crumpled, he put his hands to his face, and he began to sob.

"Anna, oh Anna, why did I have to ruin everything? Please, please, please give me one more chance. I promise you I will not fuck up again." He fell to his knees and put his arms around my legs.

"James, please don't do this. I can't stay. I made a promise to myself. I tried to get you to stop last night, and you wouldn't listen. It's gone too far now. Plus, Eve and Liam know now."

"Anna, I love you. I can't live without you. Please." He was sobbing and still clinging to my legs.

"I'll do anything, anything, just tell me what you want me to do."

"James, no. I can't."

"Anna, you love me."

"I'm not sure that I do James. How can I love the man who tells me that he hopes I die and that he would like to smash every one of my teeth in?"

"I am so sorry. I'm so sorry. Please let me make it up to you. Please, Anna."

"James, get off my legs, I can't give you another chance. You have had all of your chances."

"Why are you so heartless?" he pleaded.

My temper flared.

"What? Heartless?" I shouted. "You said you wanted me to die. I hid from you in the basement. I was scared, I was cold, and I was naked and humiliated. How can you call me heartless? I have never ever treated you or anyone else the way you treated me last night, so if you don't mind, I'd like to pack my stuff in peace."

"I can't let you go," he stood up and took a step towards me.

"You have to James. I am not staying." I backed away from him

"I can't let you go. I can't lose you. You aren't going."

"I am going."

I began to walk backwards up the stairs. James was good at this, backing me into a corner.

"James, I am going."

"No, no you aren't, I can't let you go. We are going to sort it out; you just need to see how sorry I am."

I was at the top of the stairs now and was being

backed along the landing toward the bathroom which was where I usually ended up. I tried to work out how this was going to go.

"Anna, hear me out, please."

"Okay, tell me what you want to say to me."

"I will call Respect again, and I will ask them what they suggest."

"Okay, that's good," I encouraged.

"I'll do it now. Please wait here for me."

"Okay, I will wait while you see what they suggest, but I still intend to leave James. Don't get your hopes up."

He went out to the car to make the call, and I continued packing my belongings. I wondered how I had managed to accumulate so much junk in such a small space of time. After half-an-hour or so, he came back inside. "What did they say?" I asked.

"They said I have to go on a perpetrator program," he told me. "I am going to enrol on the nearest one now."

"I think it's the best thing for you to do James, you will never be happy if you don't sort this issue out. It's obviously dogged you all your life."

"No, it hasn't, it's just when I'm with you. I only get angry when I'm with you."

"What?"

"The woman on the phone said that you need to ring them too because you started the violence."

"What?" I said again. "I was responding to your behaviour."

"It's never going to get sorted unless you take responsibility for your behaviour too Anna."

Again I felt my temper flare.

"My behaviour? You are the one who tries to control me. You push and push until I break, you never let anything lie. It's not me James; I'm not taking the blame for it."

I was shaking and crying as I spoke and the more my words tumbled out, the angrier I became. How could he try and shift the blame onto me?

"I have never treated anyone the way you have treated me. I have never known anything like it. It's disgusting; it's absolutely fucking disgusting."

I had taken a few steps forward as I tried to leave, but James blocked my way.

"James, don't do this. Don't stop me from leaving."

He stood in front of me, his breathing rapid.

"You're not going," he said simply. "I won't let you."

I felt the swirling ball of rage gathering in my chest.

"James. Let me go."

"No."

"Let me go," I repeated.

"No."

By now my heart was beating twice as fast. I was furious, and I wanted to leave. I pushed him in the chest.

"Let me go," I demanded.

He grabbed my arms and held them tightly by my side.

"You're not going," he said, backing me against the wall and squeezing my arms tightly by my side.

I wriggled and squirmed, trying to get him to let go of me, and I sunk my teeth into his chest and bit him hard. He let go of my arms momentarily, but I had lost it by then, rage was coursing through my body, and I just bit him harder and harder. I could feel the gristle beneath his skin slowly yielding to my teeth. I felt so angry that I wanted to bite a chunk of his flesh away. He grabbed my hair and pulled it hard, I could feel it coming away from my scalp, burning and stinging as each hair was prized slowly from its root, but I didn't care, I was too angry. All the pent-up anger and frustration, all the bitterness, all the vile toxic abuse that James had filled me with was spilling back out of me, and I felt out of control. I felt hatred and anger, and I wanted to hurt him.

He pulled my right arm up behind my back painfully. He pulled it hard, forcing the joint out of place and a searing pain shot through my shoulder and back.

"Stop biting me!" he screamed, and the shock of

the pain in my shoulder made me let go of him. He pushed me down to the floor and smashed my face into the ground before getting up and leaving.

Again, anger took over, and I jumped up and ran after him, hammering my fists into his back. He ran down the stairs and picked up the laundry basket which had my carefully wrapped belongings in it.

"Is this your stuff?" he asked.

"Yes, it is," I said.

He picked out the nearest item and unwrapped it. It was a photograph of my parents, and he hurled it against the wall so that it smashed into a thousand pieces.

"What are you doing? Stop!" I screamed as he picked up the next thing and did the same. My *Mirrorball* lyrics were in the basket, and I began to panic. Of everything in there, that was the most precious thing.

"James please, please stop," I begged, but he carried on. I launched myself at him and tried to pull him away, but he laughed at me. I pummeled him with my fists, but he dodged me as he destroyed my treasured belongings one by one. I tried to think of a way to stop him. If I grabbed the lyrics, he would probably manage to get them from me, but he wasn't listening to my pleas for him to stop. I guess that he was pleased that he had found a way to really hurt me.

"Please, James please stop."

His face was contorted, and the kitchen floor was covered in debris. Broken glass, bits of china and shards of wood littered the quarry tiles. Did he have no conscience? How could he do this to me? I made a grab for the lyrics, and he tried to snatch them from me, just as I had thought he would. I wasn't going to give him them though, not without a fight, and I kneed him hard between his legs. He doubled over in agony, and I began to run. I ran out into the driveway and began to fumble for the keys to Eve's car, which were wedged into my pocket. I had the picture under my arm as I fumbled for the keys and James soon caught up with me on the drive. I clutched the lyrics to my chest and began to run, but he easily caught up with me. He pushed me to the ground and began to try and prize my arms open. I kicked at him, my booted feet making contact with his stomach. I was so angry and kicking him felt good, I wanted to kick him to the ground and never stop, but he soon got the better of me. He wrestled the lyrics out of my arms and held them above his head.

"James no, please don't, I am begging you, please don't destroy them."

He marched back into the house carrying them, and I followed him, desperate to get my precious gift from Dylan back. Back inside the house, he locked the door and put the keys into his pocket. He was pacing the kitchen, the lyrics under his arm, and I stood, rooted to the spot, staring at him, wondering what on earth was going to come next. Finally, he began to speak.

"You can't leave me."

"What?" I said, surprised.

"You can't leave me; I love you too much."

My mind raced. He loved me? Why did he hurt me then? But if I played this right, maybe I could get away with those lyrics? Maybe, if I played along with his little game, I could lull him into thinking that I was going to stay and get out of the house with my final piece of Dylan intact.

"What do you suggest then?" I asked.

"I think that if you just didn't wind me up as much, we would be okay."

My blood boiled. He was blaming me again. I took a deep breath. I knew it was all bullshit, but I had my eye on the prize- my lyrics - proof of Dylan's love, proof of his existence, something that showed how much I meant to him, how special I was to him. I waited for James to speak.

"Anna, I think it would be helpful if *you* rang the Respect Phoneline to talk about your violence."

Oh, my God, the guy was completely in denial. He pulled his t-shirt down to show me his chest. He pointed to the bright red angry welts, the perfect indentation of my teeth.

"Okay, I'll call them, give me the number then."

He put my lyrics down on the side and went to get his phone. Where could I hide them? He would only be out of the room for a minute. I picked them up and put them under my arm, but he walked back in before I could think of anywhere. He handed me the number, and I went up to the bedroom and closed the door. I could hear him moving about downstairs, and I wished he would go out.

Where could I hide the lyrics? I scanned around the bedroom. The wardrobe was too obvious, as was under the bed and in my chest of drawers, which I had emptied anyway. I dialled the number that James had given me, nervous butterflies in my belly: "Hello, this is the Respect Phoneline, how may I help you?"

"I'd like to talk to somebody about my relationship," I said, my voice shaking.

"Okay, can I take your first name please?"

"Anna."

"Hello Anna, my name is Nicola, tell me about your relationship."

"My partner thinks that I am abusive, but I know that it is him."

"Okay Anna, tell me about what happens when your partner thinks that you are being abusive."

I tried to talk to Nicola, I really did, but I was

sobbing and choking on my own words. Eventually, I managed to tell her about what had happened at Eve's, I then told her about me trying to leave James and how he had stopped me from going and that since then I had just lost control completely and begun to fight him. I told her about me biting him and kneeing him in the groin, and she listened carefully.

"Anna, James is abusive, and now you are using violence too. This is a very dangerous situation. You are not safe. Anna, my advice to you is to ring someone to come to the house for you right now. You need to get to a safe place immediately. Ring the police if you have to, now, from your bedroom. If you don't leave James, there is a strong possibility that one of you will end up dead, or at the very least seriously injured. *It is not safe for you to be around him, Anna.*"

I was so shocked.

I had known that it wasn't good, but I didn't realise that it was dangerous. Was it that dangerous? Nicola was an expert; she knew what she was talking about, she wouldn't have said it just for fun. I hung up the phone and lay on my bed staring at the ceiling, then I stood up and put the lyrics behind the wardrobe. That would have to do for now.

I began to dial Eve's number. I'd ask Liam to come to the house for me. The phone began to ring and ring and ring. Great, they weren't answering! I tried Hattie, but she didn't answer either. Chloe didn't have a land line, only a mobile and I tried and tried to recall her number, but I could only remember the first four digits. I was stuck.

What could I do? Should I ring the police? I just couldn't. I couldn't bring myself to do it. Was it shame stopping me? Embarrassment? The fact that James was injured? What if he made it look like I had been the one doing the abusing? Would I end up like Daniella? I sat with the phone in my hand. I turned it over and over, trying to come up with a plan, but in the end, I gave up and went back downstairs to James.

He was sitting at the kitchen table, he had opened a bottle of wine, and he looked up at me expectantly.

"What did they say?" he asked.

"Do you want to know, really James? Do you want the truth?"

"Of course I do."

"I told them word for word, blow by blow, what has happened between us since yesterday and they strongly recommend that I leave you as soon as possible because it is not safe for us to be together."

"And what are you going to do?" James asked.

"I don't know," I lied. I did know, I was going to leave, as soon as I could, but I knew if I told him that he would start again and I wanted to avoid any further incidents.

"I need a wee," I said walking away. I sat on the toilet, trying to formulate a plan. I went to the washbasin to wash my hands and gasped in shock as I caught site of my reflection in the mirror. I needn't have worried about people thinking that I was the abuser. My face was a lumpy mess. James had banged my face on the floor, and there was an angry red carpet burn underneath my eye, which was swollen, and a large lump on my forehead. I took off my cardigan and looked at my arms. Sure enough, new red finger marks had appeared pretty much on top of the bruises from the previous day. I was a mess. I had to get away. Why had I ever thought it was safe to go back to the house alone?

I went back into the kitchen. James had got me a glass and poured me some wine. He gestured for me to sit beside him and I did as he suggested, it was best to keep the peace so that I could get away safely. I thanked him for the drink and took a small sip. I didn't want to drink too much in case I got an opportunity to leave.

"You know Anna, I know we have our problems, but I do love you. I want to be with you, and now that I am going to go to the special counselling group you have to give me a chance. I can't change if you won't help me."

In my head, I thought *bullshit.* But I said nothing. Time passed slowly, and eventually, it got dark outside.

"Let's get a takeaway and watch a film," he suggested.

"Okay," I said, hoping that he would go out for the food. I hoped in vain, and he ordered it to be delivered.

Our food arrived, and James lit the fire and put on the film. It was so strange, cosying up with him, knowing that I was going to leave and that this evening was all an act. After our food, James suggested that we go to bed, and I tried to get him to go up without me so that I could escape, but he hung around waiting for me, and in the end, I went up with him. I got into bed, I kept my clothes on, and I turned my back to him. He lay behind me, as close as he could and put his arms around me. He began to try and undress me, but I told him to stop, and he did.

"I just want to feel close to you," he told me, and I could tell that he was crying. I planned to wait until he fell asleep and then I would leave. He kept his arms tightly around me, and I stared into the darkness waiting for him to start snoring. Eventually, after what seemed like forever, he fell asleep, and I quietly climbed out of bed, picked up my precious lyrics and crept downstairs. He had locked the doors and hidden the keys, so I had to climb out of the kitchen window. I ran across the drive, unlocked Eve's car and breathed a huge sigh of relief as I reversed off the driveway and away from the house, away from James and to safety.

ELBOW

I drove to Eve's with my one bin liner full of clothes and my Elbow lyrics. I guessed that I would never see any of my other belongings again. I couldn't call her and tell her that I was on my way because my phone still hadn't been charged up. I thought that I ought to stop and try and put a bit of make-up on my face. I didn't want to turn up on Eve and Liam's doorstep in the middle of the night with my face in such a mess. It was so embarrassing. I was too scared to pull over though; I thought that James would wake up and realise I had gone. It wouldn't take a genius to guess where I was going and his Audi would easily catch up with Eve's little Fiat 500, particularly the way he liked to drive.

My heart was in my mouth all the way to Eve's, and when I pulled up outside, there were no lights on. I locked the car and climbed the steps to their front door, then rang the doorbell. I felt so bad for disturbing them and had considered just waiting in the car until morning, but it was freezing, and I felt scared.

After a few seconds and no movement or sound inside the house, I rang the doorbell a second and then third time. Lights appeared in the doorway and then Liam finally let me in. "

Shit," he said when he saw me. "Eve," he shouted up the stairs, "it's Anna. Shit, what the hell happened? What has he done to your face?"

He boiled the kettle and Eve came downstairs, bleary-eyed with bed hair.

"I'm so sorry to wake you," I said, as she came over to me and put her arms around me.

"Don't say sorry," she whispered. "What has happened? We should have come with you."

I told them all about what had happened, and I reassured them that they weren't to blame. Why were other people taking responsibility here? James was the one who had caused all of this. I wondered if he had realised I was gone yet. I imagined him angrily ringing my phone, but it was switched off and silent. Maybe he was still asleep, snoring and oblivious?

The next morning Liam went into town and bought me a charger for my phone. I didn't feel like going out because of the marks on my face. I plugged my phone in, but I didn't turn it on, afraid of what would be on there waiting for me. We talked about what I should do. What were my options? I was sure that James was going to make me pay my half of the rent and I didn't think that I had a way out of that as we had both signed the tenancy agreement making me as responsible for paying it as he was.

I could probably stay at one of my friends, just while I got some money together. I would need to buy a car too; there was no way I could manage without one. I had £600 in a savings account, and I would have to use that to buy a car with. I didn't think that I was going to be driving anything particularly reliable in the near future, but at least it would be mine and not his. It would be good not to be beholden to James in any way shape or form.

Eventually I plucked up the courage to turn on my phone, and sure enough, messages from James began to flood in. They were in no particular order, and some of them were from the previous morning when I had been driving back to our house to get my belongings. From the messages, I gathered that James had woken up about an hour-and-a-half after I had left and realised that I had gone. Initially, his messages had been nice.

Anna, where are you? I am so worried, come home. Xxx

I'm guessing you have left me. I suppose I can't really blame you. Please let me know that you are safe. Xxx

Just so you know, I am heartbroken. I have nothing and no one; my life is empty. I miss you and will love you always Anna. Xxx

As the hours had ticked by, James had become progressively more aggressive.

Why are you taking the piss out of me like this?

I can't believe you have snuck away like a coward.

Don't think that you will be welcome back here for your things. You are nothing but an arsehole.

I've gathered all of your crap together, and as soon as the tip opens in the morning, that is where it will be going.

Each message made me feel a little sicker than the last, but I was determined not to reply in anger. I wanted to wait, gather my thoughts, decide what it was that I needed to say to him and then say it, clearly and concisely, hopefully ensuring that I never needed to talk to him again. A few moments later, another message appeared on my mobile; it was from June.

James has just shown me his chest. I can't believe that you attacked him so viciously. I knew that you were bad news when he told me you had hit him. If you think you are going to get away with this, you have got another thing coming.

Anger began to swirl in my chest again. How dare she get involved? All my resolve to stay calm in my responses to James dissolved in the face of this new anger, and I began to write a message.

I have just turned my phone on and received your messages. One minute you miss me and love me and the next minute I am an arsehole! Which is it, James? All I wanted was to have a nice time and a good relationship with you. All you had to do was treat me with respect. It is not a lot to ask, but you do not seem to be capable of it. I want nothing to do with you ever again. And as for your mother and her threats, well she can just fuck off. YOU MIGHT HAVE A BITE MARK ON YOUR CHEST, BUT I CAN'T GO OUT BECAUSE OF WHAT YOU DID TO MY FACE.

I sent the message, and then I began to type another one.

Your son is an abuser. I cannot go out because of what he has done to my face. It is not the first time. I'm certain I won't be his last, and I am definitely not his first victim. Don't threaten me again or I will go to the police.

"Anna, are you okay? Who are you texting?" Eve looked concerned.

"I have just got really angry and sent him and his stupid old bag of a mother a message."

I showed Eve the messages.

"Just ignore them now, they aren't worth it, they really aren't. You are so much better than them."

"I'm just so angry, and it's so unfair. I haven't done anything wrong, yet they are making me out to be some kind of monster."

I was crying angry tears.

"I am so fucked off. Why did it have to be so shit? After what happened with Dylan, wasn't I due something good? But no, it has to be more shit, and I am fed up and fucked off."

I was feeling extremely sorry for myself and had to stop myself from stamping my foot like a five-year-old.

"I hate that self-righteous old bag and her tosser of a son. He's a smarmy, arrogant tosser. In fact, he's a big fucking mummy's boy who still needs his arse wiping! Arghhhhh."

Eve just sat and waited for me to stop ranting, and then we looked at each other and began to laugh. I wasn't sure what we were laughing at, and neither was she, I think it was the image of June following James to the toilet with a giant loo roll that had just popped into my mind.

"You are going to get through this; the good stuff is just around the corner for you. It's just unfortunate that James ever came into your life."

"I just feel so stupid for trusting him," I said, resting my head in my hands.

"He had us all fooled though. I thought he was wonderful, Liam thought he was wonderful. No one suspected that he wasn't wonderful, not for a second, and I am so shocked."

"That's the other thing though, I am going to have to tell people, and I don't think that I can face doing it."

"I will tell them for you. Who do you need to tell? Make a list, and I will tell them, you don't need to worry."

"Mum and dad, Chloe, Sophie, Hattie; although she already knows what he was like."

"I will tell mum and dad. I don't mind ringing Chloe and Sophie and telling them, and you may as well just let Hattie know that you are staying here and that you have left him, just send her a text or something."

So that is what we did. I let Eve tell my parents and my friends that I had left James and I sent Hattie a text message. She replied quickly.

Hi, I am sorry, but not surprised at what has happened Anna. Please never go back to him. A leopard does not change its spots. I'm so proud of you for getting out, you are strong, and you have just proved it. Many women don't feel that they can leave. You have done the right thing. You know where I am, let me know when you feel up to seeing me. Stay strong. X

A message from James followed Hattie's.

Oooh CAPS LOCK. You dickhead.

I showed it to Eve. "Oh my God, he is so immature!"

"He is, he is a big fucking baby."

"Cock," Eve said. "You deserve so much more."

I didn't respond to James again, and I didn't hear from June. Everyone was shocked to discover what James was really like and Chloe appeared to be wracked with guilt, somehow believing that she was responsible for the whole situation. I bought myself the best car I could with my available funds and I wrote to the letting agent and told them that I had left him because it was not safe for me to stay and that I expected that he would either continue the tenancy or pay the outstanding rent, which, after some to-ing and fro-ing, he did.

I moved into Hattie's spare room and started all over again. Here I was, ten years after leaving home, and all I had to show for myself was a fourteen-year-old Ford Fiesta with a slow puncture and a hell of a lot of anger and grief. It was safe to say I was not in a good place! I promised everyone that I would never go back to James, that I would have nothing to do with him and I kept my promise, well for the first couple of months at least.

It was one morning in March that I made the big mistake. I had dreamt about James as I often did, and in the dream, he was trying to escape from an evil spirit. He was frightened and needed my help. When I woke up, I felt sad. I missed him, and the dream had made me feel worried about him. I got ready for work and went to get into my car. Hattie was away on a residential trip, which meant that I was driving myself to work in my old banger. When I reached the car, I noticed that my tyre was completely flat, my heart sank, and I unlocked the boot and got out the foot pump. I was going to have to pump the tyre up from flat with it. Why didn't I take any notice when Dylan had shown me how to change a wheel? I attached the pump to the valve and began to pump the tyre up. My leg started to ache and feel tired, but then I began to think about June, and what a hypocrite she was, and how manipulative she was towards James and I began to get angry. The anger acted like some strength injection and suddenly pumping up the tyre became easy! I imagined that the foot pump was June's face, and as sick as that sounds, it worked, and the tyre was up in no time! I got into the car, put my new Elbow album into the CD player and drove to work. Poor James, with that for a mother, it was no wonder he was the way he was. I thought about sending him a message to see how he was, and then I told myself off for being so ridiculous. If I sent him a message, I'd be letting everyone down, including myself.

I thought about him all morning, I felt sorry for him, and I missed him. How could I miss someone who had treated me the way that James had? I don't know, but I did. I missed the nice James, the one that wasn't even real anyway. I think that if it had been any of the other days that I had received the message from him, then I would have had the strength to ignore it, but the dream had made me feel sorry for him, the music made me think of him buying me the tickets to go and see Elbow and I was caught off guard at a weak moment.

Hello, I can't stop thinking about you. I miss you, and I am sorry for everything. Love always, James xxx

I read the message, I wanted so much to reply, but I knew that it was a bad idea. Was it a bad idea? Was it? What harm could one little message do? Just one, to let him know that there were no hard feelings? Of course, one message led to another, and another and another. His tone had changed from angry spoilt child to sorrowful guilt-ridden adult, and he had been back in touch with the Respect helpline and had also begun to attend a perpetrator program. The messages went on throughout the day, eventually turning into a phone call after work. James encouraged me to ring and speak to the woman on the perpetrator program. In fact, he begged me to do it; he wanted me to hear from her how well he was doing. I told him that I would contact her and eventually, we ended the call. James told me that he was living with his parents and that it wasn't easy, that he cried all the time and that he hadn't told them about the perpetrator program because they didn't believe that he had a problem.

Hattie wasn't there for me to talk to and I didn't feel able to tell anyone else what I had just done so I kept my contact with James a secret, a secret from everyone until I saw Dee again. There was no point in paying to see Dee and keeping secrets from her. If I was to do that, I might as well put my money in the bin, so when I saw her, which was a couple of days later, I told her about the dream, the texts and the phone call. She looked worried but didn't tell me what to do. She asked if I was going to ring the woman from the group as James had suggested and I told her that I would.

"I think that you are feeling responsible for James. Your dream represented that need that you have to rescue him and then coincidentally, when he contacted you, and you realised that he was hurting, that has added to your desire to save him, and I am not sure that you being in contact with James is for the right reasons Anna, what do you think?"

I sat and thought for a moment. What did I think?

"I think you have probably got a point. I hate the thought of him being manipulated by his mum, and I hate the thought of him being sad and lonely, but he has been so horrible to me."

"But what do *you* gain by being in contact with him Anna? What is about James that makes it worthwhile for you?"

"I don't know. I mean, sometimes he is so nice, but then he is so awful too, and I don't know which person he is."

"Perhaps he is both, but do you need to worry about it? You don't have to take responsibility for him, and I am concerned that you are going to end up right back where you started."

"I won't. I won't live with him or let him get away with anything. I just think that while he is trying so hard to change, maybe I can help him and I know it's not my responsibility, but maybe there is a really good person in there, and he just needs to understand his behaviour."

"Maybe there is Anna, but it is his responsibility to find that out."

I felt annoyed, and I think it was because Dee was so right. It wasn't my responsibility and if James couldn't be trusted to change without my support then was he changing at all? Of course not.

Dee's words rang in my ears on the drive back to Hattie's, and I tried to work out what motivated me to stay in contact with him. Why didn't I despise him? How would I feel if I was watching someone close to me doing what I was doing? Probably disappointed and angry. What was it about my feelings that made me behave in such a stupid and dangerous way? I didn't know, but if I had, then I am pretty sure that I wouldn't be lying here now, trapped in this uncertain hell, at the mercy of Pam. I would be living my life, and I would have forgotten about James too. I would have gotten over him. If I could lose Dylan and still put one foot in front of the other then I could certainly live without James, so why was I such a fool?

Lying here, trying to make sense of it all, my only explanation is that I didn't accept that he was an abuser. I still harboured some self-blame, deep down in my most inner person, I still believed that I had somehow caused it, and although my rational mind told me otherwise, who is really ruled by their rational mind? Is it the rational mind that causes feelings and emotions? I think not. Deep down, I still believed that James was nice, that the James that I met right at the start was the real man and the abusive person was the imposter, the result of stress, bad upbringing, or alcoholism. My emotions told me that there was a nice man there, the nice man that I had trusted and allowed myself to believe that I had a happy future with. Once upon a time, I had known that I had a happy future and it was with Dylan. I had no doubts ever that he was the one for me and I was the one for him. I didn't imagine that death would steal him from me - it was unimaginable - so when he was gone, so was my happy future. Our future children, our future home in Edinburgh, the camper van we were going to buy together, the holidays we were going to take together, all gone. Dylan and I had made so many plans and we when we made those plans, I knew that they were our reality, they would definitely happen. We believed that we had forever to follow our dreams, but we didn't, we had hardly a moment together. When I lost Dylan, I was grieving for the man that I loved, and the future that we were going to have together. Everything that I believed was mine for the taking was ripped away from me, and until I met James, my future seemed like one long empty abyss. I couldn't make plans; I couldn't look forward because it was too painful, it wasn't my future, the one that I had *known* was going to happen. I was vulnerable, a little lost, and hurting when James came into my life and when he pretended that he loved me and that he wanted to make me happy, I let him in, but he was a wolf in sheep's clothing. It seemed that it was taking my emotions a little while to catch up with my rational mind. Was I going to listen to them or was I going to do the right thing and keep away? Was it possible to have just a little bit of contact with James and keep myself safe? I didn't know, all I do know is that I was more inclined to see the good in James than the bad, and although that didn't get me very far, or keep me safe, I'd still rather see the good than the bad in others.

James continued to contact me, and I called the woman from the perpetrator program. She was pleasant, and we talked about how James had treated me. She said that there was no chance that he would have changed in such a short space of time and that although he was doing all the right things, it took at least six months to a year for an abusive man to begin to change. She warned me that it was not safe to be around James and she also asked me why I would even want to spend any time with someone who had treated me how he had. Wasn't I worth a lot more than that? It was hard to answer her question. I didn't know why I still allowed James to contact me. In the cold light of day, with the facts glaring, it seems like the most ridiculous thing to do, but emotions don't care about the facts and I didn't stop responding to James's messages.

The date of the Elbow gig was approaching. I wondered if James would suggest that we went together. Part of me wanted to go. I wanted to see them but wasn't sure that I could cope with all the emotions that it would entail and also I was pretty sure that seeing James wasn't the best idea. Part of me hoped that he wouldn't mention it and part of me hoped that he would. I wished that I could just switch off the part of me that ignored common sense, but I couldn't, and as much as I tried to ignore it, it was there, screaming at me for some attention.

Hey. I have those Elbow tickets. I'd love you to come. No pressure xxx

Bad idea! I told myself.

I'm sorry, but I don't think that it's a good idea that we see each other.

Okay, it's up to you. I am going to go. I'll go on my own, and if you change your mind between now and then, just let me know. Xxx

No, going was a bad idea. Seeing James was a bad idea. Being around James was dangerous. I thought about him standing in Nottingham Arena on his own, and I felt a stab of pity. What was wrong with me? He had caused this. He had made it so that I couldn't feel safe around him, but I still had feelings for him. Was I insane?

I wrestled with myself for the rest of the week, and I tried to talk myself out of going, but looking back now, I can see that I made my decision the moment I let myself feel pity for James. I didn't tell him that I was thinking about it and he continued to send me the odd message saying how much he'd like me to go, and that he knew that if I did go, it wouldn't mean that I was agreeing to see him again.

It could just be a one-off.

The day of the gig dawned, and I still hadn't told James that I might go along. It had been eleven weeks since I had last seen him. I went to work, as usual, I had a couple of messages from James through the day, just telling me that his offer was still there. I went home and tried to distract myself, but I couldn't settle, so I drove to the train station and bought a return ticket to Nottingham. How I wish now that I had been strong. How I wish that I had stayed away from him.

I got on the train and sent James a message.

Does your offer still stand?

He replied instantly, *Yes of course! xxx*

I'm on the train. It's just a one-off though; it doesn't mean that I am willing to spend any more time with you.

You won't regret it, Anna, I promise xxx

But I do, more than anything.

James met me off the train.

"Oh look at you," he gushed. "You are even more beautiful than I remember. I have been such a fool."

He tried to hug me, but I pushed him away.

"I'm sorry, you are just so gorgeous, I just want to be close to you."

He was crying and smiling and emotional. We just had time to go for some food, and he kept telling me how beautiful I was, how much he loved me, how sorry he was, what a fool he had been.

"I'm sorry you feel like this, but you had so many chances. I tried everything I could think of."

"No Anna, you didn't try everything."

"What?" I said, feeling the anger bubble up inside me.

"You didn't show me any understanding."

I stood up in the restaurant, at our table.

"I am leaving. I cannot carry this conversation on," I told him, and I marched away into the night, into the familiar city centre, with bitter tears stinging my cheeks. This was not how it was supposed to be. This was not how my life should have gone. Why? Why was I pacing these streets on my own with anger bubbling inside me? Where was Dylan? Why was life so cruel? I sat on a wall and took some deep breaths. I could feel my phone vibrating in my bag, and I knew it would be James calling me. I waited and listened to his voicemail.

"Anna, I am sorry. Sometimes I talk shit. I'm worried about you. Please come to the gig. Just come and get your ticket, you don't need to talk to me or stand with me. You shouldn't miss out on this."

I sent him a text message: *Okay, I will come and get my ticket. Meet me at the entrance.*

I walked to the arena and saw James waiting anxiously for me. He was smoking a cigarette, and he tried to hug me, but I pulled away from him. He gave me the ticket, I thanked him and then walked on ahead. We were late, and the band had just begun to play. I stood a little way away from James and focused on watching the band and listening to the music. I knew that he was watching me, and after ten minutes or so he disappeared, only to return with a drink for me. As he handed me the drink, he stuffed a note into my hand.

Anna, I know that you don't think you should give me another chance, but I love you, and I am so sorry for everything that I have done. I am trying so hard to learn how to become a better person. I know I have a long way to go, but I am so committed to getting it right.

J xxx

PS, you look incredible. You are so beautiful. Xxx

I sipped my drink and listened to the music. Of course, it stirred up all my memories of Dylan, and I let my tears fall freely. They ran down my face, and fell off my chin, wetting my top. Dylan should be here, holding my hand, squeezing my bum, the way he used to at every opportunity. It was so unfair.

At the end of the show, James waited for me, looking sheepish and vulnerable. I felt the familiar pang of pity.

"Would you like me to see you on to the train?" he asked.

"Yes, that'd be good," I replied, and we walked along together in silence toward the station.

"Do you think it's possible for me to change?" he asked. We stopped walking and faced one another.

"Yes I do, if you really believe that you need to, and you work hard, then yes I do."

"Anna, please let me show you what you mean to me."

"No, you have to do this on your own and if you succeed you'll be happy regardless of whether you have me or not."

"I'll never be happy without you," he told me, placing his hand on mine.

"I think that's untrue," I said softly. We talked for a long time. I told him that I really thought that he should get away from his mum and dad and he agreed.

"They have been fiddling the books, and I think that they have done me out of quite a bit of money. They are in loads of debt because they remortgaged the house."

We had begun to walk towards the train station.

"Shit, that's horrible. You really can't trust them; they are not nice to you."

"They have been good to me though since I left the house. They've been there for me."

My skin prickled with anger. As far as I was concerned, they would have been using it as an opportunity to manipulate James.

"Fuck!" I said as we reached the station. I had

missed my train; the next one wasn't for two hours.

"Just come and stay with me," James said.

"What at your parents' house?"

"Of course not. I have booked a nice hotel. I promise I will keep myself to myself."

It was either that or wait two hours for a train. It was already gone midnight. I could stay with James, get an early train home and still make it to work on time. And so that is what I did, against my better judgement, I agreed to spend the night with him.

THE FALL

"I'm glad that you missed your train," James said, trying to take my hand in his. "I am glad I get to spend a few more hours with you."

"It's a bit of a pain for me. I can't be late for work in the morning."

"No, of course, you can't. You're the best teacher in the world. I forgot to tell you how proud I am of you for doing your job; I think that you are amazing."

"Stop it with all the buttering up! It's making me uncomfortable, seriously, just be normal."

We walked to James's hotel. Typically he had booked something very nice. He didn't seem to be able to bring himself to stay in a budget hotel, not even just for one night, not even when he was supposedly staying there alone.

We walked into reception, and he tried to put his arm around me. I shrugged him off, annoyed because I was sure it was for the benefit of the man at the desk. I felt it was James's way of saying, 'This woman belongs to me.' I noticed the man on reception raising an eyebrow; he had obviously noticed me giving him the cold shoulder.

We climbed the stairs and found the room. James unlocked the door, turned to me and said, "It's quite spacious!"

I rolled my eyes. Of course, it was.

"This is nice," I said, peering into the bathroom. It was huge with polished tiles on the floor, a walk in double shower, a free-standing bath, a toilet and a bidet.

"Who uses bidets?" I asked.

"I don't know!" James said, putting his arms around me. I shrugged him off.

The bed was also massive.

"Is this a honeymoon suite? Why would you book this for yourself?"

"I guess I hoped that you would agree to come and stay with me. I suppose I just wanted to make it special for you if you did."

"I don't think you know me at all," I told him.

"What do you mean?"

"Well if you think that it is this that counts," I gestured to the room. "All I wanted was for you to treat me well, treat me how every person deserves to be treated. You can't buy me; I'm not for sale."

I looked up at James; he had a bottle of wine in one hand and a corkscrew in the other. He looked hurt and angry.

"I'm not trying to buy you; I just wanted it to be nice if you did come. You know I like to treat you well."

"What?" I said, astounded. "Treat me well? What part of the verbal abuse, the controlling, and the hurting me was treating me well?"

"I made you coffee! I bought you amazing gifts. I took you to Paris!"

"James, those things don't matter when they are against a backdrop of disrespect and abuse. They don't take away the bad behaviour. I would have rather the abuse stopped, and we lived in tiny flat, with shitty cars and no money. I didn't want all this." I gestured to the room again. "It means nothing to me."

"You ungrateful bitch," he said, slamming the bottle of wine down.

"See, you haven't changed at all. You don't like my opinion, so you call me a bitch. I am not putting up with this."

I went to the door, but he shot in front of me.

"Hear me out," he said desperately.

I stopped and waited.

"You are right. I can see that. I am sorry. I'm just going to go in the shower and calm down for ten minutes. Please don't go in that time, and if you still want to leave when I am finished, I will walk you to the station, it's dark, and it is late."

"Okay," I said reluctantly, putting my bag back down. I sat on the big bed while James went for his shower. I didn't want to leave, it was late, I was tired and the thought of taking the slow night train home and then getting up for work in the morning filled me with dread. No, I would stay and go home in the morning as planned. I took my boots and socks off. I could go for a quick shower tonight; then I wouldn't need one in the morning. I was about to start undressing, but I didn't want to give James the come on, so I waited with bare feet for him to finish in the shower.

I heard the shower stop, and James came back into the hotel room, with a towel wrapped around his waist. He looked skinny.

"You've lost weight," I said.

"I know, I just feel so stressed, I don't eat much these days."

"I think I have too. About half a stone, I think it's down to the fact that I drink less now that I don't live with you."

"Why do you have to make digs at me?" He had removed his towel and was stepping into a pair of shorts.

"What? It wasn't a dig; it was the truth. I don't drink much now."

"It was a dig." He pulled his jeans on.

"It wasn't."

"Yes, it was. You just can't let anything lie, can you? Anna has to get her digs in; Anna has to make her point." He pulled his hoodie over his head and rammed his bare feet into his trainers.

"James, do you realise what you are doing? I have told you it wasn't a dig, why can't you just drop it?"

I was so angry. I was angry at myself for putting myself back in this position; I was angry at James for still being the same. He hadn't changed, not one bit. It seemed to me that he was incapable of change, he'd just been pretending, and I'd been inviting him to fool me.

"I am not the only one to blame in all of this," he shouted.

"It is my fault for trusting you, for believing you, but other than that, yes you are. You are to blame." I shouted back.

"If you'd just treated me like a *human being,*" he spat, picking up the hotel room key and stuffing it into his back pocket.

"What? When did I do anything other? You were the one treating me badly. I am not taking responsibility for your behaviour James. It's not my fault."

I stamped my foot at the end of the sentence. I hadn't meant it, it just happened.

"Child," he said, looking me up and down. He fumbled in his other pocket and pulled out a box of cigarettes and his lighter. He flipped the box open, but it was empty.

"I'm going to buy some cigarettes," he said, storming through the door, banging it against the wall, so it didn't close properly.

I stood rooted to the spot for a few seconds. Then my chest filled with rage. I had to get away from James, from this stupid, overpriced hotel room - yet another gilded cage that I had willingly stepped inside.

I suddenly realised that I needed a wee, I would go to the toilet, and then I would leave, get the last train back home. Fuck James and his fake changes, fuck it all. I was a stupid idiot for falling for his charm again.

I marched into the bathroom; the shiny tiles were slippery from James's wet feet and in my rage and my haste to get to the toilet, my bare feet slipped on the tiles. I felt myself go, as though in slow motion and I knew it was happening, but I couldn't stop it. When the back of my head hit the bidet and the searing, burning pain shot through my brain, I knew there and then that I had done something terrible.

As the pain filled my head and neck, I felt the warmth on my lower body; it was a few seconds before I realised that I had lost control of my bladder. I waited hoping that the pain would begin to ease, but it didn't. I tried to move, but I was paralysed. My limbs felt heavy. I tried to scream for help, but I couldn't move my lips. It was like being trapped in one of those nightmares where you know if you could just scream, you'd wake up, and everything would be okay, but I couldn't scream, and I wasn't about to wake up. I could taste blood, and I could feel it trickling from my nose and ears. I was so frightened. My breathing was out of my control. I could hear a horrible gurgling, rasping noise and it was a little while before I realised that it was the sound of my breathing. I remembered Dylan's final breaths; they had sounded just like that, desperate, agonal gasps as his life slipped away.

I had some vision, I could see the ceiling directly above me, but I couldn't move to see anything else. The room seemed terribly bright, and the pain in my head was not helped by the light above me. I tried to close my eyes, but couldn't work out how to do it. James would be back soon. He would save me. He would get me some help. I was beginning to feel very cold. My wet jeans felt uncomfortable. Inside I was crying I was so scared. Death was coming. My poor family. What had I done?

I stared at the ceiling, becoming colder and colder, and the agony in my head making me wish for death. I noticed what appeared to be a tiny opening in the atmosphere. I stared and stared, and the opening began to grow and pulse, it was like a rip in the air, and it expanded and grew until nothing from before remained. As it grew larger, the pain in my head grew smaller until it was gone completely. I could feel a lovely warmth enveloping me as the cold floor beneath me became warm and soft, and I knew that I was with Dylan. I couldn't see him, but I could feel him, and I felt the way I did when we were together. I felt safe, loved, warm and content. Whenever I had looked into Dylan's eyes, I had always felt at home, and this was how I felt right at this point. I knew that I could go where he was, and nothing else would matter. I felt as though I was basking in the warmth of his love and I never wanted it to end. I knew that he was telling me that everything was okay. This would be a good way to spend forever!

A piercing scream dissolved the scene and the world beyond the opening slipped away. I'd been found. The rip in the atmosphere grew smaller until it was gone, the cold hard tiles were beneath me again, and the temperature dropped. I'd never felt cold like it. The pain in my head returned, and if I could have made a noise, it would have been to scream in agony. I could hear the rasping breaths, but now they were slow and shallow, each one sounding as though it would be my last.

The woman who had found me made an emergency call from the hotel room, and staff from the hotel gathered around me. Someone put a cover

over me, and someone else screamed at them not to touch me in case my back was broken. I wanted to say thank you; I was so cold. I felt a hand on mine and a soft female voice telling me to hold on, that help was coming.

"Her lips are blue," someone else said.

"Where is the ambulance? What's the holdup?"

I imagined that these people felt as though they had been waiting a lifetime. I could hear sobbing and words of comfort.

"You've probably saved her life. You've done the right thing. What made you come in the room?"

"The door was open, I was passing and thought it strange, then I heard those noises she was making. Why has she stopped? Oh God, she's stopped breathing. I can't watch her die."

"She hasn't; she's still breathing, her pulse is there. Where the fuck is the ambulance?"

At last the medical team arrived. They stabilised me. Put me in a neck brace, put a cannula in my hand and gave me oxygen. The police arrived, and I could hear people speculating about what had happened.

"The room was booked in the name of Mr J Green. He was seen leaving about half-an-hour before she was found. A member of staff heard some shouting from the room, and there appeared to be hostility between the two when they walked through reception."

No! I screamed in my mind. I knew what it looked like, and I also knew that my family and friends would confirm that James had been abusive to me, but this time he hadn't done it. It was an accident. It was karma.

FROSTY

So that is how I arrived here, in the intensive care unit. I slipped in James's wet footprints. I lie here in my bed in utter disbelief. Why did I go back? Why?

The answer is too painful to believe. I wanted to be wrong about him. I wanted him to change. I felt like I loved him, despite everything, I wanted him to be the James Green that I fell for, but of course, he isn't. He is the abuser that can love tenderly, the lover who can bruise with his words and his fists, the man of many faces, the chameleon.

Pam is looking after me today, I can hear her bustling about, and I think she must have a cold because she keeps sniffing loudly. She sounds as though she is crying, but as we know, she is a hard-faced bitch incapable of human emotion. I hope it's a cold and I catch it, and it becomes pneumonia and kills me. I am sick of a life of nothing. James can stay where he is. It's karma; it's fate. My life's purpose was to bring him to justice, and now I want to die and be with my love.

"Anna," Pam has pulled her chair up next to me. This is weird; she is sniffing again, she really does sound upset. Perhaps she is about to offload some worries onto me in the way that my mum does?

"I need to tell you what has been happening. I don't think you are there anymore. I tell myself that you are dead already, but part of me nags away and tells me that you aren't, that you can hear and are aware, and that is why I have to tell you who I am."

This is interesting. Who she is?

"My dad was an alcoholic. I know you will relate to this. I know how to spot one a mile off. Your dad seems nice, but I know that they all seem nice Anna, at least if they want to.

My dad wasn't nice, he was violent, aggressive and selfish, and when I met Martin at eighteen years old, I wasted no time in marrying him and setting up home. Eighteen years old, I was just a child. Martin seemed nice. Like I said, they all do. He was ten years older than me. At first, life was wonderful. I did my nurse training, and Martin worked as an electrician. But you know Anna, there are changes in these men. Once they have you, they change, and it didn't take long. I tried to please him, I really did, but nothing was ever quite right for Martin. He never hit me, and I couldn't quite put my finger on what it was that was wrong. I walked on eggshells though, I was never comfortable and always jumpy. Martin said that he thought I spent too much time at work. He wanted to have a baby. I didn't want one, I wanted a career, but I wanted to make him happy, so when I was twenty-one, I fell pregnant. Once I was pregnant, Martin got worse.

One night, because I had been sick and woken him up, he pushed me down the stairs. I was so shocked and so ashamed that I hid my bruises and pretended it hadn't happened. He was sorry, he was so sorry, and the change in him was unbelievable. He became this loving, attentive, caring man. It was bliss; it was exactly what I had been craving. Of course, it didn't last, and when I fell asleep instead of making his dinner, he laid into me. I tried to protect my unborn baby as his fists reigned into my face and head. I crouched into a ball to protect my tiny, innocent child. I know that I should have left, but of course afterwards, he loved me more than ever. I was so confused. What was it I was doing to cause him to treat me like that?

Of course, you and I both know that I wasn't causing it, he was, but I had nothing normal to compare my life with. He was like my dad in so many ways; I just thought that it was normal!"

Pam is crying. I wonder how she is getting away with just sitting next to me and talking. Her story is harrowing, and I feel so sorry for her. I had no idea that she had been through something similar to me.

"When I gave birth to my daughter, he called me an animal, because I made too much noise and embarrassed him. His treatment of me worsened, and the first couple of years of her life, I was trapped in the cycle of abuse. His attacks were vicious and worsening. If the baby cried, I would have to get his permission to tend to her. Sometimes I ignored her because I was so afraid of him. Do you know how bad that makes me feel? I left my baby to cry because of that monster. My breasts would be spilling with milk at her cries, but he would tell me to leave her for another hour. He was so cruel. I know that I have done her untold damage. I owe her so much; I have to make it up to her. I have failed her when I should have protected her."

This is a really sad story. I don't know many people with kids, but I am trying to imagine Sophie ignoring one of her baby's cries, and it seems impossible. It goes against every maternal instinct surely? Would James have had that power over me? The power to make me neglect my own child? I like to think not, but I am not so sure. After all, I went back to him even after what he had put me through.

"So my baby girl grew up. She looked out for me, even at four years old. When he wasn't there, we had a nice time, but when he came in, she knew not to take my attention, she could sense the atmosphere. Kids know. They are not stupid. And it destroys them, Anna; it destroys them from the ground up. This is why I have to get justice; she deserves justice.

One night, when she was four, Martin came home in a foul mood. Everything that I did was wrong. I knew that I was in for it. I almost wished he'd just get on and do it because the waiting for him to blow up was the worst part of it. I put my little princess to bed, tucked her in and told her that I loved her, then I went downstairs to face the music. Sure enough, he was waiting, with some stupid excuse as to why I deserved a beating. That time though, it was like he had lost it. He just wouldn't stop, and I took punch after punch after punch. He kicked me to the floor; he stamped on me, he beat with a length of cable from his work van. The man was an evil pig. He left me for dead."

Pam is openly weeping now. I can't believe that no one is coming to comfort her, that no one has noticed.

"He left me for dead to be found by my four-year-old daughter in the morning. When I came around, she was lying on the floor next to me with her cup, waiting for a drink. I don't know how long she had been waiting for me to wake up. I could hardly move, I was in so much pain, but I realised that he must not be there for her to be by my side, so I made myself get up. I took my baby, and we smashed the window, because he had locked the doors, and we left. We took nothing with us, just the clothes on our backs, I had nothing to take. He didn't give me a penny. I somehow managed to get to the bus stop, and we jumped on the bus, the driver looked horrified, but we sat down without paying. I was so scared, but I had done it. We went to the police station, and I was too scared to press charges, but we got to a refuge, and then we left town, we changed our names so that he couldn't find us, and we started again."

I want to congratulate Pam on her bravery. She has been through so much.

"When my daughter started dating an older man, of course, I was worried. I mean, I thought it was going to be history repeating itself. She told me not to worry about her. She told me that he was lovely, he was kind, generous and charming. When I met him, I agreed. He was all of those things, and I relaxed. When she announced that she was going to move in with him, I thought it a bit soon but didn't stand in their way. After all, he wasn't Martin, and she wasn't me. He doted on her. He treated her to trips away, slap-up meals, nice clothes. Anna does any of this sound familiar?"

Of course it does. She is going to tell me that this man was an abuser too. Just how many of them are there?

"When I saw the bruises on her arms, I knew what was happening. I begged her to leave him, but she didn't. She went back; she was stubborn. But then that's Daniella all over, a stubborn little madam."

Daniella? Daniella Frost? The realisation dawns on me with utter horror. Frosty? Pam's nickname is just her surname.

"So, when I heard about you, I wanted to help you. I knew what he was capable of. He pushed my daughter to the very limit. That night, the night that she hit him with the weight, he had locked her in the house and subjected her to his usual tirade of verbal abuse. He had followed her around the house calling her names. He had wound her up beyond belief. All she wanted to do was walk away. She pleaded with him to let her go, and he just mocked her, he poked her in the chest, he stood on her feet. He forced her to strip to her underwear because she was wearing clothes that he had bought her. He humiliated her, and he hurt her. He wrestled her to the floor, and he tried to rape her. She picked up the nearest thing and hit him with it. That was how it happened, and the worst thing of all is the miscarriage of justice. She went to prison. No one believed her, not one person, apart from me, and she had a criminal record because she had been caught shoplifting at sixteen and she had also had a stupid fight when she was drunk. No one wanted to believe her, and now her life is ruined.

She used to be a vibrant, fiery girl. I worked so

hard to make up for Martin, and now that bastard has stolen it all from her. He has to stay in prison. It's the least he deserves."

Her words are punctuated with sobs. I agree, he deserves to be behind bars. This is so harrowing to hear. I can't believe I shared a bed with this man.

"I can't let him go free. I can't. It's not an option, and when you told me that it wasn't him that put you in here, I just couldn't believe it. I can't risk you waking up and letting him walk free. It's not an option for me Anna, and I'm sorry, but that is why I can't let you wake up. I thought that I could make it happen naturally. I stopped giving you your blood thinners. I thought you'd get a clot and die, but you just hung on in there, so I stopped washing my hands.

I made your cannulas dirty; I contaminated your syringes, I thought that if you got septicaemia, you would die. So many of our patients get septicaemia, no one would suspect, but you hung on in there again. I missed out your antibiotics, I gave you normal saline instead of penicillin, but you just keep recovering, and that is why I have to let it end today.

When your parents have gone this afternoon, I am going to give you some insulin. It won't hurt, you will just go to sleep, and then your body will just stop and shut down. I don't think I will get caught, but to be honest, I am past caring now. As long as that bastard is punished for what he did to my daughter I will make any sacrifice; I am not going to let her down again."

Pam has her hand on mine. I cannot believe this. I am going to die, today. I will be saying a silent goodbye to my family. I've changed my mind; I don't want to die. Please, somebody help me, please.

"Keep asking, and someone will help."

It's the whispering voice. *Please, please be right.* I beg silently and desperately.

SILVER LINING

I thought that I had already experienced a wake-up call. I thought that being here in this place was enough to make me take stock of my life properly, but right now, now I know that imminent and definite death is what truly brings life and all its meaning into perspective. How ironic that only when death is coming, and life is no longer an option do I really come to appreciate it! We have all heard of the near-death experience where a whole life will flash before someone's eyes, and that is what is happening to me right now, but in a protracted way, it's less of a flash and more of a steady flow of memories and missed opportunities.

I am waiting for my mum to come and see me. I probably have only four hours left with my mum, and there is so much that I need to say to her. All of the things that have just been left unsaid, like how much I appreciate her, how I have noticed that she loves me so much, how much it means to me when she holds my hand and talks nonsense, how pretty she looked the last time I saw her, how I like the way she has her hair, how special she is, how much I loved it when she baked me birthday cakes, how I loved to sit on her knee and hear her read to me when I was little, how she is my hero, how I wish I could spend forever with her and tell her these things over and over again until she gets tired of hearing them, how her mistakes don't matter, how her love shines through and that I was always glad that I looked like her and not my dad.

My God, I cannot believe that I am about to die. Each and every second of life is precious. I *knew* that, but I guess I have not always lived as though I did. Instead, I got caught up in life's trivialities, and I allowed someone to disrespect and hurt me. Out of everything that is going through my mind right now, that is one of my biggest regrets. My life was precious. It was precious to me and to those who loved me, and I threw away the gift that I had by wasting my time with James.

I hear mum politely enquire how I am to Pam. I wish she weren't so polite to her; I wish she didn't mind her manners with the woman who was planning to murder her daughter. I wonder how much progress I'd have made if Pam hadn't been tampering with everything? I was making progress, I was getting better, and it was my desperation to prove James innocent that caused Pam to stop trying to help and for her to find a way of trying to hurt me.

Mum sits next to me and begins to chat about

stuff: Eve, the baby, how much he weighs, that he is smiling now, that Liam went to work with baby sick down the back of his shirt and no one told him. I want to smile, I want to join in the conversation, I can hear the pride in my mum's voice as she gushes about her beautiful little grandson and I wish so much that I wasn't putting a dampener on this special time. I am so angry with Pam. She is going to murder me and rob my family of these precious early days with its new little addition. James, Pam and me too, we have all spoiled these precious days and weeks. I have to face up to my own responsibility in all of this. I owed it to myself and everyone who cares about me to leave James the second he began his abuse, by putting up with it I was telling him that I didn't value myself. And by staying when I should have been going, I was giving James a license to continue to hurt me. If I cared that little about myself, why should he care about me? And not only that, I was showing James that not only was it okay for him to treat me like that, but it was okay to treat all women like that, I was perpetuating his beliefs that he has a right to control and dominate his partner. I am implicated in all of this, and although I am not an abuser myself, right now I feel as though I may as well be.

Mum is quiet now. She is just sitting and holding my hand. I wonder what she is thinking about? Tick

tick tick, the minutes go by, the precious last day with my mum. It's like Dylan all over again. I didn't appreciate him, I didn't take the opportunity to tell him that I loved him on the day that he died and now he has gone. This time though I am desperate to tell my mum what she means to me, but I am unable to.

I let my mind wander over my time here in the hospital. I honestly don't know how long it is that I have been here. I think it must be a couple of months, although it feels like a lifetime. Lauren still works here, and she told me ten weeks, so it must be less than ten weeks. I think it must be mid-May time now. I long to see the blossom on the trees and hear the birds singing. I want to see the bright sunlight and the fresh spring green of the leaves; this is my favourite time of year.

Things are becoming clear to me now. Of course, Pam didn't want Lauren to work with her. Of course, she didn't want to risk her noticing what she was doing to me. I think about when I began to deteriorate. That is when the whispering voice started; it told me that I was in danger, whoever that voice belongs to knows what is happening and I realise with a jolt of hope that it has just told me to keep asking for help.

"Help!" I cry silently. "Help me, mum," I plead desperately. I put all of my efforts into trying to communicate something to my mum, her hand is on mine, and I try to move, but it isn't happening. My heart rate has gone up though, the steady beeping of the monitor has increased suddenly and rapidly.

"I'm just going to get some lunch." Mum kisses me.

"Please don't leave!" I scream in my mind. Is this when Pam is going to strike? Will mum come back from her lunch to find that I have died? My heart rate increases further, and I try to grab her hand to pull her back, but of course, I cannot move, and she leaves without noticing the turmoil beneath my still and silent exterior.

I hear Pam bustling about nearby. Is this it? Am I about to die? My heart rate is so fast that the alarms are sounding and I hear someone asking Pam to take blood cultures in case I have another infection. She is close to me now, and I can hear her breathing, it is heavy and laboured, and again she sounds upset. Surely if she feels this upset her conscience will stop her from murdering me? I try desperately to open my eyes. Maybe if she can see that I am still here, maybe if I can show her how frightened I am, how much I want to live, she will take pity on me and spare my life. I try my hardest to open my eyes; I know how to do it. I know *how* to move, I just can't make it happen. As I try, it feels as though my eyes are opening, but nothing is happening. I'm not going to stop trying though, and eventually, I succeed in opening them for a brief second, but Pam is not near me now, and she doesn't get to witness the flicker of fear on my face. I am glad though that I managed to move my eyes, maybe if mum comes back before Pam strikes, I can manage it while she is here and she will know that I am afraid.

I hear someone suggest that I am further sedated to reduce my heart rate. *No, no please don't sedate me, I want to be awake for my mum.* But of course, I am powerless, and the sedative works on me, plunging me into a world of nightmarish, lucid dreams.

I am angry that I am being drugged, and amazingly the fear that I am feeling, the adrenaline that is pumping through my body continues to keep my heart rate elevated. I feel as though I am thrashing about the bed, but I know that I am lying still. My mum is back now, and I hear the concern in her voice as they tell her about my elevated pulse. Poor mum, I can tell by her voice that she cannot take another knock.

I know that mum will stay here with me as long as I am in any way more unwell than usual and that brings me a little peace, but I don't want too much peace because my heart rate mustn't drop or she'll leave! I am given some more drugs, and my heart rate settles, I can feel myself drifting into sleep, I don't want this to happen because if I sleep I will miss mum and she might go. I try to fight the feeling, the sinking into the bed, the lapse in consciousness, but it is not possible and sleep wins.

As I become aware of the noise of my surroundings again, I realise that my mum is not nearby anymore. I listen for the sound of her breathing, or moving, but it sounds like there is no one here. I have no idea of the time; I don't know if Pam is even still on shift. I am pretty certain that I am still alive though, that is one thing that I am thankful for.

I think more about my life, this time about Chloe and all that she has done for me. Did I ever thank her for the way that she looked after me when Dylan died? I think that I did, but I don't think I expressed enough gratitude, I don't think I told her what she really did for me. I don't think that she knows that she is one of the reasons that I didn't just give up. She is yet another person in my life who I want one more chance to show my appreciation to.

I remember our childhood together. We had so much fun, despite the obvious sadness surrounding her huge loss. We had so many shared dreams and were there for each other when we started to have boyfriends and other teenage angst. Chloe is lovely;

I want so much to tell her.

I can hear Pam nearby again. Fear floods my chest.

"I thought you were going to become ill and do it yourself," she whispers, her voice is soft and sad and I actually feel sorry for her. I genuinely think that she does not feel she has any other option but to get rid of me to keep James in prison.

I think about how sad it is that Pam's life has been blighted by a particular type of man: first her dad, then her husband and then James. It seems ironic that she feels that murder is a justifiable action. I think about how much poison she has been filled with over the years, first as a little girl, then as a teenager and a young woman and now as a mature woman. Now Pam is carrying it on, the poison taking root and seeping and spreading out further and further into the lives of others. That is what abuse does, it festers and rots and eats a person away from the inside out until they too become toxic. I wonder whether I would have become toxic if I'd have stayed with James?

My heart is racing again, as Pam rustles nearby. She seems to be taking forever, hanging around, making me nervous, and I can feel my heart pounding dangerously again.

'Help!' I scream silently; I think that she is getting ready to do it. Her breathing is rapid, and she keeps making funny little sighing noises. She comes close to me again.

"Anna, I just want you to know that I am sorry. I have to do this, you understand don't you?"

Her voice is shaky now, and she places a quivering hand on my arm, I can feel the cold, clammy sweat on the palm of her hand.

'NOOOOOOOOO,' I scream. 'Help.' But it is no use; I am silent. She moves away again, and my heart is beating so fast that I feel like I am about to take off. The alarms are sounding again, but Pam is back in the room.

"It's okay,' she shouts, "I've got it sorted."

'Keep fighting,' my voice tells me, and I continue to try to shout, to try to open my eyes, but it is no use. I feel the fine needle pierce my skin. She has injected me in the leg, underneath the sheets. I feel her push the plunger into the syringe, filling my body with insulin that I don't need, then I feel her doing the same thing again and then again, just how much of the stuff has she given me? Now what? Nothing is happening yet, but I know enough to realise what will happen. The insulin that I don't need will pack away all the sugar in my blood, and my cells will have no energy source. I will go further into a coma, and then I will die.

Pam has walked away. I can feel my body trying to fight, intense hunger kicks in and a craving for sugar. I imagine myself spooning jam into my mouth, but it's not imaginary jam that I need, it's real sugar. I know that I am about to die. I can feel myself sinking into the bed; I can feel my body shaking and sweating.

Here I go, goodbye.

I wish I could do it all over again; I wish I'd known then what I know now. I love my family, I love my friends, and I wish I'd ignored the trivial stuff. I'm sinking further now. I'm in the warm place again, and I can hear the noise around me. I can hear Lauren, but she is far away.

I can hear an emergency bell, and I can hear shouting, but it is too late, none of them will know what she has done, they won't be able to tell what I need, and I'll be dead before they realise. Fainter and fainter they become.

At least it is over now, at least people can begin to grieve and James will stay behind bars, and that's my silver lining.

LOVE NEVER DIES

I hear the beeping of an alarm, and it's a few seconds before I realise that it is my mobile. I reach across and pick it up. I squint at the screen, it's eight am, and I turn the alarm off. I let the phone fall onto my chest, and I stare at the ceiling for a few minutes. It's just me and my thoughts. I can't believe how lucky I am, and every time I hear any beeping I am plunged back momentarily into the nightmare that I lived for eight weeks, but the beeping was my phone, not some piece of hospital equipment, and I can move to turn it off too. I appreciate that.

I sit up slowly and put my slippers on, the wooden floor in Claire's house can be quite chilly. I let the sadness wash over me as I remember staying in this room with Dylan. We had shared Sophie's old bed lots of times. It's okay to feel sad though; I am thankful for my time with Dylan. I am glad that I have loved and been loved, and it's nice to be able to feel the emotion and let my body react to it. Now when I feel sad, I can sigh. When I feel like crying, tears run down my face and I can move my hand to wipe them away. I stand up, a little unsteady on my feet, and I reach for the stick that is propped up against the wall. My balance may never recover, I have been damaged by either the antibiotics that I was on or the bleeding in my brain. I'd be lying if I said that I didn't care. I do care; I want to be fully able like I was before, but I have so much to be happy about, and it's not hard to find something to be thankful for. I can walk, and that is a miracle because I almost died.

I wander into the kitchen and switch on the kettle; I can hear Claire chatting to my parents in her dining room. I make myself a coffee and go and join them. This is the first time that I have been up to Edinburgh in a long, long time. I enjoy my coffee and then begin to get ready.

As always for me, the shower is my place to think. I let the hot water run over my face and body, but I have to sit down half-way through because of my balance. I stand back up and lean my hand against the wall and think about the events that have brought me to this day in my life. I am lucky to be here.

If Lauren hadn't become suspicious of Pam, I might not be here at all. Apparently, it's easier to kill babies and the elderly with insulin. Adults have a better chance of surviving, but in my compromised condition, I doubt that I would have had what it took. Thankfully Lauren was watching Pam. I'm so grateful that she saw her take the insulin from the fridge. Otherwise, no one would have known what had caused my sudden crash. I shudder at the thought of it all.

I wash my hair; it is quite short now. I was shocked to discover that half of it had been shaved off. It's in a nice style. I like it now, it took some getting used to though; I have had long hair since I was a little girl.

I seem to be in the habit of having deep and meaningful conversations with myself these days. I think I know what life is all about now, what is important in life, and I am thankful that I have had the opportunity to see and realise that while I still have a life to live. I am never going to stop listening to my intuition - doing that was what kept me with James - I ignored my inner voice and kept myself in danger - but thankfully, it never stopped talking. Being in a coma, I had no choice but to hear it loud and clear. I can't believe I didn't realise where it was coming from; I honestly thought there was a whispering ghost in that hospital!

I think I have come to terms with my feelings for all those involved now. James is a pathetic character. His need to dominate and control his partner comes from his own feelings of insecurity and inadequacy, and from his ingrained beliefs about women and relationships. I can see that, and I almost feel sorry for him, but not too sorry for him because it's he's an adult, and he is responsible for recognising and changing his own behaviour.

When I began to recover it was difficult to decide what to do about James. Initially I had thought that I would let him stay where he was. His crimes had been so hideous and it seemed fitting that he was punished for them, for his treatment of Daniella, for his ability to let her suffer for his own treatment of her, but I never felt totally comfortable playing God and dealing out justice, so I told the truth, and then I told the truth some more, and now I am pressing charges for the attacks that James did carry out on me. I often think about whether I have done the right thing and usually come to the same conclusion that the truth is always the answer.

Of course, Pam is now the one being charged with attempted murder. It's difficult to decide what I feel about Pam. Sometimes it is pity, and sometimes it is anger, although most of the time I believe that she has suffered enough. Life has been cruel to Pam.

I get dried and dressed, pulling on some warm and comfy clothes. I am starting to put some weight back on now and build up some muscle tone again, but my body still doesn't look quite right. I put on a bit of make-up and stare at my reflection; I look older, the whole experience has aged me. It's okay though. I take my stick and walk out into the hall where everyone is waiting for me. Mum puts her arms around me and gives me a little squeeze then mum, dad, Claire and I make our way down the stairs and out into the cool autumn sunshine. I climb into the front seat of Claire's car, and mum and dad get in the back. They have never been to Edinburgh before, and Claire takes the scenic route to show them some landmarks, as we drive towards Holyrood Park.

"There are Sophie and the gang," Claire says pointing to Sophie and her little family. Sophie runs over to the car and throws her arms around me. Hamish hangs back a little, he has a baby carrier strapped to his chest, and his three daughters gathered close to him.

"Come and meet baby George," Sophie says, taking both of my hands and practically pulling me out of the car. I link her arm and Hamish and the girls greet me with hugs. I peer into the baby carrier to meet Sophie and Hamish's little boy. He is sleeping, and his cheek is red where he is leaning against Hamish's top.

"His middle name is Dylan," Sophie explains. "I hope you don't mind."

"Of course I don't mind!" I say, a lump forming in my throat. "He's just like the girls!"

"I know," Sophie says, "and the poor wee thing wore the girls' old clothes for the first few days, we just assumed he was going to be a she!"

We sit on a bench and wait for the others to arrive. Hattie arrives on foot.

"I had a little drink in the hotel last night," she says as she hugs me. "I feel a bit fragile!"

"The fresh air will sort you out," I tell her, and I watch as Eve and Liam's car pulls into the car park. Tom and Chloe are with them, and Chloe tries to hold Archie, who just wants to pull her hair and eat her face, while Liam and Eve try to work out how to use his baby carrier. While they fumble with straps, I see Nell and Edward pull slowly, almost reluctantly into the car park.

I want to jump up and run to them. I want to fling my arms around them, but instead, I walk as quickly as my skewed balance and walking stick will allow me. We fall into an embrace and Nell takes both of my hands in hers.

"I can't believe this day has come," she says, a tear tracking down her face.

"Me neither," I say, glancing at the box on the passenger seat of their car. She looks so old now. She must be in her late seventies, but the loss of her son has taken its toll on her, on both of them.

"Is everyone here?" Chloe asks.

"Yes, I think so," I say.

"Shall we start then?"

"Yes," I say.

"Anna are you sure you are okay to do this?" my dad asks quietly.

"Yes, I want to do it," I say, and we begin our ascent of Arthur's Seat. It is hard, and I have to keep stopping and sitting down. But looking around at those who are here and remembering why we are doing this gives me strength. One foot in front of the other, that's all I need to do. Nell and Edward take it in turns to carry the small box, both with tears running down their cheeks. Gradually we pick our way upwards.

"This was our favourite place," I remind Nell and Edward.

"It's lovely," Nell says. "I'm glad that Dylan appreciated it."

It seems strange doing this climb. I can tell that Nell and Edward don't really want to get to the top, but they keep going. They keep putting one foot in front of the other too.

We reach the top and take in the view. Claire tells those who have never been here before what it is that they can see from this vantage point. I lean on my stick and think about all of the times that I came here with Dylan. I have never been here without him.

I remember the first time we came here, and I remember the time he got down on one knee and asked me to marry him. How happy we were, how unknowing we were of what the future held for us. A natural silence falls on our little group, and we all stand in quiet contemplation.

Today is the 19th October, Dylan's twenty-ninth birthday. It is ten years since we first met and just over three-and-a-half years since he was killed. Today Nell and Edward are finally going to scatter his ashes. Nell clutches the box which holds her son's remains tightly to her chest as Edward begins to speak.

"We are all here because Dylan was part of our lives." His voice is cracking already. "Nell and I have always been pleased with the friends that Dylan had, and being here with you lovely people reminds us just how special our son was. Nell always says that the friends we choose are a reflection of ourselves and I am proud to see Dylan reflected in every one of you."

His voice is wobbling and faltering now. "Nell, you speak," he says, putting his hand on her arm. Nell looks up at the small group. Chloe has linked my arm, and I lean on her a little.

"We were told we could never have children, and we accepted that and got on with our lives. We had nice lives and when our little surprise came along our world was finally complete. He enriched our lives, and we loved him so much. When he was born, I remember looking into his big dark eyes and telling the midwife that I wanted him to lead a life of joy. I couldn't bear the thought of him ever suffering.

Losing Dylan has been the hardest and most painful thing that I have ever been through, but I take comfort in the fact that he really did lead a life of joy. Dylan simply did not have bad luck. Everything that he touched turned to gold, and I can honestly say I can never think of a time when he was unhappy. He got the girl of his dreams, and I know that you made him so happy Anna. He adored you."

I smile through my tears. I know that he adored me too, he was never afraid to tell people how much they meant to him.

"If anyone else would like to say a few words, please feel free," Nell says, looking around our small gathering expectantly.

"I'd like to say a few words," Sophie says, stepping forward slightly. "I hope I can explain how Dylan enriched my life. I met him on this day ten years ago, as did Anna, and right away I knew I could fall in love with him. I can honestly say that I had never met a more genuine person. I'd never met anyone like Dylan. It didn't take me long to fall head over heels in love with him, but I guessed that he loved Anna, and when he told me that he loved Anna, I knew that he was the kind of person who would rather truly love from a distance than pretend about his feelings, so I said nothing, and I soon put my feelings to one side. When Anna and Dylan got together, I was genuinely happy for them. Knowing Dylan made me realise that I should only have a relationship with someone that I genuinely love, and I thank Dylan for making me see that because I waited and then I met Hamish and well, here we are."

Hamish puts his arm around Sophie.

"Can I say something?" my mum asks, looking at Nell and Edward.

"Go ahead," Edward says.

"I'd just like to say, that as a mother, Dylan was the kind of person that you pray your daughter brings home to meet you. And as a friend, well, he had this way of making everybody interesting. He was so interested in people, in their lives and what makes others tick, he was able to make everybody feel special." She steps back and leans on my dad.

Hattie speaks. "I don't think any of us need to point out what an amazing musician Dylan was. His talent was incredible, but he was modest and genuine, and he brought great joy to those who he shared it with. And of course, our children have lost a truly wonderful teacher."

Another silence falls on our group. Everyone seems to have said their piece.

I begin to speak. It's hard at first, and my voice

sounds strained and choked.

"When I lost Dylan, I wanted to die too. I couldn't believe that I didn't have him anymore, but if there is anything that my recent experience has shown me, it's that true love never dies, even when a person does. Dylan loved and protected me when he was here, and that love and protection has carried me through the darkest and most frightening times of my life. I doubt I'll ever get used to being without him, but I'll always be grateful for my time with him. He was truly special."

Nell and Edward are looking at me with pride shining in their eyes.

"Shall we do this?" Nell asks looking at Edward.

"Yes, I think so," he replies.

She unfastens the metal catch on the small wooden box, as the wind, which had eased a little as we had spoken, picks up again. Nell takes a handful of the white dust and throws it. The wind catches it for a second before it is scattered onto the grass, leaving a faint white tinge.

"Happy birthday son," she says, between the sobs.

Edward does the same and then we each take a handful of Dylan's remains and let them go free. I have never done this before, and I had imagined that the ashes would fly into the wind and swirl through the air, but instead, they fall to the ground, fly back into people's faces and catch in everyone's hair.

Sophie has given the girls some wildflower seeds to scatter, and they twirl round and round giggling and throwing the seeds onto the ground. I look at Chloe, and she has ash in her hair. Everyone's faces are streaked with white where the dust has mingled with their tears and stuck there, and it's me who begins to giggle first.

"I'm sorry," I say, laughing and crying all at once. "But look at us all."

We are all covered in dust. Not one of us has escaped it, and although some of it has flown on the wind and some has landed on the ground to mingle with the earth on our precious Arthur's Seat, quite a bit of Dylan is all over our faces and clothes. We have all breathed him in too.

"It's like he is saying that he wants to be part of us all," Sophie says, and she is right. We sit on the grass and chat quietly, but soon the babies become restless and one by one we begin our descent, back to our lives now. Back to whatever our futures may hold for us, safe in the knowledge that love never dies.

The End

Thank you for reading to the end. I hope you enjoyed the book, but I also appreciate that you may have concerns too.

Below are a couple of links that you may find useful. Please tell people about this book. I realise that readers wish to be entertained, but in this case it would be nice to help people who are in these types of relationships.

LINKS
The Freedom Programme:
http://www.freedomprogramme.co.uk
Hidden Hurt: http://www.hiddenhurt.co.uk/
Respect Phoneline:
http://www.respectphoneline.org.uk/phoneline.php

About the author:
This is Sadie's first novel. She has three children and and a rabbit. She works in healthcare. When she's not writing or working most of her life seems to involve picking up toys and finding things she'd forgotten she has.
Twitter
https://twitter.com/sadiedmitchell

SILENCING ANNA

SILENCING ANNA